...eath, love and anything else in between. ... h an MA in Creative Writing from Oxford Brookes y. This is her sixth novel – her first five have been *Glo...* *Mail*, *USA Today* and Kindle Top 100 bestsellers.

By the same author:

A Woman of War (published as *The German Midwife* in
North America, Australia and New Zealand)
The Secret Messenger
The Berlin Girl
The Girl Behind the Wall
The Resistance Girl

The War Pianist

MANDY ROBOTHAM

avon.

HarperCollins*Publishers*
1 London Bridge Street
London SE1 9GF

www.harpercollins.co.uk

HarperCollins*Publishers*
Macken House
39/40 Mayor Street Upper
Dublin 1
D01 C9W8
Ireland

A Paperback Original 2023

1

First published in Great Britain by HarperCollins*Publishers* 2023

ISBN: 978-0-00-845344-2

Typeset in Bembo by Palimpsest Book Production Limited, Falkirk, Stirlingshire
Printed and Bound in the UK using 100% Renewable
Electricity at CPI Group (UK) Ltd

*To the feisty female crew of Stroud Maternity Unit —
today's warriors waging a different kind of war.*

Author's note

Having travelled physically and metaphorically across Europe in previous books, I realised it was high time I 'came home' with a story of Britain's struggles in the 1940s. Why so long? I ask myself. Is it because life on different shores always appears more exiting and exotic than our own back yard? The simple answer is that war is not exotic anywhere or anytime. It creates destruction, pain and carves holes in people's fabric. And yet the lives and survival of others across the world remains intensely fascinating to lovers of history and fiction.

It might also be that, for me, London of the Blitz feels like an intensely personal story, to be kept at arm's length until the time was right. I was lucky enough not to lose loved ones in World War II, but my late father, Alan, relayed vivid memories of his war in North London. He was just five years old as it began; parenting being what it was in those days, he was one of those bombsite boys so beautifully portrayed by director John Boorman on screen in *Hope and Glory*, growing up in conflict, scrounging for shrapnel and swapping their spoils in the school playground. Being a child, his memories tended towards excitement rather than fear, although he distinctly recalled diving for cover under the kitchen table when a V2 bomb detonated only a street away. I stand as a testament to his survival technique and sturdy furniture.

My dad grew up in the Wood Green described here, as did I, and I've delighted in weaving his past and that of my mum, Stella, into *The War Pianist*. Their first home as a young married couple was a flat on River Park Road, with a memorable view of the bus depot. My aunt and uncle then moved into the same rooms a few years later. Even now, when my mum and I emerge from Wood Green Underground towards her home, we wait at the bus stop just yards away. I myself remember the Lyons teashop on Wood Green High Street with great clarity, from childhood visits every Saturday in the early 1970s: the buttery orb lighting, wall mirrors at adult height and the black-and-white chequered flooring. Even now, I can taste the currant bun and sugary orange squash I was bought as a treat. I'm certain it helped to fuel my life-long love of old, ornate coffee shops.

Nostalgia aside, stories centred on London's war can sometimes be viewed through rose-tinted images of the 'Blitz spirit', where we imagine people cheerfully sang their way through the bombings around a pub piano. Delving into real-time diaries and history, I discovered there were two sides. On the one hand, people throughout Britain *did* rally. They were more giving and kind to others. Equally though, crime continued, and people felt desperately afraid, for their families and their own futures – collated by Becky Brown in real-life recollections of the time, as 'Blitz Spirit', and detailed in Joshua Levine's *The Secret History of the Blitz*. The reality was that they had little alternative but to soldier on, and I wanted to reflect the harsh truth: war robs everyone of options. The *only* choice is to survive.

In the character of Marnie, I pictured her at the centre of another great British and global institution, and one that has influenced my childhood and life since – the BBC. In WWII especially, without social media or television, it really was the voice of a nation, represented by the grand old dame of its headquarters at Broadcasting House. Through the wonders of the internet, I discovered a blow-by-blow (quite literally) diary of a BBC worker; Marjorie Redman MBE was a sub-editor at *The Spectator* magazine, based in Broadcasting House during the Blitz. She wrote down everything – from global events to the mundane of the BBC canteen menu. Pure gold for a writer! By some incredible quirk of fate, her family lived in my adopted home of Stroud in Gloucestershire, and so I was treated to her memories of Stroud in wartime too, with Edward Stourton's *Auntie's War* adding another rich seam of research.

In balancing those experiences, however, it was important for me to contrast London's siege with a different level of imprisonment across Europe, where Netherlanders were free of bombs but under a veil of occupation and oppression. The story here evolved as a meeting of minds across the war's vital airwaves, with women as the conduit. Much like opposition in Norway – detailed in my last novel, *The Resistance Girl* – the Dutch fight against the Nazis was less celebrated than nearby France, and yet they worked under equally difficult circumstances. The stories of Amsterdam's incredible Artis Zoo as a resistance refuge threw up facts that read exactly like fiction! Readers of my previous book will also recognise a key character woven into the narrative, where we get to discover a background to the formidable Nazi officer Lothar Selig before his Bergen days.

In 'coming home' to war-torn London, the overriding theme – yet again – is one of tenacity. After six books on conflict, five on WWII itself, I am still in awe of those who simply get on with it, sidestepping rubble and swallowing heartache. Recently, the world's resolve as a whole was tested and came through, and we can only surmise it's down to the lasting humanity of those like Marnie, Willem, Corrie and Gus. Let's hope so.

PROLOGUE

Up and Away

July 1940, Amsterdam, the Netherlands

Corrie

Bang, bang, BANG!

The heavy thud of the door knocker streaks through five floors of the narrow brick house like lightning, crowding out the calm of the afternoon. Her ears prickle along with every hair on her body, mixing with perspiration from the day's heat and the clamminess of the basement room.

Rat, tat, tat. Less violent this time, but no less urgent. And not the rhythmic code they've come to expect of friends and allies. She doesn't have time to calculate if it's SS, Gestapo or Abwehr, only that it's bad.

She's up the stairs quickly and meets the wide, wary eyes of Kees, shining with fear in the gloom of the hallway. 'You answer it,' she says. 'I'll get him ready to move.'

Kees' neat, cropped head of hair nods, dawdling purposely towards the solid wooden door until the stairs and hallway are clear.

Damn this house! Corrie curses, her thighs aching as she climbs up and up. Damn every house in Amsterdam for being so tall and thin, and with countless stairs.

In his room, Hendrik has been alerted by the clamour, though from the look of confusion on his face her ageing uncle could well have been dozing. The air is moist in the afternoon sunshine, and he rubs at the rough, greying whiskers on his chin.

'Who is it?' he asks.

She's surprised at how calm he seems. Resigned, almost. 'I don't know, but you have to leave.' She grabs at a small bag made ready. 'The way we've planned.'

They climb up another flight instead of down, their movements hastened by the rush of footsteps now snaking up through the house. Clattering towards them at speed. Her defined ear counts two sets of boots easily; the rest will be waiting below, no doubt. The only way for Hendrik is up. Out. Away.

'Once you get through the attic window, remember the loose tiles to the left,' she warns him.

He nods, but an innate fear is now written across his features as they reach the top, betraying his terror of heights. He's tall and broad, but Hendrik is a man of thought, his best endeavours wrapped tightly in his brain. Racing over rooftops and broken slates is not his world, though right now it is most definitely the route to a longer life.

The footsteps quicken, climbing the stairs behind them, but Corrie daren't look back as she almost pushes Hendrik towards the attic.

'Hey, stop!' A voice behind rings out and Corrie's heart contracts with panic. 'It's just me.' With those three words, Corrie's muscles untwist. Relief that it's Willem on the top stair, his neck craned towards them and chest heaving with the climb, Kees' face next to him, and Gus – Willem's best friend – just behind. Panic over.

Willem's taut features say otherwise. The heavy knocking is not an invasion of unwelcome uniforms this time, but a dire warning all the same.

'We have to go,' he asserts. 'I got tipped off, but the troops aren't far behind me. And they're looking for three people.'

'Three?' she questions. With the treasure trove of chemical secrets locked in Hendrik's head, he's an obvious target for the Germans. 'Who else?'

'Gus and I are on their list,' Willem says.

'No. No! How?' She knows exactly why, but the idea is unthinkable, to lose all of them, so rapidly. It can't be.

'It doesn't matter how,' he says sharply. 'Come on, we've only minutes.'

She follows them to the attic, met by a fierce blanket of heat through the sun-baked windows. The catch is unhooked and Willem pulls her close, burying his face into her neck, like he used to as a small boy, when he really needed her. 'I'll get Hendrik to a safe house in the city, then Gus and I have to go,' he murmurs. There's promise and sadness in his voice.

'Where?' She's fighting tears now. This is war and the gloves are off, but saying goodbye to any child is heartbreaking. Her only son, part of her fabric in so many ways.

'I don't know,' Willem whispers, his breath hot into her ear. 'Out of Amsterdam, Holland perhaps. I'll get word as soon as I can.' He pulls away, turning before she can see the torque on his face. There's time only for a tight hug with Hendrik, a 'Take care,' and all three are gone. Their long shadows last a second or so as they scramble across the rooftops, and then she and Kees are left squinting into the sun's blinding glare, the air almost too dense to breathe.

She pulls Kees in close, kisses the top of her daughter's head for her own comfort. 'If I know my brother, he'll make it back,' Kees tries to reassure.

But will he? So many of Corrie's precious ones are scattered on the wind, across the city and beyond. Where, and for how long?

Bang, bang, BANG! A ripple through the house again, though it's a crass rhythm she does recognise, a real threat this time. Through the attic window, voices and the idle of military engines float up from the street below.

She swallows back every ounce of hurt, fear and fury, wipes the thin film of sweat from her brow, and instructs herself: 'Corrie, stand firm. Do this.'

And then she descends, one determined step at a time.

PART ONE

1

Following the Flow

Marnie

She stares at the canteen lunch in front of her, as limp and flaccid as her life, a plainly overripe slice of tomato sagging over tinned sardines, three instead of last week's four. That's rationing for you, Marnie thinks, chewing lazily on fish that tastes like last week's, too. There's time for her to nip out to the sandwich shop close to Broadcasting House, but in all honesty she can't be bothered. Instead, she wills away the lunch hour sitting alone, since most of her female colleagues have already fled London to BBC outposts in the Home Counties. It would risk the wrath of Miss Roach to eat lunch in their office upstairs, crumbs on the desks being frowned upon, even when the streets outside are layered in dust and debris, as if Hitler has shaken the contents of a giant vacuum cleaner bag across Britain's capital. 'Standards, Miss Fern,' Miss Roach chirps regularly. 'Blitz or no Blitz.'

The wall clock ticks slowly towards one p.m., when Marnie will thankfully be busy in studio four, with a decent script and a good cast, an afternoon where her brain is alive and occupied. Then that clock racing too fast towards five p.m., and the prospect of braving the Underground to her tiny flat in a North London suburb, four almost bare walls, one gas-ring on the stove and a distinctly empty larder, her only company for an equally

7

sparse evening. The best novel amuses for only so long and – having worked in radio all day long – even the stirring words of Churchill's BBC broadcasts fall a little flat.

Halfway through the afternoon, inspired by a charming old gent that the BBC employs to be the voice of a charming old gent, Marnie resolves on not going back home so soon. Instead, she'll walk in the late September sunshine towards Trafalgar Square, scavenge for whatever groceries are and spend a blissful evening with Grandad Gilbert at his tailor's shop. It's not one of her usual days to visit but he'll no doubt be pleased to see her. They'll transport his tiny paraffin stove down to the shop basement to pre-empt a raid, feast on baked beans and day-old bread, playing backgammon until one of them is forced to admit defeat. It's not what some would call a life, but it's hers. *For better or worse*, she sometimes jokes inwardly, though the irony is becoming less amusing as time goes on.

At just past five, however, Hitler has other plans for Marnie Fern: it's raining fire on the Strand. The sky is spitting a fury of hot granite missiles onto the pavement under her feet, fallout from the incendiary shells laying a path of flames for the second wave of bombers to drop their heavier, destructive load. Marnie dodges the debris scattering around her shoes, not running but moving with true purpose. Almost skipping, like a childhood game of hopscotch. Except this is real fire, and no one is playing, least of all the Luftwaffe overhead. A second later, she's forced to dart sideways with a small squeak of alarm, a flare of sparks ricocheting off a nearby wall, close enough for her to feel the warmth on her ankles and a pinprick burn on her stockings. She stops for a half second and watches the glow die and smoulder, the heat along with it. Off target. This time.

Those around her are not panicked, only equally cautious, weaving their weary bodies around the blasted pieces of concrete and the assorted rubble that was once people or things and is no longer whole. The most pressing purpose of Londoners is to reach somewhere safe – and soon. To descend into the bowels of Britain's capital city, but they do it with stealth instead of speed. Just as the posters and the radio broadcasts tell them to do. Keep calm, but *do* carry on.

After months of expected attacks but largely quiet skies in the year since war broke out, the sky watchers and RAF are now on constant alert. Tonight, as with every other night for the past three weeks of the Blitz, their keen eyes will have triggered the now familiar wail of the siren – that undulating and ghostly 'Moaning Minnie' that snakes through the streets and saturates the air, designed to give the population five to ten minutes' warning of a raid, enough for them to scurry like rats into their holes. But today it's less than five, the Luftwaffe catching London on the hop. And Marnie Fern is right in the middle of it.

Despite the onslaught, she's desperate to swim against the tide of urgency, to ignore the demonic drone of the attackers overheard as they track the perfect runway of the wide, glinting Thames in picking out the night's targets. Instead of aiming for the nearest burrow, Marnie determines to fight the shoal of people seeking shelter and keep moving towards Grandad's tailoring business tucked behind Trafalgar Square. There, she'll be as safe as anywhere, with his narrow shopfront propped up by monolithic centuries-old concrete and stone on either side. They'll make tea and hug close to the radio in drowning out the debacle above, enduring this nightly dread with the shop mannequins that show neither emotion nor fear. Grandad will offer her a tot of whisky in her tea, and as it weaves around his body he'll start to put voices to the tailor's dummies, his two oldest christened 'Frank' and 'Oscar', and she'll laugh like she did as a child, because it will be a godsend to forget where they really are, even for a moment.

On the pavement, though, she's caught between the spinning wheels of a pushchair, a frantic mother and a heavyset man who scoops with his big hand on her elbow and steers her back towards the Tube station, as if he's a knight in shining armour instead of his tweed overcoat. 'Here, this way,' he pants with good intent. And that's the end of her resolve to fight the tide. Because Marnie Fern doesn't make a fuss, kick against this man's gallantry or the dread of a lightning raid.

She goes with the flow. As she always does.

Descending into Aldwych Underground means entering a different hell. Each time she is forced to descend, she thinks it might actually be the stink that proves to be the undoing of the British nation, rather than the mighty Third Reich; a type of dense, foetid miasma that in mediaeval times was believed to have perpetuated the plague. Once on the platform, people throw off their shoes with a resulting pungency, combined with the breath of those who've been at work all day and the stale tobacco woven into their clothes. It's a veritable soup of smells, and if Hitler ever managed to bottle the stench, it would be his best ammunition alongside the bombs that are still falling in waves overhead, a pattering of dull thuds echoing down the creaking wooden escalators and into the subterranean bunker of solace and relative safety. Almost a hundred feet above, on London's central streets, chaos continues. Under it, there's an element of calm − along with the aroma.

A sudden, louder explosion causes heads to look upwards and a ripple of agitation spreads among the carpet of people, as Marnie picks her way among the bodies laid out like sardines. There's a small moue of surprise from the platform campers, a generalised comment on what 'poor bugger might be under that one', until the night's residents settle back in the status quo of low-level chatter in their small groups. To her left, a mother is cooing her baby into sleep, while opposite an old couple are bickering over their precious space, pulling the top off a tea flask and smoothing out the *Daily Mirror* crossword as they go through the motions of what has recently become their life. She gazes at them wistfully. Would she

10

wish her parents here? No, not under this firestorm. And at age thirty-two, she shouldn't need them as guardians either, but as company – *some* familiarity – it would be nice. Someone.

After just three weeks, Londoners are old hands at this roving troglodyte existence, queueing for hours outside their chosen station before being allowed to buy a platform ticket and rushing down the escalators, marking out their plot for the night with blankets, deckchairs and the ubiquitous kettle and teapot. Today, Marnie has nothing but a solid handbag and regulation gas mask, its already worn cardboard casing bumping on her hip as she walks, the ever-present rhythm of wartime living.

'Over here, dear.' An older woman gestures to a narrow space next to her against the curved, tiled wall of the platform and shuffles sideways, laying out a thin piece of fabric that was probably a bedroom curtain once, but will inevitably save Marnie's work suit from the dirt and cigarette ash of the platform.

'Deena.' The woman offers a hand. 'And this is Captain Ahab.' She swipes back the blanket covering her legs to reveal a white, long-haired cat, curled up in blissful slumber amid the surrounding bedlam. 'Pets aren't really allowed, but I couldn't leave the captain,' the woman whispers. 'He won't be a bother, sleeps all night.'

Wish I had his talent, Marnie thinks. As it is, she doesn't sleep much, between the odour that hovers like a smog over the supine mass, the low hum of mutterings, snores and grunts, and the consistent keening of a nearby baby close into his mother's breast. With her long, lean body curled around her handbag and wrapped in a short wool jacket that covers only her top half, Marnie drifts in and out, her consciousness skating over the fog, but unable to distinguish the dull thud of bombs from the clumsy efforts of someone relieving themselves in the bucket at one end of the platform. Surfacing at intervals, she thinks of Grandad and wonders if he's sleeping, or been kept awake and is taking comfort – as he so often does – in his battered old copy of *The Great Gatsby*, transported to a time and world away from all this.

11

2

The Glittering City

25th September 1940, London

Marnie

The all-clear bleats at 6.30 a.m.: a less-threatening siren distin-guished by its quicker waves of sound and a lengthy monotone. To Marnie, the resonant whine is a reflection of the collective fatigue, as weary campers pick themselves up by degrees. Aldwych station has the benefit of being no longer in use, and so they won't have to deal with an influx of slightly irate morning travellers jostling for platform space, though the blast of air from an incoming train would be a blessing now in sweeping away the night.

Deena is already gone, along with Captain Ahab, and the space beside Marnie feels somehow mournful, as if she's lost a friend. Before the war, the rush of fresh particles as she ascended the escalators from the smoke-filled Underground always felt like a welcome balm, pushing away the grubby film of travel. Today, it merely swaps one dense atmosphere for another. At just approaching seven, a weak autumn light is losing out to the chaos of a heavy attack, the smoke from multiple fires eating the oxygen not already consumed by flames, office papers catching on thermals of heat and floating down like large confetti. ARP wardens, exhausted and smut-stained, are pulling at piles of rubble in the hope of finding life underneath, and London's famed streets lie somewhere beneath the carpet of rubble and grit, glittering with glass instead of fabled gold. As Marnie pushes her way through the turmoil, words of the past come rushing back: articles in the *News Chronicle* after Germany's infamous Kristallnacht, almost two years before. In a detailed report, their correspondent wrote of broken glass being swept like 'shale in the surf' in Berlin's clear-up, the readers learning of the horror and sorrow at what Jews were forced to endure. Now that soundtrack has become London's reality too, the rough shards herded across the ground, causing Marnie to wince. Whether or not his armies are here in person, Hitler has crossed the surrounding moat of sea and impinged on British lives with the same cruel purpose as for peoples across Europe – to wipe them out. London will survive, she has no doubt of that; it's already come through much worse. But at what cost, to the buildings and the people? To its soul?

She pushes aside the noise, the acrid smell of cordite and a new, sickening odour that can only be burning flesh, and wades through the sea of distress. Belatedly, she has only one destination and one purpose. One place to go.

Despite her resolve, it takes Marnie nearly half an hour to walk over the fire hoses snaking across the filthy tarmac and cobbled roads, ambulances scooping up the dead and injured, speedily for the living, less so for those with no hope. London resets itself for another day of war.

By the time she glimpses the open plain of Trafalgar Square, noting that Nelson himself is still miraculously intact up on high, there's already a sense of foreboding. The cloak of Luftwaffe has receded but the world is still closing in. Small smog patches above the rooftops are bleached by a sun that's just peering over the sway of barrage balloons, but at ground level the sight looks and feels increasingly grey. Her steps get quicker as she nears the place. Only now does the panic of the raid grind in her stomach. *Please no*, an inner voice chimes in line with her short, rapid breaths. *Please let him be all right. Don't let it be there. Not him.*

Just behind the National Gallery, the entrance to Orange Street is blocked by an avalanche of red bricks. A rising dread fuels Marnie to clamber over the jagged spars of wood pulling at her stockings like giant splinters, stooping to prevent herself falling between the spiky remnants of someone's past, toppled like a house of cards into a heap.

'Hey, miss!' A man's short, sharp bark causes Marnie to pause, but only for a second. 'You can't go in there!' he tries again, and begins scrabbling over the brickwork towards her, his tin helmet slipping over his eyes. 'It's dangerous. Stop!'

But Marnie can't, won't, because of what she sees. Or what's now absent. The space under the sign of 'Cooper's Bespoke Tailoring' is a grey, smoky, messy void, the letters hanging limply from one end of the lintel above the shop, severed like a hot knife through butter. The door is no more, not even fragments, and there are tiny fires burning at the entrance, like beacons neatly lighting the way to a banquet at some grandiose house. But the age-old building has just gone, disappeared into the mulch of London's ashes lying inert across the pavements. The two heavy stone buildings on either side are scarred and singed but not destroyed, like bookends with space for a missing edition.

Marnie sidesteps the flames and heaves herself forward into the dense lingering cloud, choking as she screams his name. 'Grandad! Grandad! Gilbert! Where are you?' Each word sucks volume and voice from her lungs, causing her to choke and falter, and it's then she realises her sobs are punctuating the pleading. Feeling a hand on her shoulder, she startles and sees the tin-hat man in his ARP siren suit, caked in grit and dust, a red stain on his shoulder that must be blood. But his face isn't angry, and that worries her more. He's not carping at her to get out or pulling her away roughly. Instead, he looks directly at her and there's pity etched into his blackened features. The edges of his mouth sweep down with regret.

'He's over here, miss,' Tin Hat says gently. With what he must have seen over the course of the night, she's grateful he can muster any sympathy at all. He steers her to the edge of the shopfront, to where a length of material is spread across a piece of pavement cleared of rubble, a pattern she recognises as expensive tweed, part of Grandad's good stock.

Thank goodness he has the best.

It's his outline under the delicate grey fleck: slim and tall, his proud chest like a gentle mound, with the tips of his eternally polished black brogues just visible under the fabric. They are caked in dust and it's this insult upon him that fells her, causing Marnie to double and clutch at her stomach, a stockinged knee hitting a shard of concrete as she crumples, much as the building had done just hours before. His shop, his business, *his life*. All gone.

'No! No, no, no . . .' she weeps, her fingers brushing furiously at his toe-caps, and then grasping at the shape of his pocket watch, ever present on his crisp, inch-perfect suit. Tin Hat stands behind while the industry of removal and repair goes on all around, as if he's somehow shielding her from more hurt. If only.

Marnie knows she shouldn't, and will probably regret her action, but she can't help drawing back the cloth to look at his face, bracing herself for the revulsion and the maiming under Hitler's tirade. Thankfully, there's none. He simply looks serene – only his clipped grey beard lighter with a sprinkle of fine white powder. But no blood, or scars, or gouging. Even his cheeks look pink. How can a bomb have ripped through, leaving nothing but a black hole, and yet her grandfather is untouched?

Quickly, Marnie raises the fabric further, stares for seconds at his chest and swears that it rises a fraction. It does, doesn't it? Just a millimetre maybe, but it's something. It's hope. Instantly, she twists to stare wide-eyed at Tin Hat. 'He's alive!' she cries. 'I can see it. He's breathing. Do something!'

That look of pity again. Regret. The ARP man – seasoned after only three weeks of Hitler's blitzkrieg – has done this before. This is his job now, until such time as the Luftwaffe decides to wreak chaos on another city across Britain or the globe. Or until the Germans come marching onto the streets, as per the anxious murmurings on the top deck of many a London bus these days.

'He's gone, miss,' Tin Hat says. 'We've checked. The ambulance people came, and there's no doubt.'

She looks back to the chest. Static under his pristine waistcoat. Winter and summer, war or peace, Blitz or not, he always wore a three-piece, tie and pin. 'A tailor has to inspire confidence,' he'd always told Marnie. 'Wear your skill on your sleeve.'

'But how? Why doesn't he look . . .' Her mind is fuzzy with the surrounding confusion, unable to focus on a single element that makes any sense.

'Probably the blast,' Tin Hat explains, and clearly wants to leave it at that, but she won't let him, cocking her head to one side. *Tell me.* 'It will have pushed out his lungs.' It's obvious Tin Hat is choosing the words carefully, despite his own exhaustion – there's no mention of 'blast', or 'burst', but that's surely what he means. His eyes dip down, signalling the end of his explanation.

What's the point in knowing more, Marnie thinks. He's dead. The man closest to her in London, perhaps in her life, is gone. Murdered by a man with a ridiculous moustache and the fire-power to muster Armageddon.

Tin Hat guides her to a clearing surrounded by vehicles and a tiny caravan kitchen that has miraculously negotiated its way through the rubble. Someone in a Women's Voluntary Service uniform thrusts a mug of tea in her hand, and she sips without tasting or swallowing consciously, but it's true, she thinks. It does help. Gradually, she's back to a reality that's her own personal nightmare.

Someone else approaches, talks to her, though she doesn't absorb any words. A piece of paper is pushed into her hand, and although the scribble makes little sense, it's clearly details of where Mr Gilbert Cooper ('deceased') will be taken, which morgue he will now shelter within, to be collated officially as one of many. Hitler's tally of domination. Marnie rarely swears, but the word 'bastard' comes to mind, echoes and stumbles around her tired, aching head.

'Are you all right, miss?' It's Tin Hat again.

'Yes, thank you,' she manages. It's what the British say, isn't it? The posters plastered across London tell them that – they can endure. They will. Winston insists on it. Only inside are you allowed to die and scream and pummel your heart back into life and weep into your WVS tea, which swills alongside the swallowed-back tears.

Where should she go now? It's almost nine and Marnie was due in the office at 8.30, though latecomers are tolerated a little more simply because of the buses these days, often waylaid by enormous craters in their path, the Underground equally slow to wake up from its night duties. Home to North London? No, she can't sit in her tiny flat and think about Grandad's last moments. He was a proud, upright man all of his life, but in those seconds, listening to the whine of bombs overhead, he might have been terrified. As anyone would. Marnie looks down at herself. She's filthy, unwashed, her stockings are pocked and her eyes red and puffy, but she needs to be around people. For Miss Roach to make her a cup of tea 'so strong you can stand your spoon in it', according to Raymond, and for Raymond – her kindly, sometimes fatherly boss – to offer condolences. Tea and sympathy: there really is something to be said for it.

Her gait is painfully slow as Marnie walks west to Piccadilly Circus and up Regent Street towards Broadcasting House. Most of the shopfront picture windows have been blown in, and her sorrow is mixed with true distress at noting the beautiful buildings felled, either by high-explosive bombs or the small incendiaries that rain nightly over the rooftops. Those have a habit of wheedling their way through windows and igniting catastrophic fires, flames that have proved the capital's age-old enemy since the Great Fire of 1666. How did the city cope back then, without Tin Hat and the irrepressible WVS offering up a sea of tea?

Marnie knows – especially now – that buildings are not people, and can be resurrected, unlike the dead. Still, they are precious to Londoners like her. It's a wound, and it hurts. Hitler, cruel but clever, clearly knows this.

As Portland Place finally comes into view, Marnie is relieved to see the gleaming white stone of Broadcasting House untouched, the larger-than-life statue of Shakespeare's Prospero and Ariel on constant guard above the entrance. The nine floors of the BBC's flagship loom over her like the prow of an enormous ocean liner, its curved walls endlessly sweeping through London's present mire, and she's certain it's the right place to be, the ship that she needs to steady her now. In the offices of 'Production (General)' on the sixth floor, Raymond Blandon looks up as she enters and instantly gauges the distress. He sits Marnie down and calls for the very strong tea. And he waits. For her to speak or cry, or simply be. This intuition is why he's considered among the best producers at Broadcasting House, why he's able to swoop into any studio, sometimes at a moment's notice, and inject calm and magic into an ailing or dull script. Why he's the best boss she could hope for.

Patiently, Raymond holds her teacup steady when Marnie's hands begin to tremble violently. 'Delayed shock,' he says in his deep, solid BBC voice. 'Nothing to worry about.' It's then that it hits Marnie; that Gilbert Cooper might not have dodged Hitler's missiles last night, but she did. It might have easily been her under that wreckage and, in a way, she almost wishes it had been – her sometimes pedestrian, lacklustre existence swapped for his lively hunger for life. And yet the reality of her narrow escape sparks a fresh round of shakes and a second cup of tea.

When she's cried, and Raymond has hugged in his fatherly way, with his big arms around her leaner frame and the sweet odour of pipe tobacco and hair oil a true comfort, he retreats to his inner office and leaves her to sit, because that's what is needed. He has no expectation of any work today, despite a frantic phone call from studio three for a production assistant – 'No, Miss Fern is indisposed,' she hears him say firmly into the receiver. The pile of scripts on her desk which need marking up will simply grow taller today. Today, Marnie Fern needs to attend only to her grief.

3

Into the Void

25th September 1940, Amsterdam

Corrie

He's not there. Gatsby. She pushes the tiny headset into her left ear, leaning into the radio set – as if it will make any difference – but it distils her concentration. Still silence. Some days the signal is weak and she has to almost pluck the dots and dashes from the void with her trained ear, like watching a faint, winking signal from a distant lighthouse and trying to fathom if it's real.

A sea of nothing. He's *never* not been there at the appointed time, as regular as clockwork. Though the news is scant from outside Holland, Corrie knows London has suffered over recent weeks with nightly onslaughts, and yet Gatsby rarely mentions such misery in their exchanges. Diligently, they focus on the task, respective fingers working at speed to avoid the Nazis pinpointing their location, nimble on the transmitter with the lightest of touch. Dot, dot, dash. Quick, sharp and purposed.

She squints under the single, dim light in the windowless base-ment, surrounded by the stock that she will take in stages up to her beloved bookshop above, and some that she dare not display on the shelves. Her own secret library, words that would easily get her thrown into jail in times like these: Ernest Hemingway, Oscar Wilde, Thomas Mann and even Fitzgerald, all wordsmiths banned by the Nazis because they speak of freedom, of other lives that are worlds away from the Third Reich. She looks at her well-thumbed

English copy of *The Great Gatsby* and wonders how such a love story can possibly threaten soldiers who have guns but little conscience. And what it all means to her now in times like these.

Times like these. That's an understatement. It's theft, plain and simple. The Nazis battered their way in – first the bombing of Amsterdam, when she heard the insidious drone of planes overhead, and subsequent explosions on nearby Herengracht, causing her solid house to shake. That was a mere taster. Days later, Hitler unleashed a lightning annihilation of Rotterdam before the troops marched in, spreading across Holland with a very real threat of equal destruction in Amsterdam and The Hague if the Dutch didn't welcome in their 'brother' nation. So, for months now, German soldiers have been loitering around the city's bridges and taking canal trips as if on a happy holiday. Street signs are written in the stark Teutonic script and there's even a new currency for German military to use. Holland has been appropriated – by force.

Yet, slowly but surely, it's trying to fight back. That's what she's here for, in this musty space that she strives to keep dry for the sake of the precious books that are her living and her tool for staying strong. But before she and her fellow resisters can build a force to retaliate, they need information from outside. And it's sorely lacking. So when she tap, tap, taps into the sacred air above the North Sea, it's precious intelligence that she is seeking, to allow her like-minded dissidents to begin organising, in the nooks and dark corners of the cafés frequented by proud Dutch determined to haul back their own country.

And Gatsby is her reliable channel to London and the Dutch government forced into exile there, striving to build a resistance from afar. Now, it's her valued, tenuous link to Willem as well.

But Gatsby is not there. Where is her codename opposite? Why isn't he answering?

With a mixture of angst and hope, Corrie turns her dial to 'transmit' and places a well-tuned finger on the button.

'*Call sign: Daisy . . .*'

21

4

Hidden Treasure

Marnie

By midday, Marnie is flagging. Raymond has been called to a meeting and the strength of Miss Roach's tea is starting to make her shake rather than infuse calm. Sleep for her is essential, especially if the Luftwaffe comes calling again tonight, though she plans on camping in Broadcasting House when darkness descends, making use of her employee ticket for the makeshift shelter in the BBC concert hall. There'll be no Deena or Captain Ahab this time, but the chance of a bunk, a blanket and a bathroom instead – the three Bs of sanity and survival. For now, home beckons.

Emerging on the northern end of the Piccadilly Line, Marnie sees immediately that Wood Green High Street struck lucky last night; the only evidence of the raid is a few small mounds of rubble swept to the edge of the roadside. The early afternoon bustle of suburban London settles her a little, people walking at a relaxed pace, a postman whistling as he strides past. She has no real love for her small one-bedroomed flat in a terrace near to the Tube station, but it is a relief to see it unscathed. The red-brick family house where Marnie grew up is three doors away and so far remains intact, although her parents left London at the first inkling of war, decamping as far as they could without crossing an ocean, to Scotland. Securing her own flat just a few doors away seemed convenient at the time, though it's never had the feel of a real home.

Until this morning, it was the tailor's shop that acted as her respite; busy or not, Grandad always welcomed her. She would sit and watch him test the quality of tweed between his seasoned, sensitive fingers, meticulously planning so as not to waste an inch, well before war and austerity descended. Then, he would chalk up the measurements – no pattern needed – and slice with his ancient, heavy scissors that were always out of bounds to Marnie as a child, and which secretly both scared and enchanted her. Her young, fertile imagination saw the razor-sharp blades infused with magic, cutting into her soul if she ever dared touch them.

'Right, Oscar, time for you to earn your money,' Grandad would say eventually to the worn but solid mannequin, and it was always Marnie's favourite part, to watch Oscar 'get dressed', the meticulous, angular suit begin to take shape under Grandad's fingers, a wizard of the cloth at work.

'Shall I bring the pins?' she always asked, both as a child and even as recently as the last week.

'Can't do without them, my lovely. Or you.'

It's this private script of theirs that Marnie replays as she fidgets in her cramped bedroom, on a mattress that is lumpy and rigid, but more yielding than a concrete platform. If only she could sink into unconsciousness.

Part of her wants to push away those memories, to sleep and forget. And yet they make her smile into the low ceiling, at the crack that seems suddenly to have appeared alongside the single light fitting. She plays back what Tin Hat told her – 'It would have been instant. He wouldn't have suffered' – and she works to believe it, that it might have been Grandad's lungs to bear the assault, or his heart, but he wouldn't have been lying there in agony, bleeding or broken. It wouldn't have been the scenario she witnessed only last week on her way to work; men and women from the rescue squads crowding around the pulverised remains of a home, one warden kneeling with his face into a pile of bricks.

'Keep talking to me, love,' he'd shouted, projecting his voice and optimism into a hole, presumably to a life still breathing beneath the debris. 'How many kids do you have? Three, you say? Tell me their names.'

Around him, the others in the group flashed looks of gravity and one – some kind of medic maybe – pulled open his bag and produced a syringe.

'How much should I give, if I can reach her?' one man in a siren suit uttered as Marnie walked close.

'All of it,' the medic said. 'It's the best thing.'

So yes, in some strange way Marnie feels thankful; the dust on Grandad's shoes had creased her, but any thought of his suffering would break her for eternity.

She wakes mid-afternoon and palms at her face; soot, grime and tears caked to form a decided crust, thicker than any Max Factor she's ever worn. In the dim light of the bathroom, she looks awful. Marnie works constantly to brighten her face, with the features inherited from her mother that have a tendency to sink downwards quite independently, as if they're predicting some dreadful atrocity. At times, when she's focused at work and her mask slips, someone will often say: 'Are you perfectly all right, Miss Fern?' and she has to hoist up her smile and reassure them, that yes, she is fine. *It's just my face that won't co-operate.*

She scrubs away at the grime in her old bathroom mirror, a thin layer of sorrow stripped clear as the water colours to grey and then swills down the plughole. If she sinks into a bath of hot, soapy water, the tears might never stop, and there's a sick feeling in her stomach, a likely mix of grief and hunger. So far, she's consumed nothing but Miss Roach's tea, which has undoubtedly pitched battle with the WVS variety inside her.

Marnie condemns last night's skirt and blouse to the wash pile and climbs into a similar outfit, brushes out the Blitz from hair that her mother describes as the 'colour of almonds' but is really just mousey, certainly in the weak, yellowy glow. For work purposes, she tends to keep her hair short and tamed, just enough length to pin into the nape of her neck.

She practises a smile; it's satisfactory, at least not the look of the doomed or the downright miserable. Londoners are no longer allowed that luxury, not according to Mr Churchill, anyway. When they behave, her lips are her most defining feature: full, with a natural bow shape, so that on the few occasions she wears lipstick, they stand out. Fashionable red is out of the question, since the boldness lends her the look of a circus clown. She thinks of Grandad and his enduring style, his maxim that 'a well-dressed man can never be downtrodden, no matter the knocks he's had', and she applies a layer of pale cherry colouring, smudges it with a handkerchief and then goes in for a second layer. He would approve. Along with the indefatigable Winston.

Hunger gets the better of her, and before descending into the Underground again Marnie walks down Wood Green High Street, comforted by its normality and the queue outside Williamson's the bakers, the aroma of a freshly baked loaf in her nostrils as she goes past. It's the Lyons Corner House she heads to though – always guaranteed to be buzzing, and with a good line in fruited buns, a necessary stodge to line her empty stomach. As she enters, the buttery, rounded orbs of Lyons' lighting act like sunshine, bathing Marnie in memories – good ones – along with the chink of cups and saucers, the hiss of the enormous urn-like coffee steamer instantly making her heart settle. It's where Mum took her every week as a child, Dad, too, on the half days when his hardware shop was closed. A long time ago now, but still fresh in her memory.

She opts for milky coffee and a fruit bun, working to force in the first mouthfuls, but then ravenous for the rest. Just sitting there, listening to the gossip of the Lyons' 'Nippy' waitresses, calms her. She feels numb, but equally as if any touch to her skin by another human will burn holes in her like acid. *Be normal*, she urges herself. Feel normal for him, because that's what he would have wanted.

She and Grandad had talked about death in the long wait of the phoney war, those months after September '39 when the bombs fell far away in Europe and the Germans swarmed over Denmark and Norway, Holland and then France. They could only read of the first British submarines lost in faraway seas, or the news that the Germans had occupied the Channel Islands, creeping closer to British shores. For months, Hitler kept them on tenterhooks, waging war above England's south coast with fighter pilots jabbing at each into the airspace, like enemy gulls wheeling overhead and pecking viciously at each other's wings with bullets.

Even now, Marnie has never admitted to anyone – not even Grandad – that in those early days she felt a frisson of excitement, thriving on the war's emergence. Not the promise of disaster, but the mood of anticipation that war brought, a certain pledge that things would have to change. In the corridors of Broadcasting House, there was a steady bustle as the Ministry of Information paired with the BBC to uphold the truth across nations (or the government's version of the truth). The increased workload pushed Marnie's own dreary routine onto the back burner, the BBC assuming a new, pivotal role as the voice of the nation. Memos flew around at a pace, and she and Raymond were needed, with their combined talents for adopting any kind of genre – news, drama and public information. She helped produce it all. She was skilled and in demand. And it felt good, with after-work drinks at the Langham Hotel opposite, courted by other producers to join 'their firm'. She felt wanted and needed, feelings that – after this morning – are drowned in guilt and grief.

Inevitably, Hitler determined on bursting London's particular bubble, prompting nervous talk in shops and pubs about just when the city would be a target. So when the bombs fell in August, in dribs and drabs at first, then with a vengeance, at 3.44 p.m. on September 7th 1940, it came as an odd kind of relief. Less so when that first night cleared and the casualties were counted, the capital's East End docks left as a flaming moonscape. There's no relief now. Only rubble and glass and heartache.

Throughout it all, Grandad was endlessly philosophical, bent over his huge industrial sewing machine, having lost two of his experienced staff to London's mass exodus into the countryside. Perhaps never happier, though, when forced to go back to what he loved in stitching cloth.

'If Hitler gets me, I'm coming back as Oscar,' he said during one particularly fierce raid. 'At least he gets to wear a good suit.'

'Grandad! Don't talk like that!' Marnie had said, though not with confidence, given the drubbing overhead that night. Mercifully, they'd survived that attack, only for . . .

She wonders what happens now, emotions and practicalities that will run parallel with war. Who to invite to the funeral . . . *Oh Lord! Her parents!* It's not that she's forgotten them, but what with the shock . . . The fact they're so far away and the unlikely prospect of travel seems as if Scotland *is* a foreign land, instead of across the border. Their lives really are light years away.

Marnie sinks the dregs of her coffee and finds a nearby phone box, clutching at her coins and dialling the number of her parents' ironmongery shop. Breath held, she imagines the trill echoing around the nails and screws and tins of paint as the two tend customers and shelves. 'Fern Hardware,' her mother answers, all business and innocence.

Marnie relays the sadness across the miles to her mother about Grandad, hears her sobs through the receiver, then her father

27

coming to the phone. 'Marnie, are you all right?' His voice is a tremor. 'We both wish you would consider moving up here. Out of the way.'

Out of the way of what, though? Bombs, or life? The last three weeks have taught Marnie that danger is sometimes better than dreary. Until today. Yet, oddly, even now, she's not frightened, only more wary.

'I'll come and visit soon,' she promises.

The much-needed shroud of night has fallen on the streets around Trafalgar Square, but the Luftwaffe are late tonight, so no sirens yet. Common sense and exhaustion says she should be in a bed or bunker somewhere, but Marnie's heart dictates otherwise; a more urgent desire is calling her towards Orange Street. She prays fatigue hasn't fuddled her memory of the pocks, pitfalls and pavements' edges towards Trafalgar Square; the blackout is already responsible for scores of deaths, people plunging into craters or hit by vehicles with only slits for head-lights. One loose footfall and she might as well be under one of the Führer's bombs. Approaching Grandad's shop, she's relieved to see the rescue crews have gone, leaving a large sign placed against the hole that was once her universe: 'Keep Out! DANGER. Unsafe structure.' Undoubtedly it's perilous to enter, but Marnie knows a second aim is to prevent looting, a crime that's punishable by death yet remains rife across the city.

She follows a makeshift path made through the rubble to the entrance, her short, noisy breaths overshadowing the crunch of grit underfoot. There's an urgency to her yearning, to glimpse his world for the last time and recover something tangible in recalling the endless hours spent in his magical palace. Equally, she's terrified of the ugly desolation she might find.

Beyond the warning notice, everything of the shop roof and upper storeys has been destroyed, and it's a relief that the offices above Grandad's tiny first-floor flat had been empty for months.

Even exposed to the sky, there's a charred stench of bonfires and damp wool, the entire building doused by fire crews in controlling the blaze. Little is left of the front shop where customers were greeted, while the newer front-of-house mannequins bought to replace Oscar and Frank are almost reduced to ashes; one stiff and sooty hand pushes out from the mulchy mess, as if proffering a greeting or asking to be pulled from quicksand.

Out back (though there's no wall to separate it now, let alone a curtain), Grandad's main workshop has been decimated. Tears brim in Marnie's eyes when she spies the only remnant of his trusty old workhorse of a sewing machine, industrial in size and strength, now reduced to a molten block. Defunct.

'Stop it,' she mutters sharply to herself, rubbing at her lower lids to ward off the sorrow. She has things to find and there's only a thin slice of moonlight to help. Sensing that the thick wooden planks of the ground floor are largely undamaged, Marnie picks her way down the slippery stairwell as if with her eyes closed, having descended into the basement many a time during a raid. Certain that the Luftwaffe or a keen-eyed ARP warden won't spot the glow, she lights a match. And gasps.

Like her grandfather, it's virtually untouched. She flicks up at the dense ceiling and a fresh layer of guilt bears down. If she'd been with him – if she *had* fought against that tide of people on the Strand – they would have been together. They might have survived. Both of them. As it is, perhaps Grandad was caught in his flat above the shop, or left the safe confines to check on something? Actions that Marnie always warned him against, chiding him to sit tight in the basement and put the kettle on again. He'd have grumbled but done it anyway.

Maybe. The worst is, she'll never know.

The match threatens to burn her fingers, and by touch and memory, Marnie feels her way to a small oil lamp always kept in the corner. From the resulting glow, she eyes the contents: Frank and Oscar are side by side, like always, the best of buddies.

Frank looks slightly worse for wear, a shower of wreckage on his shoulders, his body knocked into a corner, causing his hairless head to crack, like a boiled egg that's been tapped. Oscar is upright, as always, and his expression serene. Unspoiled. Plenty of tailor's dummies don't have heads – just a torso and removable arms – but Grandad liked these two the moment he spotted them in a second-hand sale. No hair, smooth and bland features, but 'something of a personality all the same in those heads', he always said. Many times, Marnie caught him talking to 'the chaps' as he worked. '*This is a good fit, Frank, if I say so myself.*' '*Oscar, you're a real man about town now.*' She's winded again by her own vivid recall.

Marnie would like to scoop it all up, every scrap of memory, every fibre of cloth in reach, but it's not possible. Oscar alone would be enough of a handful, and she wonders if, come the morning, she can engage some of the bombsite schoolboys to help her for a small fee. They seem to have hijacked every cart or wheelbarrow in the vicinity, while discarded prams are now rich currency for removals. In the meantime, Marnie searches out the magical scissors she so covets, Grandad's precious blades.

She scans the old cutting table that he'd reincarnated during the bombardments, but there's only scraps of cloth and a few stray pins, one side of a lapel he was in the process of stitching. Set into an alcove at the far end of the basement are several wall-to-ceiling cupboards, with tall, thin doors. They contained his supplies of thread and chalk and were out of bounds to Marnie as a child. In adulthood, she'd never had need to look inside, since Grandad always had the pins ready and waiting. She hesitates with her fingers on the handle, feeling like a tomb raider from Ancient Egypt, robbing from the deceased. And yet her longing for those scissors is overwhelming, a palpable element of her grandfather to bring him back in a lonesome moment.

Tentatively, she opens one door, surprised to see a curtain in front of the shelves, and the outline of something hard and square-ish at mid-height. A decommissioned sewing machine perhaps, one he was keeping for spare parts? Curious, Marnie pulls back the cloth, and stumbles backwards at the sight. Why? How? What the . . .?

Not a sewing machine, or anything else you might expect in a dark, slightly dank basement. Something, however, that she does recognise, by virtue of being surrounded by similar hardware in every working day. A radio. And not a cosy, wood-grained domestic wireless that families gather around in their armchairs, clutching cups of cocoa and hanging onto Winston's every word. This is a transmitter: rectangular and upright, with sharp metal corners. Nobody has one of these casually hanging around. Unless, of course . . .

Ice snakes its way through Marnie's arteries. Her ears fill with the nervous talk about pro-Nazi fifth columnists, spies mingling in the pubs and shops of the capital, like the group of German informants caught in Gloucester recently, all posing as innocent traders. Betrayal shouldn't be her first thought, but it is, followed by a wild swing of reason. *Not Grandad.*

And yet the radio is here, covertly hidden. Why?

Cautiously, Marnie approaches the transmitter as if it were one of the time-delay bombs that so often need defusing these days. Hinged to the shelf is a half-width plank that she unhooks and pulls down, noting a stumpy length of wood alongside, the exact height to wedge under in creating a stable work surface. Whatever this is, it was planned, and used. Nothing is dusty. Around the sides of the radio there is a handset with only one possible use, like a small Bakelite doorknob attached to a metal bar. Scraps of paper sit beside it, each with a jumble of letters and numbers scrawled in pencil, and a separate pile – neatly ruled in Grandad's steady hand – denoting several grids of letters. Her heart lurches again. Painfully. You don't need to be an agent to recognise this as codebreaking material. But what for? Moreover, *who* for?

Everything deflates inside her. *Them or us?*

Much like the second when she pulled back the shroud on Grandad's lifeless features, Marnie knows she could be setting herself up for a crushing blow. Is she strong enough to withstand it? Equally, can she walk away and pretend this doesn't exist?

She positions the oil lamp and pulls up a chair, reaching for the radio's 'on' switch. The set squeaks into life, dials flickering and needles in the little round windows swinging with readiness. Marnie slips a small headset onto her ears, noting a distinct white hair caught in the wiring, and she almost gives up at such close proximity to him. Only the need to know pushes her on.

Having been around BBC technology for so long, she recognises the crystal that needs plugging into place, and a dial she switches to 'receive' mode. Turning it slowly, millimetre by millimetre, Marnie screws up her eyes in concentration, eager to tune in. There are crackles and feedback, but what she's searching for is clarity, enough for a signal to appear in that vast ocean of space above where, inexplicably, a missive can wing its way over oceans and mountains, from thousands of miles away. Despite her job, the very existence of radio still strikes her as wizardry each and every day.

Is that something? It's faint at first, but clearer the more that Marnie filters the sound in her ears: a series of dots and dashes, easily distinguished as Morse. Grandad taught it to her when she was barely twelve years old, and she never questioned it then. It was simply a great game when she stayed over with him; he'd rig up a crude tin-can-and-string arrangement from his room to hers, and they would exchange silly messages, each with a pencil and a pad to convert the signals.

Do you want porridge for breakfast? he'd tap out.

No, kippers with jam, she rapped back, to his laughter in the next room.

Only now, it's clear Grandad had other uses for his skills. Does that mean he could have been a conduit for years? Since Hitler came to power in '33? *How?* How had he masked his true identity? And from her?

Automatically, she reaches for the pad and pencil, scribbling down the letters feeding through the headphones like gibberish, as coded messages always are before deciphering. The sounds repeat themselves once more before stopping abruptly, and although Marnie rotates the dial to maintain the signal, there's nothing. How can she decipher this jumble? She turns to each grid of letters written in Grandad's hand and works through all six, using the top line, and then the second to switch each of her scribbled letters. But it makes no sense, in no language she can recognise.

She moves the oil lamp closer: on the shelf beside the radio are six books side by side: George Orwell, Ernest Hemingway, Thomas Mann, Jane Austen, Thomas Hardy and Gilbert's all-time favourite, Fitzgerald's *The Great Gatsby*. Marnie narrows her eyes again in concentration: are they here for a reason? And if not, then why?

The muddle of letters and numbers in her own scrawl *must* be saying something. At the top is 'TD 134. NG'. Is it a direction to the receiver of the message? Her eyes go to the spines of the book, and suddenly – like a magnet – they fix on one text. *Tess of the D'Urbervilles*. TD. Grandad always said it was his least favourite Hardy novel, so why would he have it alongside those he loved?

She grabs at the book, flips the dog-eared pages to 134, squints in the gloom at the print. It's faded, but definitely there – letters circled in pencil in random order, all twenty-six of the alphabet, aside from z. There, it's replaced by an 's', a common trait of coders, she recalls. How does she know that? Marnie can't fathom, other than it's a tiny nugget of knowledge lodged in her brain. With her mind in overdrive, she reasons: could 'NG' simply mean New Grid? It's possible.

Quickly, she draws herself a rough square and lays out the letters in the order they are circled on page 134, creating a new jumble of twenty-six. Letter by letter, she translates the radio message using this new grid. It's in English. And it makes sense. Of a sort.

Gatsby. Is the tailor's dummy still upright? Urgent reassurance needed. Daisy.

There's no mistake – it's for him, and from someone he's familiar with; their Daisy to his Gatsby, erstwhile lovers in literature. It's no coincidence.

The rest of the message appears obvious: poor Frank lies half-cocked in the basement, but the 'tailor's dummy' is Grandad, surely. And no, she can't give the messenger reassurance, whoever is at the other end. Though Marnie's Morse is ingrained, it is rusty, and there's no good news to share even if she could. Would she in any case, not knowing if this 'Daisy' is friend or foe to the British nation?

Eyes closed, Marnie breathes deeply, pushing back the squall of despair turning her inside out. Right now, her only endeavour must be to save her grandfather's reputation, or at least postpone any damage until she can seek out the truth. And that means moving the radio, lest the bombsite scavengers comes hunting in daylight. The rest – the disbelief, and that crushing pain in her chest – is secondary.

The metal-clad set is not as heavy as it looks, but unwieldy, and she reaches for a length of cloth to wrap around it, stuffing the scraps of paper in her handbag. All six books are too bulky to fit, so Marnie pushes all but one behind an offcut of material and closes the cupboard doors, sliding the slim volume of *The Great Gatsby* alongside the scraps. She'll chance another visit for the rest tomorrow, the scissors now long forgotten. 'Sorry, Oscar, looks like you're staying put for the time being too.'

Her breath is noisy as she clambers up the basement steps, both arms cupped under the radio set. It means she's focused on not falling as she emerges to ground level, blinking to adjust in a new gloom, and she doesn't see the figure in front of her. Not until it's too late.

5

The Conduit

Corrie

Corrie jabs frantically, her principal finger barely skating over the Morse button as the jumbled letters are funnelled through the metal at speed. The message she barely has to think about, reeling off her own scribbled encryption, over and over. It won't matter, because if he's there, he'll get it. They have a connection, she and Gatsby.

Gatsby and Daisy. Some might assume lovers, but it's not like that: Fitzgerald's famed characters needed each other. She and Gatsby are hundreds of miles apart, but coupled all the same, and with the same motive: communication. Only a link to the outside world will allow the resistance to escalate, to help rid their country of the audacious cuckoos that have invaded the Dutch nest. Hitler's interlopers insist that the Netherlands is a natural ally to Germany, in sharing a border, a culture, and a way of thinking. 'A brother nation,' Hitler has said more than once. The thought disgusts her, that she should own any part of their philosophy – a way of thinking that only serves to scatter everyone she loves: her tiny seeds against the might of his tornado.

So that's why she and Gatsby work to hone their link between Amsterdam and London. The messages she collects from the resistance cell are in a readable but cryptic form, transformed

35

under her hand to a mesh of letters and numbers, and then to Morse – the vital work of a radio 'pianist' with nimble fingers.

If Corrie is honest, it's her solace, what with Willem in London, and Kees leaving for The Hague in the last month. This fleeting stream of dots and dashes spells out 'hope' in her mind.

Now, all that may be gone too. Where is he? A brewing ripple of disquiet begins to simmer within. Bad enough that Gatsby might be hurt, but if Willem was with him . . .? She works to ignore the pickaxe in her guts, which hacks away at her being with heavy blows.

Glancing at the stopwatch to her side, Corrie sees the deadline is seconds away; any longer on the frequency and the ever-present enemy ears may pinpoint her location. Short and sweet is the key to secrecy and survival, and why she and Gatsby are so valuable to the cause with their lightning exchanges.

At last her finger lies inert over the button, and she flicks the switch on her radio to 'receive'.

Come on, come on.

Leaning into the set again, her ears scan the void coming through her headphones, picking and probing each nuance of sound. Is that something? A fraction of change in the pitch. Is he receiving? Her heart rises to a peak, and plummets a second later. What with the delay, it might not be him. If he's been discovered, it could easily be an imposter. The alternative she doesn't consider. It's too final. For him, but also, selfishly, for herself too. She's adrift from everyone she's ever loved right now, thanks to the Germans circulating around her city, smiling and smoking, trying to appear as benevolent occupiers. She walks past them daily with her basket and an expression of gratitude, laughing inside at her blissful deceit. Almost always, she's carrying innocent groceries, though often there's a tiny missive tucked into the brown weave of the basket, the paper carefully steeped in tea to blend in, a tiny strand in the web of dissidence laid across the city, to be sent on to Utrecht, Rotterdam and The Hague.

36

Corrie's ear is drawn suddenly to a noise above, the tinkle of the shop bell made purposely loud as a warning. She rips off the headphones, shuts down the machine and shrouds it under a heavy damask cloth, before climbing the stairs.

On the third step, she pastes on her shopfront smile. It's automatic these days, a convenient face of acceptance on reaching the counter and the stark uniform opposite. 'Good day, how can I help you?'

Inevitably, he wants something that reminds him of home, a novel he once read perhaps, and she leads him to the shelf of German texts she replenishes regularly nowadays. Having the enemy as customers sickens her, but it means good protection; even the Nazis would be reluctant to shut down or search their own link to the Fatherland, a place where they can access a precious piece of nostalgia.

Today, the officer is easily satisfied and leaves with his two novels, but it means she's late for her delivery across the city. In her basket are books 'for an elderly lady who can't get out', she explains to the Wehrmacht sentry. She doesn't tell them about the small packages carefully stitched to the inside of her woollen cape, evenly distributed so the weight helps it swing convincingly as she walks. The perfect shroud, if she weren't so hot under it. Today, there's also a sheaf of carefully folded papers. Forged, of course; the means of ghosting out someone desperately sought by the Germans, often for the valuable knowledge locked into their heads. And the Abwehr – Hitler's determined German military intelligence – want the key to it.

Her job is to stride with purpose along the canal at Herengracht, dip swiftly into a side street, slide into a doorway that leads to the back entrance of a church building, and deliver her goods.

She's Corrie – a conduit in so many ways, and proud of it.

37

6

The ARP Man

25th September 1940, London

Marnie

The legs, in a defiant stance, are the first thing that registers to Marnie. Heavy boots underneath are planted in the rubble, and she squints at the familiar outline of an ARP siren suit, tall and broad.

'I . . . I . . .' Panic. Her weary, overwrought heart somersaults. 'I'm not looting, I promise,' she stutters, climbing the last steps. 'It's – *was* – my grandad's shop. I came to get some things, just trinkets. Nothing valuable.'

'That's a very large trinket, if I'm not mistaken,' a voice comes back. Sarcastic but not light-hearted.

She looks down at her hoard. It's becoming heavy, her back aches and suddenly she's so tired. Exhausted from the entire day, last night's lack of sleep, grief and shock. So weary she would happily lie down in the soup of detritus on the shop floor and close her eyes.

'Just a box of things – his work tools,' Marnie lies, knowing instantly that it's transparent.

Silence, at best uncomfortable. He shifts, pulls off his tin helmet, and takes a step towards her. She lifts the radio in defence. What will he do? Why is he here alone? She can't hear any other ARP searching the ruins in the dark. At the same time, she's too spent to run through this wreckage.

'It's Marnie, isn't it?' His voice is deep, perfect English but with an accent she can't quite place.

'How . . . how do you know that? Who are you?' Panic quivers through her words.

'Gilbert spoke of you frequently,' the man comes back. 'He was very proud.'

The fact that he knows her grandfather's name acts as some reassurance, but it's not enough for Marnie to lay down her guard, or the radio. What is he doing here? Simply the local ARP warden? Grandad knew all the locals in the surrounding streets, and he might easily have spoken of his family, quite innocently. But that's not how this feels.

'I know what you have there,' he says, though it's devoid of threat.

'Just some keepsakes,' she tries again while calculating. If he knows her name, he may know she works at the BBC, and she's the only Marnie at Broadcasting House.

'It's a radio,' the man offers plainly.

Suddenly, there's little point in denying it.

His voice softens, a tone that makes an attempt at camaraderie. 'Listen, we can't talk here. Let's stow it back in the basement, make it secure and go somewhere safe to talk.'

Still on her guard, Marnie nods reluctantly. 'Somewhere public,' she says firmly.

'All right, if that's what you want.'

When the man descends into the basement before her, the foolish (and slightly reckless) part of Marnie briefly considers running, but it's only fleeting. She'd have a ten-second advantage at best, and his long limbs would easily catch up. Instead, she follows him begrudgingly, keeping close to the stairwell, her back against the rail. Down below, he reaches for the oil lamp instinctively, as if he's been here before, moving with the same familiarity as her grandfather had in the darkness. Questions burn inside: is that good or bad? Whose side is this man on?

Silently, he relieves her of the radio and returns it to the empty cupboard, securing the door with a wedge of wood. 'I'll come back later tonight and collect it,' he turns to say and, for the first time in their exchange, there's the hint of a smile. Marnie is silent, offering little argument, because that's her way. Besides, is there any alternative?

He unbuckles the belt of his siren suit and steps out of it, trousers and shirt underneath, covered by a short wool blouson jacket. As he stuffs the uniform into a haversack, he looks up, into the deep suspicion of Marnie's gaze.

'So, you're not an ARP warden?' she queries, a wave of disgust evident in her tone, that his appropriation of the well-respected role is a crime in itself.

He looks alarmed. 'No, I am. Really.' Now it's his turn to beg for belief. 'But I'm not on duty tonight. The uniform helps, that's all. Moving around.'

'For snooping, you mean?' She can't help annoyance creeping in too.

He sucks in a breath, a signal perhaps that the exchange is becoming fraught. 'I don't know about you, but I need a drink.' He heads with force towards the stairs and she has no choice but to sidestep, following him into the open, roofless shop and charred remains. This man could well be a danger to her, in which case she should walk away. But he might also answer the multiple questions jostling for space inside her head.

For perhaps the first time in Marnie's life, she throws caution to the wind and steps into the darkness.

In the pitch black of the street, Marnie's only reference is the sound of the man's heavy steps crunching over the rubble. His footfall is more certain than hers; to her annoyance, she has to keep track and be led in her own city, by someone she doesn't know or trust, to Lord knows where. There are few people about once they exit the side roads, occasional spectres in the night

40

fog, figures looming out of the gloom once they're almost on top of each other, often with a look of alarm. The unease is compounded when the warning siren starts up, an escalating wail that sets the people's pace instantly faster. The scurrying for a subterranean world begins.

'Damn!' She hears his irritation a foot or so in front.

'Where's the nearest shelter?' Marnie asks. It's a genuine question, but also a test: if he is a true warden, he will know.

'This way,' he says, and she's alarmed to feel his hand on her arm, sweeping her down a side street somewhere near Leicester Square, to the top of steps leading into another basement.

'If you think I'm going . . .' she protests.

'It's safe,' he cuts in with a huff. 'And public. More importantly, we can get a drink. If I'm going to die tonight, I want a whisky in my hand.'

She could argue, but given the events of the last twenty-four hours and the overhead whine of aircraft now mixing with the siren, Marnie simply nods. Once the ack–ack guns begin blasting at incoming Luftwaffe, loud enough to eclipse Moaning Minnie, there's very little choice.

Inside, Marnie sees with relief that it's a type of club or private bar, two rooms with booths of tables and chairs around the edges, a few dotted in the centre. The place is half full, and those present seem unfussed about the potential catastrophe outside, a succession of thuds now audible over a gentle jazz soundtrack. A thin veil of smoke and the continued hum of conversation points to a generally relaxed poise, in spite of the raid.

The man gestures towards a booth. 'What will you have?'

'Brandy, please.' It's not her usual choice, but what she needs right now.

He sidles in opposite with two glasses, and it's only then that she observes him clearly. He's in his early thirties, she guesses, with hair that's light rather than the brown of the bombsite dimness, golden more than blond, with curls cropped

41

short. An angular, solid face supports a scowl over a strong nose. Above all, he looks tired. Perhaps as much as she is.

He sees her looking and raises his glass. 'To your grandfather. He was a good man.' There's a twist to his mouth that she detects as genuine. 'No, a great man.'

Marnie nips at her brandy, the burn pushing up some courage. 'So, tell me what you know.'

He considers for a second, looks around the room and judges the background of music and bombs is enough to mask their conversation. 'Your grandfather worked for me.'

'And who do you work for?'

'That I can't say. Yet. But it's the right side.' He looks into the table as he says it, a finger circling the rim of his glass.

'And if you were a Nazi, you'd say that was the right side.'

He shoots a look, perhaps shocked at her audacity. But then, so is she. Where is this bravado coming from? It's not the Marnie Fern she knows.

'I'm not a Nazi,' he says flatly, and his eyes connect with hers, fixed and determined. They are clear, his pupils wide in the club's smoky fug. 'And neither was Gilbert Cooper. Quite the opposite.'

'So, convince me. What was my grandfather doing with a clandestine radio in his basement, and a whole host of coded messages? I'm no spy but even I know that's not run-of-the-mill these days.'

'Your grandfather was one of our best radio operators, with very nimble fingers. Someone who was helping the Dutch resistance come into being, so we can actually fight those Nazi bastards.'

Marnie desperately wants another brandy, but daren't chance her senses being further clouded. What she really craves is for this day to end, for it to be a very bad dream, and to return to her routine existence, however dull it is. She'd swap everything to be back in the basement with Grandad, perhaps terrified of the bombs but oblivious to all this . . . It feels like betrayal, even though this man insists it's far from treacherous.

He tells her, halfway down his whisky, that his name is Willem – 'and yes, it is my real name'. The accent is Dutch, though subtle, and he works for the government of the Netherlands in exile, a handful of escapees led by the nation's indomitable Queen Wilhelmina.

'I don't understand,' Marnie says. 'What's that got to do with my grandfather?'

'Did you know that his own grandmother was Dutch?'

'No, I didn't,' she says hesitantly. 'He didn't talk much about his family.'

He takes another swig. 'To be fair, it wasn't the reason I chose him.'

'Chose him? How?' She looks at her emptied glass. More alcohol is perhaps a bad idea when the world is upside down, and bombs are falling like rain outside, but she's longing for a certain numbness.

'Even at the BBC, it's unlikely that you'll have heard of the RSS, the Radio Security Services?' Willem says.

Marnie shakes her head, steeped in disbelief.

'Gilbert Cooper was a member – a civilian commissioned by the government to listen into radio traffic from abroad. German radio traffic.' Perhaps seeing her mouth fall open and her eyes cloud with the look of someone truly duped, he adds: 'He was bound not to tell a soul. Not even you.'

'I knew he tinkered around with radios,' she says slowly, 'but I imagined it was in the same way he fixed his sewing machines. I never dreamt it was a passion.'

'It was a bit more than that. It's what Gilbert did in the last war – too old for combat but an ace in radio surveillance apparently. Again, top secret.'

Now, Marnie does need the clock to turn back, to pin her grandfather down and fire questions at him, to strip back the layers that she knew nothing of. How didn't she know? Too preoccupied with her own life and work, immersed in her own melancholy?

But Grandad is gone, and the most she can do is discover more of him now. 'So, how did you come to find him, if he was one of many?'

Willem sighs. 'I was tracking what little traffic in messages we get in from Holland – it's patchy to say the least – but I noted how much detail he gleaned, and his speed at reading Morse. I made contact and put forward a proposition.'

'Which was?'

'To send and receive messages from our one reliable conduit in Amsterdam. Exclusively, for me.'

Marnie's cloud of confusion diffuses, though it's anything but clear. 'Is that Daisy?' she asks.

It's his turn to look surprised, eyes skimming the club and lowering his mouth into the table. 'You found his notes?'

'Yes. And I heard a message come through from this Daisy.'

Rapidly, his disbelief turns to something like amusement. 'Gilbert always said you'd be better than him, convinced that you'd make a perfect pianist.'

'Pianist?'

'An operator, one who's flighty with their fingers on the Morse button. Said you would' – and here he falters at the meaning – 'knock him into a cocked hat.'

Marnie lets fly with a laugh, on today of all days, but she can't help it. It was one of Grandad's many maxims, so typical of him. She looks at Willem, and feels sure he is telling some truth. Does she trust him? That may be going too far, but this man certainly knew Grandad, with a level of confidence between them. That may have been a trust of sorts.

What to think? She's flattered, aggrieved and angry, collected in one large breath that projects into her still empty glass. Woozy, too, with fatigue and alcohol.

'He was utterly devoted to you,' Willem says quietly. 'Told me he was doing it for you, and the future of your family.'

Of everything revealed so far, this statement buckles her; the

44

brandy burn, too little food and an excess of sorrow igniting a blaze inside. All of it flares painfully. Grandad knew how much she craved a family, someone to share her life with. Though they never spoke of it openly, he sensed that, as a woman of thirty-two, the dream was passing her by. Marnie had work and friends to occupy her, but the desire remained for more – someone she could laugh and share silly things with. More so now, to be able to talk of a future as the bombs fall and perhaps even to squabble over who has more space in the shelter.

Marnie's parents consistently fail to hide their own disappointment, written between the lines of her mother's weekly letters, where she asks earnestly 'Have you been out?' and 'If so, who with?' What her mother really means is: with a man, who might marry you, and save us the shame of a spinster in the family. That word: *spinster*, with all the visual image of a frumpy wardrobe, a tightly wound bun of hair and a perfusion of lavender water. Poor Miss Roach in a nutshell. In time, she feels destined to become 'poor Miss Fern'.

There was a man once, back in '33, a reporter from Reuters she met at a BBC reception. It was casual at first, in that he disappeared 'on assignment' every so often, only to rekindle the relationship on his return, a furious round of dinner-dances where he waxed lyrical about his travels to Berlin and Vienna, and she had nothing to offer in return except the drudgery of life at the BBC and typing up dull reports, as was her secretarial job then. After several months, there was a weekend away in Hastings, with a candlewick bedspread covering the double divan and everything that implies, and she felt it might have been going somewhere. Until he – Edward – simply disappeared. Not even a note, or a letter. Frantic calls to the Reuters office bore nothing except an air of embarrassment. Eventually, she'd pleaded with Raymond to make enquiries, and he came back several days later with a sheepish apology and the news that Edward had finally 'emerged' as a fascist, moving to Germany and joining the ranks of the up-and-coming Nazi party.

'I'm so sorry,' her boss had said, almost as if her lover had died. Which he had, in a way. Certainly the death knell for her trust in men. *If you can't spot an out-and-out fascist*, she'd told herself, *then what hope is there for a man with a true heart and no secrets?*

'So, would you consider it?' Willem's voice is half drowned by a furious spurt of anti-aircraft fire, though Marnie is miles away from the reality, lost in a world of her own disillusionment.

She's brought back by a fierce blast which can only be streets away. 'Sorry, what?'

'Would you consider stepping into his shoes? Working for us?' Willem's gaze is steadfast. Evidently, he's not joking. 'Look, I know it's been a difficult day, and it's far too soon, but Gilbert insisted . . . he said I should ask, if anything ever . . . He said you would be good, better than him.'

The world erupts both inside and out. Marnie gets up, bent on leaving, oblivious to the carnage beyond the door. She doesn't care – she'll risk death just for a breath of fresh air, cordite and all. She's suffocating with all the domestic smoke and bonhomie, secrets uncovered and this new truth. If it really is truth.

She stumbles for the door, attracting a few languid looks as she goes, aware of Willem behind her, but forging on.

He grabs her by the arm as she reaches for the handle. 'You can't go out there – it's madness,' he says. Then catches the glint in her eye and recoils, seeming to read her sentiments: *This whole bloody thing is madness*, she is saying. *Death, bombs, messages and Morse. What could possibly be worse about this day?*

Marnie shakes away his grip. 'I need to go,' she says, with a surprising level of defiance.

'Where?' He holds out both palms. 'In this?'

'The BBC,' she says hastily. It's her real home and refuge, in so many ways. She's dodged Hitler's wrath before and she'll take her chances.

'I'll come with you.'

'No, I'll be all right,' she insists.

He holds her firmly, with his gaze this time, and the hint of a wry smile. 'It's me who brought you here, remember. And I am a warden. It's my job. Please?'

Another crash outside, closer this time, causes her to reconsider. 'Fine. But just to Portland Place.'

Outside, the raid is finally waning, the skies overhead no longer swarming with Luftwaffe. The anti-aircraft guns send up sporadic red tracers into the dark void, chasing off the straggling bombers who are turning tail for German airspace and their own safety. Job done. London dented again.

This time Marnie follows Willem willingly as he leads her through a landscape of flames, some raging with a violent blue intensity, while others flicker like innocent garden bonfires in tones of orange and red. He's clearly switched on some form of night vision, because he skirts around the new mounds of rubble at a pace, crunching over glass and only stopping when they come across a small device not yet exploded. It's then Marnie feels the tension ripple from him, of a danger both close and imminent. Willem pulls out a whistle from his pocket and sends up a shrill calling, beckoning a uniformed ARP to come and tend to the device, exchanging a mumble of words as Marnie looks on, almost mesmerised by the intense heat and glow. Too many bombs today and too much death, and now she wants to close her eyes and her mind to it all, feels herself drifting and desperate to curl up in a shop doorway . . .

'Come on, not too far now.' Willem's voice jerks her back into the present as he reaches for her hand. His skin has the roughness of someone who pulls lives and bodies from the fallen bricks of London, his grip determined. For the first time in this long, long day, Marnie feels undaunted.

Both are breathless and covered in dust by the time they reach Broadcasting House.

'You'll be all right here?' he asks. There's smut on the bridge of his nose which, for some unknown reason, Marnie feels an urge to wipe away. But doesn't, of course.

'Yes, there's a good shelter in the basement,' she says. 'A proper bed, if I'm lucky.'

He looks almost envious. 'Well, take care. I'm sorry we had to meet in such sad circumstances. I really liked Mr Cooper. And he was a hero to us in Holland.'

She's hot from the city ablaze and their near run, but what he says warms her in a different way, something soft amid the bloody thorns of war. 'He was one of a kind,' she nods.

Willem turns to go, then spins back. From his expression, it's more than an afterthought. 'Will you at least consider it – what I said? About working for us?'

She hadn't meant to, had already dismissed it as impossible in among the revelations that have come thick and fast tonight. Something, though – perhaps running through a blazing city with stupid abandon – prompts a fleeting change of heart. 'Perhaps. How will I get hold of you?'

'You can't,' he says matter-of-factly. 'I'll find you.'

And he's gone, like a ghost sliding into a Victorian fog.

She falls into a bunk and feels sleep rushing in as she wriggles, half dressed, into the clean sheet-sack issued at the entrance of the BBC concert hall. With the seating removed, it's almost like a purpose-built, scooped-out shelter, the edges lined with cubicles (for the top-notch BBC elite), and bunkbeds in between, a line of blankets pegged out through the middle to partition the men from the women. Lord forbid there should be any funny business at the BBC.

The excellent acoustics mean all noise is in surround sound, the snores echoing around the walls in the oddest symphony ever played. Marnie hears nothing, though – not a note. Exhaustion triumphs over the angst and she sinks rapidly into the deep, untroubled sleep of a newborn.

7

Live for the Living

26th September 1940, London

Marnie

Marnie wakes at gone seven to a gentle exodus as the shelter picks itself up, filing towards the bathrooms and on to various offices and studios. She's slept through the all-clear siren, needing a few minutes to recall what day and time it is. Her mouth is parched and, despite the sleep, her head feels muzzy. The events of the previous day emerge like fragments: her grandfather's bombed-out shop, the transmitter and Willem's proposal. They and her journey to the BBC shelter slide in and out like vapour, much as Willem had appeared and spirited away again. Did he really ask if she would join some sort of secret radio army, or was that conjured by her imagination and brandy combined?

For certainty, she reaches into her bag and pulls out the small, well-thumbed volume of F. Scott Fitzgerald, turns to the fly page and the fading pencil marks in neat script: *To THE great Gatsby – yours, Daisy.* It doesn't have the ring of a love note, but of respect. She runs a finger across the letters, feeling the tentative connection and then a resounding emptiness, echoing like a clarion bell. Grandad is dead. It's a truth not washed away by sleep, or a bad dream. He's gone, and she has to go on. They all do. What other choice is there?

Marnie collects a spare blouse from her desk drawer and sponges away last night's layer of grime in the ladies. She's in one of the studios by ten a.m., grappling with the script of *The Kitchen Front* and acting as referee between the sound engineer and a very forthright presenter who insists on rooting out a particular apron for the recording, even though it's radio. By some miracle of diplomacy they manage to create a programme worth broadcasting. Who'd have thought there were quite so many ways to 'present a potato'?

Upstairs on the sixth floor, it takes only the familiar pale wood veneer of the regulation office furniture to inject a renewed sense of calm. A second glance reveals a leatherette jacket covering the largest typewriter, with no evident tincture of tea.

'Is Miss Roach not in?' Marnie calls through Raymond's open door, experiencing a fresh unease after last night's drubbing.

'Dentist, or doctor,' Raymond mumbles through his pipe. 'Frankly, I'm amazed she could get an appointment.' Marnie feels relief, that at some point today the keyboard will come to life and the air fill with Miss Roach's industrious clattering and the simmering kettle. Something like normal.

She and Raymond go over the schedules for the next week, marking up the scripts and matching their diaries. Where possible, it's always a bonus to work together, in symmetry with someone. Perhaps it's the nearest she'll ever get to a partner in life; a pseudo husband, Marnie often thinks. Though there's no suggestion of any romance, she senses that Raymond needs it too, after losing his wife so suddenly, six months before war broke out. He's read her grief so well because he knows it intimately.

He brews a fresh pot once they've finished, 'Though, I warn you, it's not the smelling-salt variety of Miss Roach. I don't know how she does it with tea on ration nowadays. I think she must squeeze the leaves with her bare hands.'

Raymond sits facing her, cup in hand, instantly more serious. 'So how are you?'

'I'm all right,' she says. The muscles in her face are tired from pretending. 'Not fine, or dandy. Just all right.'

'That's good enough,' he replies, as if he knows. Which, of course, he does.

They sip in silence for a few minutes.

'Have you thought about the funeral?' Raymond asks.

Marnie sits up. What with everything else, she hasn't. 'I suppose I should. Part of me thinks in times like these there would be some sort of communal grave. But Grandad deserves more than that – everyone does.'

Raymond stands and puts a reassuring hand on her shoulder. 'If you need a decent funeral director, I've got a name.'

Of course he has.

She has to face it. There's no one else to help, and Marnie doesn't expect her parents will travel down to London for the funeral. They were fearful before Hitler's blitzkrieg, and still terrified more than four hundred miles to the north. Only she and her cousin, Susie, are left in London. Grandad's diaries and order books went up in smoke, so there's little chance of contacting even his best customers. Besides which, who has the will amid this chaos to attend the funeral of their tailor?

At lunchtime, Marnie ventures from the bastion of Broadcasting House; the canteen talk is still heavy with news of two waitresses – sisters – who died last week when their house was bombed, and Raymond reports that it's kippers in mustard sauce on the menu. She needs some air and light. The acrid smell of cordite has dissipated, but that distinct charred odour lingers and she can taste the particles on her tongue, dry and bitter. Will London smell like this forever?

On her way to the sandwich shop, Marnie notes with sadness that a hole has been gouged in one of the crescents of white Regency houses at the end of Portland Place, like a perfect set of dentures with one tooth plucked out. And yet two doors away, a man patiently pushes a lawnmower up and down the front garden.

He's heard you, Winston – keep calm and carry on.

Silly as it sounds, she feels as if the scene is unfolding for her alone; if the mowing man pushes forth, then so must she. Squatting on a dusty bench and chewing on her dull, dry sandwich, Marnie Fern wonders: is she prepared to go one step further, outside of her quiet, comfortable orbit for a stranger she's only just met? Is she really that willing?

At six p.m., with various buses on diversion and the Underground already starting to fill up with shelter dwellers, it's quicker to walk to St Thomas' Hospital, squatting on the river's edge opposite the Houses of Parliament. The welcome sight of Big Ben's tower and the familiar clock face ushers pedestrians across Westminster Bridge, its lights doused and the muddy swirl of the Thames reflecting a faint glow amid the dusk. Marnie stands for a minute to watch it flow, as it has done for centuries, through plague and fire and war. Steady and unruffled. On the water itself, fireboat crews are readying themselves for tonight's onslaught, certain that the German fighters will again use the curving, wide seam as a ready-made 'runway' for prime targets hugging the riverside, as they have most nights. Hitler knows that a direct hit on the seat of Britain's Parliament represents a potentially fatal arrow to pierce the heart of Britannia, far more than mere bricks and mortar. The bullseye. And so far, those German bombers have only been polishing their aim.

But not tonight, Adolf. I have a job to do.

Always hating the sickly smell of hospital disinfectant, Marnie would nonetheless prefer to be visiting a friend within the wards of St Thomas' faded Victorian façade today. As it is, following signs to the mortuary is infinitely worse. Prompted by Raymond, she'd phoned the number on the slip of paper given to her amid rubble and confusion; Mr Cooper needs formally identifying, they informed her. Now, heading down the darkened hospital corridors towards death, she's glad to have glimpsed his face already, the shock less likely to grab her by the throat, and only the prospect of a deep, dense sorrow to contend with. Moving closer, a strong chemical odour hits at her senses, along with a gentle sobbing snaking through the hallways in an echo of grief.

A nurse is waiting at the reception desk, clearly run off her feet, yet nice enough to apologise for a lack of privacy. 'We've got very little space,' she says, glancing at a heavy inner door. Nothing else needs saying.

The room is large, calm and clean, and oddly Marnie feels comforted that Grandad is not alone, surrounded by ten or so fellow victims, on gurneys or makeshifts beds, all silent and shrouded. Only one big toe stands proud of its covering, and the nurse restores the dignity with a swift flick of her hand.

When the sheet is pulled back on Grandad, he is almost the same, though his cheeks are white enough to match his beard. He looks cold, as if he's just returned from the local corner shop on a winter's day, before warming his face and hands in front of the workshop stove. Marnie likes to imagine that under the inert lids, his eyes are still sparkling and a little wet.

'Yes, that's him. My grandfather, Gilbert Cooper.'

Just saying the words makes it so final. That he is a victim of the Blitz, crushed under Hitler's mighty hammer, and that this new life of theirs – the survivors – is real and relentless. She feels chided inside for her own ridiculous thoughts, that at one time war offered her some excitement. The reality is here among the cloying smell of disinfectant; the drudge of death holds dominion over the grind of life.

'Would you like me to leave you alone for a minute?' the nurse offers, before casting over the other occupants. 'I mean, if you'd rather not be . . .'

'Yes, I would, thank you.' Marnie raises a smile, her best BBC variety. 'Just for a few minutes.' She pulls up a chair and sits next to him, laying a palm on his arm through the sheet, then probing underneath to find his icy left hand when she's sure the nurse has left her alone. Or alone as you can be among ten or so corpses.

It's so cold down here, despite a September sun unduly warm so late into the summer, and only just set on the streets outside. In the gloom, Marnie takes his stiff hand and tries to rub some movement into it, so she can link her fingers into his and hold it tight one last time. If there were eyes on her, some might think it morbid, but she doesn't. Nor when she talks to him through the not quite spotless sheet.

'Oh Grandad. What do we do now?'

She's talking of herself, inevitably. How can she go on without his eternal optimism and unfettered affection? Without him to nip and tuck at her shop-bought clothes, and then craft a bespoke winter suit from fabric he'd had his eye on for weeks and haggled down to a good price? How does London survive without those who were born into it and loved every inch, warts and all? Those, like Gilbert Cooper, who cared for their city as if it were a family heirloom or a glittering palace, in spite of the filth and corners of degradation. She brings his wrinkled hand close to her face and, before her lips make contact, sees the proof of who and what he was: the pad of his left index finger ingrained with white chalk from years of his tailoring. She rubs at it with her thumb, feeling what else he'd become, in the hard, flat callus on what she now knows would have been his Morse digit, the bone above slightly bent and swollen with use. Hours in the dimness of the basement, tapping out messages. Being a hero for the Dutch.

'Oh Grandad,' she breathes a second time.

Marnie's nose rests on his knuckle as the first notes of Moaning Minnie start up, the wail seeping through the blacked-out basement windows.

No, no, NO. Not now.

Marnie doesn't move, just grips tighter. That bastard Goering and a thousand tons of firepower will not deprive her of this moment.

The door opens and the nurse blows in, flushed. 'I'm sorry but you'll need to move. There's a shelter in this basement, at the other end of the building.'

'Oh yes, of course.' The fire in Marnie's belly is instantly doused, by the need to do the right thing for this nice nurse, who's been so kind. And already, she hates herself for being so damned biddable.

After only a few steps, their path to the door is cut short by a series of huge explosions and a crash of masonry, a great din that seems directly above them. Both bend under the force of the noise as the building shivers, grit and dust shifting from crevices and settling onto the crisp white of the nurse's crown. The dim wall lights flicker and splutter.

'Do you think the hospital's been hit?' Marnie says.

'Not sure. It was the same last night, but without any damage. Maybe it's the next street. I'll go and see if it's safe. Will you be all right here?'

For a brief second, Marnie wants to quip that if anything happens, she's in the right place, but that's taking gallows humour too far. The irony is that Grandad would laugh heartily, if only he could. 'I'll be fine. You go.' In truth, she would rather be down here with the dead, who are the least afraid.

The nurse runs through the door, leaving Marnie alone again. With the lamps threatening to fail completely, she searches out a paraffin lantern in time for the lights to snuff out, leaving the room bathed in a blueish, spectral glow. And yet, the feeling is anything but ghostly.

Marnie sits quietly as the bombardment retreats slowly into the distance, waiting for the all-clear before making her way down the warren of corridors. After twenty minutes, though, there's still a thump of the time-delay devices inflicting their damage, the shouts of nearby fire crews just audible outside. Stiff and chilled from sitting, she wanders among the veiled beds, placing a hand on each as she goes, as if to offer up some tiny slice of warmth. Their stiffness doesn't faze her; rather she feels a deep composure within, despite the turbulence outside. Marnie has never harboured any spiritual belief about life and beyond, only that the dead should be treated with dignity. This she gleaned from Grandad; he'd occasionally been summoned by a local funeral director to measure up clients for their 'final fitting', and spoke of it with reverence, but never fear or alarm.

She passes a gurney where the sheet covers a slight form, the feet not quite reaching the end of the canvas underneath. Too tall for a child, fortunately, but a thin, petite woman perhaps? Yet, there's a rise to the sheet, the fabric clinging to a smooth mound. The outline is obvious – she is pregnant.

Brushing her own fingertips across the rounded abdomen, Marnie senses that either a sympathetic mortician has placed the woman's hand over the rotund stretch, or this poor girl was caught in a raid and her last earthly thought was to protect her baby, her palm frozen as she shielded her unborn. Marnie imagines it was the latter, and the sadness of it engulfs her, causing a swelling in her heart that reaches all the way down to her own abdomen; the potential surrounding both of them, of a full and lengthy life. Two lives. Gone in a puff of smoke.

In among the dead, with a scant film of brick debris coating the sheets and a blanket of bombs elsewhere, Marnie sobs. Proper, heaving breaths that force her to scoop in air and let the tears splash onto the floor, with no hope of stemming the flow. She cries for Grandad, for that woman and her unborn promise. For everyone in that space, and the scores of morgues dotted across London. Marnie weeps as she hasn't done in more than decade.

When she's dry, and calm, and the din from outside has all but stopped, she picks herself up, rubbing with both hands at the grimy paste of dust and tears on her cheeks. She adjusts the sheet on each and every soul, as her own mark of respect. 'Thank you,' she murmurs.

She leaves the mortuary untouched, yet pummelled, scarred and stung inside. And determined.

56

Marnie Fern, erstwhile wallflower and follower of the flow, has made a decision. Possibly one she might regret, but after tonight, it's clear to her there's little choice. Not when the dead tell her that the only way forward is to live for the living.

8

The People's Zoo

Corrie

The early afternoon sun is warm on her back as Corrie takes the tram to the north-east of the city, an area lately transformed to an unofficial ghetto. Jewish families have long been settled in this part of Amsterdam, but the difference now is the fear. It's palpable as she steps off the tram, where residents tend not to dawdle, pushing towards their destination and tugging children by the hand. Already, there are signs across Amsterdam, 'Jews Forbidden', or one word scrawled as a warning: '*JOOD*'. As yet, the Nazis haven't made arrests in large numbers, herding Jews out of their homes and livelihoods, but everyone knows it will come. The trickle of information filtering into Holland is not encouraging, and much like the invasion of their country, the hammer blow will come out of the blue. But where can all these families possibly escape to? Occupied Belgium, just across the border, and now neighbouring France, are both saturated with Nazis. On the opposite border is Germany, where Jews have been tossed into a bear pit of unthinkable cruelties.

The analogy isn't lost on Corrie as she pays her guilders at the turnstile to the Artis Zoo, noting the atmosphere is immediately more relaxed amid the well-tended walkways. Mothers and children strolling between the enclosures of lions and monkeys remind her of happier days with Willem and Kees, though now each creature seems a little thinner than on her last visit, their rack of ribs more obvious through the sleek fur. A good portion of German troops are also mingling, in a variety of Wehrmacht and SS uniforms, at leisure rather than on patrol. One smiles at her in passing, and she returns his benevolence – but behind her teeth, set firmly together, her disgust smoulders.

Today, the animals don't interest Corrie, only what's beyond the wire and stone of their innocent-looking pens, to where the human 'inmates' are. Since early wartime, the city's zoo has harboured a growing number of *onderduikers* – the Dutch 'divers' in hiding – under the noses of the Nazis; within the Penguin House, across the moat in the hollow interior of the Monkey Rock, and those jostling for space above the Pheasant House. Whole families of men, women and children crouch in the most unlikely of secret niches, those who the Germans have 'an interest' in.

She walks with confidence towards one of the outbuildings and past a sign that says 'Staff only', rapping on the door in the practised fashion of resistance. A man she knows as Rutger invites her in, with a wary glance left and right. Time is short and there are no greetings.

'How is Hendrik?' Corrie says.

'Frustrated,' Rutger replies. 'But all right, given the circumstances.'

'Have you enough food?' She looks around at the barrels filled with little more than pigswill, part of Rutger's task in preparing the animal feed.

'Just,' he says, 'though I can't promise they won't get some of this from time to time.' The sulphured smell of rotting cabbage and stale, pulped fruit sticks in her nose.

'It's edible,' he reassures, 'though not tasty, I grant you. But when winter comes, our extra guests may be glad of it.'

Like some sort of magician, Corrie unpacks the contents of her cape from the extra pockets she's sewn in – cheese wrapped in small packages, a little meat she could find in the shops and several eggs that have survived the journey intact. She has some chocolate, too, and a stack of books from her basket.

'For Hendrik?' Rutger queries.

'For everyone here,' she qualifies. 'Distribute as you think best. But perhaps one egg for him?'

'Of course.'

She pauses before leaving. 'I don't suppose I could . . .?'

Rutger's weathered face falls. 'Sorry, no. Strict orders. Too dicey during opening times, and there's a lot of military about.'

She recovers her disappointment and pulls a small envelope from her inner pocket. 'In that case, can you give him this?'

'Of course,' he nods warily.

'He knows to destroy the note once he's read it,' she assures Rutger. 'He'll eat it if necessary.'

That raises a smile as he extends a hand for the envelope.

'Thank you,' she says. 'For being a kind caretaker.'

As she goes back along the walkways towards the exit, Corrie stops to gaze at the Bear Palace. More so at two young Wehrmacht who seem diverted by one of the furry inmates scratching repeatedly at the door leading into the fake rock of its enclosure. 'Look at him,' she hears one mocking, 'stupid creature thinks he can get out.'

In turn, Corrie is amused by their ignorance, knowing full well that this bear is smarter than they give him credit for; with its acute nose, the creature detects humans on the other side of the door, sniffing at hideaways like Hendrik. She can't imagine what it is to be inside, the skylight above the only proof of day and night beyond, hearing those huge claws rasping at the thick wood, just inches away. The zoo staff assure them the door is bear-proof, and they – the loved ones on the outside – are forced to have faith in those judgements.

There's never any choice but to keep the faith. With Daisy still off air, unable to transmit into that empty void, it's all that Corrie is able to do.

9

The Pendulum

Marnie

The congregation is drowned out not with the sound of bombs, but by the lofty ceiling of the church and its swathe of echoey morning silence – London at peace for a change. Marnie has chosen the monolith of St Martin-in-the-Fields for Grandad's funeral service simply because it was a place he loved to sit and muse, a stone's throw from the tailoring shop and the National Gallery. 'One of my places to loiter,' he called it, especially since the death of his beloved wife, and Marnie's grandmother, in the mid-thirties. Subsequently, he and Marnie had sung their hearts out in many a Christmas service under this roof before the war.

She scans the gathering; more people than she expected, perhaps due to the death notice she'd placed in *The Times*, plus several she recognises vaguely as customers. Her cousin Susie is here too, on a rare outing away from her two small children, and Raymond, for moral support. As the vicar begins his eulogy, there's an echo from the back of the church and a waft of chilled air when the door opens. She turns to see a familiar form slide into one of the pews. Willem, if she's not mistaken.

Afterwards, they mingle on the grand sweep of stone steps outside, with Marnie making small talk with those gathered. There's no burial to go on to, as Grandad insisted on a cremation, and with rationing taking more of a hold, no chance of a wake either. Still, she's genuinely grateful that his life didn't formally end with a mere handful of mourners in a vast, empty space.

Out of the corner of her eye, she watches Willem on the periphery, staring out onto Trafalgar Square. He looks deep in thought. Reflective, she thinks. 'Handsome' is a word she strives to ignore, but somehow can't quite manage it. As the bereaved peel away, he steps forward.

'Thank you for coming,' Marnie says.

'I wanted to.' His dark navy blue suit is much more flattering than the baggy ARP uniform, hugging his broad shoulders. It's a good fit, and she spies the tell-tale double stitch that Grandad always made in the bottom of the left lapel – his little legacy for every creation.

'I see he made you something.' She nods towards Willem's jacket.

'Oh yes. How could I fail to ask him? It's my best-fitting suit.'

'Well, you would say that,' she reacts, too quickly, and too soon to take it back.

'No, I mean it. Honestly,' he protests. 'If I ever have to flee back to Holland, this is going with me, assuming I don't have to swim in it.'

Instantly, he drops his voice as Susie approaches.

'Susie, this is Willem, a . . . a . . .' Marnie's imagination deserts her. What is he exactly?

'. . . A friend of Gilbert's,' Willem fills in quickly. 'Pleased to meet you, Susie. I'm sorry about the loss of . . .'

'He was my great-uncle,' she says. Susie's barely concealed expression indicates she approves of this new man in their realm and, inside, Marnie sags at the presumption. She'll have to endure something like a Spanish Inquisition during the next visit to her cousin, given Susie's uncanny knack of reading her mind.

'So, are you coming for tea?' Marnie throws into the brief but awkward pause. 'I thought the Lyons on the Strand. Another one of Grandad's favourite spots. We could raise a cup to him.'

Susie sighs heavily. 'Sorry, Marn, but I'd better get home. Arthur's mother will be tearing her hair out by now, or else filling the children with so much bread and dripping they'll be sick.' She turns to go. 'But don't forget tea at mine next Sunday afternoon. And bring your butter ration.'

She pecks Marnie on the cheek and skips down the steps, as Raymond approaches and aims for the other cheek. 'I have to go too, Marnie – meeting at the big house,' he explains. 'I'll see you tomorrow.'

Within minutes, she and Willem are alone on the top step, looking out into the open space of Trafalgar Square, at the hole recently carved by a bomb alongside the National Gallery. Admiral Nelson, ever present, surveys his pitted domain.

Marnie fidgets uncomfortably, mindful of saying something to Willem about her decision before this new-found purpose of hers evaporates. But where are the words, on a day like this? Despite everything she's seen and her epiphany in the St Thomas' morgue, committing herself still feels – *is* – entirely out of character for Marnie Fern. Over the past week, the push-pull of her own mind has kept her awake at night, counting off the crash of bombs like petals on a daisy . . . 'I will . . . I won't . . . I should . . . I can't . . .'

'Well, I'm thirsty,' Willem breaks in. 'I'm not family, but will I do in raising a cheer to Gilbert?'

She spins to face him, surprised and grateful. 'Of course. I'd like that.'

A reprieve. A small one, plus the prospect of tea to fuel her courage.

The Lyons on the Strand is one of the flagship tea houses, and for tuppence a cup you can sit among the splendour and bustle of its many floors, pretending you're in an exclusive hotel on the Côte d'Azur, with the promise of a sumptuous bed rather than another night on a hard station platform. It's almost midday, not too crowded, and the Nippy waitress – as befits her nickname – is quick to take their order once they're settled at a discreet corner table.

'Tea for two, please,' Marnie says automatically, then checks herself: 'Unless, of course, you prefer coffee instead?'

'No, tea is fine. I am getting better at it, this British tradition,' Willem says. 'Though sometimes I think I might drown in it.'

There's a lengthy growl from her stomach, audible above the chink of teacups, the result of not being able to face even a morsel at breakfast. It's too loud for either to ignore.

'It's nearly lunchtime,' Willem adds without missing a beat. 'I'm famished. Shall we eat something?'

'Perhaps we'd better.'

'We're low on bread,' the Nippy chimes, as if bored of the endless repetition, 'but there's baked potatoes instead. Baked beans on the side, if you want.'

They both nod and the waitress skips away.

'It's hardly glamorous, but my grandfather was a great lover of beans on toast,' Marnie explains. 'We often ate it late at night during a raid, cooked on his little stove . . .' Her voice breaks off at a pained, pricking memory.

'And it was Gilbert who first introduced me to such a culinary delight,' Willem cuts in to save her embarrassment a second time that day. 'So, I think it's the perfect celebration food.'

While they wait, Marnie surveys the space, now beginning to fill with a lunch crowd; at certain times of the day, you might not guess there's a war on, if you screen out the men in uniform dotted across the tearoom. Women are dressed to look their best – hats, stockings and lipstick (though applied sparingly these days), the office men in double-breasted suits. Today, without the buzz of German bombers making their afternoon recce across London, everything appears normal.

But it's not, of course. She's just attended her grandfather's funeral, and there's a large elephant in the room, invisible yet squatted right next to the teapot placed on the table in front of them.

Unable to ignore it, Marnie tackles the elephant head on. 'Have you sorted the radio?'

Willem's eyes flick upwards, with something like relief, and the awkward creature is forced to lumber away. 'I moved the set,' he says. 'Nothing to link your grandfather, or his memory.'

'Thank you.' She sips and pauses, her self-doubt swinging like a pendulum. 'And have you found a replacement yet?'

'No, not yet. But I will have to recruit soon from the radio volunteers. It's a case of finding someone who's quick enough. The Abwehr – that's German military intelligence . . .'

'I know who the Abwehr are,' she says quickly. 'From my work.'

'Of course you do. I didn't mean to patronise.' He scans the immediate area, perhaps judging if the woman at the adjoining table will hear their conversation below the wide brim of her hat. 'It's just they are the biggest hurdle to our building the Dutch resistance, detecting one of our radio signals in minutes. Gilbert and his counterpart worked like lightning.'

Take the leap, for God's sake.

'I'll do it,' she cuts in swiftly.

Willem holds his teacup in suspension, the void only filled by the Nippy arriving with plates of potato and beans.

'You will?' he says when she's gone.

'Well, I'll try,' she qualifies. 'I mean, I've no idea if I'll be as accurate as Grandad, but when we had our silly little competitions, I was just as fast, if not quicker sometimes.'

'So he was right, about you beating him into a . . . what was it?'

'A cocked hat,' she laughs. 'But I was twelve, and now I'm . . . a lot older.'

He balances a forkful of food in mid-air, a thoughtful wave on his brow. 'I do have the means to retrain you.' He chews and swallows, suddenly serious. 'And you would do that, for Holland? I'm grateful, of course, and Gilbert seemed certain you would be perfect. But you have a good job already, a worthwhile one, and so I have to be sure. Do you understand?'

She does. And Marnie is not offended. Better still, there's no need to have rehearsed any motivation. 'I've trusted my grandfather all my life,' she says, ignoring that fleeting moment of discovering the radio and picturing the worst. 'If he thought it was right, that's good enough for me.' She cuts into her soft potato, which – in that moment – surely tastes better than anything from the kitchens at the Ritz. 'And given that his grandmother was Dutch, there's a tiny slice in me too. But more than that, it's about helping people, here, there or anywhere.'

She sits back, relieved to have said it, committed to doing something, *being* someone else, if only in a small way. To have crawled out of a shell that's been her home and a virtual prison for too long. Except that irritating pendulum sways violently again: is it convincing bravado Willem hears, or a pledge that will see Marnie Fern truly come good? Too late – he's heard it loud and clear.

'I'll drink to that,' he says, raising his teacup. 'Cheers to Gilbert Cooper and his legacy.'

'Cheers, Grandad,' she says, to an untimely wail of the siren that stops their own private wake in its tracks. 'Uh, isn't he infuriating?'

'Well, no despot is going to stop me enjoying this feast,' Willem says defiantly.

They eat with purpose but no urgency – everyone is so used to daytime raids that there's no scramble to leave.

Willem says he's on ARP call, and when Marnie assures him she'll be fine heading to the BBC, he turns towards Piccadilly. 'I'll be in touch – and soon,' he says over his shoulder.

A swarm of Nazi bombers buzzes in readiness overhead as Marnie reaches Portland Place and crowds into the already full shelter of the concert hall. Being daytime, there's no rush for bunks, and everyone simply carries on with work where they can. Scripts are being marked up, a small semi-portable typewriter clatters away balanced on someone's knee, and in one corner there's an involved discussion about carrot recipes among the cleaners, leaning on their idle mops and buckets. She spies Raymond across the hall, talking with animation to a fellow producer, but Marnie doesn't pick her way over the clumps of bodies sitting or lying in wait. She needs solitude, to lock herself in her own little bubble, as she's so expert at doing in the midst of a crowd. She pulls out a dog-eared script from her bag and pretends to read, though the words swim on the page. She's thinking about Grandad, what he would do in her shoes, and about the promise she's just made. If she's honest, about Willem too. The image of him in his smart suit stays with her, imprinted, and she's unable to shake off the scene painted in her mind, of him being measured and fitted in Grandad's shop and what they might have talked about. The Dutch resistance, or the cut of the cloth? And for a moment, she's a little envious, of that time spent: the intimacy of a man with his tailor, and of cohorts in a furtive war of communication.

Looking out at the sea of familiar BBC faces, an odd sensation runs through her. These are people she's worked with for years, endured long nights and stressful, pressured days. Those with whom she shares a bond. They have no idea about this new direction, and if she does her job properly for Willem, they won't ever suspect either. It's her secret, a confidence never owned before.

And with that thought, the thrill rippling through Marnie Fern, production assistant, is better than any Miss Roach brew or triple-strength brandy at the Langham. She's positively drunk on it.

10

Radio Days

8th October 1940, London

Marnie

Willem is true to his word, making contact within days via a note sent to the sixth floor at Broadcasting House. A week after their private memorial in Lyons on the Strand, he's outside Marnie's flat on River Park Road with a car. She's been advised to pack for a week, and duly booked five days' holiday 'to visit my parents'. She's never lied to Raymond before, but Willem insisted the subterfuge was necessary, and from the way he looked at her when they met briefly in a café in Oxford Circus to talk over the arrangements, it was evident that she'd need to get used to it.

Now, it's dark as she slips into the small black saloon beside Willem, with a driver who's not in uniform but acts like he's a serviceman.

'Ready?' Willem says.

'Yes, I think so.' There's a heavy feeling of trepidation, along with a slow simmer of angst when she sits beside him. And perhaps a small amount of excitement, too.

'Settle yourself in, it's about an hour's drive,' he tells her. 'Humphries knows the way, but it's always slower in the blackout.'

'Don't suppose there's any point asking where we're going?' All Willem has committed to so far is a destination that's 'out of London'.

In reply, his expression is half amusement, the rest given over to a playful scold.

'Thought not,' she says. 'I'll just have to trust you then, won't I?'

Her tone is teasing, while his face dims. 'In this case, yes, you will. But Marnie?'

'Yes?'

'Trust is precious. Be careful who you give it to.'

She wants to ask him what he means, to interrogate this sudden cynicism, but they are thrown off course – literally – by a violent swerve of the car.

'Sorry, sir,' Humphries apologises as he rights the steering. 'Bomb crater. Came out of nowhere.'

Once the familiar streets of North London are behind them, Marnie gives up trying to calculate their direction of travel, since the whole of London bears little resemblance to its old self. Buildings that were once her markers are now unrecognisable, with rows of missing rooftops, entire terraces of homes collapsed into a heap of ash, ghostly in their absence. The first siren of the night starts up as the car weaves free of the potholes and begins to accelerate. Marnie senses them leaving London's pitted streets behind and on to black, open roads, and when they reach journey's end an hour or so later, the bombers are a mere hum in the distance. For the first time in a month, there seems little threat of being directly under Hitler's deadly load. Whatever else awaits, she might actually sleep in a bed for an entire night, and that's surely worth the jitters running inside her.

Willem has delivered the information she needs en route, falling silent and subdued for the rest of the journey. She can't tell if his former friendliness was merely a carrot on a stick – now that she's swallowed the bait, perhaps he doesn't need to charm her any further? – or if there's some weighty matter on his mind. There's little to do but stare into the inky landscape.

The gravel spits under their wheels when Humphries draws up in front of a house, large and imposing from what Marnie can make out in the sparse moonlight. And if it's not already surreal enough, an owl hoots from a roost somewhere in the still night air.

'I'll see you in a week,' Willem says as he opens the car door. She stares back with alarm. 'You're not coming in?'

'No, but don't worry, they are expecting you. And I have every faith.'

'In what?' The courage Marnie has banked for such occasions is rapidly slipping away.

What on earth are you doing, Marnie Fern?

'That you'll knock them into a cocked hat.' He smiles and slips back onto the leather seat. 'I'll see you in London. Oh, and don't forget you have a false name here.'

Once the door slams shut there's no option but to face this new scenario, because Humphries lurches away into pitch darkness and Marnie can only go forward through the open doorway.

'Good evening, Miss Desmond. We've been expecting you.'

In the light of a new morning, the temporary home for the next few days of her alter ego, a Miss Diana Desmond, reveals itself as quite grand. Or at least it was once – a large, old stone manor house, faded and now commandeered by an undeclared arm of the military. There's a mix of green, grey and navy uniforms, and plenty like her in plain clothes too. The barrack-style hut she settled into was warm, the bed comfortable and the sleep her best in weeks, uninterrupted by raids or any worry, much to her surprise. At eight a.m., and in the former lavish dining room of the main house, 'Diana' is introduced to Nancy, Edith and Ivy, and while no one acknowledges the obvious fakery, it seems understood that each woman possesses an entirely different identity away from this strange world. Beyond this week, they're unlikely to meet again.

'Best breakfast I've had in an age.' Nancy stares in wonder at her three rashers of bacon. 'I'd happily stay here through the entire war.'

'Even the eggs are soft,' Ivy echoes. 'I feel like the lady of the house, and my valet is going to appear at any moment. Someone pinch me!'

They talk, and although the conversation skirts around their homes or former lives, Marnie feels a swift camaraderie forming, a connection in what they might achieve by going forwards. The potential that waits to be unlocked. She's only known true amity before with Raymond, and perhaps Miss Roach a. little. Gradually, her anxiety begins to fade, replaced with a solid sensation that feels a lot like determination.

Is she duping herself, or does this actually seem like the right choice?

There's no chance for much deliberation, though. After breakfast, all four are guided into a downstairs room, along with a second cohort of four, and the hard work begins. They 'warm-up' with a tricky crossword that's more taxing than *The Times* on a difficult day, followed by a lecture on Morse, drilled and tested, and then again. All before eleven o'clock. She needs to keep her wits sharp, but the ease with which this odd language comes flooding back is comforting to Marnie. And along with it, there are memories – of nights spent at Grandad's, supper and silly conversations in Morse, laughing at his suspect spellings. Some recollections she lets flourish, while others are purposely barred, too raw and distracting for her much-needed concentration.

Over tea, the conversation flows again. 'I think my poor brain is on fire,' Edith moans, though her face is glowing rather than pained with the challenge. 'Wonder when they'll let us loose with the radios?'

After lunch, all eight are led into a room lined with sets, similar to the discovery in Grandad's basement. Marnie pulls on the headset, an action she repeats almost daily at work, yet this machinery feels weightier in every way, tighter, the hum in her ears resonant before the first sounds have come through.

It's slow at first, but the pace increases rapidly – endless dots and dashes that spell out nursery rhymes and one-liners from Shakespeare, easy to guess at if she's misheard a letter. Marnie pairs up with Nancy and they sit opposite each other, swapping gossip in Morse, in plain English at first, and then gradually in simple code, scribbling and scratching with pencils at the encrypted text until their words and heads are equally scrambled. After an hour, her whole body feels as if it's made of wire, messages winging their way up and down her limbs and orbiting her skull, taut and singing at a shrill pitch.

'All right, that's enough for today,' the instructor says at last. The group retires to a sumptuous lounge, where it's quiet and the fire is lit. No one speaks for a full half hour, and Marnie sits with her head back, working to sweep away the clutter of beeps.

It's the same the next day, and the day after that, interspersed with trips to the local pub with their tight little clutch of four: Nancy, Edith, Ivy and Diana. Marnie gathers she's somewhere in Oxfordshire, but with no road signs and a moratorium on details, she's not exactly sure and – if she's honest – doesn't really care. At night, she sleeps like a baby in the hut, mentally exhausted from the concentration and, physically, the social whirl. Often, in the common room, someone will put a record on the gramophone, and there are one or two men who seek her out, pulling her by the hand onto the floor as the Andrews Sisters sing 'Oh Johnny, Oh Johnny', and while it's understood that the dance, the evening, and even life at that moment are transitory, Diana Desmond is enjoying herself. The familiar frisson of guilt, too, that any part of war could be this much fun for Marnie Fern.

Then it gets serious. On day four, the instructor begins talking of 'the enemy': words like Gestapo, SS and Abwehr are suddenly part of the curriculum, ways of avoiding, packing up the radio kit at speed and reducing transmission time to minutes. As he speaks, eight sets of eyes roam the room, and Marnie knows each woman is speculating on who will need this life-saving advice the most: which of their little clutch is destined for the field, to be sent into enemy territory, transmitting while the Gestapo hovers? She's eternally grateful that it won't be her. This might be a world away from the safety of Broadcasting House, but she doesn't crave a life on the edge, and it's not what Willem has proposed. She'll simply be someone behind a radio set, like Gilbert Cooper – in danger from a wayward bomb maybe, but not hounded by the Gestapo. But if not her, then who? Even after this brief a spell, she can't bear it to be any one of their quartet.

'Well, that was suddenly very intense.' Nancy lights a cigarette in the break and blows a plume of smoke towards her sculpted, raised eyebrows. 'They aren't pulling any punches on the consequences.'

'Any regrets?' Ivy says into the unusual silence between them, teacups left untouched for once.

'Not me,' Edith says resolutely. 'Anything's better than the living death I've left behind.' Everyone looks, but no one voices their curiosity about that life.

'Diana?' Nancy pitches. 'Are you still in?'

'Yes, of course,' Marnie says, surprised at her firm, swift reply. Deep down, though, she has the luxury of Willem's pledge; Hitler comes calling every night in the skies above London, but the RAF has so far engineered a protective net over Britain. And while Winston's radio broadcasts warn of 'long dark months of trial and tribulation', the Germans are not yet clicking their heels within earshot.

There is an added, more pressing reason to go on; notwithstanding her lack of spiritualism, Marnie has felt the energy of

Gilbert Cooper in the air these past days, a pervasion of his wonderful life around her at all times. And in that presence, a purpose. A job that she can do ably, with a real contribution.

I can, can't I?

11

A Message from Will

13th October 1940, Amsterdam

Corrie

The smell of rotting cabbage is sour and rank in her nostrils, while underfoot the discarded leaves are slimy from last night's rainfall, but Corrie has been among odours far worse than the vegetable market in the south of the city. She pulls her cloak tightly against her neck and walks towards the warehouse doors, glancing left and right under her hood. At eight p.m., it's dark and almost deserted, though in a few hours the market will be a hive of activity again. For now, the dealings inside are well hidden.

She raps out four knocks on the pane of glass, pauses, two more, and then silence. Or near enough. She can almost hear the suspension on the other side of the rickety door as someone listens and holds their breath in unison. Assessing no doubt, gauging for danger. She wonders if German soldiers or Gestapo breathe in a different way? Louder? Do they give off a pungency when they're on the hunt, like animals in the woods?

Finally, the bolts slide back and the door opens an inch, still wary.

'Zeeza, it's me,' she whispers to the face bearing suspicion, and the young woman behind the door visibly relaxes, with a mere hint of a smile.

Corrie is led through a high-ceilinged, largely empty ware-house to the small office at the rear of the space, a room within a room where each glass pane has been blacked out. Inside, two men sit at a table, smoking among remnants of coffee and beer. Her nose twitches again at the fugged, dense atmosphere, more repellent than the putrefied cabbage outside.

As per usual, there are no introductions. Zeeza she's known since she was a child, the best friend of her beloved daughter, though she visits Corrie less since Kees departed for resistance work in The Hague. Dirk she's met once or twice since war began, but Rudy has been a friend of Willem's for years; just seeing him makes her heart crank inside, as if he is a surrogate son she could easily wrap her arms around for comfort, to feel closer to Willem. This, though, is business.

'I heard you have a message for me?' she says, unhooking her hood, but not the cape.

'It came via the sea route,' Rudy says, in a detached tone. 'We think it's genuine. But we need you to verify.'

'Verify what?'

'That it's his handwriting. Willem's.'

There's a second when Corrie thinks she might need to sit down, the airless room suddenly beginning to feel too hot, but she pushes out a hand onto the table instead. His writing. Something of him. It's only been three months, but the uncertainty makes it feel like years.

They push a crumpled napkin under her gaze, the printed logo of Lyons Corner House a little faded. The added script is wobbly with the difficulty of writing on tissue-like paper, but it's clear to her.

Gatsby gone. A new contact for D soon. Recommence mid-month. WS

'It's him,' she says flatly. To speak without emotion is the only way she can contain what's bubbling inside. 'When was it sent?'

'Last week, we think,' Dirk says. 'It came overland. Can you be absolutely certain? It's not beyond the Nazis to plant this.

76

The napkin comes from London for sure, but they have fifth columnists constantly supplying this type of prop. To make it look authentic.'

'It is him, I'm sure,' Corrie asserts.

'How?' Zeeza cocks her head, her face suddenly dark and serious. Corrie thinks that for someone so young – not yet twenty-five – Zeeza has lost her innocence in past months. She's no longer the freckled pigtailed girl Corrie has known for years, her laughter spiralling down the stairs at Prinsengracht as she and Kees giggled endlessly like the schoolgirls they were. But then, hasn't everyone become harder, by necessity? Innocence is too heavy a burden for resistance.

'He's signed it "WS",' Corrie says. 'It's personal to us.'

Rudy simply stares, waiting. He want details, for surety. Because no one is above suspicion. Not even her.

'It stands for Will Scarlet. Just something silly between us.' It will have to suffice, because she won't reveal private details of how she read Willem so many Robin Hood bedtime tales – she was Maid Marion, he'd informed her at age seven, and he assumed the role of the young but brave Will. Rudy nods, satisfied, and reaches for the leftover beer, his manner instantly more trusting.

He looks up and raises a glass at her. 'Then it looks as if we're in business again. You'll have to get that magic finger of yours working again, Daisy.'

'Corrie.' She cuts him off, firmly. 'Daisy only exists on air.'

'Whatever.' He waves it away with little emotion. 'But we need that stream of information from Willem. And fast.'

She walks away from the warehouse, in turmoil under the cloak of her solid wool covering. Willem is alive, as of last week, and that makes her heart soar; she's intensely loyal to the resistance, to the fight for Holland, but always a mother first. That's not a crime, is it? Sadly, it means her suspicions are confirmed – Gatsby is dead. Someone she'd only ever known over the airwaves, by the flight of his hand, and yet with whom she felt a true bond. Man or woman she never discovered for sure, but in her mind, she always sensed her opposite was a man. A kind one at that, judging by the tiny asides that would come through at the end of a missive. *Keep well. Our hearts are with you. Hold firm.* Highly unorthodox, of course, for mere operators to add any content, but it's not as if any great secrets were exchanged. At their very worst, they could only serve to confuse the Abwehr or Gestapo, who might take the words to be infused with a secret meaning, when in fact it was just strangers engaging. Being human.

In the end, she'd begun to reply: *The fight is alive and well. Holland is strong.* That's gone now, along with Gatsby.

I'd better get used to it, she thinks as the heavy boots of several Wehrmacht echo on the cobbles behind her – there will be more to lose in this ugly world. In the meantime, she'll need to crank up the radio, and reawaken the silent, sleeping portion of her.

Daisy is on air again.

12

Assaulted

15th October 1940, outside London

Marnie

The four say goodbye and good luck at breakfast; no tears because they all knew what was in store, and now what's at stake in the months ahead. Even so, Marnie is sad to break the camaraderie. She's sure at least one of the four will be posted to London and it would be nice to meet up again, to have a friend who harbours a similar secret. Equally, it's precisely the reason they can't, and why their joint farewell is a final one.

'Diana, please take those lightning fingers of yours and stick at least two of them up to Herr Hitler, won't you?' Nancy says when it's time to part.

Marnie nods a yes, and means it. They've grown, all four of them, in the space of a week; in confidence and skills, but also as women who will have a part to play. From the war's outset, she's been drilled that her work at the BBC is vital – for information, morale, and for 'Auntie Beeb' to keep life as normal as possible, exuding a calm from the wireless across the nation. And she's always believed it, wholeheartedly, even during the trickier episodes of *The Kitchen Front*. She still does. But leaving this nameless Oxfordshire house which might not officially exist, there's something else.

Despite working with written scripts daily, she's struggling to put this new sensation into words. It's a welling inside that feels like pride, and a little excitement, too, at the furtive nugget close into her chest. Plus an edge. A sharpening. The belief that reliable, steadfast and unswerving Miss Marnie Fern has the potential to do something entirely out of character.

It's no surprise that Humphries is waiting outside, engine idling, but for Willem to be present in the back seat of the saloon makes Marnie start as she slides in. 'Oh, I didn't expect a welcoming committee.'

'Why on earth not?' he comes back. 'As of now, you're my star transmitter.'

'Really? I think you might be getting ahead of yourself.'

'Not from what I've heard.' His eyebrows go up, like someone in the know, and his eyes shine against the black leather interior. 'I've had excellent reports.'

'Let's hope I don't disappoint, then.'

Willem is keen to hear what the week entailed, so Marnie runs through the coding she's learnt and the equipment they've worked with.

'Daisy will guide you,' he asserts with confidence. 'We're such a small operation at the moment and, strictly speaking, we're off-grid. That does have its advantages.' He pauses. 'Do you think you'll be able to start straightaway? From what I hear, you're ready, and we need . . . well, it would be good to get going, don't you think?'

'I told Raymond I'd be in the office later, but after that, I don't see why not,' she replies.

What else can she say? Willem's right, too: there's no reason to delay, and no practice like the real thing. If she is to partner with this 'Daisy' operator, they'll have to get used to each other as soon as possible. Mistakes and all.

He seems buoyed, then suddenly wistful, gazing out of the window. 'Have you heard the other news?'

'About Balham and Bounds Green, you mean?' She has, with bulletins trickling in through the wireless and word of mouth, a solemn reminder that while she's been having fun in the country, fellow Londoners continue to suffer the heavy barrage of the Blitz. Nineteen dead at Bounds Green Underground when a single German bomb caused the train tunnel to collapse; Marnie shivers at its proximity to her home, as the station adjacent to Wood Green and one she's often used. And only a day later, south of the river at Balham Tube, the cruellest of ironies for those sheltering from bombs overhead when a bus crashed into the yawning crater created by an explosion, alongside a fractured water main. In all, more than sixty in the tunnels underneath were drowned. Days on, they are still counting the dead.

'So tragic,' Marnie echoes.

'It's got me thinking,' Willem says, turning to look at her. 'Are you particularly attached to where you live?'

'Not especially.' She thinks of the nights spent at the BBC concert hall, and the time lying awake in her tiny, soulless flat. Despite the bustle and the lack of privacy at Broadcasting House, she knows which one she prefers.

'Wouldn't it be better if you lived within walking distance of the BBC?' Willem says. 'I mean, this last week really proves that nowhere is safe. Not even the suburbs. You'll need a base for the transmitting, and it might sometimes be at short notice, difficult if you're working late.'

For a minute, she thinks it's presumptuous of him, and in the next breath, a blessed relief. These days, people swap billets and rooms with alarming frequency, and she has been meaning to move, yet somehow is always too busy to search for an alternative. Is this another of those nudges she so often needs?

'Have you got somewhere in mind?'

Humphries takes them directly to the grand Edwardian sprawl of Bedford College, where Willem unveils a spacious room on the first floor, with a tiny sink and stove, and a larger, shared kitchen down the hallway. It's clean and airy, surrounded by the beautiful grounds of Regent's Park, a vast improvement on the vista of Wood Green bus depot.

Marnie turns slowly in the space, open-mouthed at the sight of beloved Oscar standing sentry in the corner. 'I see you were fairly confident I'd take up your offer,' she says, gesturing towards the semi-clothed mannequin.

'Hmm, I thought the old boy needed somewhere to lodge and you'd like a flatmate who's not too demanding,' Willem smiles. 'It's only a twenty-minute walk to Broadcasting House. The college lets out the space, and we have quite a few Dutch here — the *Engelandvaarders*.'

'Pardon?'

'Strictly speaking, it means England-paddlers. Those like me who escaped after the invasion, still hoping to do something useful from afar until we make it home.'

He stops, and Marnie counts the beats of time that he's suddenly elsewhere — across the North Sea, in Amsterdam perhaps. Eventually, he shakes himself back into the room. 'More importantly, there's a basement here. Enough room for transmitting space and a decent aerial. Better still, we have the only key.'

'So, can I move in immediately?' She's purposely upbeat and enthusiastic; this reborn Marnie Fern needs to remind herself to grab at life by the horns. Everywhere — grandiose or grime — is at the mercy of Hitler's whim, and it would be a crime to let this opportunity slip away.

It's late morning by the time she arrives at Broadcasting House, having unpacked her small suitcase at the college and just had time to rinse out a few items of clothing. Raymond greets her with his typical fatherly hug and untold enthusiasm, and when he professes to have missed her, there's a truth in his voice.

'How was the journey, and your parents?' he asks. 'I must say, you don't look very rumpled for such a long haul on the train.'

Marnie utters the usual platitudes: 'Oh, it wasn't too crowded, I managed to get some sleep,' but it feels exactly as it is. Lying. And with Raymond especially, that feels so wrong. 'I'll make up the hours for today and work late,' she tells him.

'That's fine. We're lined up for a broadcast at six, and once we've wrapped up, I'll stand you a drink at the Langham,' he offers. 'A welcome home celebration.'

He smiles warmly and with real heart, prompting her mendacity to twist like a knife inside. All she can do, though, is say 'Thanks' and calculate her pledge to Willem too – they've arranged to meet back at Bedford at half past ten, where he'll take her through the first transmission.

This is life, now, Marnie Fern. *You've made your bed*, as the saying goes, *now you have to lie in it.*

The six p.m. broadcast goes smoothly, and it's good to be working with Raymond on the studio floor again, though Marnie recognises in herself a renewed awakening of the technical process when they retire to the sound room for the actual recording. Intently, she watches the engineers tweaking the levels, almost stroking at the knobs and buttons, working the equipment that's so familiar under their fingers. Her own digits ripple with anticipation.

'I think that deserves a double gin, don't you?' Raymond says eagerly as they enter the buzz of the Langham bar. The siren has already sounded but the customers seem reluctant to retreat to the hotel basement or back to Broadcasting House, their courage already cushioned by alcohol.

'Just a single for me perhaps,' Marnie says, mindful of a clear head for Willem.

Raymond is on good form, more cheery than she's seen him for a long time, and he mentions a new social club in town that he's joined, 'one that's got a convenient basement restaurant, so we can at least finish a meal!' Marnie wonders if he's met a woman for company, something to counteract the loneliness that he strives to mask at work but which still pushes through on occasions. She hopes so.

They sip and talk, conversation that's punctuated by sporadic dull blows beyond the solid walls of the Langham, while inside there's a definite sense of being cocooned, and perhaps a little immune now to Hitler's nightly visits. As the clock nears nine p.m., someone switches on the wireless next to the fireplace in time for the news, and the buzz descends to a respectful hum. Through the speaker, the nine strikes of Big Ben die away to the steadying voice of newsreader Bruce Belfrage: 'This is the BBC Home Forces Programme. Here is the news.' A metaphorical comfort blanket descends across the bar as the room tunes in.

The broadcast has barely begun when ears are sharply pricked by a faint thud behind the voice – in the bar it comes across almost in stereo, since outside there's a resounding crash a split second before it projects across the airwaves, the Langham's solid core shuddering in unison around them.

'What the hell was that?' someone cries, but there are enough sound men present to recognise the stark reality – and the consequences; drinking glasses are dropped and there's a rush towards the doors, Raymond and Marnie hot on their heels.

Hitting the smouldering air, the Langham crowd can't help but see the full horror – a gaping hole ripped through the wall of Broadcasting House, with a blaze on the fifth floor taking hold. It's sheer chaos, with staff already staggering from the building, soot-stained and coughing, rained on by a storm of paper drifting down from the sky. Marnie rushes towards the entrance, intercepting a distressed woman she recognises from nights in the shelter, steering her to sit on the kerbside while bracing her shoulders against the uncontrollable tremor pulsing through her body.

'I heard a bang a while ago, and they told us to evacuate,' the woman gasps. 'I think it took some time to go off. Did everyone get out? Please tell me they did.'

She's crying now, the shock hitting home, though almost ignoring the deep, bloody gash on her arm that's dripping crimson onto the ashen pavement. Marnie wraps the wound in her silk scarf, watching the material bloom with red. She's relieved to hand over to an ambulance woman who arrives through the melee, half wishing Miss Roach and her trusty teapot would similarly appear out of the ether.

Time slows as more and more staff spew from the BBC entrance, stumbling as they cough up the toxic vapour, and Marnie goes from one to the other, bandaging or bringing water to victims, their faces either a clownish chalk white or entirely blackened, tongues leathery with being force-fed debris. Up close and immediate, the devastation feels huge.

Finally, she stands back, staring in disbelief at the flickering, demonic glow against the alabaster white of the building: her place of safety, an eternal refuge and a castle she's built up in her mind, now assaulted, its walls quite literally brought down. She feels tears pushing at the back of her eyes and fights back with anger: *how dare you do this?* How dare Herr Hitler invade the bedrock of her life and turn it upside down. First Grandad, and now this. *Bastard.*

Raymond finds her in the chaos, his dark suit covered in a white crust, cheeks and forehead red with the heat. 'It was a delayed timer,' he says. 'Hit on the seventh floor and dropped two below – the music library took the full force apparently.' She stares at him, the gravity of her look speaking volumes. 'Sure to be some dead, and possibly a few still trapped.' He shakes his head mournfully. 'So unnecessary.'

'What can I do, Raymond? There must be something.'

'It's best if you go home,' he says. 'I'll know you're accounted for, and we'll need all hands on deck tomorrow morning to help with the clear-up.'

She feels redundant, but he is talking sense; the worst has happened, and with the rescue crews now on site, it's the experts who will begin to right the chaos. A glance at her watch tells Marnie it's already half past nine, and while the task awaiting at Bedford College is not so immediate, it is a need for someone out there in the world. It's the same fight, she reasons, either here or there, against this bloody monster of fascism.

13

A Vital Cog

Marnie

'Thank God you're safe,' Willem says as she arrives breathless in the college lobby. His face is wracked with concern, scanning hers for any wounds under a layer of grey dust. The air outside is peppered with slow blows; it's obvious that Marnie has run the gamut of bombs, pitfalls and craters to make it on time. 'I heard the BBC was hit.'

'I'm fine,' she insists, wiping away grit from her eyelids. 'Safe in the Langham when it exploded, so one of the lucky ones.'

His gaze goes down to her hand, one palm held unconsciously over the other to contain the spasm in her fingers.

'Delayed shock,' she says, then remembers the last time it happened, with Raymond giving her tea. There's no trusty brew now, only the job ahead. 'I'll be all right in a minute.'

'Sure? We can postpone.'

'No, we need to do it.' *She* needs to do this, to mask the memory of the injured being led out of Broadcasting House, and to know she is doing something other than running away.

Willem leads her through the lobby and into a back passage littered with mops, brooms and buckets. He unlocks a door to a pitch-black space and flicks the light switch, gesturing to her with a look that says, 'It's okay.' It's the second time she's followed him into a darkened basement, but this is a surer footing in every way. The dank, subterranean odour is more pungent as they reach the bottom of the stairs, but much less rank than any bomb shelter she's been in. The radio set nestled into a back shelf is the same one plucked from Orange Street and transported here, probably with Grandad's fingerprints on it still, but it's what Marnie has steeled herself for. In war, hardware is precious and personal heartache has no currency here. 'Get on with it,' she imagines the cigar-chomping Winston would say if he were here now. She's aware of Willem's eyes on her as she settles herself in the chair beside a small desk and switches on the set, anxious for that spark of energy in the metal fabric and her own.

He pulls out a stopwatch and places it alongside a clean pad and pencil laid out. 'Remember, two minutes at most – best to get into good habits from the start,' he says. 'Daisy will be doing the same.'

It's what Marnie has been practising, not only in Oxfordshire, but ever since, in private moments with her left hand couched under a scarf, tapping incessantly to keep the motions fresh and her fingers fluid, as if she's afraid of it all slipping away like sand through a timer. For her, it's mere practice, but for Daisy, the timing will be vital, a case of capture or not. Life and death perhaps.

Marnie looks up, breathing steadily over a mix of excitement and fear. 'Will she be there?'

'Should be, if the message to pick up broadcasts has reached her. She'll keep to the timetable she and Gatsby had.' His swift glance spells hope rather than certainty. 'Let's start with a simple transmission.'

Marnie pulls on the headphones, inserts the crystal and rolls the dial under her fingers. Her eyes are closed as the squeals come and go, until she locks onto it. Gingerly, she pulls the Morse button towards her, finger hovering. All around, she can sense the air crackling with Willem's anticipation.

Take that leap.

To her relief, everything she's learnt, both past and present, comes flooding back. In the second she presses down, there's a shiver snaking through each limb, down to her toes. Grandad is there, egging her on, his voice through the headphones: 'Go on, my love. You can do it. You can do anything, Marnie.' Hadn't he always told her that? And yet, this is the first time she's felt herself fulfilling it, pushing hard beyond a boundary.

The tailor's dummy is resurrected, she spells out in plain Morse from the scratched message Willem has handed her. *Respond to WS*.

She waits thirty seconds and taps out again. Willem picks up a second set of headphones and plugs in the wire, one earpiece cupped to his head. Marnie hears him mumble something in Dutch under his breath, and, although she can't translate, it has the tone of a plea or a prayer.

Her eye is on the stopwatch as they wait: a whole minute with only faint crackles to tune into. Much like in training, she closes her eyes to focus, acutely aware of sticking her tongue out slightly in sheer concentration; Grandad had often mimicked the same look when they played together. But Willem doesn't need to see this, and she clasps her lips shut, her tongue bone dry against the roof of her mouth.

She opens one eye on the stopwatch. One minute fifty seconds. 'Try it again,' Willem sighs, his hope clearly fading.

The single hand on the timer ticks loudly. Marnie has one finger poised when she hears it. Faint, but present; a string of dots and dashes to cloud the space. Her eyes sweep up to Willem and the rise of his features when he hears it too. She waits for the message to end, then to start again, pencil at the ready. It's neither loud nor clear, but enough that she can scribble down the letters: *Daisy responding. Tailor's dummy new sign, old grid. Stop. MM.*

Marnie hands the message to Willem with a quizzical expression.

'It's her,' Willem says.

'Are you certain?' She needs to press him: for her to learn the signature of Daisy as an operator means they have to know it's her on the opposite end, without a shadow of a doubt. Only then can Marnie detect any future changes, signs of the Abwehr's clever impersonation if Daisy were ever captured.

'Yes, she only signs off the MM for me,' Willem asserts. 'No one else. You can give her your new call sign, but she wants to continue with the grid that she and Gilbert used – the reference books. For speed and secrecy.'

Marnie sets her finger to work again. *Tailor's dummy here. Call sign Lizzy. Old grid intact. Welcome back, Daisy.*

She'd had to think very little about an appropriate call sign, in keeping with Grandad's book-based theme: Elizabeth Bennet – Lizzy for short – has always been her favourite Austen heroine, the one whose spirit she's aspired to from behind the safety of *Pride & Prejudice*'s pages. Wanting something more out of life, some excitement. And love too.

Within thirty seconds, there's a reply. *Hello, Lizzy. Eager to exchange. Enough for now.*

Willem leans over Marnie's shoulder as she scratches out the last message on paper, and she catches a faint whiff of Pears' soap, woven with the legacy of London's smoke-filled streets.

He straightens up, a sigh oozing from his mouth. 'Good. That's really good.' He turns suddenly, his posture screaming relief, hands clasped at the back of his head, pacing in a small circle. Even from behind Marnie can sense he's suppressing a well of emotion. When he finally turns back, his eyes glisten in the darkness, and she can't help wondering: what's triggered such a reaction? Is it simply resuming contact, or the fact it's Daisy at the other end?

It's clear to Marnie that they have a connection, he and Daisy, one that sits very close to his heart. Right inside it, if she's reading him right.

'Drink to our success?' Willem says at last, swallowing hard and producing a well-worked smile.

'Yes, but I'm not going out there again.' Marnie gestures to the world above, at which he pulls a half bottle of brandy from his pocket.

'I made the presumption of needing this.'

'Then if you can stand the mess of my hasty unpacking, we can go to my room. I've had enough of skulking about in basements for now.'

Willem nods. 'Me too. And Oscar can be our . . . what is it . . . gooseberry?'

'Not sure about his chaperoning skills, but I'm sure he'll do his best.'

They shut down the equipment, secure the room and head upstairs. The building is almost deserted, but there's activity behind some of the doors, of those who refuse to be quelled by Hitler's threats. Marnie enters her room and sweeps away the underwear she'd left drying in front of the gas fire.

'Don't worry, I only have eyes for a brandy glass right now,' Willem says, with his skill of putting her at ease.

They sit for a minute in silence, drinks in hand, listening to the background noise and the raid die away to almost nothing.

'If you pack up your old flat in the next few days, I'll have Humphries collect all your luggage from Wood Green,' Willem says. His voice is low and honeyed from the alcohol.

Marnie looks around the sparseness of her new domain, lets her head flop lazily back onto the chair. 'Do you know, I'm almost tempted to leave it all there. I've been living out of a suitcase for a week, and it's something of a release. Not having anything to choose between, and, in a way, it's practice for something that might befall any one of us nowadays – being homeless, having all our possessions go up in smoke.'

'Hmm,' he murmurs in agreement. 'I know what you mean. When I arrived in England, I had only the grubby clothes I stood up in. Aside from my ARP uniform and a good suit –

courtesy of your grandfather – I haven't got much more, and it is strangely liberating.'

Her head pulls up sharply, a quizzical brow trained on his languid pose. 'You didn't even come with a knapsack?'

From what he's alluded to, Marnie imagined Willem had needed to quit Holland at speed, but with enough time to catch a train, or scramble down the overland routes to Gibraltar, those refugee trails across the Pyrenees that political types in the BBC canteen argue about far too indiscreetly.

'No, just me and a friend,' he says. 'No room for anything else.'

'So, how did you arrive here? Assuming you're allowed to tell me.'

He looks up, his lips spreading into an impish smile. 'You won't believe me if I do.'

'Try me.'

'All right. I paddled to England in a kayak.'

'No!' Her cry of surprise fills the room. 'So you weren't joking about being an England-paddler?'

He grins broadly, clearly pleased with such a response.

'Was it dangerous?' Marnie presses him. With the reputation of the North Sea as choppy and unforgiving, she doesn't doubt the journey was hairy at the very least. Utterly exhausting too. But did he need to risk his life to escape?

'It was necessary,' Willem says plainly. 'The Nazis disapproved of what we were doing.'

'Which was?'

'There was a battle not far from Amsterdam, just after the invasion. We fought hard for three days to hold the line, before the Luftwaffe flattened Rotterdam and threatened to do more. Funnily enough, I wasn't too popular with our German guests after that.'

'And so will you ever go back? With the war still raging, and Holland fully occupied?'

He sighs, downs the last of his brandy in one mouthful. 'I want to. You can't imagine what it's like to feel so helpless, to be living this life – a free life, believe it or not – with so many good friends back there. Suffering.'

'And your family too?'

His head whips up, expression suddenly fixed and hard. 'Everyone back there is family now.'

The response draws a line in the sand that Marnie heeds; his family is out of bounds in more ways than one. 'But you can still do your bit from here – the ARP work,' she goes on. 'And I've heard there are Dutch pilots training with the RAF. How are you with heights?'

His lips purse, with a hint of regret perhaps. 'I'd relish the flying. But I have orders to stick at what I'm doing. From the highest authority.'

Marnie's eyes widen. 'Highest?'

'The queen herself.'

'Queen Wilhelmina?' Yet again, Marnie finds herself astonished by this man sitting in her room, a virtual stranger until a few weeks ago. 'Queen W', as she's known at the BBC, cuts something of a dowager figure, with a formidable reputation to match. She's revered by her country, respected by the British government and given regular airtime at the BBC for her broadcasts on Dutch *Radio Oranje*. Once or twice Marnie has glimpsed her bustling, rounded figure at the centre of a large entourage, moving through the hallways of the BBC as if on castors.

'And your queen takes something of an interest in you?' She hears the tease in her own voice.

He flashes a look of self-deprecation. 'She happens to like me very much. Apparently I remind her of some distant nephew.'

'I must remember to bow in your presence next time.'

'I'm afraid it only means I have a lot to live up to, and consequently our work here' – he dips his head down towards the basement – 'is crucial. It went well tonight, thanks to you. I'm certain you and Daisy will prove a good match.'

'You are?' Marnie is hoping he'll elaborate, open up a little more. Tonight, she's seen something of his humour, a lighter side. And he knows so much of her background, though not all, she admits. Some things are better to keep within the cool work exterior of 'Miss Fern', but there's definitely more of Willem to unmask.

He doesn't rise to her query, but cocks an ear towards the window and the sound of emergency sirens overtaking the destruction. They're both aware that London will enter a different stage now, into the early hours – assessing the debacle, dousing the flames and probing the debris for fatalities. Aware, too, that if Londoners don't stop to absorb it fully each and every night, the devastation is in danger of becoming routine.

'I'd better go.' Willem gets up and stretches, rubbing his face awake. 'I want to drop into the ARP depot and see how they're getting on. It'll be my turn tomorrow night.'

Marnie sees him to the door. 'Be careful,' she can't help saying.

He turns and stares with intent. 'Not sure there's any other way, these days. Good night, Marnie. I'll be in touch with the next message.'

Settled in her new bed, with sounds of clear-up carrying across the expanse of Regent's Park, Marnie considers the day. Along with the BBC, she has entered a new realm. Officially, she's part of the resistance – Dutch or British she isn't sure, though satisfied that it is the right side. In unison, her beloved BBC has fallen victim, its shield of safety breached, even if it was only a matter of time, since its bright, white outline will have been a bombers' target for weeks now.

As she stares up at the ornate, sculpted light fitting instead of the bare bulb and thin plaster crack of her old bedroom, Marnie can't escape the fact that the bigger change is inside her. The BBC, Raymond, Miss Roach and all that encompasses have been a defence, and she's hidden willingly behind their cloak of care for too long. After tonight, it feels as if the tables have turned; she is a minuscule cog in this gargantuan struggle, but it is a functioning piece, nonetheless.

Pulling up the covers under her chin and wiggling her toes for warmth, Marnie drifts into an easy, satisfied sleep.

14

New Resistance

15th October 1940, Amsterdam

Corrie

Corrie pulls off the earpieces and hugs herself, swivelling on her chair and grinning hopelessly at nothing but the blackness of her basement.

Someone is out there. The lines of communication are open and – as Daisy – she can be at her best, aiding the fight forward. But what prompts a second squeeze on her own flesh is him, unconsciously cupping her belly. He's there and – she has to believe – safe. Willem. It's all she's dreamt about in past weeks. Hendrik's welfare she gets regular word on from the zoo, and she's reread a single letter from Kees endlessly, while the others form part of their underground loop. But a sign from her boy had been absent for too long, imagination running riot each night as she tossed alone in her bed, telling herself he is a survivor, more than capable. But this is war; the cruelty she sees on the streets of Amsterdam each day from their supposed Nazi protectors only increases the anxiety. Street traders are threatened if they don't conform, along with the open mockery of Jewish families as they walk down the street. Capable or not, anyone might succumb to the evil that's spreading like a plague across Europe. Including Willem.

Tonight, though, he's there, albeit across a vast sea. Her heart thrums with the news, and if it weren't for the late hour she would be tempted to seek out Dirk, Rudy and Zeeza to share the good news. None of them holds Willem in quite the same heart space, but for the growth of the resistance, they need him just as much. Without his resources, and the help of the British SOE, the fight cannot flourish.

Switching off the weak lightbulb, Corrie climbs the stairs to the first floor. She makes herself a hot chocolate in celebration, even though it's the last precious grains of good cocoa. But a sip of the smooth, sweet liquid does quieten the unrest inside her, enough that she checks on the shop one last time, as she always does before climbing more stairs to bed.

During the day, the bustle of her bookshop is what sustains her, though it's become quieter as the war has taken hold and money for so-called 'luxuries' grows ever more scarce; she's loath to admit that her survival is now largely down to German custom. At night, it's the silence among the shelves that brings comfort – Corrie sleeps uneasily, but may not sleep at all if it wasn't for the solace her evening ritual affords, checking the spines are ordered, no book out of place. The written word can cause mayhem and has done for centuries, but more often than not it offers consolation. And books don't bite back, she thinks, as her fingers slide over the volumes, pages she thumbs daily in these increasingly quiet times.

Her little tour over, Corrie moves to close the door gently. There's no one else in the large, rattling house since Kees left, but she's so accustomed to tiptoeing through the emptiness that it's become second nature, enough to hear a faint scratching amid the silence of the shop. Ears on alert, Corrie is instantly static. A mouse, or worse, a rat? She works tirelessly to keep out the vermin since they could, quite literally, eat all of her meagre profits.

There it is again. But as she listens, it's less like a scrape and more of a wheeze, air escaping its tight containment. Her determination overrides any fear; she deposits her slippers and creeps into the space, avoiding the creaky floorboard near the cash desk. The noise repeats. A human gasp for sure, forced out by a need to breathe. Her only comfort is that any Nazi intruder wouldn't bother hiding, choosing to crash down the door instead.

With each step closer, the wheeze climbs higher in pitch, until there's a visible shadow cast by a small display table. And a huddled ball under it. She stands for a second, detecting a faint quiver travelling through the floorboards and into her stockinged feet. There's nothing else to do but reach down and grab at the mass, yanking at the loose clothing and pulling it from under the table as it lets out a shriek. It's obvious from his small face that the boy is more scared than her. Barely more than ten years old, he releases a lungful of air, the rasp in his pathetically thin chest apparent.

'What are you doing here?' she rails, largely out of her own fear. 'Stealing my stock, thieving from your own people?'

His eyes reflect terror, but also an exhaustion that Corrie identifies instantly: weary of struggle.

'I wasn't!' he protests in a tiny pre-pubescent voice. 'I promise. I just wanted to sleep, for a few hours, until the morning. Until I had to . . .'

She's rattled by the intrusion and in no mood for excuses but, equally, he is a child, and her voice loses its threat. 'How did you get in?'

'Through the scullery window, at the back.' He follows on hurriedly: 'I have a message for you. For the book woman. An urgent one, from a lady with a large hat.'

Corrie's fingers loosen instantly, stopped in her tracks, and his waif-like body sags to the ground.

'Let's see it then.' She's anxious now more than angry. Anything via the woman in the large hat is worrying because it's from inside the ministry – a patriot who works as a typist in the Nazi administration and passes on what she can. Information from her inevitably means a threat to someone in their realm.

Shaking, he hands over the unaddressed envelope and she rips it open, padding towards the kitchen for some light.

Inspection of Artis expected next three days. Likely to be thorough.

Corrie spins towards the child, two steps behind her. 'When did you get this?'

'An hour ago,' he stutters. 'They said I could deliver it tomorrow morning, but I came straight here. And when there was no light on . . .' His small voice trails off.

'Haven't you a home to go to? Parents to miss you?' By the look of his ragged clothing and pinched features, Corrie guesses not. He confirms it with a small shake of his head, a grimace that says his face is about to crumple with sadness. 'Where are they, your family?'

'Rotterdam,' he murmurs.

Dead, then. Lying in the ashes of a flattened city. The firestorm unleashed by Nazi bombers had been fierce, the devastation widespread, and this boy wouldn't be here if he'd escaped with anything other than his life.

'Here, have some food.' She gestures for him to sit down at the kitchen table and he nips nimbly towards a chair. Like some feral child, he tears at the bread and cheese placed in front of him, his eyes suddenly replete with pleasure.

Corrie considers the message; it's reliable, she has no doubt. Their contact inside the ministry will likely have typed the search order, now sitting in some official tray to be actioned. If the Nazis or the SD – the secret police – had any real suspicions about the zoo as a hideout they wouldn't plan a search. They would just do it, unannounced. Noisily and with force. Instead, Amsterdammers are resigned to troops routinely combing official buildings as a way of asserting their domination, provoking suspicion and fear, and always on the lookout for informants to supply them with evidence of resisters.

She doesn't relish a late night trip to Café Eijlders, over by the Leidseplein, to hand over this information, and Corrie decides it can wait until early morning. Besides, she has this boy in the house now. Looking at his grimy features and the fatigue behind his eyes, it would be inhuman to turn him out. Equally, until she's certain he's not a wily thief who will rifle through her house, she daren't leave him alone.

'What's your name?'

'Felix,' he says, still working through the bread squirrelled in his cheeks.

'Well, Felix, you can stay here tonight, but before you get anywhere near my clean sheets, you need a bath.'

15

Regards to Darcy

16th October 1940, London

Marnie

Somehow, the hole looks worse the next morning. With the flames and smoke around Broadcasting House doused, the gash in the wall appears bigger and more defined, like an ogre's great howling mouth at full stretch. A few of the emergency services are still there, shoring up the sides for safety, but it's largely the clear-up crews who bustle about. Marnie stands for a minute as a small memorial of what once was, and wonders again why and how she feels so bruised. It's just bricks and mortar, she tries to convince herself outwardly.

Within, her guilt is layered with the grim news of six dead, and one seriously injured, who may soon become the seventh fatality. None of the victims she knew well, but they were colleagues and it's rocked the BBC far more than the blast itself.

'It's chaos upstairs,' Raymond reports as he blows into their office, thankfully untouched by the blast. 'The board is meeting, and there's virtually no phone lines in and out, so we're effectively working blind today.'

Miss Roach wears a grave look and has the kettle on a permanent boil. 'Pointless,' she mutters behind her typewriter. 'Utterly pointless.'

Marnie presumes she means the war – what else? – but it's hard to tell behind her cerise puckered lips.

101

They make the best of it all day, skirting around floors five and seven, and blotting out the constant din of workmen carrying out urgent repairs. Worse still is the atmosphere in the canteen, where a reverential hum has replaced the usual noisy chatter, and there's an overriding sense of gloom. Queueing for her lunch, Marnie finds herself staring at the teaspoon attached to the counter with string and some tape, yet another method of coping with war shortages, and suddenly she's running to the ladies and locking herself in a cubicle, weeping for she doesn't know what.

A woman from the typing pool knocks on the door. 'Everyone's feeling the same,' she says with sympathy, but Marnie doesn't like to admit it was the sight of a ruddy spoon that caused her sadness to spill over.

'Look, I can request that you're moved out of London to one of the rural BBC departments,' Raymond says back in the office, staring at her red eyes. 'I would support your transfer fully.'

'Why on earth would I want that?' Marnie replies, slightly hurt, but realises he's only offering because he cares. 'You're clearly not going anywhere, Raymond, so neither am I. We have a job to do. Together.'

What she can't reveal, of course, is her other motivation for staying in the capital.

'I was hoping you'd say that,' he replies. 'But we do have to be careful – no more late nights at the Langham, better tucked up in the shelter playing Gin Rummy.'

If only you knew, she thinks. *If only you knew.*

Despite her tears, the assault on her workplace has a strange, diverse effect on Marnie. When the inevitable sirens stir the BBC's populace into the basement that evening, something in her – she doesn't know what – is drawn in the opposite direction, up onto the roof of Broadcasting House. Climbing out into a sky already glowing orange and a wind warmed by fiery destruction, she stands aghast. It's as if Hitler has taken a match to a box of fireworks and simply sprinkled the contents across London – the red tracer fire of the ack-ack guns meeting mandarin sparks from a fresh explosion, tiny pockets of greeny-blue glow like fireflies amid the rubble as the gas mains are hit below. A rainbow of destruction that's both vivid and grotesque.

And yet Marnie is exhilarated by the firepower: is this what it must feel like for the fighter pilots up there in this debacle? Terror and excitement in a vortex that's deadly but alluring. She's not alone either. Teetering near the roof's edge, microphone in hand, is Ed Murrow, one of radio's rising stars who's fast becoming something of a legend at Broadcasting House. While the general population – and a good deal of the press – shirks from the nightly raids, this young, handsome American newsman has stamped his mark by reporting from the rooftops and the streets, always in his Savile Row suit, topped off with a tin hat. His florid descriptions of the attacks as they happen, the immediacy and the chaos, have proved compelling to those across Britain. Judging by his postbag, European and US listeners are spellbound, hanging onto Murrow's rich, unfettered commentary.

Now, the regular BBC firewatchers stand sentry-like on each side of Murrow as he broadcasts. A week ago, Marnie would have shied away in his presence and turned tail. But seeing Douglas, one of the regular soundmen, visibly flinch with every thud or crash, she finds herself tapping him on the shoulder and taking hold of the equipment, gesturing to get himself down below. He seems too traumatised to argue the morals of handing over to a woman, knowing Marnie has enough knowledge to manage for the last few minutes of the recording.

'This is Edward Murrow in London,' the reporter signs off finally, but doesn't turn from London's fiery panorama. Instead, he breathes in the air now choked with cordite, his shoulders moving slowly up, then down, absorbed rather than horrified.

Finally, he turns to see Marnie switching off the equipment and moving to pack away.

'Oh, where's Douglas? Is he okay?' he says in a deep American lilt, the words edged with concern.

'Needed a cup of tea, that's all,' she says.

'And you're happy to deputise?' His features, lit by the glow underneath, blend confusion with a wry smile.

'Something about it, don't you think?' On the roof edge, Marnie's voice barely rises above the crackle of burning buildings and clamour of sirens. 'Watching it from this high up. I think it's actually less terrifying than down below.'

'Having just been among it, I agree,' he says. 'And yet, I'd hope that anyone new to it would be terrified.'

'Meaning?'

'If the US president was here right now, I think he wouldn't hesitate to join in the fight against Hitler.' Murrow is cut short by a loud explosion, near enough that they wince in tandem. 'Common sense tells me we might have cooked our goose enough for tonight,' he adds. 'Let's quit while we're ahead.'

They descend onto the lower floors, make formal introductions and then retreat to shelter below, via the studio.

'Thank you, Miss Fern,' Murrow says as they part at the entrance to the concert hall. 'I'm grateful for any brave soul that's willing to follow this fool into the abyss.'

'Well, any time you need a production assistant . . .' she says. It's one of those throwaway comments that people say out of politeness, but in her current mood, she might actually mean it.

Having felt each day drag since her grandfather's death, the next weeks fly by for Marnie. Where once she followed the news fervently, on broadcast and in print, her own world takes over; she hears in the BBC corridors that German troops enter Romania and the Italians invade Greece. Yet it seems so removed from the nightly drubbing that London and other British cities are now subjected to. Principally, her mind is fixed on the space between London and Amsterdam.

As per Willem's instructions, she checks in every day to a newsagents on her route to work and buys a copy of the *Daily Mirror*. Roughly twice a week, there's a small envelope nestled next to the racing section, containing a scramble of letters written in pencil. The newsagent always smiles at her in the same way, never letting a single hint wash across his face. With the key to the basement at Bedford College, she lets herself in on the appointed days. She has Grandad's small library of books and a timetable for transmitting that Daisy also shares, which appears random at first glance but is a carefully worked pattern spanning nine weeks, designed to stymie the Abwehr from predicting the timing of transmissions. Sometimes, it's nine at night, other times two a.m., but Marnie reasons she would be up with raids anyway. Better that she's in her own personal bunker at times; between nights in the BBC concert hall and the frantic pace of work, she often welcomes the solitude of the basement.

Even when she's decoded the original message using pages from a selected novel (and it makes her smile to discover all the texts have been banned by the Nazis), it makes little sense; information about agent or supply movements. Then, she re-codes the message to a mish-mash of letters and transmits to Daisy. Soon, their exchanges are so swift that both are left with time on the stopwatch, slowly adding the odd word as they sign off: *Keep safe*, Marnie taps out. *Have faith*. She's careful for it not to alter the meaning of the crucial information exchanged, but feels sure Daisy will understand it's a sentiment for her ears only, and not to be passed on. How? Marnie doesn't know – she just senses it, as far as you can gauge someone's humanity through the crackle of hardware and across an entire sea. If such a thing is possible, Marnie detects a softness flowing through the airwaves and above the short, sharp delivery.

In turn, Daisy responds with her own affirmations: *We feel your pain: we will triumph.* The words are easily said, and although Britain's irrepressible prime minister insists as much in his regular broadcasts to the nation, it somehow means more when it comes from a lone woman, likely to be in her own basement or attic, more than two hundred miles away and under a different kind of siege.

Then, when their familiarity becomes easy and Marnie can distinguish Daisy's 'signature' in the first seconds of transmission, her opposite in Amsterdam adds something else: *Regards to Darcy.*

Marnie is mystified, wondering if she heard it right. It's coincidence surely? A Darcy in the same circle as her Lizzy. She shifts uncomfortably.

All she can do is tap back: *Will do.*

Willem sends word in the first week of November that he wants to meet. Marnie has missed their brief liaisons, but happy anticipation soon gives way to a feeling of unease. Does he know about the extra messaging? Strictly speaking, it's highly irregular, and if the entire set-up wasn't 'off the books', they'd have been detected by British radio traffic. Has Willem found out, ready to insist that she and Daisy cease their little asides?

She's waiting for him at the Demos sandwich bar near to Broadcasting House, on her second cup of tea and almost wishing she smoked, to quell the nerves inside. 'Ridiculous!' she tells herself. 'I'm thirty-two years old, not a damn schoolgirl. *And* I'm doing this voluntarily.' The words ooze from under her breath. 'It's not as if he can sack me.'

'Sorry, did you say something?' Willem stands before her, his own teacup in hand. He's wearing Grandad's navy tailored suit and, more importantly, a smile instead of a frown.

'No, nothing. Um, sit down, I've saved you a space.'

As usual, his eyes skirt around the crowded café until he's satisfied there's enough noise to be discreet. 'I've ordered us bacon sandwiches,' he says. 'I hope that's all right. It seems silly not to when they still have it. It's getting pretty scarce elsewhere.'

'Yes, thank you. I haven't eaten yet.'

'So, how are you?' he begins when the sandwiches are set down, dipping his nose towards the tantalising smell of well-cooked rashers and taking a bite. 'Is it going well, the exchanges?'

'Yes, it is. Or at least I think so.' She wonders if he's testing her, working to hide her anxiety. 'Is there a problem?'

Willem stops chewing and looks puzzled. 'No. Should there be?'

'Not at all. I take it the answers make sense to you, or your people?'

Halfway through a swig of tea, he laughs.

'What's so funny?' she questions.

'It's the way you say "my people", as if I'm in charge of an entire department. I'm afraid it's just me and a handful of others. There are small groups in Holland, but there's no combined network to speak of yet. It's mainly just survival out there.'

'But it is helping, isn't it?' Marnie surprises herself, that she's so keen for her endeavours to be useful. Not for personal glory, or satisfaction – merely that it's doing *something*.

He nods with conviction. 'It is, Marnie. You and Daisy, you're our ears. I'm lucky to have found you.'

This is the moment, she reasons, to benefit from his good humour and satisfied stomach. 'There is one question I have. Do you know who Darcy is? I'm not asking for a name, obviously, but I'm assuming you can get a message to whoever it is?'

He freezes, trying to cover the surprise, yet a momentary flash of his eyes betrays that he knows exactly who Darcy is. 'Why do you ask?'

'Only that Daisy passed on her regards,' she says, swallowing the last of her sandwich. 'Unofficially.'

He doesn't – as she feared – react with anger or irritation to

107

their unsanctioned exchange. Instead, he seems winded. 'It's me,' he says finally. 'I'm Darcy.'

'Oh. *Oh*. Well, you know, you can trust me,' she gabbles. 'I would never . . .' Inside, her guts knot with embarrassment. Darcy to her Lizzy. Oh Lord, will he imagine she chose her own codename on purpose? No, how could she? She didn't – couldn't – know about Darcy. But still . . . what must he think? Daisy, too, as someone so obviously close to him? Intimate perhaps. *Oh Christ, Marnie.*

'Hey,' he prods at her meandering train of thought, downing the last of his tea. 'Shall we take this conversation outside?'

Wrapped up against the November chill, they find a street bench and sweep away a thick layer of ash from the seat.

'I've been thinking that it would be a good idea to move the radio out of the college basement, to vary the site of your transmissions,' Willem starts. 'I've got hold of a light transmitter, one we use in the field that's very portable, and I'm working on a series of alternative locations.'

Marnie looks at him sharply, her expression hiding nothing. Why? It's Daisy who has to be wary, surely, of the Abwehr on her tail. Not here in London. Or is that not the case any more?

She says as much and Willem shifts uncomfortably. 'I'm just being careful, that's all.'

Marnie maintains her stare. 'If there's something, then tell me – please. I have a right to know.'

'It's just a rumour, but British intelligence has circulated a warning about a group of fifth columnists tracking radio messages.'

'And what does that mean exactly?'

'Nothing probably.' Willem blows warmth into his hands and sits forward. 'Let's face it, Dutch resistance is low on Germany's priorities compared to France right now. As I said, I'm just being cautious.'

'But enough to move me around?' Marnie isn't convinced

– the tremor in her stomach tells her so. It's a well-founded rumour that a 'fifth column' of Nazi sympathisers are scattered across Britain, but no one is quite sure of their impact beyond attempts at propaganda.

'It's a precaution, with any radio operator,' Willem insists.

'But you didn't move Grandad, as far as I could tell,' she presses.

'He was different,' Willem adds sharply. 'I couldn't very well make an elderly man traipse across London with a radio, however able he was.'

'So, was my grandfather ever in danger from these fifth columnists?'

'*No!*' Willem checks his outburst instantly as a woman with a pram walks by. 'I promise he wasn't, Marnie. But you of all people know the war is escalating, and the game plan – if the Allies even have one – changes every day. They never say it outright, but where I work it's not hard to calculate that Germany is desperate to plant reliable spies inside Britain. I honestly don't know the ins and outs of it – I'm far too much of a small fish . . .'

'Fry. Small fry,' she corrects, then wishes she hadn't.

'Yes, that. It simply means I don't get told things directly. I have to gather that German spies have so far been captured and turned, and what the consequences are for people on the ground. I'm as ignorant as you in some ways.'

'Not quite as much.' She's beginning to hate her own petty belligerence but can't prevent it spewing from her mouth, lips almost as pinched as those of Miss Roach in a foul mood. In silence, they watch a double-decker bus weave its way precariously around a large cleft in the road, passengers looking down anxiously from the top deck.

'You can stop the transmissions at any time,' he says quietly. 'We can't – won't – make you continue.'

'And where would that leave you? After all that training?'

He flops back, shrugs and squints out towards the street. 'In a hole about as large as that crater. But it's still an option for you.'

Again, her answer comes automatically. 'I wouldn't do that, to you or the people you support. I only ask for honesty, Willem – I'm a simple person, nothing complicated. I just want the truth laid out.'

'Agreed. Honesty on both sides.' He stands abruptly and smooths down his suit jacket. 'But, Miss Marnie Fern, I don't believe for a minute there's anything simple about you. Far from it.'

He's gone again before she can begin to absorb or analyse what he's just said.

16

The Bank Manager

Marnie

Marnie emerges from a cinema on Leicester Square at around five p.m., moving from the flickering film reel amid the dim theatre into a different kind of darkness outside. For two hours, the drama and romance of *Our Town* – a world away in mid-town America – has proved a welcome distraction to the reality of London in the grip of winter. Now, it's back to the chill wind of a December evening. She secures her scarf tightly and blinks for a minute at the navy sky, trying to remember how it used to be before all this, when the festive lights peppered the entire West End, a swarm of fireflies coming in to land. Never a true Christmas enthusiast, the illuminations nonetheless brightened Marnie's mood. Wouldn't the Luftwaffe just love that now – a multi-coloured twinkling target to aim at? Hence the blackness of the square, into which the cinema-goers pour out and feel their way back towards the Tube, arm in arm.

She checks her watch for no other reason than it allows her to look left and right, as if waiting to meet a friend, but really to scout for anyone loitering under the awning of the cinema, now the space is all but empty. Despite Willem's assurances, Marnie's caution has flourished nicely into paranoia. Sometimes, she thinks, it's with good reason.

She lays a hand on the bag slung casually over her right shoulder, and her fingers pick out a corner of the metal container inside, about the size of a child's shoebox. The sharp edge is dulled by the stiff Selfridges paper wrapped around it, so that if anyone happens to glimpse into her bag, it looks as if she's been shopping for presents, and not in fact harbouring a miniature radio set issued by a secret service and used to contact the resistance in an enemy-occupied country. That's how bizarre her life feels nowadays. Yet Marnie can't deny there's exhilaration too, especially when she's on the move; one night a ground-floor flat in Soho, and then an abandoned shop south of the river, where she sets up the equipment quickly and efficiently – though always with one ear out for a roaming ARP warden or a looter on the prowl. Without fail, Daisy is there to greet her, a presence down the wire which calms the constant butterflies inside. They swap messages and exchange greetings. Within minutes, she's packed up and gone, picking her way back over fallen bricks and the remnants of lives once lived.

Only last week, she knocked on the door of a large and well-to-do family house in Hampstead; without a word she was guided towards a large, ordered basement and left alone. After her transmission, the ensuing raid was so fierce that Marnie was made to stay by the owner and her family, who all piled into the basement and happily shared their tea and crumpets. It ranked as surprisingly enjoyable – no names and no talk of allegiances or connections, just a slice of other people's lives. Those times remind Marnie of what she's risking and why, for people here and across the seas. It's a necessary fuel to her, when rationing squeezes harder and tempers are short, Londoners feeling both a release and guilt that Hitler has extended his blitzkrieg to other British cities: Birmingham, Manchester, Bristol, Cardiff and Coventry are now in the daily firing line. The London Blitz rolls on, but is it right to feel relieved that the annihilation is dispersed?

And then there's this evening. For the past week, Marnie has had a strong sense of being watched, perhaps even followed, from the minute she leaves Broadcasting House. There's no single face to pin down – they must work in two or threes, she surmises when her imagination runs riot. No matter how many cafés she frequents, filling herself to the brim with tea, or alleyways she sidles into, she can't shake the intense feeling of eyes on her. Despite her desire, it's impossible to confide in Raymond, though he has asked once or twice: 'Marnie, are you feeling quite yourself?' Of course, Willem is the obvious choice to talk to, if only he were around. She has one method of contact, via the newsagents, and the consistent reply to her request for a meeting over past days has been a scribbled 'not available'. Where is he? Avoiding her, or decamped back to Holland? Marnie can't help feeling distrustful and abandoned, very much alone in the twenty-three hours and fifty-six minutes she's not on air with Daisy.

Tonight, however, she is determined. If 'Darcy' isn't around to help, then Lizzy will do it herself: she will damned well bring her elusive shadow into the light. She'd been disappointed to find the back-row cinema seats already taken with canoodling couples, so had been forced to sit four rows down, sensing, rather than witnessing, someone slip into the row behind. And yes, of course people turn up to the cinema late, often halfway through the newsreels. But this felt different. Her ears tuned into the flare of a match behind her left ear and the distinct smell of a Turkish cigarette, and somehow – though she knew this must be down to her whipped-up paranoia – a man's breath on her collar, warm and constant. 'I'm here,' its rhythm seemed to be saying into the nape of her neck. Inside her best woollen suit, she shivered.

Desperate to test her suspicions by leaving, Marnie found herself trapped on both sides: a large woman to her right who'd made a huge play of settling herself into the seat, and on the other by a man who, as far as she could tell, was poorly sighted and listening intently to the dialogue. The film over, she stood smartly to glimpse the seats behind, only to find the row empty. Lingering for a time in the ladies, she finally went outside.

Now, Marnie's eyes signal she's alone under the cinema awning, even if her radar says not. With purpose, she strides left towards Tottenham Court Road and the maze of streets around Soho; with luck she might chance upon the club Willem took her to on that first night and slip unnoticed down the steps. At the very worst, she could descend into a shelter and melt into the crowds. She is torn, though, because she also wants to witness whoever is dogging her, to put a face to the intimidation she feels. Bad enough that Hitler is robbing her of a decent night's sleep with his constant battering, she doesn't need anxiety thieving what little rest she gets. There's no option but to face up to it, or them. The courage that demands and where she is to draw it from, she doesn't quite know.

One step at a time, Marnie.

After twenty minutes of skirting pavement cracks and dodging rubble, Marnie is exhausted. In the blackout, she needs both eyes on her footfall, leaving nothing but her ears to pick out anything unusual in the steps of those around her. There's a distinct possibility, too, that her overegged imagination is running wild in the world's uncertainty.

Wearily, she boards the first bus to draw alongside and climbs to the top deck, stepping gingerly on the greasy wet floor under a dimmed blue light. Staring beyond the window streaked with a light mist of rain, she feels oddly safe in a moving metal box that's dodging potholes in the dark, in a city that might become a target for destruction at any minute. It's that familiarity from her childhood, of sitting on high with her mother, atop their tiny world. Out of reach. Queen of her own little moving castle.

Lost briefly in nostalgia, Marnie notes idly as a man appears and almost falls into the seat across the aisle when the bus lurches away from the stop, possibly a little worse for drink. He smiles as he settles his umbrella between his knees, a beige mackintosh belted and his black bowler perching on a full face, with round, wire-rimmed glasses. A bank manager type, she thinks, and then fleetingly: it's Saturday and the city's financial district is asleep for the weekend. Marnie assumes, too, that his smile is aimed at a woman to the rear, someone young perhaps, with a hint of red colouring across full lips, and well-tamed curls. But the seats behind are vacant, and so the gesture is for her. It's true that the war and Blitz has fostered people's benevolence, their willingness to smile and say hello. He's just being polite. She persuades the sides of her mouth to lift a little in response and falls back into her memories.

A second or so later, there's a ripping, scarring sound that yanks Marnie from her trance, so strident she thinks it might be the start of a raid. Instead, her eyes whip towards the flare of a matchhead as he lights a cigarette, the marked odour of Turkish tobacco invading her nostrils. That very same smell from the cinema. She's up and out of her seat in an instant, swaying wildly on the stairs with the bus's weave. The wheels slow only slightly but Marnie knows she has to take the chance; clutching her precious radio bag tightly, she jumps from the open platform as the conductor hails at her to 'Stop! Wait!' Landing and catching her foot on a wide, cracked seam of wet roadway, she feels her ankle bend painfully, yet manages to keep her body and bag from hitting the concrete. Startled, she's helped up by a figure who comes out of the darkness, in time to see Bank Manager man held back from a similar leap by the now wary bus conductor. His black hat retreats into the distance as she limps away into the night and – for the first time in this war – is thankful for the blackout.

17

Missing

7th December 1940, Amsterdam

Corrie

Corrie turns over the closed sign and prepares to lock up the shop, staring out at the stark lines of black against white, like a landscape photograph in its stillness. She sighs; in peacetime, Amsterdammers coped readily with this weather, ready to hunker down with food and fuel in the snow season. Now, the thick layer of white is a cloak that both screens and smothers resistance efforts in unison, helping to conceal her movements around the city on the one hand, but hindering the passing of messages outside of Amsterdam, when bicycles are sometimes all they have in reaching partisans in Haarlem, twenty or so kilometres outside the city. That's without the icy temperatures making life difficult for those in hiding, in basements, outhouses and freezing attics. At the zoo especially.

She worries most for Hendrik, now sixty-eight and increasingly infirm, with a bad chest in past weeks that's making the zoo caretakers wary, both for his health and the safety of others. His constant hacking compromises everyone concealed at Artis, with potentially dire consequences for all.

The first exodus of *onderduikers* several weeks ago was hard enough, and that was with a decent warning of the proposed search – those in hiding were led at night through the zoo's

116

empty thoroughfares, a wave of unrest rippling among the sleeping creatures, with keepers doing their best to calm the animals. Nonetheless, the fifty or so human 'inmates' sloped away to various safe houses against a backdrop of birdcalls and monkey hoots, the lions pacing pensively in their enclosure. For four days, until the Nazi search was over, Corrie was able to visit her uncle in an attic space lent by an elderly woman near Amsterdam's main train station. She nourished him, helped to stretch out his underused muscles and talked endlessly, doing her best to exercise Hendrik's increasingly stagnant brain. But he seemed distant, locked in his own world, and the respite was all too short. Along with other Dutch patriots, the elderly woman soon became nervous of harbouring a wanted man. And so back to the zoo they all traipsed, in what Corrie felt at the time was a cruel parody of Noah's Ark, a vessel doomed to stand in dry dock for . . . well, for how long? Artis is still the safest place; having been recently searched, the feeling is that the Nazis won't come calling again soon. In a second blessing, Hendrik was allocated a space above the Pheasant House in the move. It's a little more insulated, but still crucial to keep the noise at a minimum during the day when visitors are directly below. She delivers medicine for his chest but, in reality, he needs to see a doctor.

Resigned to the weather outside, Corrie turns and calls along the corridor.

'Felix, get your boots on. We're going out.'

Footsteps beat along the wooden flooring, and his face appears around the doorway, much less wan, pinker and a little plumper after weeks of the best food she can cook up and a warm bed. When he smiles, as he seems to do all day long, Corrie is ever thankful for his presence, glad she didn't have the heart to turn him out that night of his break-in. He's a delight to have around, hard-working and a quick, reliable messenger, even before he came to her. There's no dissuading Felix from his resistance work either; in war he's matured swiftly, wise way beyond his ten years.

To Corrie, however, he's still a child who needs a mother, and she can't pretend the need isn't within her, too. Caring for him means she yearns a little less for her beloved dandelion spores scattered across the city, the country and the world. In her thoughts constantly but always out of reach; with no direct word from Willem or Kees in some time, there's only hope.

Automatically, Felix helps her with the cape as she pulls it on, pushing the packages into each pocket to disperse evenly. He loads his own jacket with smaller parcels, but he's still so slender it doesn't come across as bulky.

'Ready?' Corrie says, pulling an old woollen hat over his thick, blond curls.

He nods eagerly. Whatever the weather, she knows he relishes this time of the day, running the gamut of patrols and hood-winking the Nazis, the enemy that made an orphan of him.

It's only five p.m. but already dark, with a snow-glow on either side of Prinsengracht lighting their path around the concentric ring of walkways hugging the canals. Felix pushes his hand into hers, for effect but also by desire, she imagines; with her basket in hand and scarves around their mouths to ward off the cold, they easily pass as mother and child. Progress will be hampered by the ice underfoot, but they'll make as many stops as they can, delivering the most pressing messages and parcels first.

The first sentry point they come across is easy – young Wehrmacht who are too cold to question or search thoroughly and wave them on, stamping their thick boots against the chill. Felix beams back at them and one mutters something in German about a 'sweet boy' as they pass.

'Idiots,' Felix cackles, and Corrie tugs at his hand to remonstrate, just as his own mother might have.

Walking north towards Herengracht, the second sentry is grumpier and less beguiled by Felix's impish features. 'Where are you going?' he barks, standing back to look at them fully.

Corrie shifts in the snow, trying to separate the guilt of her cloaked body from her facial expression, anxiety rising from her feet upwards. 'East of Amstel,' she says. 'I'm a bookshop owner, making my deliveries.'

He peers into her basket, pokes and grunts at the texts she's rewrapped in brown paper for good effect. 'Show me.'

Corrie gives a resigned nod; if she's too willing to oblige, he'll be equally suspicious. As she puts down the basket and unties a single parcel, she senses Felix beside her, the same tremor as on that first night through the shop floor. Only this time, the snow underfoot is the conduit. Felix is reliable and trustworthy, yet with such traumas behind him he's apt to bolt in the face of Nazi threat. He can easily outrun the overdressed, lazy sentries, but Corrie has no hope of keeping pace on the ice.

She glances at the small face by her side, glares with a message. *Stay still. DO NOT RUN.*

His small feet shuffle and the snowy layer underneath squeaks his edgy impatience. The soldier is busy fanning through the pages of a book with his big clumsy hands in thick gloves. '*Hurry up, hurry up*,' Corrie urges inside her head. Felix is a cat on hot bricks; on his own, he would already be halfway down the street, bullets nipping at his ankles.

'You can go,' the soldier growls at last. 'Be mindful of where, though.'

'We will,' Corrie trills and pulls Felix by the hand, out of earshot. 'Good lad.'

'I don't like it when they talk like that,' he mutters. 'Telling us what to do all the time. I hate them, Corrie. *I hate them.*' His voice is small but the sentiment carries the weight of a nation.

'I know,' she says. 'Just remember we fight back quietly, for now at least. You smile on the outside, but inside you can laugh until your sides ache at what we're doing behind their backs.'

His hand, thin and wiry, squeezes at hers. 'We'll laugh a lot one day, won't we, Corrie? Out loud. We'll laugh until we're sick.'

'Yes, we will, Felix.'

They avoid more sentry points by tracking east around the smaller streets, Felix leading her by the hand into narrow alleyways he's no doubt scarpered down many a time. They deliver three or four messages to a selection of canal boats on the inner ring which, from the outside, look cold and uninviting, but beyond the blackout blinds are glowing with warmth and the offer of substitute coffee. The last drop is a house a little further out, Felix skipping beside Corrie and chattering away – until she yanks at his hand to signal instant silence. The narrow street is empty, but the air thick suddenly with a threat that Corrie can't pinpoint. Nerves firing inside, she pulls Felix into an alleyway opposite the house, staring intently at the door of the intended drop. The plant signal is in the window. Everything says it's safe. And yet it's too quiet, not a single body within sight.

By ten minutes, her toes are numb, by fifteen, Felix's face is pinched and white, and yet Corrie is loath to break cover. That ominous feeling hovers like a sticky fog. After twenty minutes, she's wondering if her paranoia is perhaps too finely tuned. Until there's a stirring opposite and the door opens, two men walking out, casting left and right as they do. They're wearing civilian clothes, but every inch of them screams German; it's too dark for Corrie to see any faces, but their stiff gait is officious and military. Gestapo or Abwehr, she can't define, but either one a threat.

It's no longer a safe house, clearly. Someone's talked. And could that someone be on the inside, in the fabric of resistance?

Corrie waits another ten minutes before moving, desperate to return to her refuge at Prinsengracht, but they have one last stop, evermore vital now. The old paint factory is at the far end of Singel, Amsterdam's oldest canal, a tall, dark building facing out into the vast, glittering basin of water. Waiting on the fifth floor are Rudy and Dirk, but not Zeeza tonight. Corrie is in no mood to linger – she wants to tell them of her discovery, collect her messages for the London dispatch and then it's home for a hot drink and bed.

'And you saw nothing else aside from these two men?' Rudy probes.

'No.'

'So you can't be certain they were German?'

'Yes I can!' Corrie is exasperated that Rudy of all people is questioning her ability to detect danger, as if she hasn't been protecting her own brood almost all her life. 'It's clear to me there's been a leak, or why else would they have been there?'

'Well, we'll take it back to the group and look into it,' Dirk adds gruffly. 'You'd better give me the undelivered message.'

Corrie is left with an uncomfortable feeling that they don't trust her radar any longer, that her emotion overrides any reliability. Waiting for her own set of messages, she catches a brief, wordless exchange between the two men: paranoia or not, they are hiding something.

'What's happened?' she says with rapid, rising panic. 'Is it Hendrik? Is he bad?'

'Hendrik is no worse,' says Rudy. He shoots another look at Dirk, who nods. 'It's Kees.'

Her knees threaten to fold at his dense delivery. Rudy pushes a chair under her, and Felix nudges in, sensing the sudden distress. She swallows, mouth dry as a bone. 'Is she . . .?'

'No,' Dirk says, then qualifies quickly: 'At least we haven't heard as much. Only that she's missing.'

Missing. People disappear all the time in war, Corrie tells herself. Sometimes it's forever, but often they return, don't they? Look at the boy standing next to her, surviving that firestorm. It's chaos in this world, and it's possible Kees is just caught up in the confusion. Isn't it?

For Corrie, the alternative is unthinkable; one of her precious dandelion spores. Having them fly is bad enough, but to be

121

blown away forever . . . not beautiful, vibrant Kees, who has so much of life ahead of her.

'The last we heard she was still in The Hague, with a small group collecting intelligence,' Rudy cuts in.

'But I thought she was in the shipyards, organising the sabotage?' Corrie queries. They'd discovered as much from partisans coming into Amsterdam – the steelworkers toiling for a free Holland were busy shortening propeller blades by a few millimetres, electricians deliberately loosening screws, small adjustments that nonetheless caused German ships to be unseaworthy. Ships that could kill and maim and lead to a Nazi victory. And Kees was their co-ordinator. Only a month ago, there was a positive slant between the lines of her last physical letter to Corrie. 'I'm living life,' Kees wrote. 'And in this war, that's really something.'

I'm fighting these bastards was the real message. She'd sent a picture, too, a tiny snapshot of her dark, thick hair cropped short again, and her huge brown eyes direct into the camera. Stunning, and always with that wry smile. As a child and adult, Kees always refused to recognise her innate attraction, insistent there was more to life than simply being on show. 'It's just a shell,' she wrote in that same letter. 'I can use the outer me, but more and more I see that the kernel inside is what defines us.'

But that letter was early November, and a lot might have happened since then.

'Is there anything else?' Corrie pushes. 'Anything at all.'

Rudy and Dirk glance at each other for a split second, long enough for her to seize the gravity.

'What?' she demands. 'Tell me!'

Rudy shrugs. 'We don't know how reliable it is, but there's word of her being connected with an officer. Here in Amsterdam.'

The way he says it leaves Corrie in no doubt. A Nazi officer. Not Kees, though? She wouldn't. And yet aren't they all doing things they wouldn't contemplate in peacetime?

I can use the outer me, she'd written.

'And?' Corrie presses.

'Abwehr, we think,' Dirk grunts.

She shivers inside her cloak. Just the mention of Gestapo sends ice up anyone's spine. SS too, yet German military intelligence is fast becoming the one to dread. Radio operators across Europe know this, fearful of their tracking devices and ability to pin down transmissions with precision. The Abwehr's ambition to be recognised alongside the Nazi elite spells danger for the resistance. The question is: has it already proved perilous to her beloved Kees?

'Ouch!' Felix wriggles his hand away, Corrie feeding her anxiety into an iron grip and almost crushing his tiny fingers.

'Sorry, Felix. Sorry.' She holds out the other hand as an olive branch. 'Come on, let's get you home safe.'

She pulls him at speed towards home and the security of the house, yet wondering if anywhere can offer true protection nowadays. First, the document drop compromised tonight, and now Kees. It feels too much like a coincidence; more like there's a mole in their midst. If Rudy and Dirk won't listen, then who should she tell?

18

A Raging Storm

Marnie

Marnie can't settle. Sleep the night before had been hampered by another raid, spinning thoughts about her odd-looking shadow, and her sprained ankle, which throbbed into the early hours. Getting to any shelter felt like an impossibility and she'd sat out the raid in bed with tea, two aspirin and a hot water bottle nestled into her foot, muttering childishly at Hitler to 'Come and get me if you dare.' In the cold light of day, she's still limping a little and restless. It's Sunday, the newsagents isn't open to leave an urgent message for Willem and her blasted ankle won't hold out for a long walk. She washes some clothes, eats a sparse lunch and takes the bus to visit her cousin Susie on Bounds Green Road, turning up unannounced with a bizarre range of groceries scavenged en route.

'I'm so glad you brought tea,' a flustered Susie says, ushering her in the front door of their tiny terraced house. 'We're almost down to our last spoonful.'

'Nice to know you've missed me, Susie.'

Her cousin slumps into the kitchen chair, cloth in hand. 'Sorry, Marn. I don't mean to sound flippant. It's chaos when the children are here, and yet when Arthur's mother insists we should evacuate, I can't bear the thought. I honestly don't know what's best.' She looks tired, and suddenly older than her twenty-eight years, pushing back wisps of hair and her troubles. 'Anyway, what have you been up to? And what on earth did you do to your foot?'

Where to start? Marnie wants to share the secret half of her life much more than the mundane, but can't. What would she say anyway? *I'm running intelligence for the Dutch government in exile, for a man I hardly know, and there's someone odd following me. Two sugars, please.*

It could well afford Susie the laugh she so desperately needs, but it won't change the fact that Marnie feels very much in the dark.

She leaves late afternoon, topped up with tea and her fix of the children while Susie tackled her chores. As always, Marnie feels torn after time at Susie's; she dreams of a life partner and a home, the cosy familiarity of her own fireside, and yet motherhood seems so hard. Is it right – or normal – to have such doubts?

'Oh, and how's that man who turned up to Gilbert's funeral?' Susie asks casually as they say goodbye. 'Have you seen him again?'

Marnie is sideswiped. 'Oh, no. Just our small wake at Lyons,' she lies. It's simply too complicated a conversation for a doorstep farewell. She's discovered so little of Willem since the day of Grandad's funeral that – if you take away the obvious subterfuge – there's very little to tell. She kisses Susie on the cheek. 'See you next week, perhaps?'

Instinctively, Marnie heads to Broadcasting House. Since her parents' move, weekends have stretched into long, empty days, with only so many cafés to visit or cinemas to frequent – and those are best avoided for a while after yesterday. The four or five female friends at the BBC she met with regularly have moved to the rural outposts beyond London. And tonight there's not even Daisy to look forward to. So back to work it is. The canteen runs a half service on Sundays but at least it's open, and there's a pile of scripts screaming for attention.

The office is eerily silent as she arrives around six, though the door is unlocked; it's not like Miss Roach to forget such a thing, but it could easily have slipped Raymond's mind. She makes tea with a small pouch of leaves brought from Susie's, conscious of Miss Roach keeping a keen eye on her own supplies. As she sits down at her desk, she notices a small envelope tucked under the pile of scripts, addressed in type to 'Miss M. Fern'. Her brow ripples in confusion. The post room last delivered on Friday morning, after which she'd ploughed her way through all the office mail. Marnie imagines she simply missed it – up until the point when she unfolds the single sheet inside, almost spilling her tea over its content.

Some people are not what they seem. You should be wary of those wanting favours. Others can guarantee your future. Tues evening 7pm. Hungaria. A concerned friend.

It's on plain bond paper, with no markings, the envelope not BBC issue. As invites go, it's not the most appealing, provoking a sudden swell of nausea as she reads it repeatedly. *Wanting favours.* Do they merely suspect what she's doing, or know for certain? Either way, it confirms Marnie's notions of being watched. But by whom? A fifth columnist – those pro-Nazi sympathisers – or worse, a fully fledged German spy? It's certainly no friend. And now she really does need to speak to Willem. But when . . . and where the hell is he?

Her mind is an eddy of doubt for the next hour or so, with very little work achieved. The siren sounds at around seven p.m., but when the new in-house signalling system indicates it's not urgent – the firewatchers on the BBC roof judging an attack isn't imminent – Marnie makes her way to the canteen for whatever leftovers they have. Despite the past weeks and that large gash in the side of the building, the feeling of safety endures within the corridors of Broadcasting House.

'Ah, just the person!'

Looking up from her withered sandwich, Marnie sees Ed Murrow beaming at her, tin hat under his arm, the shoulders of his Savile Row suit a dusty grey. 'Oh hello. Not been up on the roof again?'

'Out and about actually,' he says, 'although as it happens I could really do with your help. I know it's an imposition, but are you free for an hour or so?'

It's more than she could hope for – a distraction and a purpose, two birds with one stone. Murrow needs a production assistant as he records an impromptu broadcast in one of the downstairs studios, and she needs to stop thinking about a stranger stealing into her office with a note that has since stolen her peace of mind. What could be more timely?

Inevitably, it's more than an hour, but the time flies as they push towards the finish. Murrow is passionate and a perfectionist, with the resulting programme destined to have impact. The world outside this war needs to know what the eye of this storm feels like. And Murrow, being American, is sure to secure airtime across the Atlantic.

Ironic that when they finish around 10.45, the fury of the raid has largely passed over, though the all-clear hasn't yet sounded. Marnie needs fresh air, and to weigh up if she'll brave the journey home or the snoring symphony of her BBC haven. The shelter is often the balm she needs, but tonight there's a desire for her own company. She wants to process that note and her reaction to it.

Stepping out into a crisp, surprisingly clear night, Marnie knots a woollen scarf around her neck.

'Evening miss,' says Ralph Palmer, one of the regular doormen.

'What do you think, Mr Palmer, have I got time to sprint across to Regent's Park?' She remembers her ankle then – already less sore, but it would mean a brisk limp instead of a sprint.

'Perhaps if you're quick, miss.' He sniffs the air above like a veteran weatherman. 'The first wave looks to be heading home to their beds. But there's no telling if Adolf will send a second lot tonight.'

'I might just take the chance then.'

They stand together for a minute or so, staring into the dark veil above the empty place, dull bangs in the distance and, unusually, no noise coming from the Langham bar across the way.

'You'll need a good torch if you're to . . .' Palmer turns and starts to rifle in a box behind the sandbags. 'I've got one inside. Just give me a minute, Miss Fern.'

Marnie is left alone, still gazing, when she catches sight of something from the corner of her eye, what looks to be a tarpaulin drifting down from the side of the building. It spans a good twenty feet or so, catching on the lamppost between the BBC and the Langham with only a faint clonk, the graceful descent of a toy parachutist made from a pocket handkerchief. Cautiously, she steps out onto the pavement, squinting upwards. It's sure to have come loose from the fifth floor, where large, heavy sheets are shrouding the ongoing repairs to Broadcasting House. Against the now dull exterior, recently painted a battle-ship grey to help deter another hit, it's difficult to distinguish, but the sheets appear to be firmly in place. In a mood already running with suspicion, Marnie's mind leaps to the possibilities – that a *real* parachutist, an ejected German pilot, has bailed out after being targeted by the ack-ack guns. Should she investigate? Where is Ed Murrow when there's potentially the hottest story unfolding in front of them? Or a constable when needed? Ralph Palmer? Anyone?

Driven by either stupidity or morbid curiosity, Marnie moves towards the folds of draped material, the bottom of the lamppost shielded by a parked car. She's gone only a few steps when her ears tune into the sound of a match flare, sulphur burning, only this time it's no single cigarette – more the volume of a giant fuse. Man-made, yes, but this is no pilot. As it sizzles in the still air, she swivels to see Ralph waving frantically from the doorway. His words are muffled, but he seems to be mouthing 'Come back' and 'Get down' at the same time.

Which one is it?

The searing noise reaches a crescendo as she turns and catches her sprained foot, falling heavily to her knees. Inexplicably, a sudden reflex forces her into a tight ball, like some type of exotic beetle.

In her next breath, the world in front of the BBC implodes.

A blinding white light and two dazzling purplish rings radiate at least as high as the lamppost, as Marnie dares to peer out from under her shielding arm. Instantly, there's a monumental, sinister howling beating at her eardrums, while a merciless tornado of grit, heat and dust punches at her torso, hammering relentlessly with sheer force, driving hard lumps into her back and arms. She wants to shield against the intense pain and pressure in her ears, clamp her hands on either side of her head, but some innate whisper tells her not to leave her crown exposed.

From somewhere in the squall, a voice chants, faint but firm: 'Stay down, hold on. Just hold on.' It might be Palmer, but it's Grandad, too, from another universe entirely. Whoever it is, the words assure Marnie she's alive and not falling through hell, driving her determination to root herself into the ground and not let this vicious force peel her limb by limb from London's streets. She has a brief vision of herself whipped up by the wind and sent spinning into dense black clouds, like in a children's book she once had, but the image is tossed away by the intense pain of something hard ripping into her back. *Stay firm, Marnie.*

The blast comes in waves for what feels an eternity, a pressure that eventually decreases, leaving a deluge of dust and debris raining down, pitting at her head like the fat, icy blobs of a hailstorm. As it wanes to a shower, she's daring to unfurl when someone grabs and yanks at her arm.

'NOW! Now!' they scream at her, though the voice is fogged and far away.

With legs that barely function, Marnie staggers and half-crawls with help towards the BBC doorway, away from an orange orb that is the blazing car, spitting metal and fury indiscriminately in a wide circle, the air choked with a smell of burning petrol. She can't hear what they're saying exactly, but someone helps her through the door and into the lobby, eases her down onto the tiled floor, and only then can she see it's Ed Murrow, with even more of London's streets on his Savile Row suit than before.

'Marnie. Marnie!' He's shouting to get her attention. 'Are you hurt badly?'

His voice is weak, like it's coming from the end of a long tunnel, and she wonders if he was caught in the blast, too, but there's no blood on his face as he looms close. Not like her hands, coated red and pocked with tiny, glittering shards. She can only shake her head.

'Someone get her a blanket,' she hears him say. 'She's half naked.'

Who? Who is half naked? Did I miss something?

Again, as with the last assault on the BBC, the ambulances arrive in what feels no time at all, a woman uttering reassurances close into her ear. 'Don't worry. We'll take care of you,' and it's all Marnie wants to know.

She's aware of being examined under her blanket, patted down, winces when there's a sharp pain, and then feels herself being lifted, and in her confusion thinks it's the wind again trying to prise her from the ground. Once aloft, though, it's more like floating on air and not being flayed by the explosion.

Marnie closes her eyes and gives herself over, to fate or death or survival. As the ambulance doors close, her last thought is that she doesn't mind which one of them triumphs.

130

19

A Suit of Armour

9th December 1940, London

Marnie

In the light of a new morning, she's glad when survival wins out, even if the alternative might not be quite so painful. Marnie had woken in the early hours to a dim glow above her head, and it took several minutes to work out where she was, a faint coughing in an echoey space giving rise to the acoustics of a hospital ward. A face was there, bobbing above her, asking how she was, and it looked like the wings of an angel but was actually the white of a nurse's cap; the first sign that life had grabbed at her first and hung on the longest. Satisfied she wasn't dead, her eyelids drooped again.

Come the morning, she sits up in bed with difficulty and shifts cautiously on clean sheets, surveying her heavily bandaged hands, and feeling every one of the twenty or so lacerations sliced into her back and arms, though she's told that only five are deep enough to warrant stitches.

'You're a lucky woman, Miss Fern,' the doctor says on his morning rounds. 'We pulled out some sizeable pieces of shrapnel from your back. Your instinct to curl up was sound, but it was your winter scarf and thick suit that saved your life, like a good suit of armour.'

Lying on the chair alongside, her two-piece of jacket and skirt is a testament to his words and the ferocity of the blast.

The deep maroon material is in shreds, as if it's been mauled by a giant grizzly or hungry tiger. She can't hold back the tears on her scored cheeks, flowing not with pain or shock, but the fact it was the creation of Gilbert Cooper, master tailor, a bespoke two-piece in the best quality wool he could find, designed to keep her warm and cocooned. 'Beautiful,' he'd cooed over the fabric as he fingered the weave and prepared to cut. 'This, my lovely Marnie, will make you look and feel the talk of the town.'

Grandad didn't predict it would save her life, but there he is again, looking over her. Always.

'Miss Fern, you have a visitor.' The nurse pokes her head through the curtain. 'Do you feel well enough?'

'Yes, of course.'

She can't imagine who it will be, given that Raymond was the first through the door with a bunch of flowers this morning. On leaving, he did promise to alert her cousin, so it could well be Susie.

Raymond had oozed sympathy and concern, delivering the welcome news that Ralph Palmer had emerged uninjured, and something of a hero. 'The casualties are not quite so bad,' he added without details. 'A lot of damage, mind. It was a landmine with a delayed timer, a real menace. The blast cracked a water main and Broadcasting House is flooded, so we've been rehearsing in the basement of the Langham. I heard one man on the other side of the street had his trousers blown off, quite literally. Apparently, he looked very embarrassed, but at least he emerged with both legs.'

Suddenly, Ed Murrow's assertion of her being 'half naked' at the BBC made sense.

When the curtain ripples again, Marnie begins to explain. 'Susie, it's really not as bad as it looks . . .'

'They said your ears had taken a battering, but not your eyes as well.' Willem is smiling as he walks through, a small brown paper parcel in his hand, though his mouth tightens at the first

132

sight of her face, an entire roadmap of scratches, despite her having kept it pressed into the ground during the squall.

She shifts and palms at her scored cheek. 'I haven't looked in the mirror yet, but I'm sure it's not pretty.'

'You look fine, considering you were almost blown up by a landmine. Pretty is in the eye of the beholder, so they say.'

'Beauty,' she corrects, and then hates herself for doing it. Again.

'Sorry, beauty,' he laughs, and leans into her. 'It reminds me that a Dutchman should never attempt to quote long-dead novelists. Especially an agent who's trying to blend in.'

The ice duly broken, he holds up a wrapped box. 'The only chocolates I could find, I'm afraid. From Selfridges. I'm not sure how nice they'll be.'

'Very, I should think,' Marnie says, unpacking to reveal an expensive French brand. 'It's almost worth getting blown up for exquisite chocolates.'

'Then, that's good.' He stops. 'No, I don't mean it's good that you . . . hell, I'm making a real hash of this, aren't I? I only came to see if you were all right.'

For someone who appeared so menacing that night in the ruins of Grandad's shop, Willem seems changed. Softer, and more vulnerable.

'How did you know I was here?' Marnie is part curious, part pleased, but remains a little wary. With her hearing and memory restored, she recalls the typed message, stuffed somewhere in the remains of her handbag. *Some people are not what they seem.* While Willem has shown a gentler side, they are a long way from mutual trust, and she needs more time to consider the note alone.

'I only got your request to meet via the newsagent late last night,' he explains. 'But when you weren't at home, I rang the BBC.'

She holds up her bandaged mitts, wiggles the fingers of her left hand poking out the end. 'Luckily, it's not as bad as the right.' She lowers her voice to a whisper, mindful of the flimsy curtains around the bed. 'Don't worry, I'm sure I'll be out of here and ready for "work" tomorrow, though perhaps I can stay near to home this time?'

He looks instantly affronted, the hurt moving through his lips. 'Marnie, I didn't come to check if you're fit for work,' he says curtly. His eyes are wide but crease at the corner as he speaks. 'I'm here as a friend, a concerned one. To see how you are. And only that.'

She says nothing. In all honesty, she doesn't know how to respond. Susie cares, Raymond cares. Her parents show concern from afar. But Marnie Fern is not used to anyone else's attentions. Sitting there, upright to ease the pain in her back, she realises how brittle she's become over the years, from top to toe. Hard and unyielding. Like a spinster in training.

'Sorry,' she says at last. 'I just thought, well, you know . . . you're busy.'

'I hope I'm never too busy to feel,' he comes back. 'To be a person. Not just a Dutchman needing help.'

'Yes. I apologise, and I'm glad you came. Honestly.'

In the midst of their awkward pause, the nurse arrives to save the day with her surgical trolley in tow, laden with fresh bandages. 'I'm sorry,' she says to Willem. 'Time for Miss Fern's treatments.'

'Of course. I'll leave you to it. Perhaps I'll see you tomorrow?' His tone is suggestive, raising both eyebrows as he moves through the curtain.

'Yes, I'll be discharged sometime in the afternoon, they say. Home by teatime, I should think.'

'He seems nice,' the nurse says, readying the dressings. 'Handsome, too. Have you two been stepping out long?'

'Oh, no. No . . . I mean we're not . . .' Marnie stumbles over the suggestion. 'We're just friends.'

'It's good to have friends like that,' the nurse rambles on as she works. 'Especially now. What would we do without them?'

20

A Shadow in the Basement

10th December 1940, London

Marnie

Marnie unwinds the bandage from her left hand and bends her joints one by one to ease the soreness. Gingerly, she wipes the salve liberally applied across her skin and massages her 'principal pianist', the first finger on her left hand responsible for the speed of her transmissions. Will it hold up? Or will Daisy notice if the delivery is sluggish, enough to wonder if an imposter has replaced Lizzy at the other end?

With the handset unconnected, she tests out a message several times, checking her own clarity and finding her rhythm with the tapping.

The quick brown fox jumped over the lazy dog. It sounds a little reticent in her ears.

Peter Piper picked a peck of pickled peppers. Better. The Ps will be well practised.

Careless talk costs lives. We shall fight on the beaches. Marnie laughs inside at the words that crowd her mind. She practises until the transmission time approaches, her back smarting as she's forced to bend over the desk to concentrate fully. Tonight is unusually damp in the college basement, and she's slightly regretting her early discharge from hospital – the doctor had recommended staying another night, but her heart was set on not missing the rendezvous with Daisy. *Others suffer much worse,* she'd insisted to herself. *I'll be fine with a few painkillers.*

And she is, at heart. Except it feels emptier than normal, the space more barren. Willem had intimated at the hospital that he'd be here, but sent the dispatch via a courier instead, along with a handwritten note. *Sorry, held up. Okay to use basement. Talk tomorrow.*

Yet again, she doesn't know how to react. Marnie veers between dismissing and entertaining the content of that insidious note, between Willem not being what he seems and yet missing his company. Which one should she listen to: head or heart? And is either one right?

As always, Daisy puts paid to her apprehension. The first taps that come through calm Marnie instantly, and she's quickly absorbed in the task. Then, when the transmissions are exchanged, the element she looks forward to most, the added message from Daisy, the few words that make her feel connected to a world far beyond any basement. She's surprised, however, when it's also in code. Why? Is it not the innocent asides they're used to swapping, replaced with something the Germans shouldn't hear?

As signalled by Daisy's '*FTA*', she pulls out Grandad's aged copy of Hemingway's *Farewell to Arms* – a book they've not yet used for encryption – and unpicks the jumble of letters.

Darcy needs to contact. Urgent. Please Lizzy. We may be compromised.

The words are blunt, and the tone of the message feels pressing.

Their allotted time is almost up, but Marnie speeds to encode and tap out a reply: *Is Darcy in danger? Who is we?*

Seconds tick by, enough that Marnie imagines the line will remain silent. Is it because the peril is creeping closer, the Abwehr on Daisy's doorstep? Marnie is blind to where or what situation her opposite is in, only senses the need in her. A desperate one.

Just when she's about to give up, the line is activated. Marnie scratches out the translation, reading the nine words repeatedly. Shivering properly now.

All of us. Possible traitor in ranks. Watch yourselves.

Marnie's mind is made up. Given her fragile state, she hadn't intended to go, but now it seems vital for her to heed the mysterious note and be at Hungaria for seven p.m. The written note, and now Daisy's warning, could be a coincidence. But what if it's not? Both hint at treachery and turncoats. Common sense points to her not risking it; the unknown nature of the sender for one thing, and the fact that she can barely move without one portion of her body complaining. But when has reason ever entered into this war? She's dodged a bullet – or a bomb – not once or twice, but three times now. There must be some logic to why she's still alive. A purpose.

In the middle is Willem. What is she to make of that?

Had he been here tonight, Marnie feels certain she would have shown him the note. Now, she's not so sure. Nothing is concrete any more, every part of London's foundations grinding into dust amid a rickety existence. The result: she doesn't trust even those purporting to help them win this bloody war.

Which is why Marnie downs two more aspirin, gathers her handbag and gas mask from her room, and sets out.

It's easy to see why her anonymous messenger has chosen Hungaria. In among the blown-out plate-glass windows lining Regent Street, it has the advantage of a basement dining room, with a written inducement at the entrance: 'Air raid shelter for patrons.' Hitler's night-time visits, it seems, will NOT scupper the enjoyment of fine food for determined gourmets.

Marnie is glad to see many of the tables occupied in the cushioned dining room, with plenty of waiters milling about, accommodating well-dressed people perched on the chintz chairs as they talk over a jazz quartet on a small stage in the corner. A quick scan reveals no one person sitting alone, and so she takes a table facing the stairs, telling the waiter she's due to meet a friend.

A friend. It's what the note claimed. That remains to be seen.

'A drink, madam?'

'I'll have a gin and French please.' Wise? Perhaps not, especially with painkillers in the mix, but there's a real need in the circumstance.

Her drink arrives and the minutes crawl by – five past, then ten – and with them this whole venture begins to feel like a big mistake. Sipping nervously, Marnie makes a pact with herself, the sort a child might in hopping over the cracks in the pavement: 'If I do ten more, I can eat one sweet from my packet.' She reasons that if the next person to arrive passes her table by, she will walk away. Nothing lost, except a chink of her pride.

From her vantage point, she catches the waiter's pitying expression as she eyes the stairs intently. If only he knew how desperate she is to be stood up at this point. A pair of black brogues descends, Marnie fixed on the direction of the obviously male steps, then the slight hesitation, the approach towards the cluster of dining tables.

Go past, go past, go past. She downs the last of her gin. *Go past, so I can get up and hide at home and pretend this whole charade never happened.*

'Miss Fern?'

'Yes?'

'May I?'

He's someone you would pass in the street a thousand times and still never be confident of describing fully. Neither short nor tall, tortoiseshell glasses on a slightly rounded face, and when he takes off his hat, it's to reveal mid-brown thinning hair. In fact, everything about him is 'mid' and nondescript. A bank manager type. She stares hard. Different glasses, but yes, it is *the* bank manager man, her former shadow.

'Would you like another drink?' He gestures at her empty glass.

138

'No, thank you.' She looks away. 'I'm not even sure I should be here.'

'But you are.' That indistinct smile again. 'That tells me something.'

His smugness sparks irritation in her. 'What does it tell you, Mr . . .?'

'Smith.'

Of course he's Mr Smith.

'It tells me you're curious,' he goes on. 'About what we can offer.'

'We? Who's we?'

The waiter approaches and 'Mr Smith' orders a sherry, eyes combing the room in the same way Willem is apt to whenever they meet in public. He clasps short, stubby fingers together and rests them on the table, his smile revealing small, child like teeth.

'You have exactly one minute to tell me why we're here,' Marnie says, with a firmness that doesn't reflect the indecision raging within. But yes, she is irked – suddenly furious as to why 'they' are targeting her, Miss Fern as the soft touch, easily persuaded. Miss Fern of the BBC who is always happy to oblige. Does she look *that* lonely and vulnerable?

He sips at the sherry placed in front of him. 'There are people who, let's say, have a different view of the debacle outside' – he gestures upwards, to the siren that's just begun a timely wailing – 'and want to put an end to it. Quickly, before more of our country suffers.'

'How would that be?' Marnie has an inkling, but she wants him to spell it out, through the muddying of alcohol and pain-killers, not to mention her cowering under a landmine less than forty-eight hours ago.

He tips his mouth upwards and lowers his voice. 'What Hitler proposes isn't too different to what many people in this country desire. Living a good and prosperous life, in peace.'

'Surrender, you mean? Capitulate and live under *that* man?' Marnie feels her blood boil and the skin pinch under its scarring. Her mouth contains a growl, bent so low over the table she can feel the heat of her own breath. 'And you think I am one of them? Someone who would want a false peace while others are cruelly persecuted?'

Mr Smith, or bank manager, or whoever he is, appears nonplussed by her annoyance. 'It will happen, Miss Fern, make no mistake,' he says calmly. 'And quite soon. The Allies are on their knees, and when it does, certain groups will come to the fore. It will be a bonus if you are among those people. Besides which, your own people are not infallible.'

'I am not a fifth columnist,' she states unequivocally.

For the first time, the man appears to baulk at her words, glances around for hovering waiters. 'We don't use phrases like that, Miss Fern. But, yes, if you like – the views are somewhat similar. We don't pretend otherwise.'

'And what have I done or said to make you think I'd be interested in joining your band of traitors? Who has even suggested I might think like you?' She wants to shout this from the rooftops, but doesn't, because the realisation hits with a sickening clarity, in her throbbing head and the pit of her stomach. How can she be so stupid? It's not her – Marnie the person – that they want. It's not her opinions, if Hitler even allows such a thing as individual thought. It's Marnie the model employee and her precious access to the BBC, Britain's mouthpiece. The ears of England.

Worse is the thought that comes chasing that revelation, ramming in behind with full force: *I can't be the only one.*

'And how many others in the BBC are you targeting?' She looks directly beyond the reflection of his glasses, eye to beady eye.

'We have friends.' His flat, average voice cuts to the core with those words and, in that second, she hates his quiet but supreme arrogance, that individuals like her have so little in their lives they can be won over by false promises, assuming people are essentially self-centred. And it's all glossed over by hijacking a common phrase: for the 'greater good'. How can war or domination or killing be anything like 'good'?

Marnie loathes his type with a passion, desperate right now to slap his average, pudgy face and attract the gasps of surrounding, well-to-do diners. She doesn't, of course, because she is Miss Marnie Fern, fairly model employee of the British Broadcasting Corporation. Instead, she gets up and makes a show of being affronted, enough to grab the attention of the room.

'How dare you!' Marnie cries loudly. 'Who *do* you think I am?' A waiter steps towards her to offer help. She picks up her gloves, bends down and hisses close to Mr Smith's ear in parting. 'And don't even think about following me.'

A hand whips out with the pace of a lizard's tongue and catches hers, his fingers hot and clammy. 'Be careful, Miss Fern. Be wary of being left behind with your little Dutch friend when Hitler breaks through these borders. Which he will.' His conceited smile turns sinister in a heartbeat and the cloying warmth inside the dining room plummets.

Outside, the raid is in full swing, another deadly pyrotechnic display levied on central London. Marnie is already breathless from her flight up the Hungaria stairs, and for a moment she considers running for the shelter at Oxford Circus Tube. But the thought of its stagnant air and the wall of unavoidable noise triggers palpitations on top of her heaving chest. Dozens of incendiaries have already showered the street, dotting the pavement with small fires and forcing her path to zig-zag. A shout from behind tells her to 'Take cover, for God's sake,' but she stumbles forward. More than ever, Marnie needs to reach home, and either bury herself in the college basement, or under her own blankets. Reckless for sure, but how much more can the Führer throw at her? She'll *feel* safe in her own realm, even if she isn't.

Heat from the firestorm raging above is intense and begins to penetrate her thick coat, making her already scarred skin feel as if it's singeing all over again.

Just keep going, that guiding voice inside her says.

She forges on, unable to see much ahead but navigating by familiar shops and their signs above, driven by the need to get as far away from Mr Smith as possible. A sudden crash behind makes Marnie shrink into a doorway, instantly twisting herself into a ball again. Suddenly, she's back in Portland Place, the tumult of the world on her, the noise of Ralph Palmer and Hades in her ears. So vivid.

When she uncurls minutes later, her cheeks are wet with tears. But there's no going back, not now. Lurching onwards a few yards, she no longer recognises the façade in front of her, or the houses and offices either side, the hoardings shoring up an already bombed building. In blind confusion, Marnie has taken a wrong turn and ended up in a small square, bordered on three sides by darkened windows, and one side by brickwork cracking and moaning under the fierce blaze on the top floors, a serpent's flaming tongue licking at the night sky. She shies away from the blistering heat and into a corner, where it's devoid of fire but too dark to see her own feet. Staying put becomes impossible as roof masonry crashes to the ground, and, as she stumbles back into the centre of the square, her bravado is replaced with abject fear. Looming shadows are projected onto the wall by the orange glow – of a man, moving, the outline of a hat, the brim sharp and focused. A bowler hat. Christ, what sort of a bank manager type is he? A proficient spy or a spectre who can walk through walls? How on earth did he follow her here?

Marnie crouches low, stilled, but it's to no avail. She turns to see her own silhouette loom large on the brickwork, as if she's the central figure in some enormous puppet show and the dastardly cartoon villain is stalking ever closer. The hat's shadow creeps nearer, its brim losing definition as the projected shape enlarges. Almost on top of her. Unable to sit and wait for fate or the fifth column to snare her, Marnie leaps up, tripping on fallen bricks and releasing a sudden, shrill cry that bounces off the walls.

'Hey, is someone there? Are you okay?' It's a voice she knows, from life and across the airwaves. That distinct accent. The brim comes back into focus – of a tin hat, and the face under it blackened by soot.

Marnie's laugh is driven largely by hysteria. 'That's twice now you've come to my rescue. Did anyone ever mark you down as a knight in shining armour?'

'You mean like King Arthur or Lancelot?' says a quizzical Ed Murrow, offering his hand to pull her up. 'Perhaps you could tell my wife that. She thinks I'm running around London having a fine old time.'

Marnie winces, every ache and scratch rearing its painful head. 'Come on,' he says. 'You need to lie down, clearly. Let's get you back to the BBC shelter.'

'I need my own bed,' she protests. 'It's not far. Can you? Please.' Marnie catches the hunger in her own voice. It's rash and perilous, born of her own stupidity perhaps, but she still craves the solace of her own space.

Ed Murrow looks directly up at the sky; beyond the flames only tracer fire remains. The second wave of Luftwaffe will be on them soon, but for now there's a small window of calm. 'Hold onto my arm and let's get going,' he says.

They move out into the wreckage of the main streets, stopping briefly to wonder at the fire crews beetling about, their flimsy, wavering ladders extending hundreds of feet into the air, an arc of spray battling the inferno. How can man possibly fight against this rage of nature, caused by another man's fury?

'Come on,' Ed urges. 'We can't do much here except paint a picture of this across the airwaves.'

'Look, if you need to record, I can manage,' Marnie says, trying to appear convincing. 'I can get home.'

'It's okay, I taped it live tonight, just before I found you. I'll edit later. By the way, what are you doing here?'

'Long story.'

A second wave of calm descends in the emptiness of Regent's Park, and a third sense of peace when they each down a whisky in Marnie's kitchen.

'Thanks, I didn't quite realise how much I needed that,' Ed says. 'Are you sure you'll be safe here? The all-clear hasn't sounded yet.'

'I'll be fine,' she assures him. 'And besides, where is safe any more? You're the one who has to go back out.'

'Ah, I feel pretty bombproof with this.' He taps at his tin helmet. 'It's done me proud so far.'

'I feel much the same about my eiderdown. If Hitler wants to find me tonight, please direct him towards my bed.'

She sinks slowly into the mattress after Murrow leaves, thanks her good fortune again for a flat where the bed is softer than the one in Wood Green, and sheets that don't chafe too much on her still raw back. She shifts, with a few oohs and aahs of discomfort, before settling to think.

Willem. How much of tonight had she brought upon herself, and how much is connected to her involvement with a Dutchman she knows so little about? Someone who seems attentive when he's present, but so often invisible. Before now, she's imagined his loyalties firm and entrenched – with Daisy, and Holland. But now . . . what was it that heinous man said? *Your own people are not infallible.*

There are no easy answers, not until she can pin Willem down for a proper interrogation. She feels compelled to tell him of Daisy's warning – which may have consequences for them all – but also to gauge his reaction. More than anything, she hopes to see a look of true shock on his face, that there could be a mole. She *wants* him to be innocent in all this. Who knows though, in this war. Who knows anything?

In the meantime, the persistent drone of bombers draws closer in readiness for a fresh raid. Marnie hunkers down, imagining – hoping – that the soft fibres of her eiderdown act more like steel armour.

21

Spies Like Us

Marnie

For the first time since the landmine blast, Broadcasting House is fully open the next morning, though the scars of Portland Place remain visible: the lamppost bent and contorted in a grotesque work of art and the large crater blast turned to an impromptu pond of filthy water. Marnie stands at the edge for a minute or so, out of sight of the main door, collecting herself. After that awful night, she's intent on pushing all memories from her mind – the white light and the sound of hell sucking her into its depths – determined that it will *not* haunt or define her. Whole families have their homes bombed out from out under them, she's told herself, and all while they shelter under a flimsy set of stairs. They live on, go back to work and school. She is no different.

Her legs tell another story, quivering with each step towards the entrance now banked with a wall of fresh sandbags, until she sees Ralph Palmer, bolt upright at his station with a customary cheery smile, a large plaster across his forehead.

'So glad to see you back, Miss Fern,' he says. 'Bit of a close call the other night.'

'It's all down to your quick wits that I'm here at all, Mr Palmer,' she comes back. His very presence restores her shaky world to a version of normality. 'Thank you.'

146

'My pleasure, Miss Fern.'

Raymond's surprise at her sudden presence translates to a fussing concern, so Marnie is relieved – and a little bit guilty – when he's called to a meeting. Miss Roach steps in, using an entire day's ration of tea leaves on one cup, or that's what the orangey-brown brew tastes like. Once again, she's more than grateful for their care and concern.

Enjoying her job so much means Marnie has never watched the clock crawl slowly to five p.m. Today, though, the hands can't go fast enough as she hops from one studio to another, always busy, but constantly glancing at the time. On her way to Broadcasting House she'd left an insistent note at the newsagents, this one in a code she's certain only Willem can decipher. *Langham bar, 5.10 p.m. Urgent. Daisy needs you.*

What she means is *I* need you, but that plea has so far failed. If Marnie's suspicions are correct, the simple mention of Daisy will guarantee Willem's attendance.

At just past five, she's at a table in the corner that affords a good view of the bar entrance, a tonic water to hand. An open book on her lap signals to BBC colleagues that she's happy to be alone, and means she spots Willem the minute he blows in, eyes combing left and right.

'Are you all right?' he pants. His cheeks are flushed above the navy suit and he could well have run a good way across London.

'Yes I'm fine. Get yourself a drink – we've got a bit to talk about.'

'So?' Willem puts down his beer and sits beside her. 'Your message said it was urgent. About Daisy.' His voice is eager and strained, unable to hide the unease that someone precious may be in danger.

Marnie relays the message from Amsterdam, with as much detail as two curt lines allow.

The colour sinks from his face, as fast as some of the Langham regulars can down a Scotch after a pressing deadline. 'And you're as sure as can be that it was really Daisy?'

She nods. 'Nothing unusual in the transmission. Except that . . . well, it's really silly . . .'

'What?'

'I could almost hear her distress.'

He slumps in his seat and breathes heavily.

'Willem? Do you know what she means? Could there be a mole?'

A noisy, chattering group of men enters the bar, diverting Marnie from Willem's instant reaction. He eyes them, scouting as always, puts down his beer and leans his mouth into her ear. 'Do you know that one in the tweed jacket, dark wavy hair?'

'Uh, Burgess maybe?' Marnie murmurs. 'Guy Burgess, I think. Raymond has mentioned him once or twice. He used to work here.'

There's a sound from Willem's throat much like a grunt. 'Let's talk elsewhere,' he says, and gets up.

They walk a few hundred yards and turn into Chandos Street, slip into the nearest café that's still open, and slide into a small booth, their backs to the spit and hiss of the tea urn.

'What was all that about?' Marnie asks.

'Just being cautious,' Willem says. 'That Burgess fellow looks familiar. Pretty sure I've seen him around where I work.'

'You mean he's a spy?' Marnie breathes. 'Even if he is, surely that means he's on our side?'

Willem shrugs. 'Who knows these days? Trust is a rare currency.'

Marnie lets that slice of cynicism go. 'So what about Daisy, and this traitor? What will you do? What *can* you do?'

She watches intently as he shakes his head in something like defeat. 'I don't know. We've suspected for a while that someone in Amsterdam is feeding the Abwehr information, possibly from inside our group.'

'Any idea who?'

'No, and even if I did, my hands are tied back here. The lines – your lines – are so busy passing information crucial to the wider fight that we've no space to find out. I can't investigate across an entire sea.'

His voice oozes a genuine frustration, and Marnie wonders if it's such a good thing being a favourite of the Dutch royal family after all, valued by queen and country. He'd never intended it, he revealed to her one night after a transmission, but on landing at the Dutch consulate in London had found himself pulled into the role. 'There's so few of us here and they were desperate for agents,' he'd said. 'Being an engineer before all this, I suppose I fitted the bill.'

Willem's obvious troubles make Marnie reluctant to reveal the ups and downs of her last days, but desperation compels her to open up.

To her surprise, Willem is remarkably nonplussed at news of the note, Hungaria and the mysterious Mr Smith. 'And there's no hint at what he wanted you to do?' is all he asks.

'No, only that he – they – are looking to recruit within the BBC. It makes me wary who I talk to.'

'You should be,' Willem counters. 'I don't doubt there are hundreds of good people – true patriots – around you, but it only takes one or two to plant potentially dangerous ideas. The Nazis value radio propaganda above everything else, and one of Hitler's key objectives is to control the airwaves. But we do know the fifth column is bent on hijacking information, rather than physical intimidation.'

'Well, that's a relief. I'll bear that in mind.' Her sarcasm is unrestrained.

Willem frowns. 'Just do as before – be careful of everyone around you.'

There's a pause as each stares too long into their tea. Should she reveal anything else, the other little nugget in the missive? *Now or never, Marnie.*

'It's funny, the note said much the same thing about you,' she adds quietly.

'What do you mean?'

'That I shouldn't trust people who are seeming to help me.'

'And you think they mean *me*?' Willem's scorn is apparent, but there's an affront in his voice, too.

'I presume so. As far I'm aware, you're the only spy I know. Only . . .' she falters, before pushing on, '. . . you don't have enough trust to tell me anything. I've moved homes, been followed, risked my safety, and yet I gauge so little, other than your gratitude.'

'And what more do you want?' Willem demands, the sinews of his neck at full stretch. 'What more can I give you, Miss Fern?'

'Something of yourself!' she blurts, loud enough for the waitress to look up from wiping tables. 'I'm expected to give up parts of myself, to someone who could easily be leading me down a path to Lord knows where. I want to trust you, but I don't know who you are, Willem, not even your surname. When you recruited me, there was no hint of danger – certainly you assured me my grandfather had been safe enough. And now, here I am, being followed and propositioned by God knows who.' She stops, aware her nostrils are flaring. 'Feeling threatened if I'm honest. What am I supposed to believe?'

His breaths are quick and deep, thoughts clearly stirring. 'You're right,' he says. 'I am asking a lot. And I'm sorry.' He picks up his teacup and pushes a fingertip hard against a crack in the rim.

'Look, Willem, I don't want to pry, nor do I need a deep insight into your comings and goings. But I've always judged people by getting to know them a little. It's my barometer, if you like.'

She wants to elaborate, to explain it's what people do when they're alone and likely to be for a good while, possibly an entire life. When you have no one to chew over the day while eating supper, or swap opinions across the breakfast table. Inevitably, you crave more information to be certain of your own mind. For Marnie, it's survival. And in war, anything less has made her downright wary.

'Are you free tomorrow evening?' he says suddenly. 'I'd like you to meet someone – a person to vouch for me. Well, hopefully.'

'I'd like that,' Marnie says. 'And Daisy's warning? What will you do there?'

His face darkens as he drains his cup. 'Think – for the time being. I need to work it out.' He leaves coins for the waitress and they say goodbye at the table, Willem suggesting it's best if they leave separately.

'And it's Bakker, by the way,' he says on getting up.

'What is?'

'My surname. You might not find me in one of your directories, but it is real, I promise you.'

22

News

Corrie

There's been no further word on Kees, and Corrie forces herself to stay clear of Rudy or Dirk in the days since their disclosure, but only for fear of compromising safety within the resistance cell. It's not easy, with her stomach in constant turmoil, head pounding with worry day and night. One son on the run was bad enough, but Willem is out of the Nazi line of fire for now. Her daughter, on the other hand, could be in some godforsaken camp, possibly just a few kilometres away in the Nazi prison on the central Leidseplein. Or being feted high up in the Hotel Americain, the captive guest of some Nazi officer, a prospect that makes Corrie physically retch; Kees being a mistress, willing or otherwise, is a scenario too awful to contemplate. The word 'connected' has so many implications, all of them mushrooming into horrific visions of torture and death. Or complicity to save your own skin. Corrie is entirely torn: resistance members are schooled not to reveal secrets 'at any cost', even death. But in her heart, she yearns for Kees to survive. At any cost.

The cold winter days crawl by. Takings in the shop are minimal but crucial if she is to keep two rooms in the house warm, she and Felix living between the kitchen and one bedroom, where they curl up together each night wrapped in every blanket they have, seeking heat from the stove and each other.

This afternoon, she's sold only two books, with three browsers all day – all German – and though she's tried to busy herself with tidying, her mind inevitably wanders into dark corners.

By mid-afternoon, Corrie can stand no more. Felix is out on errands, and will go on to see Zeeza for a little of the schooling he's missed out on. She puts up the closed sign, pulls on her cape, wraps two scarves around her head and face, and plunges into the white of Amsterdam.

The canal side on Rozengracht has turned to ice with the footfall, and Corrie slides her way towards the gabled corner building of Loeki's Bodega, passing with relief into the heat of bodies lining the café. It's busy for a Wednesday afternoon, full of the unemployed that pepper Amsterdam these days. Resistance too.

The café is an instant haven, alive with memories of visits with her father when he first opened the bookshop, drinking shoulder to shoulder with home-grown Dutch writers he endorsed and placed on his shelves. Years on, despite women being in the minority, and the owner's wife, Loeki, stuck in the kitchen most of the time, Corrie is comfortable among the dark wood décor and battered cushions of an old living room. More importantly, Germans don't drink here, unless SS or Abwehr spies are daring to hover amid the sloppily dressed locals.

Now, she recognises a few faces, names from the spines on her shelves, plus a few scribes long since out of print. They nod as she moves through the thick, smoky air. At the rear, in a corner table, Dirk is sitting alone, causing Corrie to scan hopefully for signs of Rudy. He's nowhere to be seen. In a room at the back perhaps, plotting behind closed doors?

Never the friendliest of the duo, Dirk looks less than thrilled to see her.

'*Hei*, why are you here?' he says irritably. 'There are no messages today.'

But Corrie is too anxious to be deflected by his surly reception. 'I know. I was just wondering . . . if there's any word . . . on . . .'

Dirk's demeanour softens a little. 'Sit down,' he says. 'You look like you need a drink.' He signals towards the bar for a beer and it appears in seconds, the top foaming and welcome.

'Rudy has asked around,' he says close into her ear. He has a sour odour of bars and tobacco about him, of someone sleeping on floors and not having anywhere to call home. 'Our man inside The Hague shipyard says Kees stopped working there three months ago . . .'

'Three months!' Corrie can hardly contain her shock. It doesn't tally with the letter sent only four weeks previous, although Kees would never risk writing about her location. 'So where has she been since then? Didn't you know?'

Dirk takes a sip of his own beer. 'We're not her keepers. And whatever she's doing, it's not sanctioned. Not by us anyway.'

'Then what?' Corrie's alarm is spiralling. She feels sick. Foresight is no friend at this point.

'The only thing linked to Kees is a name,' he adds.

'Who?'

'You won't like it.'

'Tell me, Dirk!' She's close to boiling, and suddenly the atmosphere inside the bar is stifling.

He sighs. 'Selig. He's Abwehr, as we suspected, here in Amsterdam. An officer who's keen to climb the ranks, apparently. That's all we know.'

It must be bad, she thinks, because Dirk affords her a rare sympathetic look.

Corrie crashes out through the café door and scoops in a lungful of freezing air, stops and bends double, the sting inside only just preventing her last meal from resurfacing. One line

154

from Kees' last letter swirls in front of her, every letter of the distinct handwriting black and bold: 'I feel like I'm doing something important at last.'

Oh Kees, what have you done for our cause – and who have you done it with?

23

My Good Friend Gus

12th December 1940, London

Marnie

Exactly on time, Willem is waiting outside the vast Palace Theatre on Shaftesbury Avenue at six p.m.

'I see you've been shopping,' Marnie says, gesturing to his black trousers and tweed jacket, neither of which she's seen before. Underneath is a grey knitted jumper and the collar of a white shirt.

'Reluctantly,' he replies. 'I've realised it's not fitting to turn up everywhere in my ARP suit.'

It breaks the ice, dispelling any hint of the rancour from the previous day. They walk a few minutes to nearby Macclesfield Street, and Willem steers them towards the façade of an old pub with a large, and so far undamaged, sign: 'De Hems'.

'Welcome to my world,' Willem opens the door, 'and to my office.'

He steps inside, instantly greeted by a few of those propping up the long wooden bar. Marnie has rarely felt comfortable walking into a pub, mainly because it was never acceptable for women to enter alone before war broke out. Now, the freedoms of conflict – that 'to hell with it' attitude – mean she could stride in without censure. But she doesn't, relieved when the interior of De Hems looks and feels more like something on the continent, similar to the Parisian bars she so loved on her one and only trip out of the country.

'Do you like beer?' Willem leans against the polished wood, a swathe of colourful, glinting bottles behind him. 'If you're on Dutch soil – as you are now – I recommend Amstel.'

'That's fine. Just half a pint for me.'

Marnie is taking her first mouthful of the golden liquid when Willem's eyes settle on someone at the entrance and he breaks into a wide smile. He draws a tall, suited man into their small fold, putting a brotherly arm around broad, lean shoulders.

'Here he is,' Willem announces. 'Miss Fern – Marnie – I'd like you to meet my good friend, Gus. My *best* friend.'

Gus holds out a large, strong hand. 'Pleased to meet you, Miss Fern.' A hank of white-blond hair flopping over his forehead makes him seem a little younger than Willem, but his deep voice has the maturity of an older man. 'I'm charmed to meet one of our virtuoso pianists.'

So he's one of them, she thinks. *One of us.*

'Willem only calls me his best friend because I was the one fool enough to travel over here with him,' Gus adds with a laugh.

'Ah, so you're the other oar on the kayak?' Marnie asks, though not before glancing left and right, a new instinct from past weeks. They've moved to a table by the side of the bar, but still: 'Careless Talk Costs Lives'. The posters are everywhere, and they do hold some truth.

'It's all right,' Willem assures her. 'What little of Dutch resistance in London is probably in here. We're among friends.'

'And yes, in answer to your question – I was the unfortunate recipient of Bakker's first-class ticket to England,' Gus says.

'So what was it like?' Marnie's curiosity is boundless; the idea of travelling on any kind of vessel is scary enough in wartime, against enemy submarines and arduous waves, but in a flimsy kayak?

'It was long and wet, and he never stopped complaining,' Gus says.

157

Willem almost chokes into his beer. 'Says the man who refused to paddle a minute more unless I bailed out the bottom of the boat. With a tin can!'

They're playing it up for Marnie's benefit, batting half-hearted insults at each other, but it's easy to believe they've been firm friends since schooldays.

Gus leans into her conspiratorially: 'You know, I wouldn't recommend working for Bakker. So, why don't you come and join my unit? We're much nicer.'

'Hands off, Vander!' Willem says with mock affront. 'You can't have my best pianist. We're a team, aren't we, Marnie?'

A team. Maybe. Or could it be the beer talking, the familiar effect of De Hems on Willem causing his goodwill to rise to the surface? She's smiling, flattered by their attentions, but wary still. It's the Marnie Fern way, an impulse that may never change.

Willem insists they eat at De Hems, and he doesn't lie when he promises great food comes from their heavy Dutch oven pots, a thick stew that has a good deal of real chicken in among the vegetables. Heavenly.

'I hope that measured up to your beloved Lyons,' Gus says to Marnie, wiping his mouth and standing to leave just before eight. 'Sorry, but I've got a meeting.'

'Work or play?' There's a roguish hint to Willem's query.

'Both, as it happens,' Gus says, shaking Marnie's hand and squeezing Willem's shoulder as he leaves.

The barman arrives to clear their table, but once he turns away there's little remaining except an empty surface and the babble of the room.

'I should get off, too,' Marnie says. 'You must have work to do, or people to meet.'

Willem shakes his head. 'As it happens, I don't. Free as a bird this evening, and – since Hitler hasn't come calling yet – I'll walk you home. If I may?'

'Really, you don't have to . . .' That feeling of being the spare part is fast coming over Marnie, the unattached gooseberry in a group of girls in her younger days, the one left on the sidelines of a dance floor. It was as awkward then as it is now.

'But I'd like to.' His candour sweeps away Marnie's unease. 'If we have to be entirely professional about it, then we can talk about work.'

'Aren't you freezing?' Marnie asks, a good way towards Regent's Park. Willem is in his tweed jacket, but has no overcoat, and the wind is whipping in and out of the gaps in stonework left by months of bombing.

He shakes his head. 'I'm sure that kayak trip cured me of ever feeling cold again – Gus and I were both so wet and chilled by the time we arrived that anything since is tropical by comparison.'

'This? Tropical?' Marnie stares at a dark sky that's heavy with cloud, and possibly snow.

'You know what I mean. It's all relative, isn't it? Not so long ago we thought a dispute with a neighbour felt like war, or a rickety stairwell was perilous. And yet I read somewhere recently that more people are killed on the street by the blackout than by bombs.'

'But perhaps we shouldn't broadcast that little gem to Hitler,' Marnie suggests. 'He might decide to up his game.'

They walk in silence past a trickle of shelter dwellers descending into Great Portland Street Tube, and on to the park, where a few couples are taking advantage of a quieter evening so far.

'So, have you come to any decision about your reply?' Marnie says at last. 'I'm due to transmit tomorrow.'

'To Daisy?'

'Yes.' Who else could she mean? To her surprise, he's not mentioned it all evening. Why so cagey? Or is she being overly sensitive?

'Has Daisy messaged anything extra recently?' he asks instead, his tone curious rather than accusatory. The portion of his face she can see is in shadow, unreadable as he walks.

'What sort of thing?' To date, she's considered her and Daisy's exchanges to be entirely innocent, like passing the time of day at a bus stop. Perhaps not approved, but harmless enough.

'About anyone around her?' he presses. 'About me?'

'She only asked that I relayed that particular message to you. To Darcy. Nothing else.'

The large breath he takes in smacks of relief. 'We have suspected for a time that there's a leak, and Daisy's message pretty much confirms it, but until we find out the identity, no agent is safe over there. We're working to build a foundation of resistance, only for someone to come and hack at the groundwork.'

'Does that mean you'll need to go back?'

'Believe me, I want to,' Willem says. 'But I'm effectively stuck. It's not sanctioned, and I'm not yet in a position to parachute agents in. The country's too populated, and the Germans have well-placed air defences on the ground.'

'I suppose you could always dust off the kayak . . .'

'Ha! Yes, you're right.' He's smiling as he turns to face her. 'I do love my country, Marnie, but even I might choose to take my chances with the Gestapo rather than a pair of paddles.'

'So . . . what do I transmit to her?' Marnie is fishing again. Why won't he come clean about Daisy? He's introduced Gus, his best friend and confidant in the world, and gradually Willem is letting her in just a little, so why not around the woman whose interest sizzles over the airwaves?

'I'll have something for you by tomorrow morning, the usual collection point,' he says drily, before stopping abruptly as they approach Bedford College. 'Marnie, have you got a guest?'

She follows his gaze towards a tall figure lurking to the side of her first-floor window, half hidden by the curtain. 'Oh, that's just Oscar, earning his keep.'

160

Willem looks at her with growing confusion.

'I thought he might act as a decoy to any unwelcome visitors like Mr Smith,' she explains, then realises how silly it sounds, and how wooden Oscar appears, a cap perched on his hairless head. 'But perhaps I'm relying too much on German spies being short-sighted?'

'Well, he fooled me for a second or two,' Willem concedes. 'So I'd say Oscar is a pretty good house guest for now.

'And Marnie?' he adds as she slots her key in the door.

'Yes?'

'Do you think . . . do you see a little more of me, after tonight?'

'Yes, I do.'

She says it, but does she mean it? Wary is her watchword. More than ever, wary is how Marnie Fern is forced to be.

24

The Burrowing Beast

13th December 1940, London

Marnie

Oscar is not ousted from his position. Marnie wakes once in the night and then again the next morning, both times not with a sense of shock that a man's form is lurking in her window space, but a flush of assurance.

'Grandad always did say you were a good listener,' she mutters to him over her meagre breakfast of stale bread and weak tea.

On her way to Broadcasting House, the newsagent offers his customary smile and holds out the *Daily Mirror*, which is stiff with a package in the fold. Half of her wants to run home and decode the messages from Willem, to discover what he is forwarding to Daisy, while the other half recognises a busy day ahead. Plus, Miss Roach and her teapot are waiting in the office, and until Marnie gets better at shopping with her ration card, the reliable secretary is her best route to a stiff brew and a clear head.

'Morning,' she sings on the sixth floor. Silence. The small electric kettle is hot to the touch in an otherwise empty office, until Raymond blows in at speed, followed a minute later by Miss Roach clutching a pile of files.

'Well, you do look a lot better,' Raymond announces. 'How do you feel?'

'Fine, actually. I'm down to one aspirin a day now.' Marnie has to remind herself it's only five days since she hunkered under a blast that could have been fatal. Yet her sleep now is interrupted by the raids rather than the wounding, and her mind is focused elsewhere, though that's not for Raymond to know. 'So, what's on today's work list?'

The morning flies by in the studio, with only time to grab lunch in the canteen alone. Picking up a copy of *The Spectator*, Marnie dips her head into the radio listings, combing her eyes over the clientele on rows of surrounding tables: producers, secretaries, programme directors and young lads from the post room.

She wonders who else in the room has been approached or targeted by Mr Smith & Co., and how many among them are of the same mind, poised to do the Reich's work if the dreaded invasion comes. No one looks as if they would betray their country readily, no hint of treachery behind their work personas. So how on earth are you supposed to tell?

A return to the office causes Marnie a brief heart-stop moment when she spies another envelope placed on her typewriter, pulsing like a beacon in her vision.

Though it's stamped and addressed, she rips it open with fervour and annoyance, much to Miss Roach's surprise. And breathes again. It's from Susie, inviting her to Christmas lunch.

I can't imagine you'll be going up to Edinburgh, her cousin writes. *So you're welcome to spend the day with us. The children are still at home, for now, and we'd all love to see you.*

Christmas. Marnie hasn't given it a moment's thought. The West End shops are decked out with what they have, but with so many store windows blown in, there's not the usual impact of the festive trees and lights. A second Christmas in war and, unlike the relative peace of '39, there's no telling if Hitler will allow enough respite for celebrations. The fire crews and ARPs may well be scouring for bodies under fresh debris on Christmas

Day. Still, she's glad to receive the note and pleased to have somewhere to go, ever grateful for Susie's love and friendship. She whisks off a note of acceptance and ploughs on to the day's end.

Back home, the notes via Willem point to an address a short bus ride away, and Marnie only has time to gather her 'tools': her compact transmitter, one of the prescribed novels from Grandad's little library that she and Daisy use in rotation, and the messages, which she tucks in the waistband of her skirt under her blouse, determined no fifth columnist will lay a hand on those.

An elderly woman opens the door to a small terraced house in Islington and, much to Marnie's delight, shows her to a back room rather than a draughty basement. The fire is lit and, in an accent not unlike Willem's, she offers tea and closes the door without a word.

Even prior to encoding, the day's dispatch is a stream of cryptic messages: *The flowers are to be delivered by midnight*, or *Coffee is in the third flask on the right*. It's a puzzle within a puzzle, though, presumably, they will mean something to those at the Dutch end. Only the last catches her eye: *MM. Lie low on burrowing beast. Will attempt to send means to flush out. WS*

Grandad was always better at the cryptic crosswords they tackled, but it's not a great leap to guess: the mole. And yet there's not a hint of personal meaning, the briefest of words from Darcy to Daisy, except the tell-tale use of MM and WS. Their inner secret. And yet no real assurances. She tries to imagine Daisy's reaction, hanging on every message for a sign. For something of him.

Unusually for Marnie, she is attaching far too much feeling to the process, and she knows it. The crude messages are necessarily blunt – for secrecy, and the safety that brings to those in the firing line. Much like business, war is no time to involve private emotions and she's picking up more than a crackle over the airwaves, weaving too much into the absences. Maybe Willem thinks so much of Daisy that he won't compromise her in any way? A caution for someone you love intently and will do anything to protect.

It's what she muses over in setting up the equipment: the thought that, one day, someone might think as highly of her.

The transmission time approaches, and Marnie converts the messages using specific pages from *Northanger Abbey*, then tunes into the frequency. She readies her piano finger and begins. After the opposing dispatches are fed in from the Dutch side, there's the precious seconds before she and Daisy need to cut contact. Poised, Marnie is ready to tap out what she imagines Daisy wants to hear, that her name is on Willem's lips and in his thoughts.

Should she embellish her message? Is it her gift to give, and does she have that right? The silence whines in her ears.

Hope you are gathering enough for a good Christmas is what she taps out instead.

It's pathetic and bland, shying away from involvement, but it's safe.

You too comes the Morse reply. *Keep warm.*

Marnie disconnects, hears the elderly woman in the next room switching on the BBC news, and brings herself back to London, England, and war.

25

The Palace of Light and Dark

14th December 1940, Amsterdam

Corrie

There's almost nothing from him. Her disappointment at Willem's sparse contact has overnight turned to anger that he should send such an impersonal, curt reply to her warning, the only advice for her to 'lie low'. Perhaps she should take her concerns to Rudy and Dirk again and drive home the gravity? But that instinct to protect her loved ones holds her back. Deep down she knows that it might even be Kees – her own flesh and blood – leaking secrets in dangerous pillow talk. The very idea that her own daughter might have betrayed the cause, even inadvertently, causes a shiver under her thick cloak.

Since last night's exchange, Corrie has tried *so* hard to understand how Willem's hands must be tied by London. And yes, he's unaware of Kees' disappearance. If she were to tell him, he would likely swim across the damned North Sea in the height of winter to search for his sister. But can Corrie do that to him? To cause his anxiety to surge, without any way of solving the mystery or ensuring Kees' safety?

Even though the shop can ill afford to forfeit a single sale, she's closed up again, allowing time to tour every bar and shop in the patriots' circle to ask about her missing daughter. Few have seen her, and if they have, they can't remember exactly when.

'Please,' Corrie has begged. 'Was it before the snow, or after?' But war is all-consuming, day-to-day life exhausting, and what is one young woman among many? Corrie drops supplies over to Hendrik at the zoo, and then wanders into the red-light district nearby, batting off a few, mostly friendly advances on her way to Café Mandje, one of Kees' old haunts. Because of its openly homosexual clientele, it's where regular Wehrmacht are banned from patronising, but strangely where officers are often found drinking. And it's that which worries Corrie the most.

'Yes, I saw her,' the flamboyant bar owner says. 'But it must be a couple of months back now.'

'Are you sure it was that long ago?' Corrie struggles to accept that her girl had been in Amsterdam and yet not come home. 'Did she seem all right?' she probes.

'Yes . . . and no,' the bar woman says. 'I thought it strange she was flirting with a Nazi officer. I mean, we tolerate them in here – we've no choice – but she was either drunk or pretending to be.'

Corrie runs cold, the next question sticking in her throat. 'Was she with anyone in particular? Someone you remember?'

The owner's face falls. 'Abwehr,' she spits, signalling her profound distaste. 'Blond and thickset. Unlike some of them, he has a foul mouth. And loud with it.'

'Do you happen to know his name?'

'Sorry, no. I keep my head down. But he must drink in the Café Americain, kept going on about the liquor being better. He can take his business there, as far as I'm concerned.'

The reported sighting comforts Corrie to a degree, but the rest causes fresh unease. Why didn't Kees visit her own mother after returning from The Hague? Secrecy perhaps? If she was on a mission to infiltrate a group she would have needed to maintain her cover at all times. Or the alternative? There's one overriding sense that forces people away from loved ones. Shame.

★ ★ ★

It's already dark as Corrie leaves the café and takes the tram towards the Leidseplein. She stands before the monolith of the Hotel Americain, remembering how it glittered in days of old, before the war and blackout sucked everything from the beauty of Amsterdam, its festive glow and the vibrant centre. For years, the solid, ornate Americain and its resplendent rooms acted as a magnet for wealthy tourists to dine under the lofty ceiling of the famous art deco café, all mirrors and lights and waiters in white gliding around with bottles of champagne. Now, it attracts Nazi officers, plus – or so she's told – a good many shadowy characters; the perfect venue to swap secrets in plain sight, with agents and spies trading lies and lives. A hotbed of espionage.

But Corrie wants none of that. In reality, she doesn't know quite what her purpose is, except that it's now a magnet for her too. It's where Kees might have been, and she has to try. Her clothes are not grand enough to sit alongside the beautifully attired women who frequent Café Americain, but the trusty black cloak hides a multitude of sins and, she hopes, lends an air of mystery. It will have to do. Outside, and away from the grand entrance, Corrie scrapes into her purse for enough coins to buy a single coffee, then brushes down the black wool, tidies and reattaches her blonde wisps and launches herself into an alien sphere within her own city.

It's a different world the minute she steps through the grand double doors; sharp, sleek lines of décor and glass reflect the radiant lighting, yet dim enough to lend each table an air of privacy. The whole room glimmers, resounding with healthy laughter and conversation. It's moderately busy, and Corrie skims the clusters of people under the high arched ceiling; grey-green Wehrmacht and Abwehr alongside the cold steel of SS, mingling with the vibrant reds and turquoise of some women in their best pre-war outfits. A feminine tinkle and the deep masculine laughter of confident officers rises above some tables like smoke, signalling brazen flirtation.

Is this what you came here for, my darling girl?

'A table for one, madam?' A white-jacketed waiter approaches Corrie, and in one swift glance he seems to have sized her up as not belonging, yet he's practised enough to cover it with a smile.

'Please. For one.'

She's led to a seat in an alcove, probably empty because of its position outside the fashionable hub, which allows a perfect view of almost every table. Declining the offer of a menu, she orders a single coffee, which is pricey enough to swallow all of her cash. Still, it might be the best cup she has all week.

Corrie languidly turns the fashion pages of *Libelle*'s latest edition, which she picked up at the entrance, allowing her to examine the lively panorama. What does she do now? She has neither the hope nor desire to ingratiate herself onto a table full of German officers. Her best and only option is the staff; they see and hear all, and although rumour has it some are in the pocket of German intelligence, she has to trust that one or two remain loyal to the Dutch cause.

The waiter sets her coffee down with enough care that she detects something in his action. 'Can I get you anything else, *mejuffrouw*?'

He uses the address for a high-society woman, and there's a clear, amiable message in the way he says it. She could well have struck lucky.

'I'm looking for someone,' she begins tentatively.

'Anyone I might help with?'

Corrie slides the latest photograph of Kees from within the magazine pages, the image with her hair in a boyish cut. The waiter leaves it on the table and bends his head, narrows his eyes and squints. She can almost hear the shuffle of his memory, while she combs his face for any recognition. Anything. *Please.*

'I think . . .' he begins.

'Yes?' *Please.*

169

'I'm sure she's been here, once or twice,' he says, then with more certainty: 'Yes. Though her hair was different, longer. I know her face, though. Enchanting. It was, let me see . . . maybe a week or so ago. But not since.'

A week! Corrie's heart soars. It's the last and latest sighting. 'Was she with anyone?'

His eyes darken and his voice drops to barely a whisper, pushed out between clenched lips pulled into a faux smile. 'Look behind me. There's a man in the middle tables, slightly to your right. Two other officers and three women with him. Blond. See?'

Corrie aims her gaze into the room beyond. A good portion of the men are blond, of course: perfect German specimens, with sharp jaws and white, winning smiles.

'He's broad,' the waiter qualifies. 'And brash.'

Now she sees him. He's the one dominating a group of six, forcing his presence into the space, blowing cigar smoke into the air as his head falls back with amusement. Bold and forthright, a man confident of his own attraction. The women titter in reaction, endorsing the aura of power which surrounds him.

'Do you know who he is?' Corrie asks, aware the waiter is eager to get away. Lingering for much longer will land him in trouble.

'He's Abwehr.'

She was bracing herself for it, but it snags at her heart. 'A name?'

'Selig. Lothar Selig. He's a regular here.'

The snag turns to a squeeze on her chest muscle, deprives her of air for more than a few seconds, until the waiter coughs lightly.

'Oh, I'm sorry,' she says, 'I have enough for the coffee, but not . . .'

'No, I don't want money, only glad to help, but it's best you go soon.' He gives a quick shake of his head as she digs in her purse to pay for the coffee. 'Think of it as a gift for Holland.'

'Thank you. Very much.'

'I hope you find her,' he says, scooping up the empty cup. 'I remember she was kind and always polite. I got the feeling she was never quite at home here.'

Corrie rises to go, enlightened with knowledge but heavy-hearted with what it could mean for her beloved daughter, and the resistance.

'Be careful of that one, though,' he adds as he turns. 'He is not a nice man. Not at all.'

Stepping back into the monochrome world outside, Corrie draws more of the freezing air into her lungs, hoping it will flush the turbulence inside her. A German military truck growls past, spewing out grey exhaust fumes into the chilly white, and the grim reality is thrust at her: no one is dragged to the Americain against their will. It's clear Kees was one of those women feeding Selig's ego with her false adoration, chirping in his Aryan ear. So what was her plan?

Corrie can't help but recall Dirk's grave look and his insistence that Kees' presence in Amsterdam wasn't sanctioned by the resistance.

So what had she got herself into? More importantly, if Selig is still here, in plain view, where is Kees now?

And with Willem gone, what on earth can she do about it?

26

Choose Cheese for Christmas

Christmas Day 1940, London

Marnie

They sit – or sprawl, as is the routine on any normal Christmas Day – around the wireless while Susie's children play at their feet with their scant array of new toys. King George, in his awkward, stilted tone, does his best to work through the monarch's yuletide broadcast, talking of hardships and those away from home, the 'battered' towns and cities of Britain, and the mass evacuation of children, which elicits a groan from Susie.

'. . . our feet are planted on the path of victory, and with the help of God we shall make our way to justice and to peace,' the king signs off.

'What else can he do?' Susie murmurs, leaning her head on Arthur's shoulder. 'He's got to say something positive.'

They're all tired and a little fractious, having spent the night of Christmas Eve in respective shelters, fully expecting that Hitler would come calling just as Santa dodged bombs in the sky to visit excited children. London escaped a drubbing, with Manchester catching the worst of the Luftwaffe's unseasonal packages, but there was little sleep all round. And unlike the year before, when food and presents were still plentiful, everything seems meagre, thinner somehow. With shop-bought toys largely made of paper, Susie had pulled out her mother's old sewing machine and fashioned something vaguely resembling a cloth doll for Elsie and a soldier for Michael.

'Their faces do look a bit scary,' Susie laments, blowing out her cheeks in defeat as the children toss them aside for the paper offerings. 'I only wish I had Uncle Gilbert's skill – he always helped out in times like these.' Realising too late the hurt she's triggered, she rubs sympathetically at Marnie's shoulder with one hand and offers a tissue with the other. 'Heavens knows what I'll do if they ration clothes eventually. We'll all be walking around in rags of my own making.'

The prospect of Susie's home-sewn debacle conjures a spate of giggles, helping to stave off more of Marnie's tears and dwelling too much on her first Christmas without Grandad. Instead, she recalls his face at the table in previous years, always grateful for any well-cooked food, dishing out hand-stitched presents for everyone.

Late into the afternoon, Marnie palms at her rounded stomach; despite rationing and the absence of any kind of bird (too late in the butcher's queue for even a small chicken), she and Susie had made the table appear full, using tips gleaned from all those hours on *The Kitchen Front*. Marnie recalled the 'Choose cheese!' refrain on the cinema reels, and so they'd carved a cauliflower cheese in lieu of roast and laughed a lot while doing it, with some decent stuffing made from the sausage meat Arthur had scavenged late in the day. Marnie had scoured the shops far and wide for the children's oranges, though Michael had to make do with a grapefruit. It's not perfect, but it's enough. If nothing else, they're together.

Having volunteered for the next day's shift at work – joining a few others without husbands and wives in keeping the BBC ship running – Marnie is determined to make merry and enjoy her precious family within reach. 'Is there any sherry left, Susie?'

And as the day turns to evening, her mind wanders towards Willem and what he's doing. Celebrating with Gus, she hopes, and with the other *Engelandvaarders* from De Hems, inevitably missing home and his family, if he has any. Those he's reluctant to speak of.

Boxing Day at Broadcasting House passes in fits and starts, with time in the studio and several hours wrapped in a winter coat in an empty office, catching up with paperwork. The corridors and some of the upper offices are freezing as the repairs to the BBC flagship go on, but the bombers had stayed away the previous night, and the entire family slept in their beds. Sitting there in the relative silence, Marnie ponders who Miss Roach might be celebrating with. Raymond mentioned he was going to visit 'friends', but in past years Miss Roach has always volunteered for the Christmas shifts. Maybe she has a new friend, too? Rather ungenerously, Marnie wonders if it's her signal to assume the spinster role in full. And then hates herself for even thinking it.

Instead she focuses on the positive: she has Daisy to connect with the following night. The promise of more human warmth will push her through the sense of solitude.

She's not there.

It's the evening of the 27th – a day that's neither here nor there in the Christmas calendar – when Marnie tunes in and out of the frequency two or three times, checking the dial with her eyes and plucking at the silence with her ears. But nothing, aside from the inevitable crackle. She checks over the dispatches again, collected from a designated safe spot outside the closed newsagent; it's the right weekday and the instructions don't stipulate a break for Christmas, since there's no respite from war or occupation in Holland.

She checks the radio's batteries, as they'd been taught in training. They are functioning, and she's picking up snatches of contact on other frequencies. So what's wrong? Where is Daisy, her opposite half, and a lifeline to something more in this world?

Marnie feels a tightening in her chest, running over the possibilities in her mind and needing to temper her concerns: Daisy is simply late, that's all. Held up. Of course she has a life away from the transmitter. Yes, that will be it. She's with family and has forgotten the time. Even in war, people enjoy themselves, don't they?

It's freezing in the basement of Bedford College – Willem has suggested transmitting from the college until New Year, perhaps reasoning that even fervent fifth columnists celebrate in some way – but she pulls her scarf tighter and keeps going, every five minutes or so. After an hour, Marnie's frozen fingers can barely turn the dial, let alone tap out any messages.

Still, there's nothing. Daisy is silent. Or silenced. Which is it?

She packs away the transmitter and crawls into bed upstairs, shivering. By ten p.m. it's clear that Hitler is affording London another respite from a major onslaught – yet how much sleep Marnie gets depends not on the Führer, but whether she can empty her mind of Daisy and her whereabouts.

27

Darling Girl

27th December 1940, Amsterdam

Corrie

Corrie discovered later that the policeman had taken a while to find her and Felix, since they were two doors down at the Meijers', pooling what food and fuel they had to make a decent hot meal with a hint of luxury. For Felix, especially, she wanted these few days to include some tiny indulgence, being the first Christmas without his parents – though it was no mean feat, as she had also needed to deliver every spare morsel to Hendrik and others at the zoo. The officer, however, was tenacious, knocking on doors until he found her, and Corrie knew why the second she caught sight of his dour expression.

'I'm sorry, but we do need you to identify the body. Right now.'

In the morgue, Corrie senses it's no colder than on the street, although she can still see her breath – ice white against the tired, cracked tiles that have turned yellowy from a constant chemical scrubbing. The smell is something she can't begin to describe, but if 'dismal' has an odour, then this is it. Every bone in her body is stiff with dread, her mouth clamped shut as the mortician pulls back the sheet, and a low moan of despair escaping through her gritted teeth like a toxic miasma, uncontrolled and dense with pain.

She looks as beautiful as the day twenty-seven years before when she emerged from Corrie in front of the kitchen stove, pink and perfect with her dark cap of hair. So much prospect in a new life, clashing here with the finality of death. That short crop has grown out and her skin looks pallid, slightly grubby, but there's no denying Kees' loveliness, the large doe-like eyelids and long dark lashes. Bizarrely, it crosses Corrie's mind that her stunning daughter won't now become old or wrinkled, and that surely is a good thing. The comfort lasts only a second, until she touches the slight hand, nails bitten to the quick, and feels how rough they've become since she last held them. Icy cold, too. Then the walls of the morgue echo with her howls of distress, while the tired, overworked mortician stands and lets Corrie heave up grief until it's reduced to a hoarse rasp.

'Are you certain it was suicide?' she asks, once her mouth can form words again.

The mortician nods. 'She was found in an abandoned shop,' he says. 'At first it seemed she'd died of exposure, but there were empty bottles nearby and no wounds of any kind.' He doesn't need to elaborate on the bottle's contents. 'There was a note discovered too,' he adds, sheepishly.

'Can I see it?'

'Are you sure?'

'Certain,' she says firmly.

Of course she doesn't want to read her daughter's last desperate thoughts, the workings of a woman in such distress that death is the only option. But Corrie needs an explanation. A reason for such a loss.

Her hands stiffen in holding the single sheet of rough brown paper, stained and crumpled. She's barely able to focus but it is Kees' writing she sees, large with rounded, ornate vowels, the lines displaying a slight tremor, as if the pen had quivered on making contact with the paper.

I'm sorry. I can't bear the shame, knowing I let you all down. I tried to help — I promise. But I was naïve, and some are so cruel. I can't make others sacrifice any more for me. Please forgive me.

Corrie clutches it to her chest, her face wet with silent distress, while the only sound is a soft plash of her tears hitting the hard tiled floor. The mortician shifts uncomfortably, as if he has one other dreadful task yet to discharge. Poor man, Corrie thinks, looking at him. What a thing to face, day in and day out. But he's clearly read the note and knows her friends and family need answers in this climate of uncertainty.

'Was . . . was she married?' he ventures.

'No. Why?'

He squirms inside his white overall. 'Well, it's just that . . .'

'She was pregnant.' Corrie helps him out of his misery, hears his sigh of relief echo in the space. It's a mother's instinct that tells her.

'Yes,' he says. 'But only just. Not even three months.'

Corrie is shocked. And yet not. It explains a lot — Kees' absence from The Hague, her not coming home, and her letters. *I have a purpose in this hateful war*, she had written. It would have been too soon to know about a baby nestling deep inside her, to detect what might have become a dark shadow within. Soon, though, she would have realised. *I can't bear the shame.*

Is that the whole of her disgrace? And was Selig the father? *Was* — because there's no hope or life to come from it now. No breath from Kees to feed that tiny being. No shame to come into the light.

Corrie crunches homewards on the snow-crusted walkways, much of the pure white turned to a grey slush, frozen again to a dirty coating. *Everything in this world is soiled*, she thinks. Filthy. She dreads the night, trying to sleep, knowing her mind will push up desperate, dreamy images of Kees into the early hours, half in and out of sleep.

She has to mourn and grieve, openly. To share it.

More than anything, she needs to tell Willem, to feel him by her side.

She pulls herself sharply back to reality and sees she's missed her transmission slot with Lizzy, but then even Daisy can't convey her distress in Morse. Corrie has one avenue left, a last resort for rapid and certain contact with England that will summon him. And if this isn't an emergency, then what is? His sister is not only dead, but also a pawn who may well have released secrets to Holland's enemy before going to her grave. Corrie bites back the harsh truth about her own daughter, but – even through her raw grief – she knows it's not about her or Kees any more, but all of them. About Holland and its people. Kees has paid the ultimate price, and Corrie has to hold onto the notion that she is a victim of this foul war as much as anyone under a bomb or bullet.

But they do need to right those wrongs, whatever the damage. And for that, they need Willem.

And so does she.

28

Back in the Basement

Marnie

Even Raymond's post-Christmas cheer can't make the day shorter for Marnie, who glances at the clock every fifteen minutes or less.

'Anything wrong?' he asks. 'You're like a cat on hot bricks today.'

'Oh, only that poor Susie has to make a decision soon about the children's evacuation,' she lies. It's not entirely false, but it feels like a long time since she spoke the full truth to Raymond.

'I'd stand you for a drink, but I have somewhere to be after work,' he says.

'I'm meeting someone, too. Thank for the thought, though.' His eyebrows go up playfully.

'Nothing like that – just a friend,' she says.

The De Hems façade is harder to locate after dark, and only a hum of conversation exuding through the solid wooden doors tells Marnie she's in the right place. With no work or home address, it's her only starting point for Willem. The good-natured atmosphere hits like a wave as she enters, her eyes skating over the bodies at the bar for his distinct golden crown. Except many of the men here are blond and tall, with that Nordic look about them; he's not wrong about this being a hub for the displaced Netherlanders.

She picks out a paler head of hair above the crowd and moves towards it. Mercifully, Gus's eyes show some recognition as she sidles into his small group.

'Miss Fern,' he says with clear surprise. 'Hello again. May I buy you a drink?'

'Thank you, but no.' Her eyes sweep the room. 'I'm looking for Willem. Have you seen him?'

'Sorry, but you've just missed him. He left about ten minutes ago.'

Damn! 'Do you know where I can find him?' she presses, with no attempt to disguise the urgency.

Gus steers her by the arm from the cluster, bends his mouth towards her ear. 'Is everything all right?'

Should she tell? Willem has always stressed the need for secrecy. 'Trust no one' seems to be his mantra. But this is Gus, his best friend. He and Willem might work in different units, but he's Dutch. Resistance too. By contrast, Marnie is on her own, *feels alone*, and she needs an ally right now.

'I went to transmit to Daisy last night,' she begins.

Gus nods in a way that means he knows the name, and perhaps the true identity.

'She wasn't there.'

His look remains blank. 'And? I don't understand.'

'She's never not there,' Marnie insists. 'Always on time. She never lets us down.'

'But you know – you can imagine – what it's like over there,' Gus replies in a low voice. 'There could be all number of reasons why she missed a transmission.'

'Yes, I know, but . . .' How can Marnie begin to explain the connection? *Their* link, the one she's not even certain Daisy feels from the other end, and yet which still conducts as strong and enduring across the miles. How can she expect Gus to understand?

'I just want Willem to know, that's all,' Marnie says instead. 'I should tell him as soon as possible. I mean, I sense they have something special, that Daisy is . . .'

Gus opens his mouth to speak, but a sudden eruption of laughter across the room cuts their discourse at the precise moment she might have discovered something. The noise dies down as Gus's face adopts a more serious look.

'I suppose he did leave fairly abruptly,' he says. 'Someone from his office came in and handed over a note. I wouldn't say he looked shocked, but he wasn't happy.'

'Did he say anything?'

'I might have heard him mention that he was headed to Regent Street.'

'Anywhere in particular?'

Gus shakes his head. 'He didn't exactly say, but he does sometimes go to a restaurant there. We all keep our contacts close, Willem especially, but I do know it's in a basement.'

Basement. Regent Street. Marnie's brain makes a rapid and unwelcome connection. Could it possibly be? The site of her meeting with the fifth columnist?

'Do you mean Hungaria?' Marnie asks.

Gus moves the word around his head, his eyes intent with concentration. 'The name sounds familiar. I've never been there myself, so maybe he has mentioned it.'

'Thanks, you've been a real help.'

Gus turns back to his group, pauses and swivels back to her. 'Do you want me to come with you? I can easily . . .'

'Thank you, but no. Like you say, I'm probably worrying too much.'

Still, Marnie can't shake the feeling that her angst is justified, and someone should be worried. Someone should care a lot about the silence in her ears.

After a short walk, during which she stumbles only once over some fallen brickwork, Marnie finds Hungaria still has its plate-glass window intact, along with the enticing sign for a bomb-free

182

environment. Stress-free is what Marnie desires at this point, but that's unlikely beyond this door.

Being a Saturday night, the downstairs space is busier than on her last visit, with the lingering Christmas decorations padding out the already flamboyant décor. All the tables look to be full, with no Willem in sight.

'Good evening, madam, are you meeting someone?' a waiter says.

'Yes, but only at the bar.'

'Very good, this way please.'

She orders a gin and tonic – 'Plenty of tonic, please' – and tries to look as if it's normal for her to wait for men, assured of their arrival, perhaps with flowers and an apologetic kiss. Inside, though, there are insects moving at speed under her skin, and the gin tastes like a sour poison.

Marnie makes her drink last half an hour, sipping and pretending to be absorbed in her tiny pocket diary. But she's made a mistake, clearly. Furtive glances around the space tell her that Willem isn't here. In that moment at De Hems, she'd been so sure of her instincts. On reflection, though, it's a long stretch, given there are several other basement clubs and bars around the area. Perhaps she ought to leave the spying to the experts. Deflated, she's too weary to trawl through any more, and will have to settle for an urgent message via the newsagent, plus a second visit to De Hems.

'Another one, madam?' the barman cuts in with a pitying tone he must reserve for disappointed women.

'No, thank you. I'm just going. He must have been held up.'

He nods unconvincingly.

Sliding down from the bar stool, Marnie is faced with a glimpse of the 'bedding area' behind a discreet screen – Hungaria's well-advertised sumptuous shelter for those who don't mind paying to sleep out a raid after dinner in comfy surroundings. It strikes her as a ridiculous contrast to the unyielding concrete of Aldwych Tube. Thankfully, there's no need for either tonight, being all quiet in the streets above, but her eye is immediately drawn to the area and a door beyond. Because it opens in that very second. And there he is.

Bending to talk to a man sitting at a small table, Willem doesn't see her. Both are sideways on, and it's only when Willem lowers into a chair alongside his counterpart that Marnie is able to see both faces clearly. She'd know those features anywhere, always open and helpful; she can almost detect his comforting scent of tobacco and hair oil in her nostrils. Here, though, he looks intent and serious.

What is Raymond doing here? Shielded in a back room, in a place where she's already fended off a fifth columnist intent on recruiting from within the BBC. And with Willem of all people, a Dutch resistance spy. Or is he really? And what does that make Raymond?

Marnie reels, clutching at the stool for something to ground her and searching in her brain for any kind of context to this bizarre scene. Deep in her memory, doesn't she recall Raymond talking of dinner at a basement restaurant? He might have been here before. And in turn, what could that mean? And yet, it doesn't explain why Willem is here, or what their connection is. Can it be that Raymond has already been courted and won over by false promises of freedom? That thought is bad enough, but has she also placed her faith in the wrong Dutchman – just as Mr Smith had intimated only a few weeks ago? And is Marnie Fern unwittingly surrounded by fifth columnists?

Her suspicions spiralling, Marnie tries to piece together the scene in front of her, which is promptly capped off when the door shuts. For a brief second, she contemplates knocking or bursting in, but what would she say? What would be the point of confronting either of them here? Besides, her feet are firmly stuck to the carpet, the colourful swirl moving like a wave under her.

'Would you like a glass of water, miss?' the barman asks. 'You look very pale.'

'No, thank you. I'll be fine in just a minute.'

She needs to get out, to reach street level and breathe some air, to clear the grimy thoughts clogging what reason she has left. But the stairs seem insurmountable, and she eyes the door to the ladies. The back-room door opens again, without sight of Willem or Raymond, and two well-dressed women walk out towards the bathroom.

Feeling a sudden urge to wet her face in the sink, Marnie follows them. She waits thirty seconds before opening the bathroom door, almost tiptoeing in – she's not sure why, but instinct tells her to be discreet. Immediately, she freezes on hearing a low murmur coming from one of three cubicles, while the others appear empty. The strike of a match stops the conversation for a second, a puff of smoke rising above the cubicle door. The shielded women resume their hushed conversation. In German.

Having studied languages at university, Marnie recognises the distinct guttural edge, but with the whispers her recognition extends only to 'nein', 'ja' and 'Berlin', and it's infuriating not to know what they are saying, cocooned in the secrecy of a ladies' toilet. Clear or not, those German words represent another ugly piece of a complex jigsaw: Willem, Raymond, the language of their enemy and the fifth column grouped in one place. How? Why?

What has Willem said repeatedly? *Trust no one.*

Maybe he's had a good basis for believing it all along.

The door to the ladies opens and another woman enters noisily, a diner from one of the restaurant tables. The German exchange stops abruptly and the cubicle latch unclicks, allowing Marnie just enough time to turn tail, hurrying into the street with renewed drive. To get away. To process. To work out what the hell she does next and who to trust.

As she arrives home to Oscar holding the fort in her bedroom window, she considers that he may well stand as the only confidant she has. He won't have any answers, but at least he won't betray or judge her.

A dummy might be the perfect ally after all.

29

Friends or Enemies?

29th December 1940, London

Marnie

She hears each tick of her clock next to the bed at two a.m., then three, and finally gets up to brew weak tea, stowing the timepiece in a drawer so the endless beat of insomnia is muffled by her sweaters. She must drift again, but by seven Marnie is awake and dressed, if fairly sleep-starved. Her mind has churned for hours, with no conclusion or valid excuses having come forward. For a short while she almost convinced herself that Raymond and Willem had met purely by coincidence at a back-room card game. Could a winning streak explain Raymond's good mood of late? And yet if she crawls back over her memory, Marnie can't recall a single playing card on that table between the two men.

In the early hours, she was resolute on quitting and severing all contact with Willem instantly. She didn't need this in her life, risking for unknown people and nations. An hour later, a veil of shame hovered above the bed: sticking your head in the sand doesn't win wars, and neither does cowardice. And what of Raymond – how to ignore what she saw? She has to know if it's true betrayal.

In her own bathroom mirror, she looks as bad as she feels. Sagging and deflated, like the sad sight of a barrage balloon that's lost its fight and lies draped over bombed-out ruins. She scrapes out the last of her lipstick to make her mouth look alive. Her sallow cheeks and eyes she can do nothing about.

'What do you think, Oscar? Do I look slightly better than the walking dead?'

As ever, his silence is better than the blunt truth.

After a visit to the newsagent, where her message to Willem is unequivocal – *MUST SPEAK NOW! FIND ME ASAP. NO DELAY* – Marnie is loath to return home, or even to sit out a Sunday at Broadcasting House, just in case Raymond appears. She's not ready to confront him just yet. Susie, she knows, is duty-bound to visit her mother-in-law today and fend off more pressure to evacuate the children. De Hems won't be open until later in the evening. So Lyons it is. Much like Grandad of old, she views it as a comfortable loitering space, and a bonus when her own larder is empty.

Marnie is relieved to settle herself among the multiple storeys on the Strand, with a magazine and – unfortunately – the claggy machinations of her own mind for company. Pure distraction would be a blessing right now.

At a corner table on the second floor, she's carefully spreading a tiny pat of margarine onto a scone when a shadow falls across the table. Looming. Unless Nippies have suddenly grown a foot taller, it's not her waitress offering a second pot of tea.

'Miss Fern, thank goodness I've found you,' a voice pants. 'I must have been in every Lyons across central London.'

'Gus! What are you doing here?' Startled, she gestures for him to sit down. 'Sorry, I don't mean to sound rude. It's unexpected, that's all.'

Red-faced, he slides into a chair beside her, waving away an approaching waitress. There's little introduction. 'Did you find him last night?' Gus presses. 'Willem?'

'Well, yes,' she begins. 'And no. Why?'

Gus pulls a lean hand through his hair, swipes one palm across his face, but the worry is firmly etched. 'I don't know what to think . . . if I should say . . .'

'What is it, Gus?' Marnie's barely controlled anxiety is multiplying. 'Please tell me.'

'I think he's gone. Willem has disappeared.'

'When? What makes you think that?'

He blows out a lungful of worry and slumps back in his chair. 'We were supposed to meet this morning for breakfast, and then a walk through Hyde Park, to catch up on work. When he didn't show at my place, I went to his.'

'And?'

'I mean, he has so few possessions, it's difficult to know if the place is cleared out or not, but I feel certain he's left.'

'What makes you so sure?' Marnie asks.

'He had a tiny family photograph propped up next to the bed. And it's nowhere to be found.'

'Oh.' Some of the missing puzzle pieces slot rapidly into place. 'I think I might know why. Or at least part of the reason.'

'Willem, a spy? A Nazi sympathiser? I don't believe it.' Gus shakes his head vehemently. 'It's not possible.'

His stride falters briefly and his youthful face creases, the true prospect perhaps taking root inside him. He forges on down the Strand as they leave Lyons behind, cutting through a side street towards the Savoy hotel and on to the embankment at the river's edge. Marnie catches up to where he's standing, his face turned towards the Thames's sludgy brown flow catching against the ancient wooden piles in the mud, the wind whipping at a pained expression she knows is there, the legacy of a friendship turned instantly sour.

'There might be other reasons why he was in Hungaria,' she begins, hoping Gus will confirm that yes, Willem had been undercover, scoping out the enemy. That it's all part of the Allied plan.

But he doesn't. 'Like what?' he spits bitterly. 'He would have told me something so crucial, wouldn't have kept that from me without a reason.'

'But didn't you say you worked in different departments?' Marnie is clutching at straws, since Gus's hurt has the same enormity as the lump lodged inside her, of Raymond's potential betrayal.

'Yes, but we're still resistance, working for Holland. We didn't have those sort of secrets. We never have.' Gus turns to look at her, his eyes wet from the bitter squall. And Willem.

In that moment, the word that pushes into her mind is 'trust'. Or the lack of. Willem Bakker seems not to trust anyone.

'Do you think it might have anything to do with Daisy?' Marnie asks.

His blue eyes harden. 'Why would you say that?'

'Because of her not being on air. It didn't – doesn't – feel right. I can't really explain it, Gus.'

He stares hard into the water, then pulls away from the embankment suddenly, as if to walk away. Perhaps he thinks she's ridiculous, or a silly fantasist. A mere pianist who's reading too much into a missed connection.

She grabs at his sleeve. 'Where are you going, Gus?'

'I have to find him.'

'But where? Where will you look?'

'Home. He'll have gone back to Holland,' he says. 'If what you say is true, he's looking for Daisy. I know him. And Lord knows what lengths he'll go to find her.'

'Then I'm coming with you.' The statement flies off her tongue automatically, but it's firm and entrenched. Marnie Fern is sick of going with the flow, always being the one to stand by. It's pure madness, of course – she has no idea of the danger involved in such a journey, or the hardship, but in all honesty she doesn't care. What she does care about is people – Daisy and, as much as she's fighting it after last night, Willem too. He may well be mixed up in this ugly betrayal but she needs to hear it from him, face to face. To know *why*. And if necessary, to warn Daisy of his treachery. More than ever, Marnie is determined on not sitting in a bunker, as a prime target for Hitler's firepower a fourth time around.

And she's never been more certain of anything in her whole life.

The Reich's respite is over, it seems. The drubbing that night is the worst London has seen for a while, the Luftwaffe arriving like an armada in the air to add their own form of illumination and herald a new year. Marnie hears it from the cocoon of the BBC shelter, having returned first to Bedford College after parting with Gus and taken to the freezing basement to push out her call sign into the air again. There wasn't a transmission scheduled between them but she had to try, just in case Daisy was listening. In need. They are partners, and she's convinced it's what her opposite would do for her.

But there was nothing in her headphones, only a silence followed by the sirens and a low vibration of the airborne swarm felt deep down in the basement. Whether it was the day's events or Marnie's mood, Moaning Minnie sounded especially pitiful then. In reality, it was the same undulating whine calling for the city to scuttle into their holes and dread another year of this Blitz. She'd bypassed the Underground shelter and run to the BBC concert hall, wanting – needing – to be among familiar faces. Perhaps for the last time?

Lying in her bunk, Marnie wakes at intervals and shifts, waiting for the room to settle into its rhythm of sniffs, coughs and light snoring. In these post-Christmas days, it's not as crowded as usual, but with enough bodies that she feels cushioned against the bludgeoning outside. At some point, a rumour ripples through those still awake. 'St Paul's has been hit.'

'Not the dome or the church – so far,' someone else whispers, but it's enough that the next sizeable bang from above makes everyone shudder.

For the first time in an age, perhaps since the day Grandad died, Marnie feels an acute sense of dread at being directly under one of those bombs. That ridiculous self-assurance – of being untouchable – has faded, replaced with a paranoia that she will perish under rubble before she's had a chance to really live.

30

Pushing On

Corrie

'Corrie? Corrie . . . wake up. Are you ill? Please wake up.' There's a gentle shake to her shoulder and Felix's thin face appears over the bedclothes. Reluctantly, Corrie forces her eyes to open, settling on steam curling upwards from a cup. Aged way beyond his years, this sweet boy has brewed her something, though it's a guess as to what the weak brown liquid really is — tea, coffee, or indistinct grounds. She sips at it anyway and the bitterness brings her round.

'Corrie, shall I go next door and ask Mevrouw Heuvel for help?'

'No,' she rasps. 'I'm all right. It's just a cold, Felix. Not to worry. I'll be fine in a few days.'

It's not and she won't. Because grief worms its way far deeper than a mere chill, gripping at every artery, every organ, and strangling the flow of life until you feel dead inside yourself. For three days, since she laid eyes on the cold, stark sight of Kees' body, the door of the shop has remained closed and the fires unlit, her transmitter deadly silent while Corrie has drifted on a carousel of dreams, memories and waking nightmares, unable to rouse herself to eat or talk, much less anything else.

Now, the glimpse of Felix's face – needy but endlessly giving – leaves her contrite: she should be looking after this boy who has lost far more, almost his entire future. Instead, here he is, tending to her.

It has to stop. Kees would tell her so. Her own daughter would take umbrage at this pool of self-pity, her mother abandoning the cause and everyone she loves.

When Corrie moves down through the cold house, she discovers with a further twist in her stomach that there's little wood, and almost nothing in the larder.

'I'll fetch the wood,' Felix says eagerly. 'I know there's a cart just turned over on Noorderstraat, with its wheel off. I can take the axe and be back in no time.'

If will and enthusiasm were muscles, he would be the size of three men, but as it is, his skinny arms could barely swing the axe.

'No, I'll go,' she insists. 'You peel what potatoes we have, and I'll see if I can buy any vegetables. Maybe even some cheese. How's that?'

He nods fervently, still so easy to please with meagre food and a slice of company. Corrie pulls on her cloak and notes a package tucked on the inside, a book she'd promised to deliver, and a second, thinner parcel bound in brown paper, false papers for someone along the watery stretch of the Amstel canal. She's awash with guilt again – the delivery date was two days ago. The search for cheese will have to wait.

'Listen, I have a package to deliver. If I'm delayed and it gets late, then go next door to share the fire,' she tells Felix, pecking at his blond hair.

It's after five and already dark, with a fresh fall of snow while she's been under her own canopy. The bitter wind pinches at Corrie's cheeks as she trudges east on the canal ring, weaving across the tiny iron bridges to avoid any new checkpoints. She picks up onions and a few carrots on the way, shouldering her small hoard and determined to unload the false papers as soon as possible, which – unusually – feel as if they are burning a hole in her pocket. As she walks, her mind is catching up from her days of indolence, on the drops and transmissions missed, on whether her message via a diplomatic contact has reached Willem. Perhaps he's currently working his way overland or across the North Sea. Was it right to have reached out to him? Rudy and Dirk would say no, perhaps even Zeeza, but her mother's instinct disagrees. He needs to know. And there's still the question of the damage Kees may have done – knowledge she can't yet share with any other member of the cell.

Corrie senses, too, that Lizzy will be worried, just as she would if their situations were reversed. She'll go on air tonight; it's not their appointed day, but she'll try on the hour from seven, every hour until ten, just for a few minutes at a time. It's risky with the Abwehr so vigilant, but it's what Lizzy would do for her, she's convinced of it.

Arriving at the drop point, she stirs herself to be on alert, as they've been trained to do. The canal boat moored tight into the wide expanse of the Amstel is in total darkness, but the smoke twisting from a small metal chimney tells her there's life inside. Peering in the gloom, she looks for a second, more vital signal – a cactus placed on the window shelf in front of the blackout curtain means safety. It's there, and eight raps in a set rhythm admits her to the orange glow of the inside, warm enough for her breath to catch and freezing fingers to smart from the sudden heat. A middle-aged couple welcome her in with no hint of suspicion, clearly practised at this ritual.

'Here, sit down, you look chilled to the bone,' the woman fusses.

These are people she doesn't know, has never met, yet they greet her like an old neighbour, pressing warm tea into her hand and offering up crusts of bread, perhaps from their only loaf. In return, she prises out the brown paper parcel from her cloak and places it in the man's outstretched hand, his fingers indelibly stained with ink. Somewhere in the back of this barge, or in a room nearby, he'll have a little industry going, in providing new lives to those who need to ghost from their old identities, with papers, passports and ration coupons. He holds true salvation in those blackened fingers.

'I should be going.' Corrie drains her cup and rises.

'Just a minute,' the woman says, heading into a curtained-off area at the back of the boat.

'Oh, I didn't get any message of a collection,' Corrie falters. The resistance rules are clear: only the scheduled exchanges, nothing more.

'No, no,' the woman's voice calls. 'This is for you. Now, where is it? I had it here a minute ago . . .'

'I really must be going,' Corrie stammers. 'I have to get ho . . .' She feels a prickly heat rising behind her collar.

'Ah, here it is!' the woman says triumphantly, and reappears with a large smile and a square package. 'Some kind person gave us a sizeable chunk of Gouda, too much for us. Please, have a little.'

Gouda! Felix will be delighted and, aside from the book to be dispatched on the way home, there'll be no more traipsing through the snow for Corrie. A small piece of goodness in their lives that translates as an enormity.

Corrie's hand clutches the package, with its nutty, intoxicating odour rising up, but her thoughts are at home, picturing Felix sitting opposite her with a beam as wide as his soup bowl. Amid the distraction, she hears the clatter of boots only at the last minute, dull on the snowy cobbles and then loud on the boat's landing stage. The wave of fear on the couple's faces tells her this is no snare – no betrayal on their part. They make no attempt to hide anything, or run, because where is there to go but into the inkiness of the canal, only to die under a hail of bullets piercing the freezing waterline? Instead, the woman calmly reaches for a tiny photograph propped on the mantel – an old, scuffed image of two children – and slips it under her clothes next to her breast. She turns to the man and whispers: 'I love you,' and, though not meant for her, Corrie is grateful that those words are uttered and present, not drowned out by the cacophony of military shouts invading the space only seconds later.

31

Caught

31st December 1940, London

Marnie

Marnie's fingers are painfully numb as they rifle at speed through the filing cabinet, a bitter wind whipping through the still shattered windows of Broadcasting House onto her face, in contrast to the line of sweat snaking its way behind her left ear. She swivels her head towards voices outside the office door, swallowing hot breath and releasing it only when the conversation moves past. She's pinpointed New Year's Eve as the time to steal into the empty admin offices because of the secretaries taking extra holiday, and yet it seems that every few minutes her heart is put on hold with too many bodies moving along the hallways beyond. Any one of which might turn the handle of the door and catch her doing something decidedly underhand. And distinctly illegal.

At last! Her finger lands on the buff file containing the documents she and Gus need to flee the country, plucking out two and sliding the treasure into the pocket of her overcoat that's now everyday attire inside the building, thanks to the arctic conditions of most rooms. Marnie's heart beats at least ten to the dozen as she peers into the corridor. How do thieves manage this without serious damage to their health? Do they have a stronger constitution or less to fear? Now, it's just her guilt-ridden face Marnie has to readjust, the well-worn art of appearing both normal and upbeat.

'Hallo there, what are you doing this far up?'

Oh Christ.

Marnie spins to see Raymond lumbering to catch up, a pile of scripts under his arm. 'Oh, just dropping off something to personnel.'

Raymond looks suddenly grave. 'Not a transfer request, I hope?'

'No, no.' She's stuttering. Pathetically. She needs to pull everything back into line – face, resolve, courage. Now or never.

'Raymond, can I have a word? In private.'

'Miss Roach is at lunch,' he says for reassurance as they enter the refuge of their own office, and he lays down his pipe. There's an undercurrent of concern in his voice.

Has he guessed that she suspects his duplicity?

She takes a breath that tastes sour inside her mouth. 'I saw you, Raymond. In Hungaria.'

'Oh.' He turns his face away, shoulders dipped.

'Is that all you have to say?'

'It's not what you think, Marnie.'

'Then what is it?' She hears her voice rise to a pitch, emotion thrusting from behind. 'Please don't tell me it's a coincidence, not when I was propositioned by a traitor in that place, and where German is spoken in the ladies' toilets.' The words come tumbling out, her anger just holding off the tears.

Raymond slumps like a ragdoll into a chair, face to the floor. He pushes a hand over the sparse strands of his oiled hair, and for a minute she thinks he might be crying, until he looks up slowly. There's no anger, bitterness or purpose in the features surrounded by his fleshy jowls. Only sorrow. 'Oh Marnie, I was just . . .'

Their heads pivot towards the door and the policemen who have moved through it suddenly and with force, bearing grim expressions that relay only determination. Marnie is rigid: for a brief, sickening second, she thinks they've come for her.

'Mr Blandon? Mr Raymond Blandon?' the lead one says with authority.

He nods, and deflates in unison. Almost with relief, Marnie thinks.

'We'd like you to come with us, please.'

It's a formality for them to state the reason for his arrest – 'conspiracy to enact treason in a time of war', or something similar. The exact wording is lost on Marnie, witnessing the sorry sight of handcuffs clamped onto his big wrists, and of her boss – her mentor and hero – being led away, head bowed in shame.

'Do you have to . . . with the cuffs?' she pleads to the officers. 'He won't try anything. I know him.'

Or I thought I did.

'It's the rules, miss,' the junior one says with a look of genuine apology.

By the time Raymond reaches the office door, he's already adopted the shuffle of an age-old convict. The guilty. He hesitates for a second and hauls his head upwards and around to look at Marnie directly, eye to eye. 'Sorry,' he mouths silently. 'I'm so sorry.'

And as she stands in the now empty office, with the kettle far too silent and still, she can't help but think: what else is left here for her now?

32

The House of Custody

31st December 1940, Amsterdam

Corrie

The cell is freezing, musty and damp, and Corrie pulls her sweater over her knees as she curls in a huddle on the thinnest of mattresses over a wooden bed board. No blanket and no toilet, just a filthy pot in the corner, plus a small hole in the tiny window pane near to the ceiling, ensuring a continuous flow of freezing air blasting in from outside. They've taken her cloak, of course, though they will have found nothing hidden other than the undelivered book. Yet, the mere presence of the pockets sewn into the lining will keep her here, plus her discovery in the presence of a suspected – and now proven – forger. At best, Corrie is certain to see the New Year in behind bars. At worst, there's no guarantee she will experience life in 1941, or that Daisy will ever grace the airwaves again.

After Kees she has no tears left, and crying would gain nothing anyway, other than a fleeting warmth, drying to a cold crust on her cheeks. Oddly, she's not afraid for herself, just heavy with a kind of inevitability. Her principal sorrow is centred on Felix, whose earnest face dominates her thoughts. Mevrouw Heuvel will care for him tonight, and he's enough sense to go looking for Zeeza tomorrow and alert her. But beyond that . . .

The immediate group – Zeeza, Rudy and Dirk – might already suspect where she is, not that they will be able to do much about it. This stinking cell could easily be one of many Nazi holding sites in the area but Corrie knows exactly where she is. 'Take her to the Huis,' she heard the arresting officer say, and the brief journey in the back of a military truck confirmed it. The supreme irony strikes Corrie as almost funny; the notorious House of Custody is barely a stone's throw from the opulent Hotel Americain on the Leidseplein, wonderfully convenient for interrogating officers to indulge in good wine and cigars before soiling their hands on filthy resistance. And not far either, she guesses, from where Kees likely sealed her own fate.

Her only comfort is that Kees could not have betrayed them tonight; proven not to be the mole Corrie suspected in her darkest moments. The extortion of secrets died with her beloved girl, and she would have known nothing of the forger's whereabouts. If nothing else, Corrie's plight only confirms that the 'burrowing beast' is still very much out there.

Strangely, the top-to-toe shivering begins to lull Corrie towards a form of sleep. Her calves are aching and exhaustion overwhelms her limbs. As her eyelids flicker, one hope nudges into her scattered thoughts. Willem. She might be a lost cause now, but more than ever the resistance in Amsterdam needs him – for his leadership, and the determination he carries with him.

Hope is what we need, she thinks. *Hope that you will arrive.*

PART TWO

33

Taking the Leap

Marnie

In the flesh, Marnie thinks they appear almost comical. Having studied them only in photographs and on cine-reels, facing a real German soldier now seems other-worldly; the thick grey-green overcoats, solid leather boots and rounded helmets are straight from a propaganda film, courtesy of Britain's own Ministry of Information. She fully expects someone to shout 'Cut!' and a host of actors to scurry off towards the canteen.

It's only when any one of this very real cast salutes, or eyes up the beautiful women passing by swiftly, driving people along in their pidgin French and guttural German, that the reality sinks in. This is what awaits her own country if the war is lost, the dark future Britons dread during the endless nights of the Blitz. Now, Marnie has exchanged the bombardments for a close-up, bird's-eye view of the enemy, their pupils shifting with menace under the rim of their helmets.

Gus tugs at her arm, his white-blond hair shorn and dyed a light brown, eyebrows too, hidden under a felt trilby to be sure. 'Come on,' he says. 'It's this way to platform three.'

'Yes, of course.' She forces her attention to the job at hand, strips away the natural slump of her features and paints on a smile, thankful now for so many years of practice at the BBC.

They've been in Lille for two days, though barely seeing the streets or its beautiful sights, holed up instead in a safe house: an apartment of crumbling plaster in one of those wide, nondescript thoroughfares just off the centre. So the frenetic activity of Lille's central station and its vast echoey space is a shock to Marnie's senses, a rude awakening, too, as to how many Germans occupy a city she's only ever dreamt of visiting. But this is no illusion – the Wehrmacht are everywhere: keeping watch at the ticket office, checking papers on the platforms and eyeing all travellers with distrust.

Gus changes direction dramatically, steering her smartly around a fracas that's broken out on the platform, where soldiers shout into the face of a lone man, spewing the contents of his suitcase onto the concrete. His pleas of innocence are lost under their accusations and the hissing steam, climbing towards the arched roof.

'Let's avoid getting caught up in that,' Gus mutters. Exposing the contents of Marnie's own small suitcase would be humiliating, though not incriminating enough to get them arrested. What she fears most is a more in-depth search, when the Nazis would surely uncover small components of her transmitter spread through the hastily made belt strapped around her waist and below her blouse. Or the tiny but vital cogs of her machine secreted in the block heels of both shoes, courtesy of a clever cobbler she'd found in London as they prepared to slip away. Gus is right – they don't want to attract any attention worthy of a soldier's suspicious eye.

They locate the train bound for Amsterdam, board and find their seats in the carriage, clutching second-class tickets that befit the journalists they are purporting to be, a role that Marnie could not possibly have scripted or produced. But here she is, out of the studio, hundreds of miles from her beloved Broadcasting House. Playing a part with no rehearsal, run-through or editing. A live show.

Gus squeezes her hand and tosses a smile at an elderly woman sitting opposite in the carriage, whose return expression says she is warmed by the sight of two people clearly in love. '*Ça va, mon cœur?*' he says in perfect French.

All right, darling? To Marnie Fern, of all people.

Gus had objected at first, of course he had: told her the plan *was* madness, that she was no spy, not trained in espionage. He'd created a litany of excuses for Marnie not to attempt the journey to Holland, asserting that she'd either hold him up or endanger them both as a non-Dutch speaker. She'd listened in silence, and then quietly made her case. Would he not need a wireless operator to ease each stage of the journey? And was it not more convincing for a couple to travel together? Who else would consent to go at short notice, a companion who spoke some French and decent German? Yes, his looks were more youthful, but in fact they'd discovered he was only a few months younger. It wasn't so implausible, was it?

Marnie had hitched up the sides of her mouth and set her eyes on him, determined. 'Please Gus. I want to. It's just something . . .' Her words had trailed off, suddenly inarticulate.

He'd looked at her oddly then. 'I understand. He does have that habit,' he'd replied, but without malice.

Marnie shot him a look.

'Willem, I mean,' he went on. 'Something in him, he attracts people into his orbit.'

'No, I don't mean . . . It's not like . . .' She didn't finish. Because maybe Gus was right. Despite the love Willem so clearly holds for Daisy, despite everything distant in him – and the huge question mark over his loyalty – maybe he has drawn Marnie in. *Darcy to her Lizzy.* All the things she's done since that night in Grandad's basement have been in the pursuit of something different, for the war, to be a part of it. But driven, in essence, by Willem.

Deep down Marnie knows she can never compete against Daisy, a love he would cross a sea to save, risk being captured for. And yet, her desire to leave remained steadfast; she has to see it through, to find the answers she needs from Willem, about whether her trust was misplaced, if nothing else. Even worse, she would be left at the tail-end of dots and dashes, while the real events carry on around her. Having lost first Grandad and now Raymond . . . well, there really is nothing left to lose.

She had something else to offer Gus too. When it was made plain by the Dutch forces in England that an agent – however concerned – couldn't pursue his best friend on a whim, Gus resolved to go anyway. He already possessed a false passport and enough contacts to arrange discreet transport across the Channel and into France, but he had no working papers without his government's approval. Hence Marnie's offer to step in and make her nervous trip to the admin offices, 'procuring' the blank BBC passes from the filing cabinet. Beyond that, Gus's expert forger had worked his magic within days. With minimal doctoring of her own passport, she's been reinvented as Marnie Fernvaal, a British–Dutch assistant to Gus's writer and producer. Each knows the press passes won't guarantee free passage or immunity against arrest, but the paperwork provides enough of a reason to be heading for Amsterdam. The rest is down to pure chance, but hasn't that been the case every day in London for months now?

With a parting note penned to Susie about a temporary reassignment to the Home Counties, she and Gus left London to its bombs and rationing, the clear, front-page image of St Paul's Cathedral nestled in clouds of smoke but standing firm against the flames. And Raymond? Well, she couldn't allow herself to think about that. Too raw.

Another of Grandad's maxims came to mind as Marnie watched the cliffs of Dover retreat into the distance, on a trawler bound for coastal France: *Out of the frying pan and into the fire. You'll get your fingers burnt, my girl.*

Both burn hot and score deep and fast, so are they really so different in the end?

34

Welcome to Holland

5th January 1941, Belgian–Dutch border

Marnie

She wakes to a nagging pain in her neck and Gus's hand squeezing down on her arm.

'Marnie, Marnie,' he hisses in a low tone. 'Wake up. We've got company.'

Her eyes are clogged with sleep and she hastily rubs life into her cheeks, noting the woman opposite is still dozing and the compartment otherwise empty.

From the low light, she guesses it's late afternoon, and they're stopped at what looks to be a station in rural flatlands. 'What do you mean?'

'We're just over the Dutch border,' Gus says. 'But there are soldiers boarding. Two or three, I think. Might be time to make ourselves scarce for a while.'

Crouching in the tiny, rather fragrant lavatory while Germans search the entire train indiscriminately is not something Marnie relishes, but it's preferable to putting their BBC passes under real scrutiny. The less they have to use them, the better. Quietly, they collect two small suitcases from the overhead rack and start towards the back of the carriage, away from the obvious sounds of incursion and the impatient bark for papers snaking through the train. But mere feet from the door to the ladies, Gus stops just ahead of Marnie, swivels smartly and pushes her into a half-empty compartment, as one Wehrmacht appears and clatters past through the corridor. The seated, startled occupants say nothing as the couple sit and each pull out a book from their pockets, instantly absorbed. Marnie stares at the pages, conscious of her eyes tracking the lines for full effect but completely mystified as to what she is reading, in a neat Dutch script.

Alongside a feverish hiss of steam from the idle engine, her mind runs with possibilities. What will she do if someone addresses her in their native language? Her frantic cramming from *Easy Ways to Speak Dutch* in those three days in London suddenly feels very inadequate. Gus must sense it, because he slips his hand in hers, his skin warm but not clammy. She reads his gentle grasp as: 'Sit tight, keep silent.' He's in control, as much as anyone is.

Five minutes crawl by, then ten, time enough to hear the small group of soldiers moving down the train by degrees. Marnie's astute ear for sound estimates they are three compartments away, four at the most. She nudges Gus and looks him directly in the eye: *What now?*

'Time to go.' The words slither from the barest gap between his teeth, but the meaning is clear. Gus says something loudly in Dutch, her ear catching on the word 'ill', and the other travellers nod with consoling looks towards Marnie. The corridor is clear, with only one uniformed soldier at the far end of the carriage, scrutinising papers. This time they reach the lavatories, Gus's fingers on the handle.

'Halt!'

It's a natural reaction to freeze, and only then to think about running, to estimate the time it would take for a soldier to draw his gun, the distance to the carriage door and a leap into the unknown, even with the train at a standstill. The weighing up of life against injury and possibly death. Or a lucky escape. But this isn't a film, propaganda or otherwise. This is stark reality and those bullets just yards away are lethal.

Gus makes the crucial calculation, stopping and turning towards the voice. As he does, Marnie watches his face alter, refigure itself into that of a man who simply needed the lavatory and is ready to pull out his bona fide papers. 'Yes, officer,' he accedes.

Time to put their forger's skills to the test.

'Papers!' the soldier demands, his face rigid and determined. He looks young under his cap, his otherwise smooth skin freshly scratched from shaving.

Gus delves into his jacket pocket and pulls out his passport, while Marnie reaches into her handbag, scraping her hand purposefully against the clasp to cause pain, a spasm sharp enough to stop her shaking. The officer narrows his eyes and scrutinises for endless seconds; of all the wild thoughts to occur in this moment, she muses on the length of his silent pause and how it would be judged as far too long on BBC air.

'These aren't in order – you need to come with me,' the soldier growls. Marnie hears a unified gasp from those in the nearest compartment – of shock, and perhaps relief, that they as travellers will be spared such scrutiny; if the officers have gathered enough suspects they'll be more likely to skate over the rest.

'But, but . . . we're with the BBC,' Marnie stutters in her best German. 'Here, we have . . .' She doesn't know the word for identification, but waves the pass in the soldier's eyeline. 'Here. Look at this.'

But he's in no mood to listen; he's snared his quota and wants to get off this godforsaken train. Marnie looks to Gus for support, who only shakes his head minimally. *Don't make a fuss*, he's intimating.

Does that mean he has a plan?

She feels all eyes on her back as she and Gus are forced down the steps into the flat, grey landscape, the station barely more than a concrete platform with a squat, square building as its ticket office. Two other Wehrmacht join them, and it's obvious they are the only travellers to be plucked off the train.

211

Now their quarry has been pinpointed, the soldiers appear to have given up searching the remaining carriages. What can it mean?

It occurs to Marnie they've been targeted already. She'd transmitted briefly from a small village when they landed in coastal France, and then again from the safe house in Lille, on a frequency Gus had supplied to someone other than Daisy. The cryptic dispatch she tapped out sounded much like a poem: a signal they were coming overland, though without precise details, and with a coded single-word reply: *Received*. Now, under the Nazi microscope, Daisy's stark words of warning flash up before Marnie's eyes: *Possible traitor in ranks*.

If the Germans can infiltrate English shores with their fifth columnists, then they'll surely wheedle their way into a resistance unit in a country they openly occupy. Have she and Gus been betrayed even before reaching their destination?

Trudging with dread towards a waiting military truck, Marnie Fern is certain, too, that she's a victim of her own zeal and stupidity. And soon to be a dead one, perhaps.

With mouths set firm, the two Wehrmacht use their rifles in prodding their catch towards the back of the windowless truck, forcing both down onto hard bench seats. Hearing the train shunt away feels like all hope has vanished, Marnie having heard the BBC reports feeding through from foreign bureaus across Eastern Europe – atrocities that can't possibly be broadcast to an already fearful British nation – of the scenes where innocents are driven to isolated spots and shot in cold blood, tossed into mass graves. Despite Nazi and Russian denials, it happens.

As the truck lurches away, her mind sweeps back to London and those she loves: Susie, Arthur and the children, her beloved BBC crew – and yes, even Raymond. She feels intense sadness over Willem and Daisy, too – that she will die without discovering their fate, or the truth of their love.

Does she regret putting herself in the path of danger, willingly? Of course, if this is the end. But Marnie Fern is astute enough to picture herself sitting in her near-empty office at Broadcasting House, shuffling scripts and returning to her lone bedsit, certain that she would always have regretted *not* coming more.

35

In the Stewing Pot

5th January 1941, Huis van Bewaring, Amsterdam

Corrie

It's been six days, she calculates. That's what her rough scratch-ings on the wall mark out, though sometimes it's difficult to identify her own among the many scored across the damp, peeling plaster. In that time, Corrie has been out of her cell only twice, both times to face a frankly weak interrogation with a lieutenant who was far too easy on her. She told him nothing, and he revealed what they already know: where she lives and what they imagine her role in the resistance to be. Nothing of Hendrik or the zoo, nor the partisan base. Corrie fixated on maintaining a blank face, controlling the twitch of her eyebrows when he mentioned Hendrik as 'someone of interest'. He said nothing of her transmitter, because they wouldn't have found it in the house or the bookshop, automatically disassembled and taken by the Heuvels if they ever suspected she'd been arrested. 'Don't worry, I'll hide it somewhere no one goes, not even my husband,' her elderly neighbour assured Corrie. 'Under my corsets – any young Wehrmacht wouldn't dare to forage in there.'

Corrie guesses they are letting her stew, keeping her amid the stink of the piss pot and forcing her mind to ferment. The Nazis are old hands at self-imposed paranoia. Clearly, the light interro-gation is only a basting before the real roasting begins. She knows too that they will bring in someone else for the feast. Someone senior perhaps, and maybe even a face she'd glimpsed at the Café Americain, reeking of cigar smoke and self-congratulation. The question is: will any officer soil his hands on her?

With each sunset glimpsed through the filthy window, she congratulates herself on another day gone, hours when Zeeza, Rudy, Dirk and Co. will have been able to move safely, to reposition the few arms they have and relocate the forgers' workshops. She'll hold out as long as she can. Those in the resistance speak of dying for the cause, of never succumbing to the Nazi methods (torture is a word rarely uttered), but in reality, they know everyone talks in the end. The only hope is to give those on the outside enough time to evade detection. So she'll keep her mind intact as long as she can, and pray her body has similar strength.

Today, however, might be the day. When she catches a sense of the officer walking into the interrogation room, her body would have buckled if she weren't already sitting down. The stench of his cologne masking the cigar smoke causes a spasm in her throat; expensive fragrance wafting across the table makes it worse. He's important, SS, Gestapo or Abwehr.

As he rounds the table and his features come into focus, Corrie's chest caves. It's him. Selig. Loud-mouthed Lothar Selig. Coincidence or calculated cruelty, she wonders. If anything, Kees floods her mind and fuels her hatred even more, bringing with it a wave of resilience, if she's lucky.

At first glance, he might be seen as handsome by some, with a broad face and a long, straight nose, hair that's sandy under this stark light. But she knows there's an ugliness beyond that Aryan façade. When he sits and talks, after a lengthy pause during which he scans her file, it's chilling. Unlike at the Café Americain, he doesn't need to wield his power with volume; his threats are supremely effective in a whisper.

'I know you,' he says in clipped English, eyes lowered to her file. 'I know your type. Patriots who think they are a cut above, and sneak around undermining what we are trying to achieve in this pathetic excuse for a country.'

Corrie can only watch, begging her focus to stay, reminding herself not to wince at his foul breath of brandy and too much wurst. Selig's eyes meet hers finally and it's apparent from his dilated pupils that he's slightly drunk, the alcohol stoking his inbred prejudice.

'The Führer loathes women like you, as do I,' he seethes. 'Women who imagine they are clever, and can charm their way into our favour, or our beds, or else scuttle around playing at spies with a misguided belief that they will win.' He scoffs and a fleck of spit lands on the table. 'Triumph over the Third Reich. Imagine that.'

Still, she doesn't move a muscle. Inside her body there's a riot.

But Selig isn't finished. He's not torn himself from a host of amusements at the Americain to berate her for pleasure. He has a little spice to add to the stewing pot.

Abruptly, he sits upright. 'So, I came to ask if you'll help us,' he says, instantly genial. 'I know you'll consider it, because I'm certain you'll want to save your remaining child's life. Willem sends his regards, of course . . .'

And with that, her focus fails, a spontaneous moan oozing from between her lips. The chair feels suddenly inadequate and she employs every sinew in not toppling towards the floor.

'Reflect on it,' Selig throws as a parting shot. 'Have a good, long think about where your loyalties really lie, fräulein.'

The door bangs shut, the noise acting like a bullet as her body slumps onto the table like a toy with the stuffing knocked out.

36

The End

Marnie

The truck squeals to a halt after only a minute or so, a flap of tarpaulin gusting up to reveal nothing in Marnie's eyeline. No buildings or houses, just a flat horizon she's only ever seen in travel brochures or books. So this is it, she thinks. The location. What suddenly irks her the most is that Hitler has triumphed, over her at least. The lone soldier opposite, the one who had ordered them off the train, stands up and moves towards her and Gus, who pulls up his long, lean body in response.

He senses it too. The end.

Marnie closes her eyes in a silent plea: make it quick.

Then a sudden burst of laughter causing her lids to open smartly, her brain in total confusion at the Dutch words that ring with joy, plus the sight of Gus embracing this Nazi officer and slapping him on the back as if he's a long-lost friend.

'WILL SOMEONE PLEASE TELL ME WHAT THE HELL IS GOING ON?' Marnie demands in a volume born of fear and frustration.

Gus's eyes, suddenly alight, turn to meet hers in the dimness. 'Marnie, please meet my good friend, Rudy. In the front, there's Jan and Petrus. And we owe them a large beer because they've just saved us from a genuine Nazi search.'

217

The truck stops again a few miles along the road, parked under cover of a barn attached to a single, stout house, and they're all welcomed by a farmer and his wife into a warm kitchen with a sizzling kettle. Once Marnie is introduced as a Londoner, everyone switches from speaking Dutch, though the farming couple have just a smattering of English. Rudy and his fellow Wehrmacht hastily change out of their uniforms, allowing Marnie to calm her visible shaking, even if the quake inside might go on for some time.

'It's a good ruse for as long as it holds out,' Rudy explains over a spread of bread and cheese. 'One of our contacts stumbled across a whole store of Nazi uniforms, and figured they wouldn't notice if just a few went missing. Those of us with a good command of German can pull it off if the search parties are small and not too near Amsterdam.' He chews thoughtfully and scratches his face with a wry look. 'And, you know, there is some advantage to owning these prized Nordic looks.'

'So, how did you know we'd be on the train?' Gus asks.

'We didn't. After your transmission, we made a guess you'd be coming overland, risking the train since you'd know the Dutch ports are far too heavily policed. There's a genuine Wehrmacht search unit further along the rail line towards Amsterdam, so we've been holding up every inbound train for the last two days looking for you.'

'And the truck – it looks genuine?' Gus goes on. Marnie can tell he's fizzing with relief at being back on home soil.

'Ah, that's because it is,' Rudy says proudly. 'Our loyal mechanic friend does a good job for the Germans when they need repairs, carries out the work in double-quick time, and we get a "loan" of a vehicle while the Germans think it's still in dock. There are so many in Amsterdam they don't even notice.'

Rudy delights in the retelling, and while Marnie has seen Gus showing restraint and a mask of calm on the journey from England, now he seems truly relaxed, even if his eyes droop from the stress and length of their journey. Tonight, he seems only to relish being with friends, untainted by war for now. A bittersweet homecoming in the days ahead? Only time will tell.

Exhausted, they sleep the night at the farmhouse, and for Marnie it's the deepest she's allowed herself to sink into in days. She's woken by the farmer's wife who – through a combination of awkward phrases and hand signals – helps her dress with more of a Dutch flavour, and is very relieved when it's not the traditional white cap and dirndl dress of her host. Her hair is teased into short, pinned braids and topped off with a beret, coupled with a plain grey skirt and sweater. In the mirror, she barely recognises a reflection of her younger self. Or could it be a mere persona?

As she approaches the kitchen, Marnie hears the men deep in conversation, in English, perhaps to protect the patriot farmer and his wife from too much information. What the couple don't know, they can't possibly tell.

'So, are you here on the orders of the queen?' Rudy asks earnestly. 'To bring us a plan and ways of importing arms?'

From the doorway, Marnie hovers, watching Gus's shoulders sag visibly.

'Sorry, boys. This trip isn't official.' His voice is thick with contrition. 'I came purely for Willem. Have you seen him? Do you know where he is?'

Rudy shakes his head; from her vantage point Marnie detects unease. 'No – we thought he was going to be with you.' He lowers his voice. 'When you turned up with her . . .'

'Marnie,' Gus interjects.

'Yes, with Marnie. Anyway, it was a total surprise. We assumed you and Willem would be together. The group hasn't heard from him at all.'

Gus's fist resounds on the table. 'Dammit! I felt sure he'd come back to Holland. Marnie suspects Daisy has disappeared. From the airwaves at least. And perhaps in person too.'

'She's right,' Jan confirms. 'Corrie vanished on a routine drop, an operation that was almost certainly targeted. As far as we can tell, she's in the Huis.'

'Oh Christ,' says Gus, his anxiety bouncing off the kitchen walls. 'You know what that means, don't you?'

'Knowing Willem, he's planning to get her out,' Rudy sighs. 'Silly bastard. No wonder he didn't come to us. We'd have told him what a fool plan it would be.'

Gus runs his hand through the short cut of his hair. 'Then we'd all better get our ears to the ground and find out what we can do.' There's no mention of Willem's potential betrayal. Not yet anyway.

Marnie looks on as Rudy turns to Gus, brows knitted together. 'There's one more thing.'

'Yes?' From his tone, Gus senses the news is bad.

'Another reason why Willem might not be thinking too straight.'

'What's that?'

'It's Kees.'

37

Amsterdam at Last

6th January 1941, Amsterdam

Marnie

Holland is a picture postcard, an image frozen by the snows and framed by Marnie's imagination. Wrapped in a blanket, she squats on the seat in the back of the Wehrmacht truck and peers out, watching the flatlands, the dykes and an occasional slow-turning windmill fall away to become the outskirts and then the central streets of Amsterdam. The gabled buildings – imitating life-size doll's houses – stand tall, nestled side by side like great stalks of wheat, so that if they've tilted slightly over the centuries, they all lean together in solidarity. The wide seam and the industry of the Thames she's used to, but the canals and small iron bridges appear as if a cut-out landscape has been dropped onto open water, with houses tacked on like those on a Monopoly board.

For an occupied nation, the streets are busy in daytime, but as with the Blitz, Marnie imagines that life has to go on; people need to shop, eat and earn. Women especially beetle about with wicker baskets, hopping on and off blue and yellow trams which glide up and down the solid thoroughfares over the canal bridges. There are more trucks, too – military mostly, allowing their own purloined vehicle to move easily through the streets under the shroud of Nazi insignia. Up front, Jan and Petrus are in their Wehrmacht guise, with a kitted-out Rudy in the back, 'guarding' Gus and Marnie.

'It's only a few kilometres until we drop the truck back at the garage,' Rudy tells them. 'Then we'll regroup and get you to the safe house.'

Marnie hangs onto the word 'safe', because it's the only constant in this panorama of Nazi domination that mars the postcard view: hundreds of uniformed bodies, street signs in German script, and the stomp of boots which echo over the grating engine. She turns to Gus, who looks wary. As far as she can tell, he and Willem left Holland weeks after the occupation, when it became clear their names were on the wanted list. Both would have seen the incursion, but not the subsequent wave of Nazism seeping into the roots of their city over eight long months. When Marnie thinks back to London, the bombs are bad enough, a net thrown across the skies each night, but it's always temporary – the RAF punching holes in the Luftwaffe's web until it clears and all that remains is smoke. How would she feel turning up to Broadcasting House each morning, to see its sign carved out in Teutonic script, forced to welcome the insidious Lord Haw-Haw as a hero of the airwaves? And yet this is life, for the Dutch, the French, Norwegians, Danes, Finns, the Belgians and more. Being told what to do, how to be – *who* to be – in their own country.

There's a cursory stop at a bridge beside a canal and Marnie stiffens as they hear Jan up front talking to the sentries, but mercifully no one peers into the back to check. It's only when the truck lurches on that she's aware of the tension held within – muscles, breath, hope, fear. Every element constricted. For how long? Until she reaches the safe house, or back on English shores?

Once the garage doors are closed and the vehicle hidden, she and Gus are led into a back room, where the uniforms are discarded and a brief discussion ensues.

'Look, this is too big a problem for our small group to act alone,' Rudy starts. 'I think we have to make contact with other units, and perhaps London too . . .'

'I can help with that,' Marnie says quickly, perhaps too keenly.

'I'd rather leave London out of this,' Gus counters. 'They're a long way from parachuting agents in to help us, so I'm not sure what good it will do. Besides which, I'm certain both Willem and I are pretty much considered deserters by now. We'll have to rely on who we've got. But, Rudy, let's keep the group as tight as possible, eh? As few people as we can manage with. Though we could contact those in Haarlem and see what they know.'

Rudy nods. It's unspoken, but there's a palpable air of caution in the room. While Gus appears to trust Rudy's take on the situation, the small band gathered is mindful of any leak inside the resistance. The Dutch, especially, are all too aware of that age-old fable which says a tiny hole in the dyke needs to be plugged, firmly and quickly. Or there could be a tidal wave to contend with.

'I didn't imagine we'd be travelling by tram,' Marnie says, low into Gus's ear and away from the small queue formed at the stop.

'Quickest way to get there, and the least suspicious,' he replies. 'Hiding in plain sight.' It's arranged their suitcases will be dropped off later, and with his hand linked into hers, they could be any couple travelling across the city. 'So, for now, we're just Amsterdammers going about our business. Relax, Marnie. It's the best way of not getting caught.'

'All right, I'll try.'

'And maybe smile a little? People do, you know, even in wartime.'

How many times has she heard that? The need to contort her facial muscles into a less serious expression. At the BBC, it was a genuine concern, or a light courtesy. Here, in occupied Europe, there's more than appearances at stake.

Stepping onto the bright yellow tram is like being whisked back to the number 29 bus bound for Wood Green, with women sitting side by side, gossiping with shopping bags on their knees, several children staring out of the window, their small legs swinging above the floor. For a second or two, Marnie feels the tension lessen; ordinary people really are the same the world over. She's always hoped it to be true, even under the bombs, and here is the proof. It cuts through some of her fears, shaving away the uncertainty of leaving her safe, benign orbit.

It's a calm that lasts for the briefest of minutes; the atmosphere inside the carriage switches instantly when two uniforms board the tram. Not the commonly seen Wehrmacht, but the darker lead grey of the SS, those Marnie has seen on newsreels – Himmler and his like. The ones to be really afraid of. The chatter ceases immediately as one officer steps confidently through the now moving carriage, like some kind of ticket inspector rooting out suspect travellers. Rudy has already warned of the Dutch identification cards, soon to be mandatory and branded with an extra marking for Jews, but they're not in circulation yet. And so this Nazi is simply sniffing out those he intends to harass by stealth.

Marnie feels Gus's breath in her ear. 'Say nothing and smile as if you have to,' he barely whispers.

She blinks to centre herself. In seconds, a shiny eagle icon and the glint of a silver skull looms within inches, and her saving grace is to focus on the near-black serge of his uniform, to picture Grandad gauging the cloth between his discerning fingers. 'Mmm, a nice quality weave,' he would have said, and it's only that which stops her fainting, when Marnie is not a woman prone to collapse.

She barely looks at him or hears his words above the sudden, deafening rush in her ears at coming face to face with the SS. Bad enough to hear the drone of the Luftwaffe overhead and become intimate with a landmine. This is utterly terrifying by comparison.

Gus is replying hesitantly in German, as do most in the carriage, and she realises they're discussing her. Gus squeezes her hand and, like some ventriloquist's doll, she yanks up an awkward grin as the eyes of the SS man comb her face for signs of a dangerous dissident or a Jew. The seconds seem endless, until she thinks her lips will paralyse if he stares much longer.

Finally, the officer pastes on his own fake satisfaction, swivels on his heels and heads towards a dark-haired woman and her child at the back of the tram, the unfortunate two that he promptly escorts off at the next stop. The mother doesn't object, protest or rail at him, simply rises and follows with her child. As she passes, Marnie sees the resignation in her eyes: *What would be the point? They have the power.*

Pressure inside the carriage lifts when the officers leave, though the conversation is muted, given the prospects of that poor woman and child. Is it callous that life continues in this way? Marnie thinks back to Londoners and the way they've become accustomed to the sight of bodies on the streets each morning. Tiny shrouds over child-like corpses still elicit shock in small clusters of onlookers, but not like in the earliest days of the Blitz. The living are sad and respectful, but they move on towards work and shopping, as does Marnie. It's called survival, and the Dutch have their own brand.

'What did you say to the SS, about me?' she asks Gus as they step down after two further stops.

'That you'd just had a tooth extracted, and you couldn't talk. I think I might have tapped into a deeply held fear of dentists in him.'

She laughs, hysteria fuelled again by deep relief. 'And he believed you? Perhaps they're not as clever as they'd like us to believe.'

'I told you. A smile goes a long way in this war.'

Once they reach it, the safe house isn't really a house, but an attic in the rafters of a church on Keizersgracht, with no sign of any clergy. Instead, a middle-aged woman converses in Dutch with Gus and climbs the backstairs with difficulty, wheezing audibly with each step she takes. The space is cold, though not freezing, thanks to a small, contained wood burner in the corner, already lit. Even so, Marnie thinks the thick woollen overcoat donated by the farmer's wife might well become her best friend in days to come. There are two mattresses, separated by a large square of fabric hitched onto one of the roof beams. It's dark and basic but clean.

A week ago, this scenario would have horrified Marnie, sharing a room with a man she barely knows. Even the shelter at the BBC demanded a certain decorum, where taking off your stockings was frowned upon. The freezing temperatures, however, mean she'll undress only to wash, and even then perhaps not too often.

Still breathless, the woman leaves and Gus pokes at the fire. 'Not exactly the Ritz,' he says, in a clear attempt to break the ice.

'I wouldn't know – the Ritz is far too posh for me. This really isn't too different to my old flat in Wood Green.'

Sitting opposite Gus on one of two ancient armchairs near to the fire, Marnie probes for answers. 'Okay, so what's next? How do we find them?'

Fatigue has bleached his face, and he flops back into the sagging upholstery. 'I don't actually know – yet. Not until we put the feelers out across the city. My biggest fear is that Willem has already tried to find Corrie on his own.'

'But isn't that reckless? Willem has been so careful with our transmissions, always planning. Never rash.'

Gus sighs heavily. 'Not with Corrie, I'm afraid. She's his blind spot. He will have done anything to find her. And probably got himself . . . well, I can't bear to think of it.'

They no longer speculate on a more underhand purpose Willem might have had; the news of Corrie and Kees seems reason enough for his sudden flight back to Amsterdam. To save Corrie rather than silence her.

Gus rests his head back in thought; seconds later, sheer exhaustion wins out. Marnie wraps her coat tighter and closes her eyes too. Despite the previous night's sleep, she craves more. Her mind, however, has other ideas, jumping and flitting with possibilities.

What is it with Daisy – or Corrie, as she now knows her? There's a relationship with Willem, obviously, but it's more than that; a spell that seems cast over him. What makes her so special to him that he would risk his life and the future of the resistance?

Her body surrenders eventually to a fitful sleep, dreaming of the SS man as a conductor on the number 29 from Trafalgar Square. In her clear vision, she is physically tossed off the bus for having no ticket, the leering faces of the other passengers cackling as Marnie stands alone under a downpour of shrapnel, fire and WVS tea.

227

38

The Volcano

Corrie

He comes again two days later, as the weak morning sun moves slowly across the grubby window and Corrie is battling the toxic weeds of doubt sprouting inside. Since that last encounter, Lothar Selig's words have rattled around her head, the long hours plagued with images of him pressing a gun against Willem's temple, though she knows Selig wouldn't be the one to pull the trigger. The elite don't often soil their hands, forcing others to do their filthy work instead.

Now his words are all too real. His face, too, inches in front of her, breath sour from sausage and coffee this time. He appears less smug, and that would be a relief, had his conceit not been replaced with fury – a purple flush of wrath percolating up his neck and into his wide jaw and fleshy cheeks.

'Fräulein,' he begins, in a voice that caps the volcano bubbling underneath. 'I was hoping to bring you good news of your fellow resistance – someone very dear to you. That he had co-operated fully, in return for your life.' He pauses, presumably for dramatic effect, but Corrie has control of her muscles. Just.

'He won't talk. I know Willem,' she says flatly, her pupils fixed and unmoving.

'Oh, but I think he would have,' Selig goes on with relish. 'If he hadn't chosen to desert you, and run back to his little resistance friends, without a second thought for those left behind.' Here he pauses again, his eyes snaking over her skin, watching for the slightest flicker. 'His own mother, of all people.'

'I'm glad.' She can manage just two words without her lip quivering.

Selig gets up smartly, the chair scraping on the concrete floor, and begins circling, the flap of his heavy coat causing small gusts around her legs. 'Are you? Are you really, Corrie? May I call you that, fräulein? Because I have a feeling you and I are going to become quite intimate over the next days. Extremely close. And your son knows that. Oh, he knows it all too well.'

Another pause. She swallows sticky phlegm coating the inside of her throat.

'And still he chose to break out, to frankly make a mockery of the Reich. And of you.'

The sudden crash of his fist on the table makes her jump, but she reins in any further reaction. A second, then a third thud causes the wood to bow under the assault, perhaps to illustrate the force her body might have to endure, his fury channelled into strength.

'What do you think of that, Corrie?' he fumes loudly. 'Does that not make you angry? Betrayed? Because that's how I'd feel, if someone who I loved and cared for had condemned me to a very nasty fate. Betrayed.'

'I'm still glad.'

He laughs, reverting to his smug self, as he snatches up his leather gloves from the table and begins to leave with his best attempt at swagger. And even though she's terrified inside, isn't sure how long she'll hold out at their next encounter, Corrie is relieved to have survived this round.

'Until tomorrow, fräulein. I look forward to it. Because when we find him – and be sure we will – you will face a swift and vital choice, one where your son's life hangs in the balance.' He scoffs from the doorway, clearly revelling in his own joke. 'Dwell on that word "hang". Picture it, fräulein. Use every part of your imagination.'

She's back in the stewing pot, curled in the foetal position in her cell, both because it's the only way to preserve heat and because it comforts her to conceive of someone wrapped in her arms. Willem and Kees as babies, or Felix's skinny limbs.

Selig could be lying, of course. Willem might not have escaped as the Abwehr man is at pains to convince her. It may be his attempt at a double bluff, to goad her into talking, a rash reaction to Willem's supposed treachery. But if he has escaped, it's a miracle, and there will be a reason behind it. A move designed to save her or the resistance, or both.

She heard no sirens or alarms around the complex last night, which means Willem must have been held somewhere else. The Oranjehotel perhaps? The specially created high-security prison just north of The Hague that's anything but a resting place – isolated on the coast, enough that those who are cruelly liquidated in the surrounding dunes might never be found. Of late, plenty of resistance have ended up there. Willem might already be lying in the sandy wastes.

But that can't be, she tells herself, *because I'd know if he was dead*. Just as she can detect the sentiment of Lizzy across all those miles to London, as her heart cranked at Kees' fate before that policeman uttered a word, she feels Willem's presence somewhere. His determination, too, and with it, her own resolve to survive.

Present or not, it can't stop an enduring fear bedding itself into her fabric, the dread of another close encounter with Herr Selig.

39

Proving Useful

Marnie

A watery sun splits the blackout curtain roughly covering a small window in the rafters, and Marnie peers cautiously through the gap. She's keen to avoid putting either Gus or their hosts at risk by being spotted, but the view is so enticing; the curve of the canal from the back of the church and the colourful barges nudging into jetties, lining up like London buses in rush hour. Despite the low growl of military vehicles, it seems so quiet – no constant chipping and banging at masonry in repair, or piles of debris being swept, herded and demolished. As much as this is no holiday, Marnie is desperate to get out and see more of the life she glimpsed yesterday so briefly, minus the SS.

Gus's bed was empty when she woke at seven. Clearly, he can move faster and gain more intelligence alone, but some small part of her feels abandoned. And it allows space for contemplation. Time she'd rather not have, forced again by a decent night's sleep to dwell on her purpose here; the inner pendulum that's travelled with her. What possible good can she do? Worse, she might put someone in harm's way. There's no escaping the truth. It was *her* insistence that made Gus acquiesce, her deep desire to feel useful. Now, having come so close to compromising her guide on the tram the day prior, she feels only ashamed. Resolved too, that if she continues to prove dangerous or useless, she'll seek out the first British diplomat or journalist she can find and work her way home, assuming it's even possible.

Laboured breathing worms its way up the wooden stairway to the attic, the heavy rasp of the elderly caretaker, who calls herself Ellen. She carries a tray of breakfast, and Marnie rushes to relieve her of any more burden, relaying thanks in some international language of smiles and gestures. Ellen only huffs in catching her breath and looks to her rear, where another head appears. It's not Gus, but she sees quickly it's not Wehrmacht or SS either. A small black cap, and then the gamine form of a woman comes into view, the look of a teenage boy in lace-up boots and trousers, with a woollen blouson jacket. She should be freezing, but her cheeks are pinched and flushed.

'Zeeza,' Ellen announces, then picks her brain for the odd English word she knows. 'Friend. Good.'

Zeeza steps forward, pulls off her cap to reveal a boyish cut underneath, with a soft feminine face, the combined look of a pixie and Dickensian street-urchin.

'Gus sent me,' she says in accented English, her mouth set firm. Obviously, Zeeza is here under resistance duty and duress. Ellen begins her slow descent down the stairs, and Zeeza waves away the offer to share Marnie's small plate of bread and jam.

'Do you know where he is?' Marnie asks. 'Gus, I mean.'

'Scouting for information, I should think. Combing the bars and cafés. He'll be back sometime in the afternoon.'

The delivery is factual, without feeling, and Marnie chews quietly, hating herself for feeling so ridiculously attached to Gus, like a child clutching at their mother's skirts. A pathetic limpet.

'He thought it wise if I spent the morning teaching you some Dutch,' Zeeza begins. 'Just enough to get about with, to answer questions, and not to get caught. I hear you speak some German and French, that you're good with languages, so it shouldn't be too hard.'

232

'Thank you. I'm grateful,' Marnie says. 'I really am.'

The pixie flicks up her large brown eyes. She looks unconvinced.

'I want to help – genuinely,' Marnie entreats. 'I know how it must look, but I came because I thought I could make Gus's passage easier, and to help with the transmissions, now that Daisy – Corrie – isn't here.' She's babbling and she knows it.

'Corrie will be back,' is the clipped reply. 'I know she will.' Then, slightly less harsh: 'In the meantime, I suppose we can do with all the help we can get.'

It's an armistice of sorts. And Zeeza proves a good teacher, coaching Marnie in how to move her mouth around the Dutch vowels, simple greetings and courtesies only the Dutch would know, plus answers to stock German questions and ways to pass through a sentry point without attracting attention. Marnie's head is fit to burst, but she's flying too, awash with that same feeling from the days back at the Morse training house with Nancy and the others, her former years at university and that joy of soaking up knowledge. Of pushing forward.

'Time for a break,' Zeeza says. 'There's only so much you can absorb.' She pokes at the fire, and boils water for more weak tea.

With both hands wrapped around a hot mug, staring into the flame of the open wood burner, Marnie searches for the right moment. 'So, how long has Willem known Corrie?'

She tries to say it casually, but Zeeza's eyes flick again, switching from russet to mud brown in one blink. 'Better get back to our practice,' she says. 'I have to go soon.'

They are saved any more awkwardness by a succession of quick steps on the stairs. No wheeze either, but a cheerier '*Hoi, hoi,*' as Gus comes into view. Marnie watches Zeeza's face glow, and wonders for a second if there's a hidden attraction on her part, and hence some jealousy in Gus arriving home to Amsterdam with a strange woman in tow.

'How are you getting on?' he asks.

'Fine,' Marnie says. 'Thanks to Zeeza, I now might not embarrass you. Or, more importantly, get you hauled into jail.' Is there a chance some slight humour will melt Zeeza's frosty demeanour?

'She's being modest, Gus.' Zeeza nods, unsmiling. 'She has the basics already.'

'That's a good job because I'm going to put you and your radio to work,' Gus begins, 'and for that we need to go out.'

Quite naturally, they adopt the hand-in-hand guise of a couple in weaving their way towards the water, choosing to avoid the hub of military activity around the busy portside. Instead, Gus navigates Marnie towards a less industrious side to the left of the station, where the wind whips off the water, and she pulls her scarf over lips already dry and cracked. Even London in the depths of winter never seemed this cold.

Gus trades a handshake and minimal words with a boat owner, and they step onto a large, wide goods barge piled with boxes and containers, setting off amid a cloud of grey diesel against a low weak sun. She doesn't ask where they are going, or any details, because she's learnt to trust Gus, in the way she briefly trusted Willem once. Fully and without reservation.

The barge motors north-west over the dark water, the bow rising and falling with other traffic negotiating the expanse between each slice of the shore. Marnie perches on a hard wooden seat among the boxes, sheltering from the cold and the German patrol boat looming ahead, although their pilot only waves confidently as they pass.

'This way,' Gus directs when they alight on the sparse north shore, leading her to a collection of low-level . . . well, they're not buildings, but merely huts. Each is wooden and clearly hand-built, a patchwork of offcuts and pallets like sheds on the allotments back home, though these are surrounded by scrub rather than cosseted greenery. In the waning light, everything looks dim and drab. Is this their new safe house?

An elderly man opens the door to the only cabin with a curling wisp of smoke above and, to Marnie's relief, a rustic comfort and warmth from a small stove pushes outwards. 'This is Jacobus,' Gus introduces. 'Time to practise your new-found Dutch because he doesn't speak any English.'

She does all right, she thinks – the usual niceties, with plenty of nods and smiles. The old man brews tea that's little more than hot water, but welcome all the same, while she and Gus piece together the transmitter, and he hoists a makeshift aerial onto the tin roof.

Once set up, Gus pulls out a sheet of plain paper and a well-used Dutch text that she has no hope of translating, except in code. Gus scribbles his message, but once she's encrypted it, Marnie is in her comfort zone of tapping out the random letters. The alphabet is the same and that's all she needs. She breathes warmth onto her fingers and sets to work, while Gus checks his watch for the timing. It feels good to be working again, being useful.

Then they wait. The old man reads silently in the corner, as if he's accustomed to lending out his humble home for resistance work, while she and Gus sit out the anxious moments.

'Where is this going?' Marnie asks.

'Haarlem, about twenty kilometres towards the coast,' he says. 'Normally, we'd pass handwritten notes via bicycle couriers, but it's almost impossible in this weather. Half our bike wheels haven't even got tyres.'

'And you've friends there?'

Gus nods. 'A good contingent of patriots. They have contacts close to the Oranjehotel, and they might know if Willem is there.' His face drops. 'Or has been.'

'A hotel?'

Gus is halfway to explaining the grotesque irony of the nick-name when there's a crackle through the headphones and Marnie is rapidly onto the response.

Together, they decrypt the jumble of letters back into Dutch. 'Shut it down,' Gus says. 'We're out of time. We can't chance that the Abwehr are scanning for radio traffic even this far out.'

With the light now dimming outside, the old man brings out a single candle and Gus takes the message nearer to its glow. 'Shit!' His tone needs no interpretation, and neither does the shock on his face. 'They do know where Willem is.'

'In the prison, this hotel place?'

'Mercifully, no.' But Gus isn't relieved. Not in the least.

'Then where?' Marnie can't bear the suspense and, for the briefest of seconds, she asks herself why. Why *does* she care so much?

'He's not in the Oranjehotel,' Gus qualifies. 'Not any more. But it sounds like he really should be in a hospital.'

40

Mending the Fabric

Marnie

The snow is banked high on either side of the narrow road as Marnie peers out from under a rough canvas at the bleached yellow sunrise, wondering if she's destined to see all Dutch countryside from under a grubby tarpaulin. Though, lying in the back of a farm trailer, in among a consignment of earthy potatoes, it still seems preferable to the Wehrmacht truck and that imagined journey towards a single bullet and a lonely death.

'Are you all right?' Gus asks, as the tractor lurches over rough ground, the trailer – and them – bobbing in its wake. 'Not quite as comfy as a London bomb shelter, is it?'

'No, but the smell is much better.' She's only too grateful for his attempt at humour, knowing how anxious he's been since the message about Willem. Instead of returning to central Amsterdam as planned, they'd stayed the night in the hut, she in the armchair, and Gus huddled on the floor. Sleep for both had been sporadic. The old man, however, proved more lithe than he looked and was up and out in the early morning, returning with details of a passage back to the southern shore, plus a connection with a farmer moving his load. Vitally, the route avoids moving around under the Wehrmacht's gaze.

'Are you sure you want to come?' Gus had asked as they prepared to leave. 'Willem doesn't sound too good. I can get Zeeza to escort you back to the safe house.'

'I want to come,' Marnie replied, with a fresh wave of confidence. 'I'm no doctor or nurse, but I was a first-aider at the BBC. I might be able to help.'

Mainly, she craves to see Willem in the flesh, even if it is broken, to see his body intact, and perhaps feel that wave of calm he once spread over her. Not forgetting that he has those answers from home, too, explanations she desperately needs, proof that she is not foolish and naïve. Crucially, that Willem Bakker is the man she imagines – wants – him to be.

The tractor stops at a smallholding just inland from the coast, gusts of wind carrying a salty odour from across the empty flats.

'Haarlem is just three kilometres from here,' the farmer says, pulling out two bicycles from his barn. Both have tyres, but each has one punctured wheel and nothing to repair them with. Still, it's a lot to be grateful for.

They share a hot but hurried mug of coffee substitute, and the farmer waves them off, his eyes darting back and forth across the landscape, on constant watch for German transport. 'Keep to the lanes and the dyke paths,' he warns them. 'It's too narrow to get the army trucks down there.'

Marnie is soon sweating with the effort under her thick coat, pushing the pedals on gravel and dirt that's rutted under the patchy snow, her calves aching and her chest sucking in the freezing air like a set of bellows. Even tackling the stairs to the sixth floor of Broadcasting House each day was no preparation for this. Several times, the wheels catch on a stone and she's almost tossed off, swerving wildly.

'Are you still upright?' Gus calls backwards at her volley of squeaks and groans, his own face reddened by the exercise.

'I'm fine,' she grunts, shrouding another lie. Everyone makes sacrifices and this is minute in comparison.

It's nearly an hour before the layout of a small town rises up in the distance, a tall, central spire acting as a beacon and spurring their legs to pedal faster. Though her mind is focused on reaching Willem, Marnie can't help but marvel at the surroundings; quintessentially Dutch, straight from the pages of the history books. There's a meandering river weaving between a warren of mediaeval buildings, a mix of gabled, red-brick houses, some tall and willowy, others squat and wide. They pass through the sprawling market square next to the soaring spire; with a few women in their traditional white cotton caps, she half expects to see a local ruffian in the town stocks and Robin Hood striding out of a narrow alleyway. According to Gus, Haarlem has become a good hiding place for dissidents, and Marnie understands why. With its puzzle of nooks and crannies, she can already picture the attics and basements behind closed doors, adjoining corridors and hollowed chimney stacks. So which one is harbouring Willem?

Having parked the bikes, Gus leads her on foot down a maze of small lanes before knocking on the door of a closed tobacco shop. They hear a window open above, look upwards until the sill resounds with a thud. A minute later, the door opens and a woman ushers them into a dark hallway.

Marnie catches a little of the Dutch being exchanged. 'How is he, Diet?' Gus asks impatiently, and the woman's face fails to hide the gravity.

More light seeps through the tiny windows with each flight of stairs they climb. On the third or fourth floor, Diet turns the handle to reveal a room in semi-darkness.

Though she is less prone to alarm nowadays, Marnie's hands nonetheless spring to her face at the sight of him, despite the gloom. Next to her, Gus releases a moan of anguish. Willem's face is a mass of cuts and bruises, one eye a pulp of plum tissue, his mouth contorted with bruising. And that's only above the covers. She wonders if it was equally shocking for Willem to see her in hospital, that day after the landmine. There, at least, she was surrounded by clean sheets, sterile trolleys and nurses gliding about a light, airy ward.

Gus hurries to the bedside, kneels and buries his head in the blankets as Willem stirs to extend a hand. Gus mumbles his distress in Dutch – a mixed blessing that there's life here, but horror at the mutilation of his best friend.

Marnie watches from the doorway, at Willem moving his seeing eye towards her, his head tipping up slightly. 'I'm all right, Gus,' he tries to assure through his warped lips. 'Really. Looks worse than it is.'

He's lying now – Marnie recognises that – but even with the minimal movement of his face, she senses Willem is wholly relieved to see them both. In an instant, the bond between the two men tightens further, closer than brothers.

In obvious pain, Willem shifts to prop himself up and sips water with difficulty, the liquid dribbling with the swelling. 'Feel like a damn baby,' he mumbles.

Diet hovers, refusing to let humour brush off the serious condition. 'He needs to see a doctor,' she says in competent English. 'But the local medic went out to a woman in labour last night and hasn't come back.'

'I can wait,' Willem protests.

'You might, but that wound cannot!' she snaps back. 'It's open and it will get infected. Then where will you be, eh? Gangrene, that's where.'

'Show me,' says Marnie. 'I can't promise, but I might be able to help.'

Willem's mouth twists into a wayward smile. 'Is there no end to your catalogue of skills, Miss Fern?'

'Well, I didn't come all this way just to make small talk, Mr Bakker. I'm only sorry I don't have any chocolates for you.'

'Then I'll just be grateful for good company.'

If the sight of Willem's face prompted alarm, the gash under his left shoulder blade forces Marnie to visibly wince; a long, raw furrow with ragged edges, exposing a tangle of crimson and purple muscle. Around the wound, his broad back is a sickening spectrum of abuse – red, orange and purple bruising, in a way Marnie can almost see the outline of boot prints pressed into his torso. But it's the gaping flesh that needs most attention, where the blood has begun to congeal and create a worrying slough. For now, Marnie's nose tells her the bacteria is at bay. But for how long?

'How did it happen?' she asks Willem.

'I was lucky, the bullet just skimmed as I bent to leap a fence. If I'd have been any more upright, I wouldn't be talking to you now.'

'You may be talking, but it's a bit more than a graze.' Marnie's mind goes back to her own injuries after the landmine. The shrapnel had caused deep abrasions, and it hurt. A lot. Enough that the scars snag and catch her out a whole month later.

She turns to Diet, swallows and wonders if what she's about to say is the truth. 'I can stitch it, if you have a few things.' She reels off a list: alcohol, a fine embroidery needle, thread, boiled bandages, small scissors and a continual supply of simmering water. She doesn't add that a good dose of confidence would head up her wish list. 'Diet is right – it needs closing up,' she tells Willem. 'And cleanly. I'm going to have to take my time. Can you bear it?'

'As long as I have a decent slug of that alcohol. Oh, for De Hems, with a good, stiff brandy to hand, eh?' He pauses, reality pushing through his wit. 'I need to ask, Marnie – have you done this before? I know full well you're a quick learner, but please tell me this is not your first attempt at surgery.'

She shakes her head. 'Not the first. I did the advanced first-aid course at the BBC, and sewed up a nasty cut on a sound man's finger.'

'That's good,' he nods. 'Just one more question.'

'Yes?' Marnie swallows. She might have to admit that the wound was a quarter of the size and nowhere near as deep. And that she might be seriously out of her depth.

'The sound man. Is he still alive?' His tone is light, but with a serious undercurrent.

'Very much so, I'm glad to say.'

'Then off you go, Doctor Fern. Sew away.'

It's progress, she thinks. He trusts some part of her, but it's at a price. And can it work both ways?

Willem drifts into sleep as Marnie clears away her tools, drained by several gulps of brandy to dull his senses, plus the obvious pain. Gus had clutched at his hand throughout, wiping away beads of sweat; she couldn't see Willem's expression, but felt the tension of his teeth set together and his intermittent flinching. Marnie burnt from top to toe throughout the entire 'procedure', desperate for a sip of water, but unwilling to soil her hands, scrubbed until they were sore before she began. The clearest principle she'd learnt for first aid was in flushing the wound and not introducing any means of infection. The alcohol not inside Willem was used to douse the tissue, before her eyes crawled over his raw flesh in picking out minute slivers of metal, finally using the steeped, sterilised thread to knit the skin in a lengthy scar line. Fairly neat, too, Marnie considered; all those hours as a child trying to emulate the fine stitching from her grandfather's hand had finally borne fruit. She's never been able to piece together a garment, but a human seems a different matter.

At the time, her focus was entirely on the fabric she needed to mend. It's only now, while rinsing her hands of his blood, that she reflects on the feel of his skin under her fingertips, the sparse patches of smooth, unbeaten flesh and how he'd seemed to relax when she put pressure on those. Odd, too, that it reminds Marnie of the night they met, when she'd been tempted to wipe smut from his nose after the raid, but knew then it was a touch too far. Despite the events since, where on that spectrum do they stand now?

In Diet's kitchen, Gus stares into his cup of real coffee, their first since reaching Holland.

'It's the last of my supply, but he looks like he needs it,' Diet murmurs, cocking her head towards Gus as she joins Marnie at the stove. 'And you certainly deserve it.'

She tells them Willem was found on the roadside outside Haarlem by a local man, hidden or fallen next to a canal, half-conscious with delirium. 'I've been doing my best, but I'm no nurse, and I've got others to see to. Now you're here, I think he'll do better – that's the first proper exchange I've heard from him. Or humour.'

'We're grateful,' says Gus, 'and I promise we'll move him as soon as possible. Did he give any clue as to where he's been?'

'Not yet. By the state of his body, it's almost certain he's been held by Germans, though Lord knows how he would have escaped. In his confusion, he's muttered two names constantly. "Corrie" and "Kees". Sometimes with real distress. I suppose you know who they are?'

'Yes,' says Gus, and the conversation is capped; Diet doesn't want to know and Gus can barely bring himself to discuss it. Only Marnie sizzles with curiosity.

'Sorry, but I'll need to get back to Amsterdam today,' Gus begins, to a look of clear disappointment from Diet.

'I can stay,' Marnie cuts in quickly. 'I'll help look after Willem.'

'Will you?' Diet's face brightens. 'I haven't dared leave him, and I've elderly ones to shop for. I'll make you up a bed in the next room. It'll be nice to have some real company.'

It's late afternoon by the time Gus leaves. He goes up to check on Willem, and presumably to pump him for any information, but their patient is still out cold. 'Though he's breathing steadily,' Gus reassures Marnie. 'Snoring too. Tough as old boots, I think the English say.' He leaves Marnie's radio behind, with the codebook, arranging to make contact at nine a.m. the next day. 'Once he's fully awake, get as much out of Willem as you can. If he has any idea where Corrie is, we need to know immediately.'

'I understand.'

Gus turns as he heads out the shop door, his face still bearing the burden of his best friend's welfare. 'And thank you, Marnie. I don't mind admitting that I had my doubts . . . you must have guessed that. But you've helped Willem, and us, too.'

'And that's all I wanted,' she replies. 'To contribute.'

41

Bluffing

Corrie

She's stewed so much she's almost dry. Anxiety dries up your spit, and the meagre water on offer means Corrie is dehydrated, with skin like chalk and a nagging ache in her kidneys. She feels like a husk.

It's all part of the plan, she imagines, as is Selig not turning up today to enjoy goading her. Sometimes, the fear of pain is worse than the act itself, and it's been a topic of conversation between resistance members, though always avoiding any direct mention of torture. *But I can do it*, she thinks, *I can match this bastard*. Already she's forcing herself to conjure up the level of pain that a string of kicks to her torso will bring. Ones with a force of hatred behind them. She's focused on that moment of impact, when she will instantly switch her mind to picturing Amsterdam in the sunshine, sharing a beer with Hendrik on the canal side that spring before the Germans arrived, the first day her father allowed her the pick of the bookshop shelves, and endless summer days when the children were young. Those vivid memories will sustain her through a good deal of agony, she can only hope.

Corrie heard him yesterday as the corridors echoed and he hovered just beyond, talking to the guards. All staged for her benefit, no doubt.

'No interrogation, not yet,' Selig had ordered. 'No one touches her without me here.'

'But Major Weber has said . . .'

'*I* will talk to Major Weber.' Selig sliced off the challenge with venom. 'For now, I want her fit enough to move at short notice. This is Abwehr business and I have uses for her. Understand? Nothing happens without me here.'

That brief reprieve was soon overtaken by the dread she's now attempting to keep at arm's length. What can he mean by 'uses'? He must know she won't do anything to harm the resistance. Not willingly, or without extreme provocation. And now he doesn't have Willem as bait. Or he claims not to have.

It's the many facets of this constant bluffing, the layers of untruths that Corrie loathes so much. That people – Dutch, German, Jew or gentile – can no longer trust each other to be true to themselves, or those they once considered to be friends. The war has made so many fearful, and necessarily meek. Worse, it's stripped whole cultures of any trust they had between each other.

And where is a world without that?

Here, she tells herself. In a freezing cell with dehumanising stink rising up through the flagstones.

Corrie turns over on the skimpy mattress, pulls her knees up to her chest and takes a chisel to the wall in her own mind. If you crave it enough, tap endlessly into thoughts of liberty, your mind can be set free. She closes her eyes; the books on those imaginary shelves will soon take her to a thousand different worlds, full of life and love.

42

Home Truths

Marnie

Marnie is dozing beside Willem when she hears him stirring under the covers.

'Easy, easy,' she warns. 'Try not to lie on your back for now.'

'I'm not sure if I can find an inch of me that's not on fire,' he croaks, shifting uneasily onto his side.

'Diet is out trying to find some aspirin, so you can have that on ration.'

'Blast – bacon and eggs, and now painkillers. Is there anything that's not on ration?'

'Sympathy?' Marnie offers.

'I'll take a dose of that, Miss Fern, but not too much, or I might never get out of this bed.' His fingers skate gingerly over his face, touching on the crust of both lips and the swollen eye that is now mercifully open and only a little bloodshot. 'Am I still stunningly handsome?'

'Criminally so.'

'That's all right then. The Nazis can happily take a finger, but I'll never survive without my looks.' The laughter at his own vanity sparks a fit of painful coughing.

Marnie helps him sip some water, his hand clasped over hers in steadying the cup. His flesh is pale, while her cheeks colour and burn rapidly, a reaction that makes her flush inside. Luckily, she's able to distract him with a firm purpose. 'I've been charged with interrogating you.'

'Well, you're much better looking than the average Abwehr, and you don't have a dirty great cosh, so go ahead.'

Though Marnie is reluctant to take herself back to the BBC and all it now represents, she imagines tackling a script that – in Raymond's words – needs 'a little teasing'. In other words, a complete overhaul. Begin at the beginning with any challenge, she's come to realise. Page one.

'All right,' she says. 'On that night when you disappeared from De Hems, Gus says you got a note and left quickly. What was on it?'

Willem closes his eyes, either to focus or to breathe away the enduring pain. 'It was a message to tell me that my sister was dead. Kees. I assume you've heard.'

'Yes. And I'm very sorry for that.'

'I knew it was from Daisy, because it was handed to me. We had a diplomatic contact, known only to us. She would have never used that line of communication except in a dire emergency, so I had to go.'

'But I don't understand – if it was so urgent, why go to Hungaria that same evening?'

At her words, Willem's eyes expand with surprise.

'I saw you there,' she explains. 'Gus said you spoke of a place with a basement. I sort of put two and two together in the hope that I hadn't made four.'

'It's not what you think, Marnie.'

'Then what is it, Willem?' She's struggling to keep her simmering frustration under wraps. 'Tell me, because I haven't a clue what you were doing there, in a place where I'd batted off a fifth columnist, in a back room with my boss. And my friend. The boss who was arrested just days later in front of my very eyes and marched off to face charges of treason.'

Willem pushes himself to sitting with difficulty. 'If you'll just let me explain.'

'Please do, Mr Bakker.'

He couldn't leave London until the early hours, he tells Marnie, and there was unfinished business to complete. 'After your meeting with that Mr Smith, I began to ask a few questions,' he says. 'I tapped into a contact within British security, about any suspected infiltration at the BBC.'

'And?' Marnie isn't sure if she's ready to hear the truth, but it's too late to be squeamish about it now.

'They already had Raymond's name on file, though it was only as a "person of interest". My contact mentioned Hungaria as a potential meeting place for those with pro-Nazi sympathies.'

'So you went there, to do what?' she pushes. 'Arrest Raymond? Ingratiate yourself so you could embroil him further?'

'No!' Willem is alarmed, verging on annoyed. 'I went there to warn him.'

'About what?'

'About you, Marnie!' He sinks back, a hand over his sore, beaten belly. 'I went there to warn him off. Yes, I pretended to be in sympathy with their views to gain access, but then I told him, in no uncertain terms, that he was endangering you. That you would be under the spotlight if he didn't leave the BBC.' Willem pauses. 'Look, everything we'd done since Gilbert died – even before that – had been under the radar, if you'll excuse the pun. British security left us to our own devices, more or less. And because we've been suspecting a leak somewhere in Holland, it suited us. So, imagine how it would look if the British discovered you were running around London with a transmitter by night and working side by side with a suspected fifth columnist by day? They would put two and two together and make a great deal more than four.'

Marnie is winded. More so than that day before she left British shores, witnessing Raymond's face flood with shame and blanch

249

white with fear in the same second. She saw the loneliness her boss had been at pains to hide with his jollity, the long evenings at home since his wife died. Maybe that's how they recruit, Marnie justified to herself – they prey on those whose world has been tipped upside down by war and sheer bad luck to create a vacuum that may never be filled. Pro-Nazis would have promised a better world, just as Hitler continually pledges to the German people. It was wrong of Raymond, and he'd been weak. And yet, Marnie still finds it hard to condemn him, still loves him for his generosity and kindness. For being the Raymond she knows.

'So was it you who tipped off the police?' Marnie assumes.

'No,' Willem says. 'It wasn't. I should have, but I thought of the hurt it would cause you. I simply told Raymond to resign and go elsewhere, and that if I discovered he hadn't broken ties with those traitors then I would hand him in. He didn't know I was leaving the country – I hoped the mere threat of it would frighten him into cutting loose.'

'So, who did?'

Willem shrugs. 'British security possibly. He was in their sights anyway. It was only a matter of time.'

'And you did all of that, in the middle of your own turmoil, to protect me?'

Willem reaches for his water, his face turned away. 'Yes. Why wouldn't I?'

They need a break before ploughing on, at least Marnie does. She brews the tea Diet insists is a tonic, and then watches Willem's nose wrinkle at the acrid smell. 'What on earth is in this?' he grimaces.

'Just drink it,' she says tartly, slipping back into the role of interrogator. 'Let's talk about Daisy. Corrie.'

He takes a breath. 'I arrived back in Amsterdam exhausted, and filthy. I should have gone to one of the safe houses and spoken to the resistance unit first, but I went to our house instead, desperate to see her.'

That pricks at Marnie – *our* house, even when she understands his depth of feeling for Corrie. She works doubly hard to keep her features even. 'What did you find?'

'It was empty, ransacked and freezing inside, obvious that no one had been there for days. I cleaned myself up and went knocking on the neighbours' door. They told me she'd left on an errand and hadn't returned. There was a young lad there called Felix who seemed especially sad.'

'What did you do then?'

'I went hunting for information, in the bars and cafés I knew were good points of gossip. It didn't take me long to discover she was in the Huis van Bewaring.'

Marnie watches his face crease at the memory, of his sheer dread dawning in that moment.

'I wasn't thinking straight, Marnie, and I know that now. I was spinning from the news of Kees and couldn't bear to think of the same dismal fate for another person I love. On top of that, I'd sunk too many beers on an empty stomach, and it made me reckless.'

'And so you went there, to this prison? How on earth did you think you could do it on your own, against the German Reich?'

He looks at her with remorse, like a small boy caught pilfering. 'There was no rational thought, Marnie, that's the point. I borrowed a Wehrmacht uniform from someone I knew, and tried talking my way in. I had no plan, only a frantic need to find her.'

Marnie stares in silent disbelief.

'Precisely,' Willem says with a half laugh. 'I didn't make it past the second door. Not surprisingly, it booked me a room at the Oranjehotel. But in the midst of my own little holiday at the hands of our German guests, I did discover something. Before my glorious escape.'

'And what would that be, Willem Bakker, aside from the fact that you are not immortal?'

His face grows dark in the fading light of the bedroom. 'There's a particular officer who has a failing.'

'What sort of failing?'

'He's as determined as we are to wheedle out secrets. And to win. At all costs. I'm also banking on the fact that he'll do anything to get hold of me now.'

His name is Selig, Willem tells her. Lothar Selig. Rising in the ranks of the Abwehr. The Nazi man was well aware of Corrie's alignment with the resistance, Willem too. And he knew Kees. Intimately. Somehow, he also knew of the close family connection, despite Kees having adopted a separate surname.

'He took great pains to tell me about how Kees had flirted and courted him, but that he detected she was a plant from the outset.'

'Do you believe that?'

Willem's head shakes fervently. 'Kees was better than that. She'd been months undercover in The Hague without attracting suspicion, so he must have been tipped off.' He takes in another big breath, eyes flashing with anger. 'He called her a whore, Marnie. I swear if my hands hadn't been shackled I would have killed him, then and there.'

'So it's a good thing they were. Or you'd be dead by now.'

Willem doesn't look convinced.

'So what now?' Marnie asks. 'Is there a way to get Corrie out of this . . . what is it, House of Custody?'

'Not with a straightforward break-out – it would be suicide for the resistance. More lives than we can afford to lose.'

'What then?'

Willem smiles in a way that unsettles Marnie, displaying renewed elements of recklessness. 'I'm going to lure her out by teasing at his ambition, and his ego,' he says with conviction. 'And if necessary, offer myself up to Selig in exchange. He knows by now that I've been in England, close to the government in exile. That makes me a very good catch for the Abwehr. And for him, there's a principle at stake now.'

Marnie is appalled and shows it. 'That's absolute madness, Willem! You barely survived this beating, and I'm certain you won't live through another. They will drag information out of you, despite your resilience. Every person has their breaking point. How can that possibly help the fight?'

She's not surprised at his sacrifice for the woman he loves, but horrified at a plan so doomed to failure. If you can call it a plan. Marnie is shocked, too, at the reaction inside her – a sick feeling in her gut, and a sharp pinch to her heart muscle. She doesn't relish any suffering, but there's a violent reaction within her to thoughts of a world without Willem. *Her* world without Willem.

He's set on the path, though. 'Believe me, I don't intend making a reservation at the Oranjehotel any time soon,' he says. 'The trap will be carefully orchestrated, in our favour. A finely spun web, you might say.'

'And what if it goes wrong? What if the Abwehr are fairly clever, and second-guess your motives?' she presses. 'If this Selig character is working his way up the Abwehr, he is no fool.'

'Then we'll be two steps ahead of him.'

'And if you're not?' She's acting as devil's advocate to save his life.

'Then the most precious thing I have left will be safe at least. That's all that matters.'

When Marnie transmits to Gus the next morning, her message consists of a single line: *Idiot is recovering. Come and save your friend from himself.*

43

The Plan

Marnie

It's a further day before Willem can get out of bed, and another twenty-four hours until they can move him from Haarlem, still stooping from the severe bruising to his torso. Bicycles are out of the question, and there's no handy German transport available, so it's down to whatever is available.

'I hope this is not an omen,' Willem says as he lies back in the coffin under a shroud, his face tended and powdered to a convincing death mask by Diet. 'But I have to say, it is quite comfortable. Shame no one really notices.'

'Just behave and be quiet,' Gus scolds him like an older brother. 'If the sentry points insist we open up the lid, then you'll have to hold your breath. So damn well practise being dead!'

'Yes, sir.'

His face disappears under the wood that's been carefully doctored with air holes, and Gus glances knowingly at Marnie's taut expression. 'The only way, I'm afraid. I'll see you in Amsterdam. Zeeza will get you there safely.'

The coffin is just a ruse, she tells herself. Not real life. Though what constitutes reality is in question right now. Marnie hasn't allowed herself over recent days to think of her past life, or her parents, blissfully naïve up in Scotland, and Susie, who must be wondering why her cousin hasn't at least written from her fake BBC posting in the countryside. Supposing Susie tries to contact Raymond via the BBC? That will spark genuine concern on the British side. If Marnie ever returns she'll have some explaining to do.

If.

'If' has never been under consideration before; she's always had 'when' in mind. But the deeper into this war she goes, the more her absence becomes a possibility and her thoughts become maudlin.

'Marnie, are you all right?' Diet asks as she prepares to leave.

Zeeza, at least, is in slightly better spirits as they are thrown together again, even verging on friendly at times. Around Diet's stove, she drills Marnie in more exchanges they might encounter, and they manage a three-way conversation in Dutch, the sort of light chatter friends have in a café; Marnie might not actually freeze if a German soldier barks at her in either Dutch or German.

'We'll leave for the city after lunch, and get to Corrie's before dark,' Zeeza says.

'Aren't we going back to the church attic?'

Zeeza shakes her head. 'We've had Corrie's place under watch for days now. It's been searched and the Reich has abandoned it. If we don't occupy it, someone else will. And then there's Felix.'

'Who's Felix?'

'Oh, you'll like him,' Zeeza assures. 'I'm sure he's going to like you too.'

Once again, Amsterdam strikes Marnie as so quiet, despite the hum of trams and buses, the putter of canal boat engines and the hurdy-gurdy of music machines pushing out their fairground-style tunes on street corners. The soundtrack of constant repair is still conspicuously absent, and then when darkness comes, the void of a siren and drone of incoming danger.

255

In its place, there's the sight of soldiers scowling under the rims of their helmets, or harassing those women with dark features scuttling home to avoid confrontation. Again, the military presence prompts a ripple of dread in her, heavy black boots on the old cobbles amplifying the sound. Marnie wonders: are their soles deliberately designed by the Reich to be louder? It's the psychology of warfare that Hitler employs all too often, as if the sound dial on footwear is turned up to elicit terror. In the same way that the mere prospect of a raid at home has Londoners scampering for the shelters every night, the anticipation here acts as an effective cosh. Hitler may be mad, she decides, but he's a bloody intuitive madman.

When they arrive at the house and shopfront on Prinsengracht, Zeeza appears relieved that the door and windows are undamaged, though the frontage gives off an empty, unattended feel. Marnie squints upwards at the gables above four lean floors, and then back at the pristine porchway, its walls lined with beautiful art deco tiles of a deep green hue. Nostalgia for home nips at her, of proud women in Wood Green scrubbing their own tiled doorsteps, despite the ever-present film of grit hovering in the suburban air like smog. 'I'll give that bloody Adolf a brush and bucket and he can come and clean this every day,' the women carped under their hair curlers. 'Or else I'll send him the damned bill.'

Inside, Corrie's house is a chill of emptiness, drawers and cupboards turned out in the living quarters and the bookshop in complete disarray, crawled over by German search parties.

Zeeza scowls her contempt. 'Oh, it would really upset Corrie to see it like this.' They set to work righting the chaos, Zeeza in the kitchen and parlour, and Marnie in the shop, which she considers more of a pleasure than a chore. The books have been swept off the shelves in swathes, no doubt by Germans looking for hidden messages, leaving them dusty rather than damaged. The majority are in Dutch, and so it's both intuition and recognising the odd phrase that guides Marnie into reordering the stock. She's never set eyes on Corrie or exchanged a verbal word, and yet her presence is palpable in this space, just as Grandad hovers constantly in the hinterland. Marnie fingers the texts that Corrie has selected for sale and feels that connection again, floating between the motes of dust. Despite Willem's certainty that his strategy will work, Marnie wonders if this – the sharing of words and physical space – is the closest she and 'Daisy' will ever come. Life in Amsterdam seems so tenuous as part of the resistance, even more so than under a carpet of bombs back home. Here, death doesn't shower its wares from above, but punches you squarely in the face, from the barrel of a gun or on the receiving end of a thuggish boot, the image of Willem's disfigured body still fresh in her mind.

Voices down the hallway interrupt her morbid train of thought, light and happy words exchanged in Dutch, and when she ventures into the kitchen, Zeeza is fussing over a young boy with a mop of blond hair.

'Marnie, I'd like you to meet Felix. He was living here with Corrie until . . . Anyway, I think it's time we relieve the neighbour of her responsibility.' Zeeza reverts to Dutch. 'How's that, Felix? You'll come back home?'

The boy, built like a beanpole that's about to sprout upwards, beams his gap-toothed smile and nods several times.

'Oh, and he doesn't speak a word of English,' Zeeza adds, 'so I'm guessing your Dutch will improve.'

The three spend the afternoon shopping for the few groceries they can find, where Marnie practises her Dutch on a friendly stallholder. With no raised eyebrows and the right wares in her basket, it passes as a small triumph.

They gather wood on the way back and then tackle the bedrooms upstairs, which are less disturbed but in need of an airing. Much to her surprise, Felix takes an immediate shine to

Marnie, trailing her around the house and proving himself a walking dictionary. Both fall into a game where she holds up an object – a lamp or a pillow – and he recites the word in Dutch, while she obliges in English. By the early evening, they share not so much a vocabulary, but an understanding certainly.

Felix chops the vegetables for soup, reaching into the small hiding place near the stove for Corrie's precious stash of nutmeg, grating a tiny amount into the bubbling broth. He grins with an air of cheeky collusion, and Marnie is honoured to be admitted to his small world of secrets, however inconsequential. She's always liked children, Susie's especially, even if she doesn't always possess a great affinity with them. Perhaps it's because she knows that, after what Zeeza has revealed about his life so far, Felix is a near adult in a child's body. Already, this ten-year-old seems to understand the value of watching and listening, that the tiniest of actions can have rewards – and consequences. Like death. His face exudes innocence, but there's nothing naïve about Felix and his reasoning.

Zeeza disappears once the main work is done, no doubt keen to escape her role as babysitter. She returns at six with news, flushed with the chill from outside. 'The others will be here soon,' she announces.

'Others?'

'The cell will gather for a meeting, in the back kitchen. With the blackout, we'll be well hidden.'

'Er, I'm not sure there's enough soup to go around,' Marnie says. Is this what's expected of her – that she'll act as a kind of domestic host?

'Oh, it's beer they'll want,' Zeeza says dismissively. 'And they'll bring their own.'

Suddenly, Marnie is uneasy, but isn't sure why. In the past two days, she's become used to Gus's absence, replaced with Diet and Willem as allies. Zeeza blows hot and cold, and Marnie wonders if there's still a tincture of jealousy, she having arrived as a 'couple' with Gus. But it's more than that. That word rears its head again, nudging into her thoughts; in among tonight's gathering, is it possible the mole will be present?

By seven the kitchen is full of people and smoke, beer bottles crowding the wooden table. Marnie is glad to see Jan and Petrus again: 'Look, no uniform today!' Jan gestures to his everyday clothes. Rudy is there too, and behind him a new face introduced as Dirk, who gives a swift nod of acknowledgement before reverting to a firm scowl. At ten past, there's a rhythmic rap on the back door and in walks Gus, Willem limping beside him. He's upright at least, his features shrunk back to his familiar look, bar the lingering cuts and bruises.

He greets the room with a triumphant '*Hoi*' and then heads towards her, offering up the traditional Dutch three kisses on alternate cheeks. 'Hello, doctor,' he says, a glint of mischief in his eyes. 'What do you think of your patient now?'

The room jeers like overgrown schoolboys, raising and clinking beer bottles. 'Make no mistake,' Willem rounds on them in English, 'this woman saved me from a nasty encounter with gangrene. And she has more expertise in other areas, so we'll welcome Miss Marnie Fern as one of us.'

The group toasts her acceptance, Dirk included, though Zeeza smiles weakly in the corner next to Gus.

Willem passes up the offer of a beer, keen to get down to business. He pulls out a folded piece of paper, drawn with a basic map. 'The priority is to get Corrie out without any loss of life or violent repercussions from the Reich. Which means it's vital we place this Selig character in a sticky situation, awkward enough that he won't dare admit his stupidity to his superiors.'

'How do we do that?' Rudy questions. 'He's the golden boy of the Abwehr right now. German high command is watching him closely for promotion.'

Willem's old smile spreads wide. 'Exactly. His ambition is our weapon to reel him in. We lay a trail of radio messages they can intercept' – his eyes flick up to Marnie – 'about a resistance operation working out of a warehouse south of the canal ring. When they can't resist the bait, we'll be there as a welcoming party.'

Eyes go back and forth in the room as the candle on the table flickers.

'It will be carefully controlled,' Willem insists. 'We'll dispatch the guards' – he says this with military determination – 'and take Selig hostage.'

The room gasps. 'Christ,' someone murmurs next to the stove.

But Willem is unrelenting. 'We'll force him to request that Corrie is moved from the Huis, for a prisoner exchange.'

'Swapped for whom?' Jan questions.

'For me,' Willem answers plainly, but puts a hand up when Jan goes to protest. 'But, of course, I'm not going anywhere. It's a bluff.'

'And what do we do with Selig afterwards? Kill him?' a wide-eyed Petrus asks. 'Because you know it will spark carnage. For civilians and innocents.'

'Nothing would give me more pleasure than ridding the world of such a man,' Willem says calmly. 'But the embarrassment if he has to admit his folly to high command should be enough to quash any repercussions. My guess is he'll cover it up. If he doesn't, then he'll be likely ghosted out of Amsterdam. And Holland.'

There's an eerie silence, cut only by the swallowing of beer. It's Rudy who voices the collective doubt of the room. 'It's madness, Willem. For you and the rest of us. I say we go for a break-out at the Huis, properly this time, using the uniforms we have and bribing the guards in advance.' Agreement ripples across the room, though Gus remains stock-still, out of loyalty perhaps.

'And what if that fails, as I did?' Willem is swift to bite back. 'Corrie could be dispatched instantly. Gone.' His teeth are clamped shut, and Marnie wonders what emotion he's holding behind them. Clearly, Corrie means a lot to everyone, but everything to him.

But Rudy won't be derailed. 'Everything is risky right now,' he says. 'The best we can hope for is damage limitation. Who agrees with me?'

A murmur spreads, eyes down out of obvious respect for Willem, but nonetheless siding with Rudy's plan, as if the thought of kidnapping a high-ranking Nazi would be putting a detonator under a powder keg. Marnie watches light and hope seep from Willem's face, and yet he pulls himself up.

'All right, if that's the group decision – we go with a break-out,' he says with reluctance.

Later, when the fog of people and smoke has dispersed, leaving only Willem, Gus and Marnie in the kitchen, Willem is already mournful: 'I only hope we have more success than I had.'

'*Anything* has to be better than your disaster,' Gus pitches, but he's trying to lighten the mood, forcing Willem to laugh at himself again.

Gus pulls up a chair opposite, suddenly serious. 'Do you think she's still alive?' As the closest friend, he poses the question that no one else dares to.

'She's alive.' Willem nods firmly. 'Selig knows her value to us. To me. He'll be keeping her as bait. Besides, I can feel her, Gus. I know she's there.'

44

The Enduring Wait

12th January 1941, Huis van Bewaring, Amsterdam

Corrie

He hasn't come. For five days, Corrie has expected the scent of Selig's musky, predatory presence beyond the door, and for him to enter with his self-satisfied look and to get serious. Very serious.

But nothing, bar several trips out to a draughty room with a single table and two chairs in it. A Wehrmacht lieutenant sits opposite and asks a stream of questions while she maintains a steely gaze into the battered wood of the table and says nothing. He displays no malevolence, and she almost wants to say: 'Why don't we have a conversation about the weather? Or books – what do you like to read? Because that's better than this stupid game.'

Still, he rattles on from his interrogation script, until they are both bored and she's returned to her cell. The cold is unrelenting, but they have given her more clothing, and socks, though no shoes. The fabric is worn and sour-smelling, the fibres scratchy, but on inspection there's no lice, so that's a luxury in itself. Yet Corrie holds a deep suspicion over this relative comfort: why is she being treated with kid gloves by the Reich? What do they have in store, and what is Selig planning?

She wants to think about Willem, about Zeeza, Hendrik and the rest, but she can't. Kees nudges at her constantly, the guilt of a mother latching on and refusing to let go. When the thoughts force their way in, the ache in her stomach snakes upwards to her chest, sitting heavily like a tumour of black plague that she fears will spill a foul, noxious hate if she gives it too much credence.

Instead, Corrie wanders back to the bookcases lining her memory, tries to picture the shelves in her shop, running her fingers over the spines and mentally selecting a lengthy novel that she's read before, so retelling the story taxes her mind and keeps it sharp. She yearns for it to lure her into sleep and forget, but still to be vigilant for the predators that hover beyond the door.

Alert for anything that the hound Selig might spring upon her.

45

The Break-Out

13th January 1941, Amsterdam

Marnie

The cell meets at dusk, in a separate safe house near the station, for the finer points of planning, which has been necessarily quick. Rudy reports that he and Jan – dressed in their Nazi guise – followed a young Huis guard at his shift end the previous evening, luring him into a precarious position with a woman and alcohol. And photographs.

'Since he's not only married and keen for promotion, he's now willing to help us,' Rudy assures. 'Corrie's cell will be left unlocked, and it's up to us to get in there on some pretext and march her out.'

As a wanted man on the military radar, Willem is sidelined to the Nazi truck that's their escape vehicle, albeit with deep frustration and a face like thunder.

'Trust the group,' Gus whispers to him. 'Corrie is resistance and we all want her out.'

'Do I have a choice?'

'No, my friend, you don't.'

Zeeza is to stay in the truck to help with a seamless escape, and Marnie will place herself on the Leidseplein with Felix to create a diversion if it's needed. She's glad to have a purpose – the idea of sitting in Corrie's kitchen and waiting for news is unthinkable – but it's a long way from hiding in a basement tapping out codes into the wilderness. How does she feel? Terrified, and yet resolute too, that determination wheedling its way in again.

Under his Wehrmacht helmet, Rudy perfects the steely-eyed expression of a guard. 'Everyone ready?'

They all nod, and Marnie wonders if it's how soldiers feel when they're facing a fierce battle. Or an onslaught.

'Then let's go.'

'Seamless' is not how Marnie would describe it. She's at a tram stop with Felix, pretending to read a paper while eyeing the pillars of the Huis gates a few metres away, ignoring the looks of passengers when the two of them allow several trams to come and go without boarding. Nervously, Marnie watches another of the group's 'borrowed' trucks drive in through the gates, Willem's cap pulled so far down she hardly recognises his face in the driver's seat.

Then they wait. For eternity.

'How long?' Felix asks. He's skipping up and down to ward off the cold, but surely with some nerves, too.

'No idea.' The time it takes to spring someone from jail through the front door is not a topic that ever came up at the BBC.

By twenty minutes, Marnie is beyond frozen and desperate to leap on the next tram that arrives. Still, her focus is on the entrance, though her ears pick up the urgency first, a resounding engine snarl that's all too common across Amsterdam. The squeal of tyres, however, is neither familiar nor reassuring. With a volley of bullets, shouting and general chaos, the truck roars from the Huis entrance, lurching forward as a body half hangs from the back of the tarpaulin, hauled in frantically by several hands. It's not good.

Instantly, she and Felix sprint the few metres, close enough to see Willem's face as a mask of alarm in the truck window.

He accelerates at speed as Marnie thrusts herself forward across the entrance, Felix jerking clear of her grasp and throwing himself down to 'fall' on the ice as a military jeep races in pursuit.

Please stop, please stop, Marnie pleads silently to the jeep driver, and any other force or deity listening.

He does. Just. Felix lies almost under the front wheel, a soldier leaping from the vehicle, yanking him clear and screaming: 'You stupid boy! Get up! Get up!'

'Sorry, sorry,' she entreats in her best German, dusting Felix off, chiding in her most maternal voice: 'Silly boy. Are you hurt?' Delaying, even for a few precious seconds, so that by the time the soldier climbs back in, Willem's truck is no longer in sight. The question remains: where is Corrie? In the truck's rear, or back in the Huis?

They make their way to the agreed meeting point of the garage, unsure if success or disaster awaits. Marnie, especially, wonders how she'll find Willem: elated in the arms of his loved one, or despairing at her possible demise?

Zeeza lets them in by the side door, and her grave expression provides the answer. Marnie sees Gus before Willem, and he gives a brief shake of his head, as if someone has already died.

'What happened?' she whispers. The other, despondent forms are scattered around the room like mourners.

'The young guard was true to his word – we got as far as the inner door,' Gus says. 'Then an officer confronted Jan and all hell broke loose. It's only by some miracle everyone got out.'

'Do you think they were tipped off?' Daisy's on-air warning resounds in her ears: *We may be compromised.*

Gus shrugs and looks towards Willem pacing at the back of the garage, then sitting heavily, head in his hands. 'Best to leave him for a bit,' Gus advises.

'So what now?' Marnie asks.

'We split up to various safe houses – it's too risky to go back to Corrie's. Then regroup for another plan.'

'And what about Corrie?'

Gus sighs and gazes across to Willem's obvious pain. 'All we can hope is that she's more valuable to Selig alive.'

46

Noah's Ark

13th January 1941, Amsterdam

Marnie

It's only when they are back in the Nazi troop truck and en route for the safe house that Marnie gauges Willem's true distress, the tension exuding from his tightly wound body.

'I'm sorry,' she says quietly, realising how inadequate it sounds.

He says nothing, only reaches for her hand and squeezes her fingers, a touch that both gives and draws courage from her. 'I won't give up,' he adds, eventually.

'I know you won't. None of us will.'

Behind the wheel of the troop truck, Jan is in civilian clothes but, in darkness and with his knowledge of the city, they skirt around the roadblocks, stopping only briefly to deposit the group at several drop points in twos and threes. As fast as she's becoming used to this nomadic life, and grateful for anywhere to lay her head, Marnie is perplexed when they pull up in a part of the city so far unknown to her. The earthy, visceral odour is at odds with the Amsterdam she's come to know.

'We're here,' Jan calls from the cab. 'Good luck.'

The remainder – Marnie, Willem, Gus and Felix – jump down and are led quickly through a side door by a man who's ready and waiting. In the gloom, Marnie blinks but sees little, notes the familiar sounds of Amsterdam alongside the scrape of a hoof and a breathy snort of an animal. Could this be a farm in the city's midst? But isn't that a monkey's chatter she hears?

'You're behind the lions' enclosure, just for tonight,' the man whispers and leads them past cages with iron bars and steel mesh, a ripple of unease spreading as animals stir in their wake. He opens a door, as a fusion of pungent odours hits at them, of straw and hay, excrement, musk and rotting vegetation. 'Sorry, we didn't have much notice,' he apologises. 'It's just for a few hours. There's some clean water on the table, with bread and cheese, but don't use the paraffin lamp – it's too noticeable. I'll be back at first light.'

Willem has stirred himself and thanks the man, he and Gus laying out some empty sacks as an impromptu carpet. It reminds Marnie of the London shelters, the new mothers just getting on with it, the old woman and her cat that night in Aldwych station. From what she's gleaned listening to the *Radio Oranje* broadcasts, the Blitz has not abated – England's cities ceaselessly under fire. There seems to be no end to the misery inflicted, so that being stuck in a room reeking of an old privy counts almost as a luxury.

Morning hits them via two senses; rays of bright winter light pour through the windows high in the walls, along with the noise of Artis Zoo waking up – snorts and sneezes, creatures stretching their limbs and shuffling towards a welcome breakfast. For a second, it strikes Marnie as not so different to the wake-up routine in the BBC shelter, and that brings comfort as she irons out the consequences of lying all night curled around Felix on a hessian sack on a cold concrete floor. Gratitude goes to her overcoat yet again. Willem, Gus and Felix unfurl themselves with similar groans of discomfort. So what happens now? Marnie wonders. Will they have to hide out here for days or weeks, regardless of Corrie's fate? For the remainder of the war even? And could Nazi occupation *be* forever?

There's a rap on the door and the man from the previous night appears. 'I'm Rutger,' he says. 'Your keeper, for want of a better word.'

He leads them outside to the zoo that isn't yet open, with several attendants brushing the walkways and emptying the feeding buckets. Felix is wide-eyed, as if he's on some sort of holiday, peering at the penguins taking an early swim and the bear scratching at the floor of his enclosure. Rutger leads them across the site and towards a building that Marnie guesses is some kind of bird house, judging by the pictures on the door. Up a narrow back staircase, they come into a dim loft space where four or five people are sound asleep.

'They spend most of the night awake and sleep in the day, to keep the noise down during opening hours,' Rutger's hushed voice explains. 'Last night they were busy making room for you.'

Under the low ceiling, a large corner of the attic has been set aside, with four mattresses laid out carefully to afford each 'resident' a sense of their own area, a curtain hung from the rafters between each one. The material is moth-eaten and flimsy but acts as the sturdiest of walls when any semblance of privacy is precious. Suddenly, Marnie longs for her own little bedsit, with only the silent Oscar for company, and yet realises, too, how fortunate she is – to be alive, among allies, to feel part of something. This will do. It will do nicely.

Willem is already across the room and leaning over one of the occupied bunks, a mattress raised up on pallets to form something like a proper bed. His arms are around the sleeper, voices stifled but their emotion pulsing with relief.

'Hendrik, how are you?' Marnie hears Willem mutter in Dutch, then: 'No, she's not with us. Not yet.'

Mumbled reassurance comes from a grey-haired man, who sits up and aims a broad smile at Willem, relief etched into his aged face.

'Settle in,' Rutger says as he leaves. 'The zoo opens in half an hour. I'll bring the day's food at closing time, around five thirty. Until then, you need to be as quiet as possible. Okay?'

They all nod an understanding. Quiet is the watchword now. After last night's frantic endeavours, silence is survival.

By the zoo's closing time, Marnie has slept as much as she can, principally without shifting an inch, and the room begins to stir into life. Besides Hendrik – who she learns is Willem's great-uncle and something of a surrogate grandfather – there's a family of four in the attic. Meneer and Mevrouw Levy are a couple in their mid-thirties with a boy of twelve and a girl of ten. Like Hendrik, Paulus Levy is – or was – a scientist at the university, both in the physics department, each with a different expertise; combined, their intellect is something the Germans increasingly crave to advance their weaponry. It's vital knowledge they would aim to extract, Gus tells Marnie quietly, and then toss the donors aside like a hulled-out shell.

'My grandmother on my father's side was Jewish, and Ima's parents too,' Paulus says over the evening stew that his wife cooks up on a tiny stove. 'And though the Nazis aren't arresting Jews in great numbers yet, we think it's only a matter of time.'

Willem nods. 'Soon, every Jew will be marked out officially, and it'll be more difficult to hide.'

'Which means our forgers are going to be busier than ever,' Gus cuts in. 'Better we get in now and be certain of good-quality travel papers.' He looks pointedly at Willem. 'For when we need to go.'

'Let's just see what we hear in the next day or so,' Willem says to the group, eyes down on his food. He's not giving much away, his turmoil over Corrie tightly controlled since they arrived at the zoo, and Marnie notes Gus watching him constantly, like the friend he is. What fierce struggles are playing out in Willem's head, a clash between duty and loyalty, comrades and kin?

By late evening, the Levys ease into their routine, eked out over the months they've been here. As the animals are settled for the night, the *onderduikers* don keepers' jackets and venture outside, two at a time, to breathe some fresh air for twenty minutes or so, with strict instructions to stick close to the enclosures. After eating whatever Mevrouw Levy cooks up – and she seems to be a magician with limited ingredients, just two steel pots and an iron griddle – they clean the room, taking turns in washing bodies and clothes in a small side room with a cold tap. 'We play board or card games together, then read or draw until the light comes up,' Paulus tells them.

It's the shelter existence currently played out in cities across Britain, though more comfortable than Aldwych, and without the human stench. The pheasants underneath don't seem to voice any objection either. But will they have to do this for months? As a working woman, and with her role at the BBC, Marnie is accustomed to constant movement, running from one studio to the next. It's what keeps her mind fresh and fuels her enthusiasm. Since landing on Dutch soil, life has been truly nomadic. Sedentary just isn't her style.

'So, can I show you our lovely zoo?' Willem says, to Marnie's surprise. He's trying his best to smile while holding out one of the keeper jackets. Outside, the chill hits them, but she welcomes the prickling on her skin, and the air is fresh enough, if you ignore the inherent animal musk.

There are a thousand questions circling Marnie's mind, like bees around a hive, but she respects the silence Willem seems to crave as they walk.

After a few minutes, she can't contain herself. 'I'm really sorry the plan didn't work.'

'Me too.' He turns and looks directly at her; a brief sense of that time shared in London, when he gave credence to her personal sadness over Grandad amid the widespread city grief. 'She's not dead, though, Marnie. I know it. I can feel it.'

'So, we hide out here for a while, until we can try again?' She looks up into the night sky and wonders if daylight will now be rationed. 'I've no complaints, believe me, but I don't know how your uncle and that family have managed for months, so contained. If I go a little bit stir-crazy, will you promise to ignore me?'

He stifles a laugh. 'Only if you do the same for me. I spent just three days at the Abwehr's pleasure, in solitary when I wasn't being beaten, and it felt like a lifetime.'

'I never did ask – how did you manage to escape? I heard very few people get out of the Oranjehotel.'

'Pure luck,' Willem says. 'I spotted a guard I'd seen at a café straight after the occupation. Let's just say he was in a compromising position then, and I let it be known I had a good memory. He gave me a window of opportunity, and I took it.'

'Though it wasn't without risk. A good deal of it judging by the state of you in Haarlem.'

'Nothing's without risk these days, Marnie.'

They snake around the enclosures in silence, pairs of knowing eyes trailing their progress in the darkness. Willem hesitates by an aviary, staring at a large exotic owl blinking his wide, white stare beyond the bars. 'Easy to forget there's still beauty in the world,' he murmurs. 'I never really noticed it as a child, because a trip here was so exciting. My mother brought us a lot.'

Is he talking in the past tense about his mother? Marnie wonders. Dare she ask? Or will he shut down again over his family? *Why not? Nothing to lose.*

'Do you miss them, your family?' she says, then feels stupid and cruel when Kees flashes up. Of course he bloody does.

Willem looks wistful rather than offended, rubbing at a scab on the back of his hand. 'I can't seem to grieve over Kees,' he says. 'I suppose it's because I refuse to imagine a world without her. I hadn't seen her in months, but I knew she was doing good work – our work – and that made her present to me. The idea that she will never return once this . . . horror is over. My mind can't seem to allow it.'

Somewhere in the distance, an animal shrieks loudly, piercing the melancholy between them.

'It's a protection, until you allow yourself to think about it properly,' Marnie says. 'I cried over Grandad and the waste of his passing, because I had the space. Seeing him alive and then dead was strangely calming, when I came to process it all. His death was nonsensical because he died under a dirty bomb, but his life . . . well, it makes sense now.'

Willem's expression is suddenly more animated, eyes bright to match the owl's. 'Are you sure you're not a psychologist, as well as a producer, pianist, physician, and all-round talent?'

'No, I'm not. Just a pragmatist.'

'Pragmatist?' His brow knits. 'I don't know that word.'

'A realist,' she explains. 'I believe in the here and now. Black and white. I told you before – there's nothing complicated about me.'

'But you are real,' he shoots back. 'And very present to me, Marnie Fern. And I'm just glad you are here.'

47

Eruption

Corrie

When he comes again, there are no games. His anger is instantly unsheathed, the uncapped volcano in full lava flow. Bubbling with hot, fresh rage, and the entire jail hears it.

'The fucking audacity!' Selig bellows, his fist slamming the table in front of her, hard enough that Corrie sees the guard by the door visibly quake. Her resolve only just stands firm.

'To stride in here and expect to walk you out,' he rages on. 'What do they think we are? A bunch of amateurs waiting around to be duped?' He looks to her for a reaction, but when she remains mute, sits down opposite, the chair creaking with his solid bulk. He swallows. 'So, fräulein. You must be very pleased with yourself, knowing that he tried to come for you. And failed, of course.'

Still, she doesn't react, except with her own seething magma inside, firmly capped, eyes into the table. *Don't goad him, Corrie.*

'It tells me something, fräulein,' he says, his breath like a snorting bull against the ice-cold of the room. 'It tells me that your precious Willem is desperate, and that you harbour more secrets than perhaps we've given you credit for. So maybe we shouldn't wait any longer, eh? We should finally stop dancing around and find out. Properly.'

'Do it.'

He laughs at her, head thrust back with throaty amusement. 'Oh, my brave little fräulein,' he says on recovering himself. 'You have no idea. Really you don't.'

Might as well start now, Corrie reasons. She closes her eyes, draws the scent of newborn Willem and Kees from her memory bank and pulls equally on her stock of courage. 'Have you children, Captain Selig?'

He looks taken aback for a second, and she takes his silence as a no.

'Then you cannot ever fathom what a mother will do for her children, or what she will sacrifice. How she would suffer, and die for them. Not happily, but willingly.' She flicks her eyes upwards and fixes them on the reddened, sweating visage of Lothar Selig. 'Let me assure you now. I am that woman.'

His big hand twitches in response and she tracks the movement – she won't be able to dodge his determined blow across her face, but she'll at least see it coming. His fingers, however, go to his brow and the beads of perspiration sitting proud. He stands and pulls at his coat lapels, as if he's about to offer her a dance, and strides out. Perhaps she's been saved, temporarily, by the Café Americain and some other poor wretch he'll be pawing over in the next ten minutes, in his unblemished, unbloodied uniform.

Back in her cell, Corrie is unsure of the exact effect of her short but impassioned speech. She meant it, certainly, though the bloodied images fixed in her mind of her own battered body are still terrifying. But she said it, and somehow that makes her willpower all the more real. And she was returned here immediately, rather than to some torture chamber, complete with sink and running tap to nicely emulate the sensation of drowning – again and again, she's heard, as they bring victims back from the brink of death. It's a favourite of Nazi interrogation and common knowledge in the resistance. In all honesty, it's that which Corrie dreads the most, the drawn-out, interminable seconds of a last asphyxiating, watery breath, where no amount of sweet memories will dilute the terror.

As an antidote to that particular thought, she pictures Willem, Zeeza and Rudy, and the others. It's a comfort to her they at least tried, and that helps as she shivers under the meagre blanket. They came for her, a solace she might have to take with her to the grave. It's enough, Corrie decides.

It might have to be.

48

A New Look

Marnie

Gus arrives back in the loft minutes after Willem and Marnie's stroll of the grounds, with a face that's difficult to read.

'So?' Willem presses him eagerly.

Gus sits heavily, looking unusually weary. 'I met with our contact in Nazi HQ. She's seen no trial or execution order relating to Corrie.'

'That's good, isn't it?' Marnie says.

'On the face of it, yes . . .'

'But it doesn't mean she isn't being tortured as we speak,' Willem cuts in matter-of-factly.

'True,' Gus agrees. 'But our contact also says there have been rumours. Selig is apparently livid at the escape attempt, yet seems even more determined to hold out for the bigger prize.'

'Which is?' Marnie realises she knows the answer the second the words leave her mouth. It lands with a sickening thud in her stomach, as Gus shoots a dark look at Willem.

'Have you seen Rudy and Jan? What do they say?' Willem urges.

'I have,' Gus says. 'They agree – reluctantly. We go with your original plan.'

Willem smiles, not with any smug satisfaction, more like relief

278

that Corrie has a chance of survival. Even if it means he will be separated from her forever.

'Be sure I will not sacrifice any of the group,' he says. 'If it's necessary, I will go with Selig, and quietly.'

'You know you're insane?' Gus states plainly, with little humour

'Says the man who got into a kayak with me to paddle across the North Sea. Willingly.'

'Willingly?' Gus splutters. 'You practically put a gun to my head!'

For a brief moment, the gravity of this latest endeavour is wrapped in jest, as if they're laughing over a beer at De Hems.

Willem, though, is quickly back to business. 'We don't have much time, and I don't trust that Selig won't switch his tactics on a whim.' He turns to Marnie. 'So, our fabulous pianist, you're a vital piece of the plan, and this is what we'll need you to do.'

This is a first, Marnie thinks. In London, she's occupied basements and warehouses, and earlier this morning the top storey of a flour factory, where she had to wipe off a cadaverous mask of white before stepping back out onto the streets. Never a canal boat, until now – but then this is Amsterdam. And she is living a type of dream found within a travel brochure, Nazis sprouting up in place of tulips.

Today, however, is no dream. With her small set unpacked and tested, she pulls the headphones over her ears, the immediate silence drowning out sounds of water slapping against the barge sides. Christ! What would Gilbert Cooper think of her now? Anxious, certainly, but she likes to imagine his waistcoated chest puffed out with pride too. His Marnie, part of a fighting force.

The messages she taps out are in code, of course – the Abwehr would suspect if the exchanges were anything but covert. And they are necessarily quick, too, with someone on constant watch in the street and whatever building, boat or basement she's within. Much like Daisy before her, the Abwehr's ears are tracking and all too close, easily more of a threat than fifth columnists. She lingers on air long enough for them to intercept, though too short a time to be pounced on by any stalkers nearby. Gus is alongside, since Willem is deemed too high on the Nazis' watch list.

The message content she doesn't understand even when translated, but Gus assures her that these bogus exchanges with the unit in Haarlem represent a path to the falsified warehouse meeting. 'You're laying a trail of temptation, like in Hansel and Gretel,' he explains. 'Cryptic enough that the Abwehr will consider themselves very clever in working it out.'

She and Gus have criss-crossed the city by tram throughout the morning, hand in hand with their practised lovers' look. At one checkpoint, they were asked for their destination by a sentry and, rather than stand mute, Marnie looked him straight in the eye and replied in her best German. When he waved them on rather than threatening arrest, she was surprised and galvanised. *Perhaps I can do this.*

She might have spoken too soon. 'Damn!' Marnie fiddles with the tiny dial, checks the crystal, and still there's a ghostly silence in her ears. 'Gus, I think we've got a problem.'

'Unrepairable? Are you sure?' Willem says, his face creased with worry in the gloom of the loft space. His hands go to his head in despair. 'Shit!'

Gus nods. 'I can fix most basics, but Marnie's radio is dead.'

Willem paces almost on tiptoe, mindful of the zoo visitors down below, though he seems to need the motion to think. 'We need at least one more dispatch to go out today before the Abwehr are convinced the meet is on. So far, it isn't enough.'

Felix's thin face and wide eyes sidle into view. 'I know where there's another radio,' he says eagerly. 'Corrie's friend has one, and I've been to her place. I can show Marnie.'

Willem looks first hopeful, and then concerned. 'It's more exposure, Marnie, and a lot to ask.'

'I'm in,' she says. What else is she here for?

Despite the topsy-turvy hours of the last few days taking their toll, Marnie is glad to be out in daylight again, with the last remnants of snow nudging into pavement crevices. It suits their purpose that shoppers have scarves wrapped tightly across nose and mouth against the bitter wind. She and Felix are lodged in the window of a café, facing their destination on the narrow Tuinstraat, weary in having walked the entire journey from Artis to the western side of the ring. Felix has polished off his Stroopwafel in minutes and is now eyeing Marnie's own biscuit hungrily.

'Go on, then,' she says, pushing it towards him. For now, the hollow growl of her stomach has been filled with a decent coffee and a side order of angst, Gus having left Artis for meetings across the city. Felix is with her, but she is the adult here and it feels as if she is flying solo. There's no choice but to get this right, with too many people relying on her skills. Corrie principally, but Felix and Willem, too.

Every thirty seconds or so, her eyes flick towards the row of shops opposite, and the sign above one: 'Dames-Kap Salon'. With its picture of a coiffured female head and net curtains at the window, it could be any hairdresser's shop in a hundred high streets across Britain. Several middle-aged women have gone in and out, their hair clipped or teased into a style with pins. After thirty minutes' surveillance, Marnie and Felix are satisfied there are no patrols hovering.

'Ready, Felix?'

He nods and scoops up the last of the crumbs on his plate. As planned, they enter together, to the tinkle of a bell above the shop door, and once inside, Marnie is instantly at home. The row of metal drying hoods above faux-leather chairs and a pungency of setting lotion in the air remind her of Saturday mornings at home, reading a comic while her mother completed the weekly ritual of shampoo and set. Here, two women are busy chatting, hair fixed tightly to their heads with curlers, yet more evidence that people really are the same the world over. Thank goodness.

A woman greets them in Dutch, bending to hear Felix as he speaks low into her ear: the verbal password only they would know. He spins towards Marnie, mouthing 'Go with her,' and leaves to keep watch from outside. With a smile, the woman gestures to a sink where Marnie is expected to lie back in the chair, playing along as a new customer. It leaves her feeling vulnerable, but she succumbs soon enough to the bliss of warm water and soap on her scalp, hoping the stale odour of her dry, scratchy strands doesn't cause offence.

The hairdresser – who calls herself Sonja – makes simple conversation in Dutch, where Marnie is only required to issue a nod, a 'Yes' or a 'Hmm' every so often. Hair dripping, she's steered towards a chair facing a large, oval mirror, watching Sonja attend to the other customers behind. Back at the attic, they have only a small cracked looking glass to share, and now Marnie is drawn – reluctantly – to confront her own image in this harsh light of day. Yes, her cheeks look slightly pinched, not surprising with the rations, and her skin is pale from a lack of sun. The rest, though, comes as a welcome relief; she'd expected to look a good deal older, for the travelling and uncertainty to have affected its toll, those famous downward features to be losing out against gravity. Yet, to her amazement, Marnie Fern looks quite all right. Even with no make-up, there's a sparkle reflected in her eyes, a new animation to her face. Could this be down to a life with purpose? One that's perilous, but filled with a sense of belonging?

Beyond the mirror, Marnie watches Sonja tease out the curls, take payment from the two customers and usher them out, singing 'Same time next week' as she shuts the door and turns the key.

Flipping the closed sign, she wraps Marnie's hair in a towel and heads towards the back of the shop. 'This way,' she beckons. The familiar weak bulb lights a basement crowded with bottles of shampoo, plus the odour of old, dank wood. Sonja uncovers a recognisable box, the same dimensions as her own, and within seconds Marnie has the crystal in place, pulling out the scrawled message that Gus has provided.

'Ten minutes,' Sonja warns in broken English. 'Then open the shop, or . . . Wehrmacht.' Marnie understands – nothing can appear out of the ordinary.

As with her dispatches through the day, once her fingers are on the button, she *is* flying; in seconds, there's Grandad pulsing through her finger, London, the BBC, Willem, Daisy, everything that had made – and still makes her – whole. Only Raymond hovers uncomfortably on the edge.

She's packed up and ready by the time Sonja's face pokes through the basement door. 'All good.'

In the salon, Marnie goes to push her still damp hair under her hat, as Felix arrives back at the door with reassuring news that the street remains clear.

'Are you having a . . .?' Sonja attempts in English, miming the action of scissors with her fingers.

'Well, er, I just thought . . .' But the hairdresser will brook no refusal, and Marnie is piloted firmly towards her previous seat.

'She thinks you deserve it for your work,' Felix translates, then adds with a grin: 'And she says you need it, too.'

There's a good deal of laughing and hand signals before Marnie settles on a cut, pointing to a picture of a woman with a short, cropped style. If she's honest, it reminds her a little of Zeeza, and she's not yet cured of that deep desire to fit in fully. By the time Sonja is done, Marnie's reflection provokes more surprise; she fingers the boyish crop of hair, feathered around her ears

283

and fringe, notes that the new, leaner shape of her face means she can carry it.

Even Felix tugs at her skirt and smiles to show approval. 'You look like my cousin,' he says, though it's not tinged with any sadness.

It's getting dark as she and Felix walk with purpose towards Artis, his jaunty steps expelling some of that energy he's struggled to contain since they arrived in the loft. They pass a general store, one Marnie recognises as stocking the few sweets available on the shelves. She palms the guilders in her pocket and hesitates as they pass. The others will be waiting for them, but there are no further messages to dispatch now, only for others to check if they've had the desired effect.

Besides, Felix is so full of optimism as he grips her hand tightly, and yet never demanding. Any child in this war deserves some sweetness and light, this boy more than most. 'Come on,' Marnie says. 'A few bon-bons for each of you – we'll take some back to the Levys.'

He is like any ten-year-old: a child in a sweetshop, a pig in clover, the bookworm in the biggest of libraries, with his wanton gaze on each jar as the store owner counts out the sweets and bags them up. They're both so involved they don't notice the customer standing patiently behind.

'Are these ones your favourite?' a voice says in faltering Dutch.

The shopkeeper is unfazed, no doubt used to German custom, but Marnie sees Felix stiffen and swivel, his delight falling away. The soldier at their rear is barely nineteen, Marnie estimates, and trying hard to extend some courtesy, as they've been instructed by their superiors: befriend the Dutch, they are not our enemies, but brother Aryans. He smiles at Felix and reaches into his pocket, perhaps for some change to buy extra treats. Marnie, though, is too busy watching Felix's bravado disappear, replaced with a rising trauma that becomes a twitch in his left leg, then his right, his stare fixed on the rifle slung over the thick grey-green of the army overcoat. His small boots shuffle on the tiles wet from slush.

Don't run, she pleads inside. *Please don't run*. Felix looks to Marnie for assurances, while she's frantically translating the awkward Dutch into English, and back again, pulling out her stock phrases and hoping her accent isn't as clumsy as this young soldier. 'Yes, he likes those,' she manages.

'Please, allow me,' the soldier offers and places coins on the counter, handing the sweet bag to Felix. The small boy is dumbstruck, his mouth manifesting a nervous tic, while Marnie presses a hand firmly on his bony shoulder. He can easily wriggle free and run like the wind, but this soldier's trained reflex will be to chase, to point his gun and maybe to fire, to ask questions later. Through the grasp of her fingers, she speaks an impromptu language: *Stay. Stay calm.*

It's fruitless. He bolts. With the speed he's cultivated over months as a messenger, Felix ducks out from under her hand and is out of the door, as Marnie sees shock, realisation and confusion run across the face of the young Wehrmacht, before he reaches for his gun – as his superiors have trained him to do – and make for the doorway.

'No!' she cries, hands up in deference and defence. 'No. Please. *Please*. He's just . . .' – she struggles to find the word in German – 'excited. About the sweets. Please. I'll find him.'

Gun still cocked, the soldier considers, but doesn't push past her. He looks scared enough even having the weapon in his hand, perhaps relieved the situation has already defused.

'Thank you, thank you for the sweets,' Marnie rambles on. 'He'll enjoy them.'

Wordlessly, he nods, relief in his eyes. Marnie takes it as her cue to exit, scouting left and right, but with Felix nowhere in sight. Slipping and sliding in her haste, she peers down each side street, calling his name in an urgent whisper. Finally, his familiar cap and blond tufts peek out from behind a low wall.

'Oh Felix,' she says, pulling him into her coat, though she can't be cross with him.

'Sorry, Marnie, but I don't like them,' Felix croaks, still clutching his bag of sweets. 'I don't like them one bit. You won't tell Willem or Gus, will you?'

'No, I won't,' she assures. 'Come on, let's go home.'

He pops a bon-bon into his mouth, rolling the sweetness around his cheeks and skipping over clods of ice and snow. Marnie, though, can only think of his raw memories, of the soldiers Felix will have witnessed before the bombs took out his family, and how such close proximity must evoke that horror. Equally, she imagines the spring in the step of that young Wehrmacht leaving the shop, who will no doubt spend the day thinking he'd made some small step towards an alliance, instead of letting enemy resistance slip through his fingers. *How complex and cruel is a world run on hate and mistrust*, she thinks, forging with Felix towards the zoo, a place stocked with beasts, but where the rules of survival seem abundantly simpler.

49

Melting Ice

Marnie

'Thanks to Marnie, that's the last of the transmissions,' Willem says as he huddles by the stove next to her. He looks across to Gus for more news gleaned from his scouting.

'Our ears inside the Abwehr headquarters thinks they've taken the bait,' Gus confirms. 'Right now, Rudy and Jan are putting the word out for tomorrow evening.'

'How many?' Marnie asks.

'Hopefully twelve of us,' Gus replies. 'With weapons, enough that we can see off a troop, if that's what Selig brings with him.'

'And if there's more of them?' She feels compelled to act as devil's advocate again; to her, it's like the entire cell walking into the lion's den, the analogy all too close for comfort.

The two men exchange looks. 'Then we'll deal with it,' Willem says. He coughs, unconvincingly. 'And there's one other thing – we'll need Felix with us. As a courier.'

'No!' Marnie's reaction is unequivocal. 'That's impossible. Willem, he's a *child*, for God's sake.'

His response is calmer but equally resolute, his eyes directly into hers.

I wish he wouldn't do that.

'Yes, he is,' Willem agrees, 'but more than anyone, Felix also understands, and he's been running resistance messages for

287

months. When we need to dispatch Selig's order for Corrie's release, he can cover the ground quickest.'

Still, she won't let up. 'And what if he gets caught in the crossfire, because it's obvious to me there's going to be a firefight. Very possibly a bloodbath. Do you want that on your conscience?'

'No, I damn well don't!' Willem is almost off his chair with frustration, then sits, as if to suppress his own temper. Instantly, his voice becomes cool, a seam of something she's never heard before – stone-cold and dogged. 'I don't like it either, but this Selig character will not be strung along forever. You have to understand, Marnie, that this is our battle. If we have no resistance to build, then as a country we might as well start singing the German anthem and calling our babies "Adolf". It's not a game.'

'I never said it was,' she counters with irritation. 'I'm here, aren't I, out of my cosy comfort zone?'

'Yes, you are. But these are our rules now.'

She looks to Gus, and it's clear where his loyalties lie; he's Dutch, resistance through and through.

Marnie tastes the sourness of defeat. 'Okay, if Felix goes, then I'm coming too. Because I am not sitting in here twiddling my thumbs and wondering if you're both on your way to the morgue.'

Again, the exchange of looks between brothers-in-arms. 'She has a point,' Gus says. 'She and Felix can stay in the back of the warehouse. We'll make sure there's an escape route if things . . . don't go to plan.'

Reluctantly, Willem nods. 'Agreed.'

Hours later, Marnie's still feeling it – the crackle of tension between them, invisible but divisive, in the same way that the flimsiest piece of fabric between their bunks acts like castle walls to a personal kingdom. In London, she and Willem had crossed swords several times, but there was no lasting acrimony, always overtaken by the task at hand. Now, Marnie wonders if this undertaking is one too far. Too huge and too personal for Willem.

Through the curtain, he tosses and turns on the mattress, pretending to read, though Marnie has yet to hear a single page flip. She breathes, more heavily than intended, frustrated at her own inability to rest.

'Fancy a walk?' Willem's voice comes through the thin cloth. 'I'm sure the animals would appreciate some company.'

'Yes, why not?' The crackle, like a thin sheet of ice, shatters and melts into the floor.

A glittering frost crunches underfoot as they stroll among the deserted walkways to a background of snuffles, catcalls and the light snoring of a whole other world at rest.

Willem stops by the penguin pool, transfixed by a lone creature twirling underwater, clearly enjoying its solitary space as the others sleep. 'I think I could watch them forever, spinning and swimming without a care in the world. They were always my favourites when I was a child.' His heavy breath billows white against the darkness. 'It's the earliest memory of my father, bringing me to see the penguins. My only memory, in fact.'

It's the first mention of his father Marnie can recall, of any family aside from his sister and a brief reference to his mother. 'Do you miss him?' she can't help asking.

He palms at his face, as if to sweep away such indulgent nostalgia. 'You don't miss what you've never had,' he says matter-of-factly. 'He left when I was small. I've not seen him since.'

'Oh, I'm sorry.'

'Don't be. My mother more than made up for it, my grand-father and Hendrik, too.' A tiny slice of moonlight just catches the twitch of his lips. 'And you? You've hardly mentioned your parents.'

'Haven't I? Oh, I love them dearly, but I feel we might well live on different planets, especially as the war goes on. They don't really understand what I want out of life.'

'Which is?'

289

'Something more than I had,' is all Marnie Fern can think to say. 'Coming here, meeting everyone with such purpose – it's taught me there's no exact path for any of us. And that perhaps it really isn't too late for people to change.'

He shifts, causing his fingers to skate close to hers as they stare at the penguin doing his acrobatics, and she's struck by how much she wants to grasp at his hand and grip it tight – not out of lust so much, but to feel his fingertips under hers, the tiny pulse of life flowing. Because of what's before them, and because it might well be the last time, under a moonlit sky that feels impossibly surreal.

'Well, don't go changing too much, Miss Fern. You're fine just as you are.'

'Well, thank you, Mr Bakker.'

'Oh, and by the way, I like your hair. It reminds me of my sister.'

'Kees?' She's filled with a wave of remorse at being a trigger for his grief a second time.

Willem pulls two small, dog-eared photographs from his pocket and holds both towards her; a small girl and boy alongside an adult, clearly his younger self and Kees, plus their mother, presumably. The other is a portrait of a beautiful young woman, dark doe eyes and full lips not quite smiling into the camera. He's right, the hair is almost identical, the gamine style cropped close into her head.

'I'm so sorry if I . . . I really didn't mean to,' Marnie stutters.

'I know that. And to have a reminder of her is . . . hey!'

An icy spray of water flicks up to shower them both, the penguin flipping away smartly under the water, having hit his target with the accuracy of the best Luftwaffe pilot.

'Do you think he's trying to tell us something?' Willem says.

'Maybe it is time to get some rest.'

They head back to the Pheasant House in near silence until the door looms large.

Marnie hesitates before the stairway. 'Are you scared, about tomorrow?'

'Of course,' he says, without missing a beat. 'I'd be inhuman if I wasn't. But it's also the human in me – in every one of us there – that makes us stand up to men like Selig.'

50

The Palette of Imprisonment

16th January 1941, Huis van Bewaring, Amsterdam

Corrie

Corrie is right. Selig was never going to hold back forever, though still not ready to soil his own hands. Instead, he's sent in the previously insipid lieutenant, who proves that his own forte – his enjoyment – is in fact more physical. Gone is the bored voice of pseudo interrogation across a table. When he slaps her cheeks the first few times, she watches his eyes light up with true fervour. As the blows get harder, stinging the flesh and forcing her head to bend sideways on the stalk of her thin neck, Corrie discovers that it helps to focus on the redness rising in his face, the zeal bubbling inside as he screams vile expletives at her, insults on her person, country and beliefs.

Far from breaking her, this vehemence actually helps in her resolve towards silence, aside from the spontaneous cries and moans that any single body under attack pushes out as a reflex. But she says nothing, betrays no one, even when her skin breaks and blood soils his knuckles. The more satisfaction he displays, the more fulfilment she gains in watching his flesh perfuse from pink to crimson and then scarlet, until he flies from the cell, breathless, his own fury at a fever pitch.

Back in her cell, Corrie curls up tight, knees to her chest, and imagines herself as the tiniest of beetles shielding from the dangers of the world, even if her skin feels nothing like armour. Something from the mattress digs into her back and she welcomes the discomfort, as a distraction from the soreness of her belly. She slips a hand under the loose trousers they've given her, and the chill of her fingers cools the red-hot ache that will soon bruise to a vibrant shade of purple, gold and a sickening green. The palette of imprisonment. The small groan from between her swollen lips is instinctive, much like the lyrical mooing of women in labour as a release, and of her own self during childbirth. At the time, she'd laughed with her mother at mimicking a farm animal, and then creased her features and mooed some more as she birthed her own babies. The pain disappeared in seconds as she looked at their tiny, pouting faces, though Kees was soon wailing her indignation at being born.

Kees. Her precious girl will never get to feel that now, the hot and cold pain spliced with the ecstasy of her own baby moving into the world. Neither will Corrie share in it with her. Ever. It's that and not her present pain which makes a tear roll onto the stinking, grubby mattress.

Now, she wonders what colour her own lips are, the blood crusted from cherry to burgundy perhaps, a shade of ruby-red as she pulls her fingers away, and braces the ache in her belly again. This time, it didn't go beyond a straightforward beating, so there will be more, she's sure of it. Without Selig present, the lieutenant will have been sent in to tenderise, to instil the fear of what else is to come – the faux drowning, and perhaps a shiny blade to slice her papery skin. The broiling and the final roasting is still to come for Selig to witness.

With every ounce of her will, Corrie steers her mind from the range of depravity they might enforce. Instead, she fixes on collating her memories, the ones she will utilise when Selig comes again; of Willem, Kees, her parents and Hendrik, of joyous Christmases around the kitchen table, skating on the canals in winter when the children were small. Every image will – she hopes – carry her through to the end. Because it will come.

Willem came for her once, perhaps even twice, from what Selig has hinted. She can't expect such a sacrifice from the resistance again. What is it that people say? 'Third time lucky'?

Somehow, she doesn't think so. Not now that Selig is into his stride.

51

Calm Before the Storm

17th January 1941, Amsterdam

Marnie

They leave in relays from Artis, Willem first, Gus fifteen minutes later, and then Marnie and Felix at just gone six p.m., the daylight hours having dragged with attempts at sleep, the Levys clearly sensing unrest creeping across the loft.

Felix's eyes are like saucers against the evening gloom as he and Marnie trudge the icy pavements to the tram stop and take it directly south towards the suburbs. She scans their fellow passengers and wonders what they see: a woman and her small charge, perhaps, out to collect groceries before huddling up by the fireside. Can they possibly imagine where she and Felix are destined, and to what purpose? Would they even want to?

She'd insisted on being present that afternoon when Willem had gone through the plan with Felix, where there was no cushioning of the cell's motives towards Selig, even if he did skate over the potential killing of soldiers as part of the process. 'Then we'll need you to take a note to the café at the Hotel Americain and give it to this man.' Willem held up a mugshot of a rakish man in a waiter's uniform. 'He'll pass it on to a customer in the café.'

Felix nodded. Delivering messages was his forte, and he clearly gauged the magnitude of placing it in the right hand. 'Wait until you see it passed to a fellow Abwehr officer and make sure that he's read it,' Willem instructed.

Felix nodded a second time.

'Then you come straight back to us. They won't be able to follow you at short notice – not a tail you can't outrun anyway – but watch your back. Take a longer route if you need to. We can wait.'

Felix smiled then, brimming with pride at his standing along-side the grown-ups. 'They won't catch me, Willem, I promise.'

On the tram, Felix pushes in close to Marnie, his hand linked into hers, palms warm and his slim fingers clutching hers. They're all feeling it. Last night, he'd crawled into her bunk, claiming he was cold, but she sensed his shivering was more likely from a nightmare. As they hugged together for warmth, Felix drifted finally into sleep, twitching violently and muttering '*Moeder, Moeder*' repeatedly. A word she recognises: Mother.

Now it's Felix who keeps Marnie's anguish under control, her facial muscles working at full stretch, and she's thankful for him. Without this boy's courage, she would never have stepped beyond the zoo this evening.

They alight the tram in a dim, lifeless street, where Marnie scans upwards for an apartment above a hardware shop on the crossroads – a sign to look out for in the window. A bright yellow bulb means warning, a soft orange glow is a signal for go. But given their suspicions of a mole, can she trust it?

The dim light above forces her to decide – to rely on Willem's conviction and detailed planning. He cherishes Corrie, that much is clear, but she knows he also feels deeply for the entire cell. And that includes her now. She is part of that family, by default perhaps, but wasn't he the one to draw her in? Not to Amsterdam, but into the fight for Holland that's led her here.

With her ears tuned for the snarl of any military vehicles behind, Marnie and Felix walk further south to where the canals don't reach and the houses fan out to a combination of scrub and small market gardens. It's almost deserted, with only voices rising up in the distance. In the daytime, she knows this area would be a hub of activity, like Spitalfields or Brick Lane market. By night, those areas of London's East End are a relative desert, chip papers and remnants of the vegetable stalls rolling like tumbleweed across the paving stones. Here, pieces of wet vegetation are ground into the snowy mush from the day's limited trading.

Felix squeezes her flesh. 'This way,' he says, tugging her further towards darkness.

They arrive at a warehouse looming suddenly out of a wasteland, its black wooden panels melting into the surrounding emptiness. Felix delights in rapping out the rhythm of a password, and Zeeza's face appears at the door jamb. She flashes a welcome at Felix but quickly reverts to a serious, determined expression. Marnie soon sees why.

At a quick count, there are twelve of them beyond the door, those from the gatherings in Corrie's kitchen, plus a few more. At least five are women. Faces are drawn, along with the weapons they hold, a varying array of machine and handguns at the ready. Aside from the Wehrmacht combing the streets, with arms that often seem like toys, she's never seen so much firepower.

Willem has hold of a short, stubby machine gun, the strap slung across his body. More shocking is that he looks so comfortable with it, Gus too. He nods wordlessly at her, and she can almost see the electricity flying through the smoky clouds, cigarettes being smoked one after the other, pitched and stamped onto the floor.

'This way,' Zeeza commands, and shows them to a small office with multiple squares of blacked-out glass windows, a candle already lit inside. 'You're to stay here until we need Felix.'

'How long?' Marnie asks. The idea of tolerating this much tension for hours on end seems unthinkable. And yet, she'd still rather be here than back at Artis – safer but essentially blind.

Zeeza shrugs dismissively, in that 'however long it takes' way, shutting the door and leaving them both to settle into two chairs behind a desk. Marnie pulls out some precious paper and pencils, donated by the Levys as a good distraction for Felix, and surveys the space. There's a small meeting table in the corner strewn with coffee cups and newspapers, plus a side door to the office with a lock. The escape route perhaps? For now, she feels cocooned – claustrophobic, in a way she's never felt even in the smallest of basements or bomb shelters. As if Selig and his elite Abwehr corps might parachute through the roof at any moment, leaving no chance of flight for anyone. Clearly, she's been left to her imaginings for too long, and needs a good dose of the practical *The Kitchen Front* to bring her back to her senses, with an altogether different battle over a simple apron. What sheer joy that would be now.

After ten minutes, the door handle turns and Willem steps through, having pushed the weapon around to his back, out of sight.

'Hey, all right?' he says, and pulls out a certain smile, the one Marnie recognises as his contrived speciality. Felix nods keenly, eyes darting with anticipation.

Willem sits on the corner of the desk, and points at the side door. 'That's your escape route,' he explains. 'If you need to use it, make your way back to the church safe house – Felix knows the way – but not to Artis, in case you're followed. Understand?'

Felix nods again.

'Good. Someone will find you there,' Willem adds.

Marnie notices he doesn't say 'I', as in 'I will find you'. The reality is that he can't make those promises, and the thought punches at her squarely. That she might not see him again after tonight. Or Gus. She has no man in her life, but why is it that the men in Marnie Fern's orbit all seem to fade away – her father up to Scotland, then Grandad, and even Raymond? Now, potentially – very possibly – Willem and Gus. Is it her as a person, bad luck, or simply war?

Distant in thought, she's startled by the feel of flesh on hers, and not Felix's thin digits this time. Willem has reached for her hand, briefly holding it in his, rubbing his rough thumb in her palm.

'Thanks,' he says. 'For coming. For trusting.'

'I didn't think you went in for trust.' She's trying to sound glib, but any light touch is sorely lacking.

'I do, with certain people.'

'Well, I'm glad. What I don't like is that your sentiment sounds so final.'

Willem takes in a large breath, stroking at the crown of Felix's head with his other hand, who's bent over the desk with his paper and pencil. 'Just covering all the bases. Making sure you know.'

'I do. Somehow, I imagine that's where you reached with Gilbert.'

'We did,' he nods. 'And he would be so proud of you now. Also fairly annoyed that you'd put yourself in danger, but he wouldn't be able to hide his admiration. I know that for sure.'

The scratch of pencil lead marks time like a ticking bomb.

'How long until this "meeting" is supposed to start?' Marnie asks. *How long have we got to suck in the last remnants of normal life?*

'Ten minutes.'

'What if he doesn't come?'

He shrugs. 'Then we find another way, cast more bait. But I think he will. We've had word that a small unit has been mustered.'

'Why small?' Marnie questions. 'Surely this Selig will come in with force?'

'Not if he wants the glory for himself, to claim the Abwehr command has decimated an entire resistance cell. Don't forget, I've seen his ego first hand. That hunger for success.'

'That's what worries me,' she comes back.

'But he's misjudged us, and ignored one crucial point.'

'What's that?'

Willem swings his gun around so that it sits close to his belly, opens the office door. 'That I'm much hungrier. Keep safe, Marnie.'

52

Captive

Marnie

She sometimes wishes it wasn't so acute, but Marnie's hearing tunes in automatically to a pinprick of sound in the outer warehouse as her watch counts down the minutes to seven. There's little talk, only a nervous shuffling of feet. At a minute to, she hears a weak rap on the door and the weapons cocked in response, pictures them facing the door with gun muzzles pointing, faces stern. What's behind their expressions? She's running with dread, so how must they be feeling? Felix has stopped his drawing and is wedged in close to her, a small hand grasping at her coat. She's broiling and freezing in every atom of her body.

The first bullet is a dull thud, followed by the hail of a theatrical gun battle from some overegged cowboy film, back at the Gaumont picture house in Wood Green High Street. It's a short, sharp cacophonous exchange, punctuated with screams and shouts of despair and the odd part of a word in German and Dutch cut off, a window of the office splintering under a spray of firepower as she and Felix shelter under the desk in this new and equally terrifying blitzkrieg. Suddenly, shouts override the din, and the hail of bullets slows. She hears Gus's distinct voice scream 'STOP! STOP!' and then footsteps over a shale of glass, the sound of London streets left behind. What carnage will Marnie find now? What death and utter destruction beyond this door?

The silence is deafening as the seconds tick on; she can't hold back, needs to know, even if it's the worst sight possible: Willem lying in a bloody mess. Lifeless, like Grandad. 'Stay here!' she commands Felix, and lunges for the door.

Beyond *is* carnage. Amid a dull silence, she counts four uniformed Wehrmacht lying dead, splayed out as if they knew little of what was coming, eyes closed, thankfully. One in a slightly different uniform is standing against a pillar, a gun trained closely on him, hands aloft in surrender, and the silver adornments on his greatcoat tell Marnie that he is the prize.

A better sight is Willem's gun aimed at this Selig man, and Willem behind it, his knuckles white with the tight grasp. Upright and uninjured. The ice in her lungs thaws slightly, then her eyes go to the collection of bodies in the corner, surrounding another. Gus and Willem are accounted for, she takes in the stunned faces of Rudy, Jan and Dirk. So who's been hit?

'Stop the bleeding, stop the bleeding!' someone shouts in panic, and Marnie runs towards the group. The slight form of Zeeza is on the ground, head back, face contorted with pain, a small moan leaching through her gritted teeth.

'Let me see,' Marnie says firmly, pushing her way in. Zeeza's ankle is a mass of red, with a pair of bloodied hands securing a cloth tourniquet below her knee.

'Lower,' Marnie directs. 'She can't afford to lose too much blood.' Already, Zeeza's normally pink cheeks are drained of colour, beads of sweat on her brow. Marnie picks up the ankle to a cry from the injured woman, but she needs to see properly and now is not the time for gentle nursing. The bullet has gone through – good for infection, bad for blood loss, though it can't have hit an artery or they'd already have a corpse on their hands.

'I need alcohol and bandages,' she instructs. The group must have predicted injury of some kind, because both arrive swiftly in front of her. 'Brace yourself,' she says and the tiny, tough woman nods, her mouth a thin line. Marnie clears the mass of blood, douses the wound in alcohol – to a colourful curse into the air from Zeeza – and then wraps the wound tightly. 'Have you a doctor ready to help out?' she says into the space.

'Yes,' Rudy replies. 'A few minutes' drive. We can use their troop vehicle outside to transport her.'

'Then do it quickly,' Marnie says. 'It's way beyond anything I can help with.'

By some miracle, or due to the element of surprise, Zeeza appears to be the only resistance casualty, and by the time Marnie turns again, the man who must be Selig has been forced onto a chair, hands tied behind his back. He's not struggling or complaining, nor looking with defeat into his lap. Quite the opposite. A sneer ripples around his prominent lips, and his narrowing eyes are bored into Willem, with a look that's not even hatred. It's pure disdain. Marnie reads his message loud and clear: contempt for everyone and everything around. Does he know that Willem is a worthy match for his scorn?

It's like watching two gladiators in the arena, a battle of wills as much as strength. As Zeeza is carried out of the warehouse, time becomes critical.

'Here we are,' Willem begins flatly in German. 'It appears, Herr Selig, that you are suddenly quite alone. I have something I want from you, and you need something from me.'

'It's *Captain* Selig. And what could I ever need from the likes of you people?' The lack of fear in his voice is chilling. Marnie witnesses the arrogance and self-belief in the way he cocks his head, almost inviting violence.

But Willem is too focused on his goal to notice. To him, the plan is paramount. 'A friend of mine is staying at one of your residences, and we would like her back,' he says.

'And how can I possibly do that?' Selig shrugs against his tethers.

303

'A simple note from you is all we want. A clear instruction to have her brought here. The rest we'll do.'

Selig breathes heavily through his nose, sneers audibly. 'And then what? You'll cut my throat in the next breath. Why on earth would I consider playing this game?'

Marnie sees Willem's impatience begin to surface. Time is ticking, they have bodies to dispose of and a scene to clean. 'I'm a man of my word,' he says, still calm. 'We know full well that news of your death will spark a bloody wave of retribution. And unlike you, we don't welcome that.'

Here Selig actually laughs, loudly and thick with derision. 'What makes you think it won't happen if you let me live?'

'Because you'll look a fool.' Willem's voice is icy and convincing. 'I know that what you or your Nazi cronies can't abide is failure. And tonight is your failure, *Captain* Selig, and yours alone.'

Selig sniffs, nostrils flaring. 'How can I be sure that you won't let this little episode be known, either now or in the future? That I won't lose either way?'

'You're just going to have to trust me, aren't you?'

Briefly – but only briefly – the Nazi man looks beaten. Outsmarted. Only those looking at him face on would have glimpsed the lightning look of defeat, recovered quickly with a fresh injection of arrogance.

'You're welcome to her. She's no use to us any more,' he relents. 'Pathetic woman. She gave us everything at the first sign of any inconvenience to herself.'

Casting around the room, Marnie can see that no one believes this of Corrie.

Willem ignores Selig's denunciation, reaching behind for the paper and pen they have ready. Gus loosens the hand ties and Willem directs Rudy to train his own gun on the captive, while pulling a small table towards the chair. He leans close into Selig's broad face, and thrusts the pen at his hand.

'Now write,' he commands.

53

Moving

Corrie

She's chewing slowly on the last morsel of her bread ration, moving it warily around her cheeks to where it doesn't hurt, when the key is rammed noisily in the lock with real force. Corrie startles, then hauls herself upright automatically, working so as not to appear stooped or beaten. Perhaps this is it, the roasting? They've had enough, decided they won't waste any more time on her. Her mind calculates the reason why and lands on an unpalatable possibility: Willem has been recaptured, if he ever did escape, and they are pressing *his* body and mind instead, for more information than she could ever provide. Wringing the life out of him.

You can't think it. Stay strong for him.

Yet as the door swings open, the lieutenant stands before her with an expression of anger rather than happy expectation, as a soldier appears from behind and throws a pair of old, oversized shoes towards her feet.

A grubby overcoat is tossed onto the bed. 'Put them on,' the lieutenant barks.

Corrie's mind reckons again: if she's destined to face a noose or a bullet, they wouldn't bother with shoes. The dead don't worry about dirty feet. And yet she heard Selig clearly: no one

305

was to do anything concrete without his say-so. So where is he, and why is she seemingly on the move?

Shoes slapping against the flagstones, she's led from the cell into a silent passageway, squinting to shield her eyes from the white, bleachy glare of corridor lighting. Faces of the few young soldiers milling about are blank – neither pitiful or hateful – and Corrie wonders if this is part of the process, to wrong-foot her, just for the sheer fun of it. To instil some hope in what will be the last moments of her life. But she determines they will not have the last laugh, letting her thoughts steer to those she loves – her precious spores sprayed across a country and a world at war, some of which are ashes now: Willem, Kees, Hendrik and Felix and Zeeza. They are lodged firmly in her heart, in readiness.

She's distracted when the freezing air hits her skin, taken aback by the clarity of the night sky, her skin pocked by a light sleet that's whipped up. It feels cold but invigorating, stirring a dormant spirit. Acutely so. *Already they haven't won.* She'll die feeling alive.

But it's not the courtyard they head for, where Corrie imagines the deed has taken place many times before, other resistance hanged or shot in cold blood. Instead, she's led to a waiting vehicle – a staff car rather than a transport wagon, and that further piques her curiosity. What on earth is going on?

The lieutenant now takes his place beside her in the back seat that smells of old leather and diesel, mingling with the scent of the musty coat around her shoulders. He says nothing, a look of complete derision on stony features, while his hand rests next to the holster on a pristine, shiny belt. They drive out of the Huis gates, and then south, beyond the canals. She doesn't know what time it is, beyond a point in the evening when most Dutch are holed up in front of their stoves, shutters closed against the war and weather. Aside from Germans on patrol or parading at leisure for women who choose to engage them, the streets are almost empty. The driver clearly knows where they are going, because no directions are given, and they motor on in silence. After ten minutes, almost no lights are visible beyond the car window, not even a chink. Breath eludes her for a second at the thought of an end so lonely, beyond people and their homes. Death is death, but to be left for the neighbourhood dogs to find and sniff at . . .

The car comes to an abrupt halt. 'Out,' the officer says in a short, sharp tone.

Despite every preparation in her mind, Corrie's body has its own ideas, her flesh quivering and heart stomping to its own beat. *You can shake but do not weep. Do not beg.*

She peers into the blackness and just makes out the warehouse where she's met with the partisan cell before. *Oh Christ.* She lurches at the silence and almost loses her footing on the icy ground. Have they brought her to witness an ambush inside, fellow resistance perhaps already slaughtered, with her own body adding to the pile of corpses? At such a sight, her tenacity may crumble into dust. But where is Selig? There's no staff car – nothing in fact. Why wouldn't he be here to crow at his own blood-soaked success?

For the first time, the lieutenant comes close enough that his nose wrinkles with her unwashed odour. He extends a hand and tugs at the arm of the coat, pulls her roughly towards the door. In his grip, though, she detects some reticence. Instead of enjoying himself or what's to come, he's wary. Maybe a little scared.

He knocks at the door, shifting from foot to foot in the few seconds it takes to open slightly. In the narrow crack, there's Selig's big face, his body in shirtsleeves, braces loosely over his shoulders. His hair looks dishevelled, as if he's been enjoying the company of a woman, voice clipped and short with physical effort.

'Ah, thank you, Meyer,' he says curtly, and puts out a hand to grab at Corrie's coat.

307

'Are you . . . all right, sir?' the officer questions. To him, it must register as unusual to say the least, both Selig's request and his behaviour, the location more so.

'Perfectly fine. Like I say, I have plans for her. And no one needs to know about this. No one. Understand? A private endeavour – for the Führer.'

The clack of Meyer's heels resounds on the cobbles. 'Yes, sir. For the Führer.'

'Thank you. You're dismissed. Heil Hitler.'

Meyer turns away, and as Corrie is pulled beyond the doorway, she sees the glint of a knifepoint pushed into the back of Selig's shirt, opens her eyes fully to the scene in front.

And her mouth, quite literally, drops open in disbelief.

54

Gladiators

17th January 1941, Amsterdam

Marnie

Marnie watches a myriad of expressions on Corrie's face as she absorbs the tableau in front of her with shock and disbelief. Clearly, she can't fathom being among so many of those whom she loves and trusts. Marnie, too, is full of wonder at this woman she's despaired of ever setting eyes upon: Daisy to her Lizzy. In a first, brief glance Corrie looks older than imagined, and petite, with short, blonde hair that's dulled with grime, skin dry and eyes sunken with fatigue or worry, plus the obvious signs of abuse, one eye a bluish shadow. Though it's hard to imagine anyone looking healthy under those conditions; Marnie's own appearance is nothing to write home about these days, a long way from the prim and well-turned-out Miss Fern from the sixth floor.

Of course, Willem is the first to rush towards her, Corrie disappearing under his broad frame. Even beneath his clothes, Marnie sees utter relief ripple in Willem's back and hears their tears of delight. The love of his life – marked but safe, for now at least. She can't imagine what that must feel like, similar to seeing Susie or her parents liberated from danger perhaps. Only tenfold. There's a second while she laments never being able to experience such emotion, and then swipes away the self-pity.

Now is not the time.

With a gun still trained on Selig, the others crowd in one by one with their heartfelt welcome, kissing and hugging, Felix swallowed into the cluster of bodies, gripping onto Corrie's body tightly. Another pang next to Marnie's heart.

She checks herself. Is it jealousy? More like envy in feeling the outsider. Again, the reminder that she brought herself here. No one put a gun to her head. She is exposed to this by her own design.

There's little time for the joy and relief in the room to sink in. Selig sees to it, having had enough of happy reunions.

'So what now?' His boorish voice projects across the room. 'I hate to spoil everyone's happy families, but shouldn't we get on with this charade?'

Marnie is aghast at his audacity. Isn't he afraid, in a roomful of resistance, all thirsty for revenge? Any one of them could pull the trigger in a split second, and the restraint is obvious, particularly in Willem. She watches his expression darken in a second as Selig is dragged to his feet and the two men come face to face, gladiators in a different arena now.

What Marnie detects on Selig's face is certainty; the power of the Reich's retribution, and the scores who will be rounded up and shot, civilians and innocents, if he dies tonight. Willem, Gus and Rudy know it too, bent on avoiding a widespread massacre.

'As much as I would love to pass the time, we have to leave,' Willem says.

'Such a shame,' Selig sneers. 'And we were just getting to know each other.' He spits on the floor in defiance. 'I'll just have to content myself with having known your sister much more.'

All faces in the room swivel nervously towards Willem, in time to watch his body go rigid, neck muscles tense under the dim flickering of the lightbulb.

Selig sees it too, and clearly he can't resist. 'She was so much nicer, and very obliging.' He adopts a dirty leer. 'Extremely keen to please.'

'You LIAR!' Willem lunges violently, but Gus is quicker, has seen his friend's fury stoked.

He leaps onto Willem in an instant, the only one tall enough to restrain him from killing Selig with his bare hands. 'It's not worth it,' Gus hisses into Willem's ear. 'You have Corrie. She's safe. It's what we came for. *Leave it.*'

Selig, though, will not. For a minute, Marnie imagines he has some kind of death wish, but then she sees it peak again – his supreme confidence, barely shrouding an innate evil. No wonder he's rising fast in the Nazi ranks. Once, she heard Rudy tell the group that Selig was considered too mean even by Nazi standards in his last posting, the rumour being he'd been passed on to the Abwehr for 'taming'.

It hasn't worked. Tonight, he's far from tamed.

'Do you know what she did to me, what she offered?' Selig rambles on, a smirk spreading across his lips. 'And I took it. I took *her.*'

'SHUT YOUR FUCKING MOUTH!' Willem veers violently from Gus's grasp and spits the words into Selig's face, nose to nose.

Yet again, Selig is unstoppable in his low, goading vitriol. 'She was beautifully sweet at first. Oh, and she tasted so, so good. You can always tell when they're a virgin. From innocence to a whore in one fell swoop . . .'

His words die under Willem's knuckle on his jaw, the force felling Selig and knocking Dirk's hands from the restraints, causing the tethers to come loose. In seconds, Willem and Selig are spinning and brawling, no longer the gladiators' arena, but a bear pit of ancient days, clawing at each other's eyes and faces. No one can get near enough to the circling mass of limbs to restrain either, guns twitching nervously on the perimeter of this impromptu ring. Marnie glimpses Corrie's face across the room and sees abject fear – she's come from one pit, tossed into another. Precious minutes with her loved one, only to lose him again?

And Marnie, what does she think as her lungs suspend? She doesn't know, except the thing she most wants in the world right now is for Willem not to die. Not after they've survived tonight. Beyond that, she can't – or doesn't want to – examine the reasons why.

Gus is almost dancing around the two entwined men, trying to grab at either and stop the wrestling. He pulls back sharply; in the dim light, the glint of a blade shines brightly. In Selig's hand, perhaps hidden in his boot all this time. By the sleight of the other hand in a split second, the metal is up against Willem's chest, pressing into his shirt. The room freezes, a gasp from somewhere, Selig's face showing a malevolent triumph.

Until a second lightning move and suddenly the Nazi is flat on the floor, Willem looming over him, and the blade switched to his hand now, the point nudging into the skin of Selig's thickened neck, threatening to draw blood and extinguish life.

Willem is panting hard, the knife pulsing inwards at a rhythm as he struggles to bring his heaving breath under control. 'So,' he manages. 'How much of a whore is my sister now? Tell me, you bastard – you forced yourself on her, didn't you? DIDN'T YOU?'

Anyone else might see the danger in admitting such a thing to Willem, akin to Selig thrusting the blade into his own body. Not him. He smiles and scoffs under the knife. 'Oh, she was so naïve, Bakker. Thought she could flirt and fuss around me for secrets and suffer no consequences. But she wasn't so strong physically.'

The room is held in abeyance, all eyes on Willem's reaction.

'Give me one reason why I shouldn't rid the world of a Nazi and a woman-hater right here?' he seethes.

Still, there is no fear in Selig that Marnie can see, only sneering contempt. 'Do it,' he urges through set teeth. 'Do it, and see where it gets your precious resistance. Do it, you fucking coward.'

The blade twitches, Willem on the very edge of control.

'Don't.' Corrie's small voice punctuates the air. Willem doesn't take his eyes off Selig's sweating face, but Marnie detects the slightest change in him. If you could actually see ears prick up, then this is it.

'It's not worth it, Willem,' Corrie goes on in a quiet, calm voice. 'He's not worth it.'

The knife twitches again, Selig's skin denting inwards.

'Kees wouldn't want this sacrifice,' she induces him. 'Don't do it in her name.'

Nothing stirs beyond breath for what seems like an age. Outside, a plane drones overhead, Allied or Luftwaffe busy with the grinding process of war. Still, the weapon holds firm, Willem's body and reason fighting his contained rage.

'*Please*, Willem,' Corrie urges.

Marnie is watching Selig's face intently and his bizarre, grotesque enjoyment; he might die, his expression is saying, but he'll take everyone with him. The Reich high command are right: he is the meanest of bastards.

He pokes at Willem's fire one more time. 'Do it, you weakling. Do it for your cheap whore of a sister. For Kee—'

'Don't you dare say her name!' Willem screams. The blade swipes.

'No!' Corrie shrieks. 'NO!'

She and Gus rush forward as the floor smears with scarlet, Selig's hands around his face, hiding what surely must be a look of shock now. He'd invited it, and Willem obliged, and yet he's still alive, not shuddering and gurgling the last breath of a throat cut from ear to ear.

Corrie yanks hands away – Willem and Selig's – to reveal a deep crimson gash running from top to bottom of his left cheek, seeping rather than pumping blood. The Nazi man is swallowing back the inevitable pain, quashing any display of distress escaping from his bloodied lips. Willem stumbles backwards, guided by Gus, as Corrie and Marnie tend to the wound. No one in that room would lose sleep over Selig coming to harm, but for him to die now would be a disaster, after all they've achieved.

Marnie grabs at a cloth thrust into her hand, presses firmly at the wound as Selig flinches. The room waits. After a count of ten, she lifts the fabric and watches for the flow of blood. Stemming now. Is it? Yes. She can see the wound is deep – Willem scored with malice, certainly. It will scar, but it's not fatal. Looking at close quarters into Selig's eyes, Marnie thinks she can see his realisation, and maybe some relief beyond his mask of malevolence.

'What . . . what do we do now?' Rudy says nervously into the room. 'Does he need the hospital?'

They all look to Marnie, whose role as some kind of 'sawbones' medic seems to have been established since her arrival, largely her own doing, in a desperate attempt to justify her presence among them.

'He'll live,' she says, then swipes a look at Selig. 'More's the pity.'

From where or what version of Marnie Fern does that come?

Willem is in the corner of the room, his trembling hands smeared with blood, leaving Gus to take control of the debacle. He's silent and contrite, clearly aware how close he was to bringing down the wrath of the Reich onto the resistance with a flash of his temper and hating himself for it. Corrie sits close, murmuring reassurances into Willem's ear and wiping at his tainted, wringing hands.

'We clear out of here, all of us, as planned,' Gus commands. He looks directly at Selig, but without sympathy. 'As much as it pains me to do it, we will call help for you as soon as we're clear. Because we are human. I'd remember that if I were you.' He moves closer to Selig's face, which is now a congealed mask of red, voice down to a low growl. 'Remember, too, that if there is revenge, if civilians or resistance are held to account for any of this, we can end your career with the Reich in a single telephone call. If it becomes known that you let an entire cell disappear into the ether, you will end up licking the Führer's boots for forgiveness. If you're lucky.'

Finally, Selig is moved to silence.

55

Daisy and Lizzy

18th January 1941, en route to Artis Zoo, Amsterdam

Marnie

By the time most of the group clamber into the truck, Willem has regained his composure and a measure of his authority. He clutches at Corrie's hand as she squeezes beside him and, sitting opposite in the darkness, Marnie can just make out his face, which is drained but awash with relief. She wants to introduce herself to Corrie, but it doesn't seem like the right time, not when they are newly reunited. That familiar gooseberry feeling returning.

Perhaps Willem senses it. 'So, I think a formal introduction is in order,' he says as the truck pulls away.

Corrie raises her head, with an expression of bewilderment.

'Daisy, I'd like you to meet Lizzy,' he announces with relish. 'Your partner on the airwaves.'

'Lizzy? You're here?' Corrie murmurs, glancing quickly at Willem and then back at Marnie as her mouth widens, overriding the tired, maimed eyes and cracked skin to light up her entire face. No doubt aware of her unwashed self, she only pushes out both hands and grasps at Marnie's. 'Oh, it's good to meet you at last,' she breathes. 'I feared I might never get to thank you.'

'For what?'

'For keeping me going, your words of encouragement. Helping us. For being there.' Her sinewy fingers are bony, and yet her firm grip has the loving touch of a long-lost friendship. Throughout the months, Marnie has often wondered if she's simply imagined the bond behind the Morse. But clearly not; Corrie had sensed it too, strung together in the dot–dot–dash. And if she hadn't already known it, what with Felix, and Willem and Gus, Marnie is glad she's faced risk and jeopardy to be here, in the back of a truck, escaping danger. Truly.

'Yes, me too,' is all she can manage, openly lost for words. Perhaps later, she can elaborate, express everything running through her now.

Willem isn't finished, though, still overrun with enthusiasm and delight. 'We can dispense with the subterfuge for a minute. This is Marnie Fern, from the illustrious BBC no less.' He puts his arm around Corrie's tiny shoulders. 'And this is Corrie Bakker, my beautiful and brave mother.'

Marnie almost chokes, her turn to run with confusion, for her brain to scrabble in catching up with her heart, soaring and plunging in equal measure. *Did he really say mother?* Corrie is his *mother?*

Yes, she sees it now – the likeness, even in the darkness, and the lines of parenthood etched on Corrie's otherwise young face. All manner of emotions push their way upwards; she might laugh, or cry, be gloriously happy and riddled with fury at the same time. Anger towards Willem, who's kept such a secret from her for all this time. Why? And yet when she looks at him, a man who is pulling his long-lost treasure so close into his body, she can't show any disdain. Like everyone else who was present in that bloodied room, she can only feel triumph.

It's two a.m. before they arrive back at the zoo – Marnie, Willem, Corrie, Gus and an exhausted Felix – the last of the group to be dropped at varying safe points across Amsterdam. In the attic, Willem and Gus dampen the Levys' obvious anxiety, as Corrie is tearfully reunited with Hendrik.

317

'We'll be gone from here soon,' Willem assures Paulus Levy, though Marnie notes he doesn't pledge the family's safety. She heard him and Gus agree in the truck that they had twenty-four hours at the most before Artis – and everyone in it – becomes compromised. Before Selig could come prowling.

Once she's cleaned up and Felix is settled, Marnie retreats to her bunk, bent on sleep and resigned only to rest. She's exhausted, but wired – that age-old thrill of a crucial deadline back at the BBC. Except what just happened in her once humdrum life was not a thrill. It was sad and ugly, death vivid on those Wehrmacht faces, violence edging into every second of that vile encounter with Selig. And yet, despite Grandad's peaceful image in the morgue, she has to remember that his death too was vicious and unnecessary. 'An eye for an eye' – isn't that what people say?

Wouldn't it be better that everyone kept both eyes, for a clearer view of what humanity should be?

Through the flimsy curtain, Marnie can't help hearing Willem and Corrie's murmurings, feeling like an eavesdropper on their intimacy again, even though that affection has now shifted on its axis, as mother to son. They are lying on his mattress, a blanket over them both; Marnie can see the silhouette of his long arm stretched around her, as if he's determined never to let her go again.

'With the animal stink in here, all of you might not be able to smell me as much,' Corrie jokes in a low voice.

Willem laughs, without a care; Marnie pictures Corrie's head on his broad chest, his nose nuzzling into her hair and the generations falling away – Willem the same age as Felix, once curled up next to his mother, and now her cradled in his adult arms, he as both child and protector. It's abundantly clear why Willem wouldn't let her go, why he travelled hundreds of miles and risked death to rescue her. With true fortitude. The love she sees now is something easily construed; what she had with

Grandad, perhaps more than with her own parents. And what Marnie wouldn't sacrifice now to have it back.

Can she stay angry at Willem for such a natural instinct?

She must drift, because it's six a.m. before Marnie wakes to the sound of the Levys preparing to bed down for the daylight hours. Corrie is still asleep, Felix and Hendrik, too, with Gus and Willem huddled in the far corner, their voices low. When Marnie rises to use the makeshift bathroom, Willem catches her eye.

'Too early for a walk, check on those penguins before opening?' he says.

She nods. 'I need some air.'

It's threatening more snow as they wander past the elephant house, the wind brisk enough to swipe away Marnie's fatigue.

'So go on, then, ask me,' Willem says quietly. 'I know you want to.'

She pulls her coat tighter. He's right – she is burning with curiosity. Equally, does she really want to know why he harboured such an enormous secret, all the while imagining he and Corrie were lovers with a past? Or has she been spectacularly deluded, by Willem principally, but also by herself?

In the end, her need is too great. 'Tell me then. In London, why didn't you let on that Daisy was your mother?'

Willem turns and looks at her. Into her. 'Trust,' he says.

Her anger surfaces, swift and hot. 'Trust?' Marnie throws at him, trying to dampen her voice in the empty walkways. 'You thought I couldn't be trusted? To what . . . to tell someone? Who the hell would I tell, Willem, and why?'

His eyes narrow, cutting off her bitterness. 'Not you, Marnie,' he insists. 'I doubted my trust in others. Look, you've seen how the Nazis exploit emotions, what Selig did to my sister. Daisy was our best local operator, and I am an agent, and we both needed to serve. Only a handful in the resistance knew of our relationship – Gus, Rudy, Jan and Zeeza – and we made a pact to keep it that way. Corrie adopted her maiden name as war broke out to distance ourselves. That way, if either of us were captured, they might not twist the screws of emotional blackmail.'

'But they did find out, didn't they?' Marnie says. 'Which means your mother was right – there is a mole somewhere.'

He reaches for her hand. 'Almost certainly. But you can see why I tried so hard to protect her, can't you? She means the world to me. And now, with Kees gone, there's just the two of us. Trust in others was a luxury we couldn't afford.'

Marnie's fingers tingle, thinking of Grandad and their own glue. Then there's the warmth of Willem's hand on her chilled flesh, still pumping with life – exactly what she wished for not so many hours ago.

He cups both palms over hers. 'And, I have to admit that what you imagined – maybe some other kind of relationship between Daisy and me – proved a convenient distraction.'

'From what exactly?'

'You, Marnie Fern.' He switches his focus to their hands. 'If you thought my attentions were elsewhere, then I wouldn't have to face up to where they really lay.'

She stares. Silent and stunned. What is he saying? That she – plain old Marnie, spinster in the making – has become the object of those affections? 'I . . . I don't understand,' she stammers.

He laughs, low but freely. 'Perhaps if I tapped it out in Morse it might be clearer to you? I like you. I like you a lot. And I've come to admire you more over these months. All those things that *you* imagine make Marnie Fern plain only bring out the shine for me. You're honest and without airs, kind and funny, and you think of others. You're a brilliant pianist, and pretty good at sewing me up, too. So, if we weren't holed up as fugitives in my own country, wary of sticking our noses beyond these cages, I would whisk you away to some foreign clime for another sort of adventure.'

320

Instead, he takes her somewhere she's not been for an age, with his mouth close to hers, their lips just stroking, before his hand moves to draw in her neck, and there's no doubt of his intent when they fully connect. No code needed. She doesn't need to search deep in her own memory for the feeling, because she's never had this . . . such touch and elation in unison, the stirrings of everything she's imagined and hoped for in one kiss. The feel of a man she knows she loves, wholly, within her grasp.

He pulls away, eventually, a satisfied smile across his lips. No facial effort required, either, in the beaming expression of Miss Marnie Fern.

'So what do you say?' Willem ventures. 'To life's adventure?'

'Right now, I'd settle for a cup of tea at Lyons on the Strand.' It's a trite riposte that's a convenient mask for her own astonishment. Yet when she leans in to kiss him again, he can be in no doubt as to her sincerity or her answer.

56

A Mother's Intuition

18th January 1941, Artis Zoo, Amsterdam

Corrie

Corrie watches the return of Willem and Marnie from the corner of the attic, where she's perched on Hendrik's bed, relishing his closeness, like those last days in Prinsengracht. In the interim, he's aged beyond his years and she worries that – with his body weakened by hardship – his will to survive may have been dented too. The time now is a blessing.

'Willem likes her, doesn't he?' Hendrik says in a raspy tone, propped on his makeshift pillows.

Corrie turns to face him, surprise apparent. 'You don't miss much, do you?'

'I may be sick, Corrie, but I'm not blind. And there are things that even science can't explain.'

'Silly old man,' she teases, fussing with his covers. 'Now rest. I'll bring some tea over.'

As she moves towards the stove, slowed by the bruises still blooming on her flesh, Corrie glances at her son, side by side with a woman she knows, and yet doesn't. There is space between their bodies, but something happened on their walk, she can tell – a connection. Willem is changed. Even as a child, he couldn't hide things from her, his rounded cheeks always flushed when he attempted the smallest of untruths. Kees, well, she was a different matter – as a young girl and a woman in the making Corrie found it difficult to read her. Look how that turned out. By contrast, Willem was always an open book to his mother. She sees the guilt over Selig's wounding hasn't been brushed away – the jeopardy he might have placed them in – but a fog has been lifted. As if he can see a way through. Maybe some kind of future? With Marnie, perhaps?

Corrie searches inside herself: how does that make her feel, so soon after gaining him back, the joy of him in her arms again, the dream of their reunion realised, not slumped in a Nazi cell? Only to lose him in a different way.

Oddly, she's not perturbed, because she's trusted Lizzy from the beginning. In the guise of Daisy, it's something Corrie is unable to explain, and may never experience again over the airwaves. But it was there, and seeing Lizzy in person now, she's conscious of that unspoken bond. The fact that Felix has taken to Marnie only makes Corrie more certain; increasingly, she puts her faith in the judgement of this small boy, because he's lost everything, left with only himself to rely on.

'Here, let me do that.' Marnie approaches the kettle and gestures for Corrie to sit down. 'How are you feeling after some sleep?'

'Better than I look, honestly.' She smiles. 'I've discovered that sheer delight is a very effective medicine.'

'I think you're right,' Marnie says. 'There are plenty of hurdles ahead, but Willem is . . . well, different already. With you here.'

Corrie suppresses a wry look.

'And I'm very sorry about your daughter. From what I hear, I would have liked to have known her, someone so determined.'

'She was. Perhaps too headstrong, but that's what comes of us being a tight little group for so long.' Corrie takes the teacup from Marnie, and beckons for her to sit close. 'My husband was, well, let's say . . . unreliable. He left when Willem was small, and Kees just a baby. For years, I passed myself off as a widow to avert the shame, even though it was entirely his. He left me with two children and never a care for us. My father died soon after and the bookshop passed to me – sad at the time, but a real godsend too. I learnt the hard way never to rely on anyone but myself. It meant Willem had to grow up very quickly.' Corrie is surprised at her readiness to open up so quickly about memories that have always been painful to speak of. But with the dots and dashes replaced with words, and the freedom it now gives, she finds herself eager for Marnie to know their history.

'Is that why you're both so close?'

'Yes, I think so. When Hendrik wasn't there, Willem became the man of the house, always watching out for us.' She pauses, peering at Marnie with puzzlement. 'He told me what happened in London. I wonder, didn't you feel angry at him for leaving you, for . . . oh, what's the word? Didn't you feel *slighted*, after all you'd risked in your own life up to that point?'

Marnie stares, clearly surprised at such a searching question, that Corrie has already sensed what's between her and Willem.

'Honestly?' she says. 'Yes, for a short time, I felt let down. Back home, I imagined I simply felt rebuffed and ignored.'

'Then?' Corrie queries.

'Then, when he introduced you as his mother, I realised that what I'd been harbouring was in fact jealousy, for someone I took to be his lover. I just hadn't allowed myself to recognise it. But I understand why he did it, and the depth of his feeling for you. Because of what I had with my grandfather.'

'Gatsby? Tell me about him, if you can. I'd love to know.'

So Marnie does. Corrie hears about the real man who afforded such hope in those early months of occupation, of the substance behind his radio presence. Finally, she can form her own image of the unseen Gilbert Cooper, his life, talents and his innate humour, and she understands why Gatsby helped her feel useful, in the same way his messages maintained her faith.

'He sounds like a lovely man,' she says. 'I'm sorry for your loss, too.'

'At the time, it was the worst,' Marnie recalls. 'Grandad wasn't religious, but he had a certain belief in fate. I feel sure that if he could see us here, he would judge this as right. It's all happened for a reason.'

Corrie considers the scene in front of her, the escapees and the displaced, the pulling apart of her previous good life, and what she now has within reach, more so as Felix sneaks in between them to claim his share of their warmth. There's no comfort and no certainty for anyone, but it's replaced with a sense of togetherness she's never known before, even when her precious spores are sure to be blown far and wide once again. It will take a lot for Hitler – or Selig – to rob her of the fortune held within herself.

'I think you're right, Marnie,' she murmurs into her cup. 'This war is an abomination, the occupation an illegal sham, but there is some value in what it's brought. We just have to make sure our sacrifices don't outweigh what we've gained. That's the secret to winning.'

57

The Burrowing Beast Surfaces

18th January 1941, Artis Zoo, Amsterdam

Marnie

Poor Gus. He looks exhausted, still grimy from the warehouse and forced by necessity to zig-zag across Amsterdam through the early hours as the vital link between a handful of safe houses. Sleep for him has been entirely absent.

'What's the word on Zeeza?' Willem asks with concern.

'At the home of a sympathetic doctor and doing all right,' Gus reports. 'She'll be out of circulation for a while' – he nods pointedly towards Marnie – 'but very grateful for your quick action. She says thank you.'

'Any word on Selig?' Willem asks.

'Not yet. I let his location be known around four, when we were well clear of the warehouse. Nothing since. He might actually be lying low.'

'I hope the bastard is busy licking his own wounds.' No one censures the venom in Corrie's quiet sentiment, since she of all people deserves to voice it.

'Well, whatever he does, we need to clear out of here tonight,' Gus goes on. 'Papers are almost ready for Willem, me and Marnie. Corrie moves tomorrow . . .' he catches the flash of concern on her face, '. . . with Felix and Hendrik. The Levys are to stay, as there's no word that Artis is a target.'

He tries and fails to stifle a yawn. 'We need to transmit to confirm a pick-up point for the papers. Where is the radio now?'

'Still at the hairdresser's,' Willem says. 'I wanted to keep it as far from the zoo as possible.'

Gus frowns. 'Then someone will have to go.'

'I'll do it,' Marnie cuts in swiftly. 'I know where it is.' There's another look from Corrie, but it disappears rapidly, as if she's conceding how foolish her exposure would be. Instead, she hands over the baton to Marnie with grace.

'You can't go alone,' Gus says wearily. 'I'll come with you.'

'You will not,' Willem cuts in. 'You can barely stand upright. If anyone is going, it's me.'

They set out at ten, and it's only the warm touch of Willem's hand in hers that allows Marnie to recognise the man walking beside her. At a glance, he looks more like some bohemian academic wafting into Broadcasting House for a recording on the Roman classics.

Corrie had needed to suppress her laughter as she fitted Willem with a shaggy wig from Rutger's box of tricks, plus a pair of rounded tortoiseshell glasses, the lenses of which are thankfully not too thick. 'If I close one eye I can see pretty well,' Willem said.

Willem having not shaved, and a large trilby pulled down over his eyes, meant even Gus barely recognised his best friend. 'Although you might have to smile a bit if you want to look less shady.'

It would be an eagle-eyed Wehrmacht who picks out Willem from their rogues' gallery of wanted men, with only a fuzzy reproduction for reference.

Even so, Willem is reluctant to risk a routine check on the tram, so he and Marnie walk towards the salon, and for the first time it feels as if they are properly alone, without a prowling lion or curious monkeys for company. Nothing has been said since their early morning walk; as with Corrie, the communication is through their fingers, in the way Willem grips tightly, running the tips back and forward across her palm, electricity far more potent than any radio waves. In reply, Marnie squeezes tight at her good fortune.

Sonja must be keeping vigil because she unbolts the salon door as they walk past. '*Hoi.*' She nods to Marnie and exchanges a stream of urgent words with Willem in Dutch.

'She had a visit from two Wehrmacht yesterday,' he explains. 'Claimed they were looking for hair dye to send home to their wives, but they had eyes everywhere.' Sonja looks relieved when he pledges to remove the radio after today's use.

Down in the basement, Willem plugs in a spare set of head-phones while Marnie locates the frequency. They swap looks as a stream of Morse comes through at the appointed time, and Willem scans quickly under the dim bulb, words clearly arranged as an anagram. Unscrambled, it confirms a location for the crucial collection of papers. Marnie tunes in again for the repeat message, ensuring she hasn't missed anything. Her ears prickle, an unset-tling low buzz in the background. She hesitates, not wanting to tap out the expected, routine reply, that the dispatch is received.

'What's up?' Willem says.

'I don't know,' she says slowly. 'Something doesn't feel right.'

'What?' Through the warp of his strange spectacles, Willem's eyes are narrow with worry.

'The execution is almost too perfect, too clinical,' she says. 'The transmission didn't hesitate at all.'

'I know this operator,' he tries to assure. 'Perhaps not as skilled as you and Corrie, but they don't make mistakes.'

Now Marnie questions her own ears. She closes her eyes in replaying the dots as they came through. Is she being too cautious? And yet, paranoia is well placed when it could so easily be a trap. A worm of doubt squirms inside her.

'We've no time for delays,' he says, already a foot on the steps to warn Sonja. 'Send the routine "received" reply, then shut it down and we'll get out of here.' Marnie taps out the reply, knowing all too well that trust can be misplaced. But this is Willem, and what other choice does she have?

Upstairs, and with the boxed radio squeezed into Marnie's shoulder bag, Willem is warning Sonja to quit her flat above the salon for a few days. She presses a hastily wrapped package into Marnie's hands, tugging at her own strands of hair as she speaks.

'It's to help with more disguises,' Willem translates, peering through the opaque net of the curtain. 'The street looks clear for now. We shouldn't hang around.'

Marnie can't begin to assess what's running simultaneously through her mind and body as they exit the salon, a contraband radio under her arm, nestled next to several wigs and hair dye. Not even a fluent Dutchman could explain away the contents of her bag to an inquisitive patrol. Briskly, and with eyes sweeping the landscape left and right, she and Willem walk towards the tram, cut down a narrow canal path, and then out the other side.

'Shit!' Willem stops in his tracks as they round the corner – Rudy and Dirk straight in front of them. 'You two scared me half to death!'

'Sorry,' Rudy says, as if he's simply out on a morning stroll. 'What are you doing here? You're supposed to be lying low.'

'I could say the same for you.'

Dirk looks darkly from under the brow of his woollen hat. 'Messages need delivering,' he mutters.

'Is everyone all safe, accounted for?' Willem asks. Marnie notes his neat sidestepping of Rudy's question. He's told her repeatedly: everything is on a need-to-know basis, no matter who is facing you.

'Yes, safe. So far,' Rudy says. His face brightens. 'Can we walk with you?'

Willem falls in step with the both of them, until Marnie notices a frisson of unease ripple through the group of four. In less than a heartbeat, the mood switches. Her eyes go to Rudy, his open face, and Dirk's familiar joyless look, a glint in his continually suspicious eyes.

'Actually, while we're in this part of town, we have a few other errands to run,' Willem says, with what Marnie knows is that smile, the convincing undercover one. *Why? What's suddenly changed?*

'Oh, okay. Good luck.' Rudy turns away with a wave, though Dirk hesitates a little, his hand going up to his face, much less casual. Unease rips through Marnie, eyes strafing the scenery for Abwehr watchers. Is Dirk giving someone a signal that it's time to swoop? Was she too slow on today's transmission, long enough for the Abwehr's tracking equipment to pinpoint the salon? To have been following them?

Except that she sees nothing, hears no shouts or rush of boots, only Dirk's hand still at his face, leaning towards Willem and just catching the whispered words thrust over the chug of canal boats and swish of water. '*Noah's Ark. Exodus.*'

Dirk swivels and jogs to catch up with Rudy. Marnie doesn't need to see it or feel the touch; she senses Willem stiffen alongside, before he grabs at her hand and lunges forward.

Noah's Ark. Exodus. There's only one place resembling anything like an ark – Artis – and only one meaning for exodus. Thoughts spin in line with Marnie's feet, which are barely touching the ground. Perhaps not Dirk then; the man with the sullen face and suspicious manner is *not* the elusive mole. Quite the opposite. He could well be their saviour. And so why was he at pains to hide his face, throwing the words behind him, out of earshot of . . .

Rudy. Keen, eager and ever-present Rudy?

'Is it what I'm thinking?' she says, matching Willem's brisk pace towards Artis.

'I'm afraid it might be.' The words barely make it past his lips set together. 'We need to get back to Artis. And fast.'

58

I See Everything

18th January 1941, Artis Zoo, Amsterdam

Corrie

Corrie tunes into the general consensus as they gather around the pallets that make up the communal table. Being early afternoon, their voices are lowered to a hush, even when tensions run high amid the impromptu council of war.

'We have to leave now?' Paulus Levy is aghast, his eyes a sharp white in the gloom. The tremor in his voice trails away, glancing at his children as they sleep.

'As a precaution, yes,' Willem counsels, with a renewed calm. 'It's not certain the Germans suspect Artis as a hideout, but we can't take chances, so we all go this evening.'

'Why not instantly, if this Rudy knows?' Mevrouw Levy interjects, anxiety rising with her voice. 'He could lead them here any minute. You're not Jewish . . .'

'But we are all hiding, which makes us wanted,' Willem insists. 'And we're not sure Rudy does know the exact location. That night we arrived, the group was all agreed – each hideaway destination was kept strictly secret, and Rudy was dropped off in the truck before us. Only Jan the driver knew, and if he's the leak I'm certain we wouldn't be sitting here now.' The group hangs on his words. 'Everything does point to Rudy being the one, though I'm confused as to why there haven't been mass

331

raids already.' He shrugs. 'I can only guess that this isn't a straight-forward betrayal. We have to hope for that.'

'Willem's right,' Corrie says softly, her hand on Mevrouw Levy's quivering arm. 'I know it's a wrench for you, but we have to trust those who can help. We shouldn't act rashly.'

'You would agree with him – he's your son!' Ima Levy spits back.

Corrie recognises the accusation is born of fear. 'You're right – he is my son, and that's why I trust him,' she says quietly. 'Queen Wilhelmina happens to rely on his knowledge, too. Is that good enough for you?'

It silences Mevrouw Levy, who leaves the circle to appease her nerves by chopping the scant store of vegetables.

The flash of tempers calmed, Willem continues. 'Gus is out again securing the safe houses. The Levys will go to one in Haarlem; Hendrik, Corrie and Felix to the coast; and Gus, Marnie and I head to The Hague, to link up with a few resistance there, attempt to make fresh contact with London.'

'And how will we get away from here?' Herr Levy questions, anxiety oozing from every sweating pore. Corrie tries to imagine how she would feel in his shoes – unwanted in his own country, with dependent children and a wife seemingly on the edge. Yes, she has Felix, but he's more resourceful than most adults, and her son is the one sitting in front of her making plans, helping others. Her pride knows no bounds in watching him. Kees, too, if she were here – she'd throw both arms around her brother, accuse him of a being a 'bossy boots', and yet do almost anything he asked. Because she trusted him, they both did. Implicitly. She watches Marnie now and sees that same faith marked in her face, her concentration absolute.

Despite this burden of responsibility and the prospect of a fresh betrayal, Corrie notes a lightness in Willem. It's partly down to Marnie, clearly, but something else too; he seems to have recouped what was previously lost in the mire of war. Her son has learnt to trust again. Not everyone, because that would be crazy in these times. But Marnie certainly and, by virtue, more of humankind.

Corrie knows, too, that there's a price for her son's new-found happiness – he will slip from her grasp again. Tomorrow, the ill wind of Nazism will blow once more and disperse her beloved spores far and wide.

What can she do but be happy, if it means survival for them all?

What little belongings they have are soon packed, a quiet but nervous hum rippling across the attic as they wait for the hours to pass.

The wonderful Rutger has come up with an impromptu plan, though being a keeper, it necessarily involves animals 'and the prospect of a fairly strong smell', he reports. 'Sorry. But it is the most convincing way.'

The zoo has one closed truck for transporting animals, large enough for a small herd of mountain goats that have apparently developed a 'timely and mysterious illness', he delivers with a sardonic smile. 'One that's very possibly infectious to humans. For the benefit of the checkpoints, I'll be taking them to a specialist vet.' Behind the driver's cab is a specially built compartment to house *onderduikers*, cramped but suitable for short journeys.

'I'd defy any Nazi to make it past the goat smell, those butting, sharp horns and the fear of infection just to have a poke about in the back of the truck,' Rutger adds.

'But what if they simply shoot the goats, as being dangerous or useless?' Ima Levy pitches from the back of the room.

Everyone stops and stares. She has a point, thinks Corrie, albeit not a very helpful one. 'Then we'll have to hope one of them is an animal lover,' she says brightly. A good deal of life since May 1940 has rested on hope and faith. What's the point in changing tack now?

★ ★ ★

Gus returns mid-afternoon and reports the plans are all in place. He, Willem and Marnie spend some time with Rutger arranging the timings, while Corrie gets to work with the hair dye, on eyebrows too, in trying to match the colour of the wigs from Sonja. The children's laughter at the adults' strange new appearances lightens the mood before they share a last meal and try to rest before the move.

Willem sidles over to Corrie's bunk just as she lies down briefly after readying Hendrik.

'How are you?' he says.

'I'm fine.'

'Liar.'

'Willem Bakker! You can't call your mother a liar.'

'I can, when I know you're faking it,' he says, and nudges in, side by side on the mattress. Just like when he was a boy cooching into her bed, she thinks, except now his arm stretches around her shoulder, her small head nestling in the crook of his long limb. *How times have changed.* She breathes in every second and pockets the memory somewhere safe, in order to bring it out again intact. When she needs to. If she has to.

'Do you know, I've actually gotten used to the smell in here, the animals wafting up,' he murmurs. 'I'll almost miss it.'

'Liar,' she says.

'Huh. You always could see through me.'

'Will you try to get back to England?' she asks after a moment's silence.

'I think we'll have to. As much as I want to stay, I realise how much Holland needs the British SOE. If we have any hope of building a strong resistance against the likes of Selig, we'll need to organise the dropping of agents, radios and arms, linking us all together. And for that I need to be in London.'

'And there's Marnie,' Corrie ventures, sensing his instant twitch where her flesh nestles his shoulder. Just like the tiny tic he exhibited as a small boy whenever he felt unmasked.

'Yes, Marnie, too. I want to get her home safely.'

'Although, you didn't force her here, did you? She came of her own accord. I don't think she's expecting favours from you, or an escort.'

He inhales, deep enough that Corrie's head rises against his ribcage. 'But we – I – do owe her a lot,' Willem says. 'I asked for help when her world – and her city, don't forget – was in jeopardy. And she came through, leaving her solid life behind well before she boarded that boat from England.'

'I see,' Corrie murmurs.

His head lifts up and twists, inviting his mother's gaze. 'Do you see, really? Everything?'

'Yes, my lovely boy. I see it all.'

'And?'

She smiles. 'And I say you must go to London and change the world. But first you must look after yourself, and Marnie too, if that's what you want.'

'It is. And you, will you come with us, eventually?'

'Maybe. Perhaps when it's over. But I have Hendrik, and Felix – family now. And thoughts of you, and memories of Kees. That's all I need.'

She stares up through the skylight, and wills the earth to bring on the darkness and the cloak of safety. Let the wind blow and the spores separate.

As long as they keep whole.

59

Flight

Marnie

The obvious anxiety in Mevrouw Levy's fingers acts as a distraction to Marnie's own disquiet, the poor woman's digits twitching as if she were warming up to play a piano concerto before a packed concert hall – or when Marnie herself is about to take a turn on the transmitter.

'Just take a deep breath, Ima,' Paulus urges, grasping and rubbing at her hands, infusing any certainty he has into his wife. Alongside, their children clutch at their mother's skirt, unsure of what to make of the current running through the room.

Mevrouw Levy is not alone; a low churn of nausea has sat within Marnie for the past few hours, as she'd tried to keep busy with Corrie in washing and dressing an increasingly frail Hendrik. They're all fretful and lacking in sleep; the day seems endless and Marnie wonders when she might ever feel rested again. Right now, there's nothing to do but keep pushing towards a better level of safety.

Willem and Gus are out helping Rutger load the goats, hats pulled down and scarves wound tightly, and it's a godsend the weather still demands plenty of layers.

The men return as darkness descends. Marnie's eyes snap to

336

Willem's face, at the reassuring smile he wears for the Levys, then at Corrie, who's too busy to note his pretence.

'Everything all right?' Marnie nudges in as he pours dregs from the coffee pot.

'With the Levys, yes,' he whispers. 'They'll go first, then Corrie. But there's a change of plan for you, me and Gus. The Hague is compromised. We need to link up straightaway with the escape line.'

'And where's that?'

'The Belgian border, and then across the Pyrenees to Spain.'

He says it like they're about to hop on the number 14 to Piccadilly, but Marnie almost chokes on her own coffee. Europe has always been on her wish list of holiday destinations, but perhaps at leisure, with a nice hotel or two.

'How?' she questions. 'Are the roads passable?'

Gravely, Willem shakes his head. 'No roads. On foot.'

'Shanks' pony', as Grandad would have said. *Oh Christ.*

Willem swallows. He's not finished yet, she can tell.

'What other surprises have you in store for me, Mr Bakker?'

'I hate to ask, but can you face one more transmission?' His eyes relay the importance, how they might not have a place to go if she can't or won't.

'How risky is it?' she asks. 'That the Abwehr are listening after this afternoon?'

'Moderate. Less, if you're quick.' He smiles and drains his cup. 'And you're still my best pianist.'

'Don't let your mother hear you say that.'

The Levys are led out of the attic late afternoon, and the sight of them leaving two by two doesn't escape Marnie. Noah and his entourage had the same desperate need of escape. The attic feels suddenly deserted, so that she's glad when Willem returns from the yard ten minutes later.

'They're away safely,' he reports. 'Rutger will drive them as far as the city limits, where they'll be met by more transport.

All being well, he'll be back in an hour. Get your scarf and hat – we need to go a few streets away to transmit.'

With the radio in her shoulder bag and hats pulled low, she and Willem leave cautiously by the keepers' back entrance, move quickly across the road and into a warren of narrow lanes towards a small café. Both are shown into a windowless back room, empty of people but rank with stale cigar smoke.

Willem keeps watch as Marnie sets up quickly, the café owner poking his head through the door with a brief thumbs-up sign. The message is in Dutch, strange and vague, as always, but once encrypted it's just a jumble of letters again, and Marnie takes herself into the detached universe of radio waves.

'Do we need to wait for a reply?' she says once it's dispatched.

'Unfortunately, yes,' Willem replies. 'We've no meeting site until then.'

The minutes are agonising. The proprietor brings them coffee, and though Marnie is wary of drinking too much, it's good ersatz and she may need its stimulant qualities later. Finally, the airwaves dash out a reply, Willem snatching at the answer to encrypt rapidly.

'Damn!' he breathes with frustration. 'They can't meet until tomorrow. We need to transmit again, insisting it's today.'

'Surely there's somewhere we can bed down tonight?' Marnie asks.

He shakes his head in defeat. 'Nowhere that Rudy won't already know of. It has to be today. But your fingers will have to be like lightning on this one.'

She knows it, sits for a minute gathering her focus. *Come on, Gilbert, if you are some kind of presence, I need you here. Now.*

'Now, Marnie,' Willem urges gently into her ear.

Her fingers fly, no pretence of brain-eye-finger coordination. Just pure instinct on this one. The reply comes instantly, forcing her to stay on air. *Say again*, it reads.

She looks to Willem for confirmation. Is this the Abwehr

listening in, goading them into betraying their own position? 'What should I do?'

'We've got no choice. Go again.' But he's not sure either, she can tell.

Again, the wait, still on air. Longer than they've ever dared. Too long.

Finally, the answer comes through: a rendezvous, and today.

'Right, let's go,' Willem says, in the exact second the bar owner crashes in with news that troops can be heard approaching, and Marnie gives thanks for those noisy Nazi boots that warn of the enemy.

'This way,' the barman beckons, and leads them through the kitchen and out into a back alleyway, slamming the door behind. Willem grabs Marnie's hand, sending a message in his tight grasp, and they merge into the warren of streets as a smiling, loving couple. A Nazi troop truck passes the front of the zoo and they freeze, but it bumbles past, leaving a trailing white cloud in the darkness.

Back at Artis, Rutger has returned, with news that the Levys are on their way to Haarlem. In the yard, the slow business of loading more hideaways into the space behind the goats is in progress. Stooped and unsteady, Hendrik is being helped up while Rutger controls the curious goats amid an earthy stench.

Willem approaches with news of the latest plans. 'All of you in here?' Rutger's brows go up. 'It'll be a squeeze, but if we have to.'

The compartment is already packed tight – Corrie, Willem, Gus and Hendrik standing like sardines – when Hendrik begins struggling for breath and needs to lie flat, leaving not an inch of space, let alone any spare oxygen.

'Marnie and Felix can sit in the cab with me.' Rutger thinks on his feet. 'I'll say it's my sister and nephew just getting a lift.'

They've driven barely a few streets when a new checkpoint looms ahead, marked out with searchlights. Rutger flashes a look at Marnie: *could it be just a coincidence?*

'Let me do the speaking,' he instructs.

The young Wehrmacht who approaches seems nice enough, until he notes a staff car pulling up at the checkpoint, followed by a jeep of armed soldiers. In the presence of Nazi hierarchy, he gets officious. 'Papers,' he demands. 'Open the back.'

Rutger appears casual enough as he jumps down from the cab, but Marnie sees the rigid tension in him. Crucially, she feels it in Felix's wiry hand almost crushing her own.

And no wonder. The officer to emerge from the staff car is all too familiar, though his face is no longer coated in blood or sweat. Instead, as he draws himself up, eyes scouring the cityscape, the light beams pick out the line of a raw, prominent scar. It makes him look instantly meaner. Marnie doesn't doubt he *is* meaner for it.

Felix's entire body begins to tremble as Lothar Selig strides forward with confidence towards the truck, muttering something in the ear of another Wehrmacht as he walks past the cab. Marnie assumes his presence means his Abwehr were tracking the signal of the last dispatch, just not accurately enough to pinpoint the café. His arrival at the checkpoint can only be bad timing. The worst kind.

'It's all right, Felix,' she whispers into his ear, though it's only words against a groundswell of trauma rising from this poor boy. She pulls him firmly into her body as protection for all.

They hear the back of the truck opening, soldiers reeling noisily from the stink, their complaints and Selig's insistent bark that they 'Get on with it.' Rutger is weaving some lie in German about the goats belonging to his uncle, easy enough in the unmarked vehicle, with no visual ties to Artis.

A determined stomping alongside the van causes Marnie to tighten her grip on Felix, but it's no good. They're ordered out of the cab and towards the back, where soldiers are already battling with curious goat horns. And where Selig is. Marnie is thankful Corrie persuaded her at the last minute to darken

340

her hair with dye, but if the Abwehr man looks her straight in the face – as he did that night – then the cover is blown. Everyone's cover.

She feels fear switch to a ripple of intent in Felix, feet shuffling, the sinewy muscles of his thin shoulders tensing, as in the sweet shop. She knows exactly what his instincts are, and what his young mind might be calculating: a distraction, drawing away the eye of the tiger from the sitting prey. Selig the tiger. Felix will have done it a thousand times in pilfering apples from a grocer, for survival. But there's a world of difference in being chased by an irate shopkeeper and soldiers with guns.

Don't do it, Felix. Don't run. Not this time.

The small boy must see it just as Marnie does – Selig's eyes lifting up towards her, the momentary glint of recognition and clear signs of suspicion. As a large hand goes up to touch the ugly line of stitches sweeping down his cheek, she feels Felix squirm from under her grip. Like lightning, he launches his small body at Selig's legs with every ounce of strength. The thickset German is toppled more by surprise and tumbles backwards to the ground, while Marnie – and everyone else – watches in shock as Felix grabs Selig's handgun from his holster. Again, the boy must know that one wayward child is a weak target, but a child who steals an officer's handgun warrants a chase.

'NO!' Marnie screams, as much to Felix as the soldiers leaping out of the truck in pursuit, one stopping to cock his weapon and fire at the tiny slip of a boy now dodging traffic and bullets, disappearing into the darkness. She hears shouts, and a shrill cry of alarm – from Felix, or passers-by caught in the skirmish?

With Selig still down, Rutger exploits the scattering of troops, securing the back of the truck and dragging Marnie into the cab within seconds, where he revs the engine and screeches away from the checkpoint.

She squints hard into the wing mirror, seeing Selig pull himself up to standing as one of the soldiers reappears, dragging a writing, indignant Felix by the scruff of his neck. The Abwehr man looks with venom at the quarry that has slipped his grasp yet again, then back at the boy who might be a token catch, but a golden ticket all the same.

'Felix!' Marnie cries. 'We can't leave him there!'

'The rest of us being caught won't help him,' Rutger pants. 'He knew what he was doing.'

All she can do is watch helplessly as Felix, and possibly his future, recedes into the distance.

She doesn't remember much of the journey ahead, only that it's fast and short through blackened streets, taking corners at speed, with Rutger's frantic breathing beside her, and the imprint of Felix's impish face in her mind: a pure mix of defiance and fear, and then a new horror dawning within. *How will I tell Corrie?*

They swerve into the same garage she and Gus had first arrived at in Amsterdam, the doors clamping down on the world outside. Marnie jumps down, and horns or no horns, stink or not, she fights her way towards the truck's secret compartment.

Corrie's face is already a rictus of fear; she will have heard the shot, felt the truck lurch with urgency. 'What is it?' she says in a voice thick with dread. 'Where's Felix?'

What can Marnie say? 'I'm so sorry,' she tries. 'He just went. He bolted.'

60

The Guillotine

Corrie

It's like waiting for the guillotine, or the firing squad, instead of the urgent travel papers that Gus, Willem and Marnie so desperately need. Corrie, though, awaits news that promises to be either feast or famine – the sight of Felix's face peering through the door, dirty and contrite, or word that his maimed body is in the morgue, beaten into submission by a regime exercising no restraint. It's Kees all over again and, with it, the agony of ignorance.

Willem tries his best to comfort in the interim, even though it's gone midnight and half his brain is on the arduous journey ahead. 'I'm certain he won't talk, at least until we're all safely away,' he assures.

'But he's only a child!' Corrie spits back, the worry feeding her anger.

'And he's more of a man than some in our midst,' her son counters quickly. 'There's nothing we can do until we get news. If I can escape the Germans, I'm damned sure Felix will try. He may surprise us some more.'

'But what if he's already . . .'

'You can't think like that,' he says. 'All we can do is put out the word, and use our leverage where we have any.'

343

Images of Felix – *her* boy now – flood Corrie's mind. But she's forced to accept the sometimes cruel rules of resistance; saving people takes precedence over a solitary person, even a child. And Felix knew the risk of running, calculating that his legs were speedier than the Wehrmacht. This time, he was wrong.

There's only one advantage to this torment, she thinks mournfully, and that's as a distraction to the impending goodbye. The one where she gets to look at her only present child and wonder if his future will rob her of being a mother forever. Corrie has seen so much good in past days, but this is the reality of occupation – domination and subservience to that bastard in Berlin who thinks he can have it all. *Demands* to have it all.

The three leave from the garage in the early hours. She throws her arms around Gus first, as someone who she's known since boyhood, always lanky and smiling, his own mother long dead. 'Be safe, and don't you two get into trouble,' she instructs him, as if they're simply off on a school camping trip.

She fingers Marnie's short strands next. 'Look after him, won't you?' The responsive nod and tight hug is all Corrie needs, certain of the bond they've cemented over such a short time.

Willem is hovering, one eye on their contact who's impatient to go. It's almost as if he daren't approach his own mother. She sees it in his eyes – that this really might be the last time. It's up to her to make the move forward, and to sever the attachment again.

'Make a life, Willem Bakker,' she says, under the broad awning of his arms, 'and make sure it's the right one for you.'

'*Moeder*,' he murmurs into her hair. 'I will be back, I promise.'

'No need for promises, other than to stay alive. Or to try. Not for me, but others.' Her emotion barely contained, she looks past his shoulder at a tearful Marnie. 'You hear me?'

'Yes.'

It's the hardest thing she's ever had to do, pulling away and steering him towards the door. It's probably what the condemned did in ancient times and still do now when facing the gallows. Push forward. No point in delaying the inevitable.

'I love you, remember that.'

He stares, nods, and turns, and his big, wide back – not a pubescent form any more – disappears through the door, while Corrie awaits that second guillotine to fall.

61

Over the Abyss

13th February 1941, coast of Gibraltar

Marnie

'*Adios.*' The man on the dockside waves as they both scan the darkened port from the relative safety of the merchant ship. Safer still, Marnie hopes, when the anchor is stowed and they're moving away from the Gibraltar coastline and into the inky unknown, though they've been warned it's another battleground beyond the harbour confines, of enemy submarines, convoy chasers and German patrols. Until they sight English shores, there is no 'safe'. It's merely one step closer.

Marnie hopes this is the last in a long line of goodbyes, good wishes and hugs of gratitude she, Willem and Gus have dispensed since leaving Amsterdam. For more than three weeks, life has gone by in a blur, even if some days have been slow and grinding, step by painful step at times. It feels both a split second of her life and a yawning chasm of time.

'All right?' Willem says, his usual refrain when they enter each new phase of the journey. As always, she spares him the increased burden and simply says, 'Yes, fine.' They're both aware it's a lie, but equally they share a trust that will allow fresh honesty on hitting English soil. What's the point in Marnie admitting she's utterly exhausted, so weary she could weep, her feet are in ribbons and her bones screaming for relief? There's no other choice but to go on. What drives them is the work ahead, to

346

reach a place where they'll gain the first intelligence of Corrie and Hendrik, Jan, Zeeza, Dirk and the rest. Of Felix, too, even if the news is bad. And from where Willem and Gus can feed the Dutch resistance with arms and agents from afar. There are so many reasons to keep pushing forward.

Willem looks as weary as Marnie feels, and it's only Gus who seems relatively unscathed by the journey, a meandering trail that's demanded travel by train and bus, the back of a truck and squeezed into the boot of a car, rusty old bicycles, donkey and cart, and a good deal of Grandad's 'Shanks' pony'. Each and every stage has seen them on constant guard, from that very first contact in Amsterdam, wary that messages could have been seeded by the Abwehr, or guides paid by the Reich to lead them into a fatal abyss.

Through the exhaustion, they've each maintained a constant alert, checking religiously, hoping, and – at times – simply holding their breath. The relentless tension has proved gruelling, creating tears and angry words, followed by recriminations and apologies. But never a thought of giving up or giving in. In her dreams, or the waking sleep of constant movement, Marnie places herself at the window of her small bedsit, a cup in hand and readying for work, conversing with Oscar. It's what keeps her going through the dark times. She often steals a look at Willem in the endless hours of waiting, and knows he's thinking of Corrie, and Kees possibly. That's his fuel.

The energy to keep moving day by day comes from the people; Marnie has lost track of how many safe houses and hotel rooms have been bestowed by good partisans along the way, eating precious food from their tables, from Maastricht to occupied Paris, where the enticing City of Light twinkled in the window of a tiny apartment, their hideaway for almost a week. So much of her wanted to break free and run down the Champs-Élysées with Willem, even if they would have needed to dodge the swathes of German uniforms in tasting good coffee at a sidewalk café. 'Another time,' he'd promised. 'I mean it. We'll come back to a free Paris.'

On to Toulouse then, using the best eggs and fatty bacon as fuel for the nail-biting journey through the densely patrolled 'forbidden zone' on the French–Spanish border. And how will she ever recount those three infinite days crossing the mountainous Pyrenees on foot, losing feeling in her toes for almost the entire journey, breathless with the freezing, thinned air at a dizzying height, so blind with blizzard and darkness that they had to troop in a line clinging onto each other, for fear of toppling down a sheer rock face? It was a blessing at times not to see the fatal drop only a few feet away, huddling afterwards in ramshackle huts with others on the well-trodden path, sharing lumps of sugar for energy and cognac to warm the blood.

'It's still a damn sight better than a kayak,' Willem said in an especially low moment, at which Gus roared with a manic laughter, bringing some light into the drear of the cabin and prompting ripples of conversation.

How familiar and yet so distant brandy with Raymond at the cosy Langham seemed then. Marnie thought of Ed Murrow, too, and wondered how he might report the scene, still in his suit and tin hat, no doubt. A lifetime away.

Crossing the border into neutral Spain should have been instant relief, and yet it remained perilous with so many Abwehr circling, intelligence agents preying like hawks in the streets and bars of Barcelona and Madrid. Still, there must have been some influence from London, because the three were cleared by the embassy and bound for Gibraltar much sooner than others on the escape line. Perhaps the formidable Dutch queen had seen fit to forgive Willem and Gus for their desertion?

After a day and a half at sea, Willem and Marnie are up on deck at dawn to watch the soaring, imposing white cliffs of Dover come into view, with Gus still sleeping below deck.

She's never been overly sentimental about homecomings, and even when Willem squeezes her shoulder, Marnie is at a loss to read her own feelings. The Blitz is still raging, and yet it's a different level of danger they'll greet now, ARP uniforms on street corners instead of Wehrmacht, falling masonry that might do for them instead of a bullet, or the dreaded stink of a shelter. No Selig, but no Corrie either. No Felix, perhaps forever. She welcomes the relative safety and laments the loss in equal measure.

And what of her job at the BBC? Will there be one, and what will it be without Raymond and his comforting tones?

The ship docks, but it seems like an age until they can descend the gangplank and feel British soil underfoot. How does that first step feel? Marnie doesn't know, incapable of emotion somehow, either good or bad.

'Welcome home,' someone says, and that does lift her features. 'Where are you headed?'

Mystified, she looks to Willem. For weeks, they've been led – by guides, necessity and circumstance. A choice for her own destiny is almost too much to contemplate.

'London,' he says firmly.

The streets of the capital appear quiet and oddly empty, and then Marnie remembers it's the weekend. Despite Hitler, people do still have them, a respite from work, if not the bombs. Is the landscape more scarred, tumbledown and less upright than when she left? It's hard to tell, much like arriving back from a real holiday, where leisure time has stretched out the days and there's an expectation that home will have borne dramatic changes. When, in fact, life merely carries on. It's still London in the Blitz, only a little more crumpled, a few more toothy gaps in the red-brick terraces.

'Shall we get a taxi?' Willem suggests when they emerge from the Underground, Gus having diverted to his own digs.

'No, I'd like to walk through the park.' It's not as if they have any luggage, just a small knapsack each and the clothes they stand up in.

The late afternoon dusk is a mute, flat grey, but overall Regent's Park looks to be throwing off the worst of the season, flowerbeds no longer under the siege of deep winter. It cheers Marnie, and her only worry is in reaching Bedford College and finding it maimed, so desperate is her craving for somewhere familiar to lay her weary head. She'll never think of sleep again as anything less than a precious jewel.

On the approach, the building is as they left it, solid and ornate. A true refuge. Willem halts at the entrance, his tall frame a silhouette against the fading light. Suddenly, after weeks together, sleeping in the same room alongside Gus's light snoring, it feels awkward. As if they have to readjust to another life and start again.

'So, I'll see you tomorrow?' he ventures. 'Unless, of course, you need a few days to yourself. At some point soon, we'll all have to be debriefed.'

Marnie cuts him off, smiling. 'Won't you come in?'

'For that cup of very British tea we've been craving?'

'I doubt I have any tea. I was thinking more of breakfast.' Marnie Fern is resolute. Changed, for the better, she thinks, and utterly certain of what she wants.

Willem looks upwards and smiles. 'I think you've already got company.'

Head tipped, she spies Oscar in the window, keeping his constant vigil, cloth cap slightly askew.

'Oh, he won't mind,' she says. 'And at least he won't talk in his sleep like Gus. Come on, we've plenty of catching up to do.'

'Then lead on, Miss Fern. I'm right behind you.'

February 7th 1955, Broadcasting House,
Portland Place, London.

Transcript: Activities and recollections
of BBC employees during the war years
1939-45. Archive material only. Tapes:
Mrs Marnie Bakker (née Fern). Continuation.

Interview by Thomas Fallon (TF).

TF: Thank you, Mrs Bakker, for co-
operating on this second session. Can
we pick up where we left off: on your
return to England?

MB: Yes. In all honesty, I was surprised
to have a job back at Broadcasting
House, though I imagine it was because
the war had taken plenty of men to
fight. I'm fairly sure, too, that Ed
Murrow had a hand in my return. I
slotted back into being a production
assistant, and was then promoted to
producer within a month or so.

TF: Effectively, in Raymond Blandon's
position?

MB: Yes, although I could never have
hoped to fill his shoes.

TF: You remained loyal to Mr Blandon by all accounts - did you visit him in prison on your return?

MB: I did. Several times.

TF: You forgave him, for what he'd done. For treason?

MB: I didn't see it as forgiveness, or treason even. He did wrong and the justice system recognised his remorse, which is why his sentence was lenient. Raymond was lonely, and he was promised a way of alleviating it, by people who preyed on the vulnerable. If my time in Europe taught me anything it's that none of us know how we'll react in the heat of the moment, or what we'll do for survival. I truly believe Raymond had no malice towards our country. He paid a heavy price for his loneliness.

TF: And what of your own endeavours after your return, besides the BBC? Did you continue with the SOE Dutch section?

MB: Only on British shores. I was placed with them as a part-time radio operator for the remainder of the war, in SOE headquarters. So no more draughty basements!

TF: Was there no desire to return to the Netherlands undercover?

MB: Every desire, but I was married, and then pregnant a few months after our return. I had a family, loyalties of my own, and I knew Corrie and her compatriots understood that.

TF: It must have been a difficult time, not knowing about those in the resistance, and Corrie, who had by then become your mother-in-law?

MB: It was harder for Willem and Gus. What little resistance was left scattered to ensure survival after Rudy was exposed as the leak. His actions caused a lot of damage but it could have been far worse. We discovered later that Rudy's own family had been threatened by Selig, and he mitigated it by passing on some information, but disappearing from Selig's view when he could and filtering other intelligence. We have to be grateful he didn't stoop to a full, fatal betrayal. My own view is that he was weak and afraid, rather than treacherous.

TF: What happened to Rudy?

MF: Disappeared, from Holland at least. No one heard from him again.

TF: What was the result of his betrayal?

MF: Initially, with some safe houses raided, there was a scramble to find new hiding places. A month after we left Amsterdam, Nazis began arresting Jewish men and the entire country staged a national strike - a brave move - but it also gave the Abwehr and the Gestapo a perfect excuse to clamp down on resistance groups. In the aftermath, eighteen dissidents were publicly executed in Amsterdam alone.

Selig seized his opportunity to exact a personal revenge. Sadly, Jan and Dirk were arrested and never emerged from the Oranjehotel, although Zeeza led a group to safety in Utrecht, including Corrie. At that point, the cell in Amsterdam was effectively wiped out and had to be built up again. Ironically, the only refuge never to be raided or suspected during the entire war was Artis Zoo. The animals proved to be the best guardians. Along with Rutger, of course.

TF: And Felix? Was he ever found?

MB: Oh, Felix! Seems he had more than his share of nine lives. Incredibly - and don't ask me how - he managed to convince Selig of being held captive and forced to run messages by the resistance cell, after which he pledged to spy for the Abwehr.

TF: And did he?

MB: (laughs): Yes, but only what the resistance chose to feed through him. For a short time, until he joined Corrie in Utrecht. Until that point, Selig had been riding high in the eyes of Nazi command - he'd convinced them of decimating an entire section, only to nurture a ten-year-old boy who subsequently emerged as a double agent. Nazi command lost their patience then and his time in Holland came to an end, although not his persecution, we understand.

TF: Do you know what happened to Lothar Selig?

MB: He was sent to Norway, to infiltrate SOE and resistance on the western coastlines, where again he effected some real damage. And then he disappeared from our radar.

TF: And Felix now? Did he and Corrie survive the war?

MB: Narrowly. Both of them were resistant in Utrecht, and then back in Amsterdam. The Jewish purges began in earnest in 1943, and so they worked tirelessly to hide Jewish families and help the transport out of Holland. The Levys, we heard, were ghosted to England in 1942 and set up home in Oxford, where Paulus resumed his research at the university. There were times when we lost contact with Corrie for months on end, fearing the worst. With good reason, apparently. Against the odds, Hendrik survived until the Dutch Hunger Winter of 1944, but his body couldn't battle the starvation. Corrie and Felix moved to England, to live nearby, in 1947, and Felix is studying at Cambridge now. No one's surprised - he was always such a bright boy.

TF: And you, Mrs Bakker? How was the remainder of the war for you?

MB: After Amsterdam, it was relatively safe, but also very busy. I had two babies before the victory - Jan was born in 1942, and Kees in 1944. Enough to say that Corrie is now a doting grandmother. At the time, though, I moved to be near my cousin, Susie. As a working mother, I needed all the help I could get. And the BBC still felt very much like a second home.

TF: What of your husband?

MB: Inevitably, he was torn. Part of Willem's heart - his soul, in fact - remained in Holland, and once the SOE began parachuting agents in he couldn't keep away. Both he and Gus undertook several precarious missions. It was a tense time, as I was often tracking his messages as he travelled overland. The SOE and resistance lost plenty of agents during that period, through a combination of bad luck and treachery, but also some poor decisions on our part - the codebreakers and SOE. We have to own up to those mistakes.

It didn't deter Willem, though. In the preparation for Operation Market Garden in '44, he insisted on parachuting in. As you know, the Allies suffered plenty of casualties during that massive assault. He and Gus were listed as 'missing in action', and those days were especially hard, with Kees just a few weeks old. Corrie was transmitting again, and we shared a good deal more than airspace. She imagined never seeing her son or her grandchildren, and I understood those fears.

TF: And the outcome?

MB: He and Gus were found eventually, both badly injured and hidden for weeks by a Dutch family, at great risk to themselves. Seems like those two were bent on using up Felix's leftover lives! I must admit, I had a few stern words with my husband at our reunion. Those injuries meant neither could travel again until the liberation in May '45. We all made the journey to Amsterdam just a few days after - seems there were some benefits to being SOE, not least cadging an army transport flight.

TF: How was that reunion, with Corrie and Felix?

MB: Indescribable. Magical. With my own son beside me, I understood what Willem and Corrie had been through, and how difficult it must have been, watching your children walk into the abyss, whatever their age. There were plenty of tears, especially from 'Uncle' Gus.

TF: And finally, more than ten years on, how do you look back on the war?

MB: It seems churlish to say with fondness, because of the atrocities, the devastation Hitler caused and the families torn apart, losing my grandfather, too. But for me as a person, it was pivotal. I started the war as an old maid in the making, and it released me from a destiny I couldn't easily break out of. War tore up the rule book, for so many women, and

Marnie Fern especially. At work and at home. I grew up, but I also gravitated towards youth, lived the life I'd missed out on. And, most importantly, I met the man who helped me gain what I desired most: the love of my own family.

What can I say, other than the time and conflict were oddly healing. War, in all its grotesque forms, completed me.

Acknowledgements

People often assume that once you're over the hurdle of your first publication, writing subsequent books comes easily. It doesn't. And that's why I'm indebted to the ongoing support from so many quarters in the evolution of this novel. Massive thanks goes to my wonderful editor at Avon – Molly Walker-Sharp – (who now reads me like a book) and her keen eye in framing what's good and what's not. Also to my agent Broo Doherty at DHH Literary Agency, an expert in a quick online 'chivvy' and general author/muse dog counselling. The entire team at Avon and HarperCollins worldwide, too, without whom no book of mine would ever see the light of day. My gratitude goes to copy editor Rhian McKay for battling patiently with my ancient O-level grammar and putting it right.

On the home front, there is a legion of 'people props' to mention: Gez, Sarah, Micki, Annie, Kirsty, Hayley, Ruth, Marion, Isobel, Kelly, Heidi and Zoe – shared dog-walking, coffee and chat is the stuff of life with this great bunch of friends. Equally, I couldn't do without trips to Coffee #1 in Stroud and the lovely baristas for my daily top-up of more than a good flat white.

In the writing world, I am so lucky to be part of a wonderful Gloucestershire posse: sharing the ups and downs in writing makes it infinitely easier; so too a timely bit of plot-busting with scribes Sarah Steele and Mel Goulding. Elsewhere, I relish regular cocktail catch-ups and book talk with Loraine Fergusson (LP Fergusson) and Avon's Lorna Cook (also known as Elle Cook).

These are the wonderful people I know, and yet there are so many more who I may never meet face to face: swathes of readers, reviewers, buyers, sellers, bloggers and librarians who connect solitary writers to the outside world and get our words out there. You are crucial; never underestimate how far a good review, a kind word or a tiny tweet goes to pushing out more chapters. A thousand thanks.

And, of course, my mum Stella. My biggest fan. If a woman of eighty-four accosts you in a supermarket and urges you to buy my book, it's probably her. Say hello. She's very friendly.

Germany, 1944. **Anke Hoff is assigned as midwife to one of Hitler's inner circle. If she refuses, her family will die.**

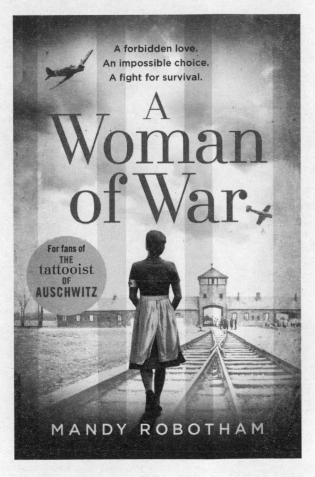

A forbidden love.
An impossible choice.
A fight for survival.

A Woman of War

For fans of
THE
tattooist
OF
AUSCHWITZ

MANDY ROBOTHAM

For readers of *The Tattooist of Auschwitz* comes a gritty tale of courage, betrayal and love in the most unlikely of places.

The world is at war,
and Stella Jilani is leading a double life.

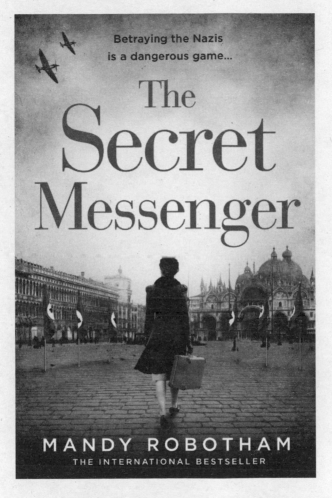

Betraying the Nazis
is a dangerous game...

The
Secret
Messenger

MANDY ROBOTHAM

THE INTERNATIONAL BESTSELLER

Set between German-occupied 1940s Venice
and modern-day London, this is a fascinating tale
of the bravery of everyday women in the
darkest corners of WWII.

Berlin, 1938. **It's the height of summer, and Germany is on the brink of war.**

A country on the brink of war.
A woman who will uncover its secrets.

The Berlin Girl

MANDY ROBOTHAM
THE INTERNATIONAL BESTSELLER

From the internationally bestselling author comes the heart-wrenching story of a world about to be forever changed.

A city divided.
Two sisters torn apart.
One impossible choice . . .

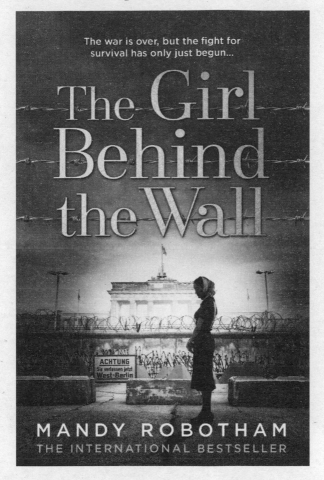

The war is over, but the fight for
survival has only just begun...

The Girl
Behind
the Wall

ACHTUNG
Sie verlassen jetzt
West-Berlin

MANDY ROBOTHAM
THE INTERNATIONAL BESTSELLER

Set against the dawn of the cold war,
this is a timely reminder that, even in the
darkest of places, love will guide you home.

Norway, 1942. **Rumi Orlstad is grieving
the loss of her husband at the hands of Hitler.
And now she will make them pay.**

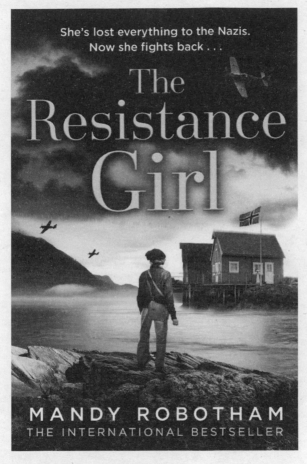

A heartbreaking tale of the sacrifices ordinary people made to
keep friends, family, strangers – and hope – alive.